THE WORLD OF A BILLION DEATHS . . .

The sky was as dark as the blackest nightmare as the C.A.D.S. teams rode up the steep ramps from the hidden exit of the underground Omega base. One at a time they shot up the concrete and out into the new world that awaited them, their bikes roaring with 600 horsepower of energy, their immense black suits of destruction covering their bodies in protective cocoons.

Something was different. Every man could feel it — not through the advanced sensory mechanisms of the suit — but in his guts and soul. The world had changed. The cloudless impenetrable sky was charged with fury and death. It was as if the earth were filled with hatred at man for what he had done to it.

Where was the moon, the stars? They scarcely dared wonder as more and more of the roaring bikes poured from the tunneled earth up into the world of a billion deaths . . .

ASHES
by William W. Johnstone

OUT OF THE ASHES (1137, $3.50)

Ben Raines hadn't looked forward to the War, but he knew it was coming. After the balloons went up, Ben was one of the survivors, fighting his way across the country, searching for his family, and leading a band of new pioneers attempting to bring America OUT OF THE ASHES.

FIRE IN THE ASHES (1310, $3.50)

It's 1999 and the world as we know it no longer exists. Ben Raines, leader of the Resistance, must regroup his rebels and prep them for bloody guerilla war. But are they ready to face an even fiercer foe — the human mutants threatening to overpower the world!

ANARCHY IN THE ASHES (1387, $3.50)

Out of the smoldering nuclear wreckage of World War III, Ben Raines has emerged as the strong leader the Resistance needs. When Sam Hartline, the mercenary, joins forces with an invading army of Russians, Ben and his people raise a bloody banner of defiance to defend earth's last bastion of freedom.

BLOOD IN THE ASHES (1537, $3.50)

As Raines and his ragged band of followers search for land that has escaped radiation, the insidious group known as The Ninth Order rises up to destroy them. In a savage battle to the death, it is the fate of America itself that hangs in the balance!

Available wherever paperbacks are sold, or order direct from the Publisher. Send cover price plus 50¢ per copy for mailing and handling to Zebra Books, Dept. 1641, 475 Park Avenue South, New York, N.Y. 10016. DO NOT SEND CASH.

C.A.D.S.

BY JOHN SIEVERT

ZEBRA BOOKS
KENSINGTON PUBLISHING CORP.

ZEBRA BOOKS

are published by

Kensington Publishing Corp.
475 Park Avenue South
New York, NY 10016

First printing: November 1985

Printed in the United States of America

CHAPTER ONE

Charlie sat at the wheel, his eyes squinting thru the window as Alma switched on the ceiling light for the third time to check the wrinkled half-torn roadmap on her lap.

"I think we should have reached Diablo Junction by now," she said nervously. "It was only supposed to be twelve miles from the last turn we made."

"I *told you*," Charlie said impatiently, as Amy began to whine in the back seat, trying to block her brother who began poking her again. "I *told you* that we should have kept going straight no matter what the highway sign said back there. This isn't Route 38. This is County 4."

"Even if it is County 4, we should have come into Domingo by now," replied Alma as she creased the map then reached around to swat her son Walt with it. "Sit *down* and stop bothering Amy."

"But she's bothering *me*, Mom."

"Turn that damned light off, Alma. I can't see the road," Charlie yelled.

Alma switched off the light with a loud sigh. It was all *his* fault, trying to take the back roads to avoid traffic on the Interstate. Now where the hell were they and how would she call her sister in Albuquerque to tell her that they'd be late? There wasn't even a roadside stand with a telephone. As a matter of fact, there hadn't been a roadside anything for at least a dozen miles. Charlie signalled his exasperation by slamming down on the accelerator pedal. They quickly hit 75mph and Alma's eyes grew wide with fear.

"Charlie slow down! We might hit something."

"What? Hit what Alma?" Charlie yelled, keeping his foot on the accelerator. Damned woman was always complaining, thought Charlie. And those two in the back seat should have been abortions.

Suddenly there was a bright light like a flare ahead on the road. Charlie slowed slightly. It was coming their way. Could it be a car on an intercepting road ahead? They could ask directions if they could get the driver's attention. Charlie blinked the headlights on and off as Alma rolled down the window and yelled into the cool desert night wind.

"Hey Mister! Slow down—we're lost!"

The yellow light grew brighter. There were two, then three of them, making odd loops that seemed to rise and fall in the night. Then a strange droning sound was in the air. Charlie braked to a sudden halt on the macadam, the tires screeching.

"What the hell . . ." he started to say. Suddenly the car was swept by a powerful blinding white light. The shrill whine became a frightening scream, like that of several jets tearing overhead. Both children were yelling at ear-piercing level, "A saucer! Mom! Dad! LOOK! It's a *flying saucer!*"

Alma and Charlie gaped at the brilliant lights which they now could see emanating from the helmets of four futuristically garbed Martian-like creatures at least eight feet tall. Slowly the figures floated toward them, hovering about ten feet above the asphalt road. Their metallic space suits flashed brilliant red lights and jagged short antennae rose from their huge steel heads, which had one mirrorlike *eye*. Charlie floored the throttle—but nothing happened. His wife beat on his neck.

"What's the matter!" she screamed. "Get going! Get the hell out of here!"

Suddenly, Charlie realized that in the midst of his terror he had engaged the handbrake. He released it with the accelerator still floored and the car screeched forward, throwing the kids onto the floor. He drove frantically past the apparitions, weaving wildly to the right, almost getting the rear wheel stuck in the sandy shoulder of the road. Alma was screaming at the top of her lungs, the kids were screaming from a combination of terror and joy, and, for the first time in his life old Charlie was screaming too.

"Martians! Martians! They've come to take us!" he yelled as the car bounced down the New Mexico two-lane road, disappearing within seconds over a rise.

These were the gods of the Technological Age. Within their battle suits, their mortal bodies possessed the power of whole armies of the past. They operated the most elaborate one-man fighting machine ever conceived as they flew over the roadway.

Col. Dean Sturgis looked through the visor of his helmet set at Optimum Perception Mode—all systems on simultaneously—and viewed the plains rushing by all around him. He could see the heat outlines of every living creature for miles ahead—rabbits running, snakes undulating along, the cactuses standing tall and hard. The multi-mode view through the helmet gave him a vision beyond the spectrum of the human eye—heat waves, electrical body currents, the density of moisture in the air—information that shimmered and danced across his visor in computer-created images and readouts that years of training had taught him to interpret instantaneously.

He felt exhilarated as he leaped high in the air, the valve jets on his lower back kicking in just as he left the ground, keeping him hovering aloft as he surveyed the terrain.

"You really gave them tourists a scare," laughed Billy Dixon over his helmet mike.

"What the hell were they doing down this way in the middle of the night?" asked Tranh Van Noc, his vowels mellowed by his Vietnamese accent. "What do we do, Commander? Should we go get them?"

"Leave them alone. They're scared enough," answered Dean Sturgis coolly. "I doubt they'll be a problem." He was suspended in the air with the bluish metallic suit's backpack jet keeping him up a good 20 feet. "I don't think they got a good look—and if they did, no one will believe them."

"The strobes can be blinding, especially four sets aimed on them at the same time," Fenton Macleish cut in.

"Let's get on with the maneuvers," Sturgis said. "We've got to test the full firepower of these C.A.D.S. units tonight. Reduce jet, ground me," he intoned into the mike and the suit's computer obeyed the voice command while printing out "affirmative," in glowing red letters at the bottom of his view screen. Sturgis, encased in the space-suit-like garb, slowly descended to the surface, kicking up sand around him. Tranh and then Billy and Fenton dropped quickly down beside him.

"All right, form up," Sturgis ordered. The three soldiers of the Omega Force lined up single file in the darkness of the endless desert. "Now you've all checked out pretty well in weapons usage—at least on the test ranges you've been good. But tonight we're striving for a little more realism—and we're going to use the full range of the computer-assisted visor screen—on my command. Let's run through the various screens and their uses. Fenton," he said, "What's *Mode Blue*?"

"I'm only on loan you know, to these colonies—but I'll hazard a guess," replied the Englishman. "Enemy units ahead?"

"Right," Sturgis said. "Directly ahead that is. What mode gives a reading for up to five miles, Tranh?"

"Macro-mode. Full coverage in 360° panoramic view," Tranh said softly through his mike.

"Good," replied Sturgis. "And remember—the functions of the visor screen are your aces-in-the-hole. Not something to be afraid of. When we're out there fighting, and we will be, your survival will depend on your ability to use every mode instantaneously, and to take full advantage of your superior firepower. Understand?"

"Understood," the three voices answered back through the darkness.

"Remember," Sturgis said, "the wrong screen at a critical moment and it's like being blind. If you don't know what you're doing, switch to Clear. Now let's get shooting."

Sturgis could feel his adrenaline flowing. The prospect of firing the full range of his suit's armory always did that to him. It was the power of a god, in the hands of a mortal. Nothing but nothing could stand in his way.

"Now come on, all together; Jump Mode," he said to the suit computer, "Synchronize unit."

He ordered Infra Screen and the view before him lit up like daylight. The strobes of all four suits' helmets cut off, saving the men's eyesight from the strain of the flashing lights. The computer wasn't told that. It was just exercising its own built-in "common sense." The C.A.D.S. suits, a triumph of science and engineering, were truly the ultimate war/defense system. They had been created to work *with* men, a symbiotic meshing of human and machine.

They leaped across the desert in bounding jumps of

nearly 100 feet, touching the ground for just a moment and then shooting up into the air, 30 feet above the desert that sped by them below. The starless night surrounded them in a blanketing caress of darkness. But through their computer-assisted visors they could see the world, streaming with life and energy.

The orange pulsing outline of a heat trace from a living creature on the desert floor below came into view. Sturgis directed the view screen "Enlarge five times, infrared mode, creature at 40° due east."

The screen focused on the thing—it was a rabbit, and through the Sensing Mode Sturgis could see its bright heat outline. It hopped tentatively forward toward a cactus and froze as it heard the C.A.D.S. above. The rabbit's heart, clearly visible through the life systems sound probe, was beating furiously. Sturgis took pity on the creature. Their jet blasts had shaken the tranquil night of all these desert animals—coyotes, rabbits, armadillos . . . But they would leave them alone in their night, in their primitive paradise. Suddenly, his screen blipped out the words Life Form Predator—67° west. Still in magnification mode, he looked in that direction. A coyote, bearing down on the unfortunate rabbit. So it wasn't their noise that disturbed the rabbit, but the creature's sixth sense, his instinct for his enemy that scared him. Instantly the computer read out Intercept Predator-victim: One second. The coyote pounced and the rabbit disappeared between the beast's snapping jaws. Sturgis was fascinated, but in mid-jump, he had to watch for his next landing spot. Theoretically the suits were still being broken in, and theoretically the computer could make a mistake and land them on a cactus. Only it never happened. But orders were to take special precautions until the computers had fully checked out. He landed softly, his plastic/steel boots digging their cleats into the soft floor of sand. He looked back in MAG ×12 and saw the coyote spiriting away its prey. I guess the desert isn't so peaceful after all, Sturgis thought. But then the whole world was like that. The stronger preyed on the weak and the still stronger preyed on them. But the battle suits that Sturgis and the other men wore made them—in the war of survival—the strongest of all.

C.A.D.S. That acronym sounded so tame compared to the hell-power it represented. The USAF designation for Omega Command sounded mundane too. Little did the world know that the White Sands Agricultural Experimental Station was the base of the deadliest bunch of men the world had ever seen, men trained in mega-death. One of the psychological things the training had to combat was the "It isn't fair" syndrome. A lot of the new men, never in combat, didn't understand that war wasn't fair. How could they cremate a man who had yet to turn and draw his puny weapon? How could they destroy a tank that ploughed unaware through the desert before them? A split-second hesitation could mean death in this business. And somehow Sturgis had to make them understand that.

"Move to target testing area three," Sturgis commanded. "Ready on my signal, maximum jump capacity, remember to lean into it . . . and put the new A.A. and G.I. Modes on. If they malfunction, turn back to normal screen and advise. Let's *go!*"

There was a sudden whoosh of air as the four gladiator-like figures leaped, scattering dust in their wake. To Sturgis it always felt like he was being lifted by some kind of damned skyhook rather than the force of the jets. He glanced about. The three others were parallel to him, at the same 30-foot height.

"Now! *Lean!*" he commanded, and slowly they started forward.

11

Sturgis soared along on his jets a good ten yards above the cactus-dotted desert, being careful to lean into the jump so as not to lose control and land on his ass. He turned on the I.R. (Infrared) screen and the night vision probes which combined with R. Mode (Radar Mode) to project on his visor a bizarre yet detailed picture of the terrain about him.

It was incredible. Not only did he see the world as if it were daylight — in brilliant luminescent colors — but he could perceive what no human eye could pick up — the energy waves of the night air, sheets of wind, shifting patterns of heat and cold air rising and falling to the ground. The world was in motion, wild motion everywhere — ever changing, alive with bugs and bats, predators and prey. The entire spectrum of the energy band, twisting like the aurora borealis through the dark night. And Sturgis could see it all, a vision that in the past only poets and madmen had been privy to.

Below and to the right a lumbering armadillo, startled by the blast of his jet backpack, scurried across the desert in search of safety. Sturgis could see the creature's heat trail as it quickly waddled across the desert's cool ground. He could even see like red smoke its hot exhale of life's breath. Cactuses stood out like fluorescent pink statues encased by a blue aura of their own life force. The bizarre beauty of the night desert was awesome. Sturgis was startled by a sudden broad motion above him and to his left. It was a pack of bats returning to their caves, darting about in the sky like red meteors. The C.A.D.S. suit was functioning perfectly tonight. The science team had been working feverishly on the latest improvements of the contractor's original design for the vision modes. They had outdone themselves, thought Sturgis.

"You boys on scan Macro, Infra and Radar?" Sturgis asked over the intercom.

"Yesah," said Billy. "Ain't it somethin'?"

"Something *else*," emphasized Tranh Noc.

"We British would say it was bloody fucking incredible," Fenton Macleish piped in, the rear figure in the flying four-man formation.

In the middle of the New Mexico desert lit only by a few hesitant stars on this moonless night, the four men bounded along.

"What's the target tonight?" asked Billy. "Got to be something big if we're going to use combined firepower."

"Coyote Mesa," Sturgis answered. "Is *that* big enough for you? Plot coordinates Coyote Mesa," he instructed the computer.

Plotted, came the running luminous red words at the bottom of his vision. The others read it too, as they were linked in Syncro-Mode—which flashed out all information simultaneously to each member of the team.

Move unit to coordinates plotted, max speed.

The suits turned on their after-burners and they tore at maximum speed across the desert floor. The C.A.D.S. suits couldn't fly per-se—they could jump a hell of a distance though—fifty to a hundred feet at a shot. Within minutes they saw their target ahead, a giant mesa, nearly a thousand feet in height, covered with scrubby bushes and weed-like growth.

Prepare fire control modes, Sturgis instructed the C.A.D.S. Prepared, the computer responded. He saw the small red sighting lights go on in Billy's LPF unit, and in Tranh's Electro-Ball tube.

All systems go, ordered the computer. Commence firing, Manual Directed Automatic Fire Mode.

Billy was first, and from beneath his arm, which he merely pointed out as he whispered the word Fire, a long stream of white-hot burning liquid plastic shot nearly 300 feet onto the wall of the huge stone mesa, igniting the scrub brush.

Now it was Tranh's turn. He pointed his left arm and electro-balls, apple-sized high-explosive shells guided by electro-sighting, ripped out with an ominous roar, crackling blue electricity shimmering around them as they flew. Then the impact. The mesa wall crumbled as if hit by a tank shell at point blank range. An avalanche of screaming rock exploded outward, sending huge boulders crashing to the ground below. Such was the explosive power of the E-balls. Tranh lobbed another volley and sighted for still another but Sturgis flashed the Hold signal through his communicator.

The colonel next shifted to his Combat Active Screen and instantly his visor filled with a blue grid over the Infra and Macro Modes already functioning. Sturgis pointed his left hand and sighted a red dot on the grid until he got it steady where he wanted it—in a fissure in the sheer rock.

"Fire Automatic-space-two sec," he commanded.

Hawk eight-inch missiles began slamming into the wall one after another as huge sections of the cliff face collapsed and tumbled to the desert floor below with every shot fired.

"Cease Function," Sturgis ordered as he lowered his arm. The team could hardly see through the dust cloud blowing in from the fallen mesa ridge. Sturgis waited a minute for the air to clear.

"Now we'll see what all four of us can do. On signal, Fire!" he yelled and the Omega attack team opened up with all they had.

A hailstorm of electro-balls, Hawk missiles, exploding submachinegun bullets, plus liquid plastic fire rained down on the mesa. The sky lit up like the Fourth of July, sparks and white-hot rocks flying off in every direction. The entire solid-rock plateau shook and rumbled as cracks ripped up its side like a paper bag being torn open. Then, as if its very atomic substance could take no more, the mesa erupted like a volcano of stone, a billion pieces of boulder ripping through the cold night air like a shower of meteors. The Omega Squad shot backwards, their suit jets automatically kicking in when the computer sensed the oncoming torrent of the exploding mesa. Several huge chunks of rock slammed into the suits, but they had been armored with the most explosive and shock resistant combination of alloys and plastics known to man. Against the C.A.D.S. armor, these huge rocks flying at the speed of sound felt like the slightest bump to the inhabitants inside. In moments the mesa was reduced to a heap of smoldering rubble.

"Jesus Christ," Billy whispered, "I never thought that — "

It was awesome. Even Sturgis, who fully knew the capabilities of the suit's weaponry better than anyone, stared in awe at the empty space where the mesa had stood. Complete and total *annihilation*. That was the only word to describe what the C.A.D.S. could do. His jaw was set in a grim expression as he commanded the unit to return to Omega Base. The attack team acknowledged and the four men turned and entered Jump Mode. They were all somewhat unnerved and humbled by the experience. What had science and technology wrought? Was this the work of the *devil*, or a saving grace from the gods? Would these C.A.D.S. suits ever be used? Sturgis hoped to hell they wouldn't . . . particularly since the unit had been specifically created to penetrate nuclear ravaged territory to counter enemy troops, seizing strategic areas before the enemy could regroup. The Omega Force's C.A.D.S. suits had special filters and radiation resistant coatings designed to eliminate the effects of alpha, beta and gamma rays.

Sturgis thought of the earth as a huge nuclear battlefield. The idea was too terrifying to consider even for this veteran warrior. He silently prayed that the Omega Force would never see action.

The squad returned to their radio homing devices hidden on the desert range and shut down their jet boosters.

"All right men, slow down," Sturgis said as he coasted to a stop, "the Tri-wheelers are around here somewhere."

Just then he heard the beep-beep-beep of the proximity signal through his earphones. Their camouflage work was getting better all the time! There, under a large grove of mesaweed, really a camouflage net, were their vehicles. White Sands was truly immense and this section of it was far from the base facilities, so they had used the Tri-wheelers — capable of speeds of 150mph — to bring them to their attack site.

"Okay, let's start stripping away and stowing this netting, men," said Sturgis and the team quickly scrambled to stow their gear in the storage wagon attached to the back of Sturgis' vehicle. They got themselves seated, still in their jet-black suits, and strapped themselves into the low slung seats.

They started the engines — the whining sound much like the noise of conventional motorcycles. The real secret to the Tri-wheelers' power was the nuclear battery charged liquid fuel used in their jet-combustion engines. The fuel's atoms were activated by the introduction of free-radical particles, all this giving the Tri-wheelers the power and acceleration of a high performance racing car.

They tore across the desert at high speed, sending up billowing clouds of lazy dust against the horizon. The Omega Attack Squad spread out in V-formation, heading into the dim glow of the sunrise that was quickly brightening in the east, the night sky now changing from black to blue.

Sturgis looked back over his shoulder and could still see the thick column of smoke to the west where they had demolished the mesa. The cloud of dust glowed pink in the breaking dawn.

Ahead of them lay the camouflaged Omega Base. Ostensibly it was an experimental farm, a garden in the desert to test new breeds of plants and trees. They roared up to the western entrance, which was hidden under netting, and passed beneath and into the compound. Moving slowly now, they drove downward along a sloping ramp, lined on each side by Tri-wheelers. Then they parked their vehicles and shed their gear, assisted by the servomechanisms without which the C.A.D.S. were dead weight. Then, in stone silence, the black coveralled men walked past row after row of potted orange trees being watered before the heat of day came streaming down through the camouflaged netting. The white coveralled men who tended the plants turned to watch the four Gods of Destruction move past. Colonel Sturgis walked down the long cinder-block corridors, past the science labs, the mess hall, and finally reached his room in the dormitory, a stark block affair without amenities. His concrete room was a 10′ × 15′ cell with a single bed, a desk, and a chair. It was a cold morning and he adjusted the electric heat thermostat at the base of the wall, crushed his cigarette on the floor, and turned off the light.

Sturgis lay down on the thin-mattressed steel bunk and tried to relax. He kept seeing the mesa dissolving into red-hot slag whenever he closed his eyes. The power, the sheer power of it all. And somewhere in his gut he knew they'd be using them—soon.

Suddenly he heard a rustling sound from beneath the bed. He reached for his .45 strapped to his waist and then just as quickly fell back on the bed laughing. It was his dog, Excalibur. The white pit-bull looked up with a hopeful glance and Sturgis reached over to scratch his head. A man who didn't recognize his own damned dog . . . he must be losing brain cells, he thought.

"Come here, boy," Sturgis said. The 60 pound cannonball of the toughest breed of canine ever bred, renowned for its tiger-like fighting abilities in India, jumped up on the bed and lay next to the colonel. Soon, the man drifted into an uneasy sleep.

CHAPTER TWO

White Sands Base had a long and significant history behind it. It was there, on July 16, 1945 at 5:30 a.m., that the earth was explosively thrust into the nuclear age. It was the site of the first atomic detonation—a blinding blast of star fire the likes of which had never been seen before. The test of the new atomic bomb went so well on the former army gunnery range—now dubbed White Sands Proving Grounds—that it wasn't long—August 6, 1945—before a similar bomb was dropped on Hiroshima, and then on Nagasaki, spelling the end of the Second World War. And the end of the age of innocence.

A lesser known milestone at White Sands occurred on September 26, 1945—the first test of the Tiny Tim missile, a sounding rocket, the first of a series of high-atmosphere rocket tests that led to the Jupiter C model which blasted America's first space satellite into orbit.

Renamed the White Sands Missile Range in 1958, the camp continued to serve as a test site for short-range missiles for several years. Then its flat dry grounds were used as a training camp for astronauts as well as an emergency runway for distressed space shuttles in the 1986–1990 era.

The base was scheduled to be decommissioned in 1991 after being rated an antiquated facility. At that time the camp was run down, the main buildings sat dilapidated along the one-lane road that ran past the perimeter of the isolated 4000 square mile facility. It was now officially designated an agricultural experimentation site, with trees now filling the vacant lots surrounding the perimeter and constant deliveries from sealed trucks carrying huge crates marked Fertilizer or Soil Samples. In reality, however, a steady stream of high-tech equipment and weapons were transforming the unassuming "agricultural station" into a sophisticated military complex. The hidden world in the underground concrete bunkers that stretched off nearly a half mile in each direction — a world of men and machines — brimmed with activity and planning, all preparations geared to one great climax . . . war.

The morning of December 22 broke through a cloud-covered sky with temperatures hovering near 20°F. Damned cold for a desert. The men sleeping in their living quarters grumbled, pulling their blankets another inch or two over their faces. But in an hour the clouds burned off and the sky turned a bright blue. Clear and crisp. Colonel Sturgis took the pit bull for its morning constitutional. Excalibur liked to go over the perimeter of the camouflaged airplane area — something about all that tarp made the dog think that something was hiding — and he'd set his body in a tense fighting stance and stare straight ahead. The next stop was the orchard where Sturgis had trouble keeping him away from the apple trees which he loved to chew like a beaver. They had a difficult enough time growing in the severe climate without Excalibur bothering them.

By now the sky was as brilliant as burning crystal with the perfect circle of the sun glaring down in a shower of benevolent warmth. A beautiful day. It was hard to believe sometimes, on a morning like this when the senses burst with the crisp beauty of the earth and sky, that all was in fact not right with the world. How easily it could all be turned into a glowing black hell. Sturgis shuddered, whether from the sudden stiff breeze or his own thoughts he could not tell. He walked on around the edge of the fenced-in station, the pit bull pulling him along.

Suddenly, he heard a strange wailing sound like that perhaps of moose in mating season. Could only be one thing, thought Sturgis—Fenton Macleish.

Sure enough, Fenton was standing just beside the old hay barn decked out in full plaids and kilt. He was refilling his bagpipes with air as Sturgis spotted him. The Englishman looked at his colonel with a wide grin and commenced blasting out his own eerie rendition of "God Save the Queen." As flat and off-key as the song sounded, the roaring bellows of the bagpipes made Sturgis' heart beat a little faster. The drone of the pipes had a certain omnipotence to it as if the gods were singing along. Suddenly, the pit bull opened its powerful jaws and began howling along with Fenton's playing. The two of them competed for decibel victory until Sturgis dragged Excalibur off and back to his quarters, the echoes of the pipes resounding throughout the compound. The music was sweet, but sad. It made Sturgis feel old for some reason. Thirty-six wasn't old in civilian life—but for a combat soldier, it was getting on. Maybe—if Robin would still have him back—maybe he should just get out of the damned military business. He was covered with scars, cuts—remembrances of his past opponents. For what? What the hell was it all for?

The tugging on the leash drew him down the corridor. He put the pit bull in his room in the dormitory and then walked to the mess hall, late as usual. Damn! Chipped beef on toast. Not a real breakfast at all.

"That's what we get," said a man dressed in civilian clothes in line next to him, "for keeping odd hours." The man watched Sturgis inspect his plate with disgust.

"Guess so," Dean said to the man, a tall, ruddy faced guy in a gray suit with an ID tag that said "John Watkins, Ferris Industries," one of the subcontractors of the C.A.D.S. suits jet pack. The civvie extended his hand.

"Watkins' the name, and you?"

"Sturgis. Col. Dean Sturgis." The men had a seat at one of the smaller tables.

"I've heard your name come up a few times," Watkins said with a wink. "You like to have your fun—with the women and the booze." He winked again. "Okay by me. I'm a fun loving guy myself."

"Yeah, sure," Sturgis replied dryly, eating his warm tough food with slow, disinterested bites. The guy was a jackass, he thought. How did they always manage to hook onto me?

"I understand the pack is working okay."

"Tolerably," Sturgis said, wondering what the guy was getting at. "You here to check up on it?"

"You bet. Old Mr. Ferris, our president, promised he'd walk you guys through modifications—so, here I am."

"I'd like more power," Sturgis said coolly, cutting a piece of hard black bread and buttering it with a stiff slab of margarine.

"More power? That's the one thing we can't do, buddy. It's already at the safety threshold—the suit might come apart with bigger jumps."

Just as they were going to get into the why of it, Tranh—Sturgis's closest friend—sat down.

"Interrupting something?" he asked with his soft calm voice.

"No, but you might have some input. We're talking about the jet packs for the C.A.D.S." Sturgis said, stuffing a slice of the cold black bread into his mouth.

"Not enough oomph," Tranh agreed.

Watkins gave the Oriental a strange look. Sturgis intro-

22

duced Tranh Noc to the businessman. Watkins shook hands across the table, his hand felt like a dead fish in Tranh's firm grip.

"You Chinese?" the technician asked suspiciously. Tranh and Sturgis eyed each other, sensing the taint of prejudice in the businessman's voice.

"No, Vietnamese," Sturgis said, "Vietnamese-born *American*. We go back a long way."

"Right," Tranh said. "You've heard of Viet Nam. The last bastion against communism—that the U.S. swore they'd never let down."

"How interesting," Watkins said absently. "Well where were we . . ."

"The C.A.D.S. jet pack," Sturgis answered, setting his dark brown eyes firmly on the civilian's face.

"Oh yes. Can't be done. It's a miracle we got it up this much—the power . . ."

"It's coming in at about 40%," sneered Sturgis, "of the specified power."

"Software problems. Design modifications—safety—meant more weight."

"Bullshit," Sturgis hissed between his teeth. He wasn't in the mood to play games with this bimbo.

"I beg your pardon?" Watkins half gasped, drawing himself up in his chair.

"*Bullshit*, I said," Sturgis repeated. "The manufacturer had a 200% cost overrun and delivered 40% of what he promised. I'm rating it unsatisfactory in my equipment appraisal report."

"You do that sonny, you . . ." Watkins snapped and threw down his napkin, then stood up stiffly. "I've heard of you, Sturgis. You're a—a—a troublemaker. People wonder about you, you know. About your motives, your . . . well, your loyalty."

Sturgis stood up, and put his hands around the man's collar, pulling him forward, halfway across the table.

"Listen, pal, you can say what you want to about the suit but don't ever question my loyalty. I've spent more time saving my country's ass, pulling it out of trouble, than you make in dollars each year. Furthermore, it's not just me and Tranh criticizing the suits. These things are being tested by two hundred men. In one suit assembly we found sixteen malfunctions, in another eight, in a third twenty-three. You guys have already been responsible for five deaths. We've spent months rebuilding things that *your* quality control department should have caught — if you *have* a department like that! Now I'm telling you — get it straightened out — or we — meaning me, will come down there and kick somebody's ass. And since you're such a know-it-all smart ass, I'm holding you personally responsible — not your company buddy, but *you*. Understand?"

The civilian nodded vigorously. He didn't seem so full of bravado now with Sturgis looking straight at him with fire in his eyes. The man backed away slowly, his face ashen. Then he turned and walked quickly out of the mess hall without another word.

"Maybe you shouldn't have done that, Sturgis," said one of the officers seated at a nearby table. It was Major Van Patten, chief military scientist at the base.

"You mean maybe I *should* have," Sturgis grinned.

"Yeah," Van Patten said with a sigh. "Maybe you should have. I've been doing it the diplomatic way for months and it hasn't paid off yet. Still, the general will hear . . ."

"He knows how Ernie died," Sturgis said bitterly. "And Druze, and Sanders, and . . . well, you know the casualty figures. I don't have to remind you."

"Yeah, we know," Van Patten said softly, "but we have no choice. Believe me, Sturgis, there's — there's not much time left." With that Van Patten turned and continued his breakfast. The men ate in silence, each thinking his own ominous thoughts.

At last Sturgis finished his food and rose. "Come on Tranh, let's visit the firing range and see if the E-11 Electro-ball system is being tested yet. I'd like to have a look at the new auto-loader before I find it on my suit one morning without anyone even telling me."

They walked up a small concrete ramp and then down an endless narrow corridor lit every 75 feet by a half-hearted fluorescent tube. Finally they reached the underground *Target and Test Facility*. It was damned big, Sturgis always thought whenever he entered the huge natural cavern 1,000 feet below the desert sands. It was a formation ideally suited to the hundreds of tests that had to be conducted before authorization of any of the suit's weaponry systems was established. Here, robot mock-ups, crude servomechanisms wheeled around amongst the stalagmites jutting from the floor, steered by men safely sheltered in control booths nearly a thousand feet away. Sturgis and Tranh walked up the stairs to a room marked Control One and opened the door. Fenton was at the controls of one robot, apparently tired of the bagpipes. The Englishman nodded hello and went back to watching the visual transmission of the robot's chest level camera which showed the robot moving at a good clip through a deep part of the cavern.

"That's the one with the new Electro-ball system?" asked Sturgis, as he and Tranh took seats behind the operator.

"You're bloody right it is, and it's gotten stuck three times out there. I'm taking it up to Cavern G to try the E-11 out."

They watched through the video eyes of the robot and saw the high granite walls of the billion-year old rock appear on one of the many view screens above the operator's control panels. It would take a lot of firepower to even chip those 300-ton slabs.

Fenton made some adjustments on the panel and pressed the "fire" button. They saw the robot arm and the Electro-ball tube come up. Suddenly, there was a blur from a small, crackling blue ball flying several hundred yards toward the wall. The granite was lost for a second in a cloud of dust. Then it was clear again — enough to see that the wall was split in half.

"Will you look at that . . ." Fenton said. "Six shots delivered in less than a second, and it split the damned thing. Some sort of cumulative effect from the rapid fire."

"Good," said Sturgis. "Let's hope we can get the thing on the suits soon."

"Not enough fire power? Last night wasn't enough?" asked Fenton, remembering the destruction of the mesa.

"Too much is not enough in war, Fenton, didn't they teach you that in the Queen's Black Guard?" Sturgis grinned.

"You Yanks do everything bigger over here in America, don't you? I'm sorry we Brits ever let you colonies off on your own. You're quite a menace," said the Englishman sarcastically.

"Mind if I take the controls?" Sturgis asked.

Fenton shrugged and relinquished his seat. Sturgis took over the robot's controls, turned it, and headed it back. It was almost beautiful deep in the cave where they hadn't blasted every damned formation to bits. The walls gleamed with an almost translucent sheen. But soon Sturgis saw the ugly scars of the weapons tests, and the piles of debris that even the robot with its multi-wheeled feet had difficulty maneuvering over. Sturgis brought the robot back down through the vast cavern. Tranh watched as it appeared from behind a stalactite grouping.

"It's here, sir," he reported to Sturgis.

When they got the robot up for inspection they discovered shrapnel pieces lodged over half of the robot's protective outer skin.

"Would have killed us to fire the E-11," Sturgis said angrily. "Good thing old Charlie here did it for us. Time for some modifications."

"Modifications? Did I hear the dreaded word?" asked a voice behind then. The pockmarked face of weapons-chief McAllister appeared.

"Such a waste of tax money, Charlie is. Getting himself injured all the time. What did it now?" The chief asked.

"The new 11 unit," Tranh said from his seat.

"These damned contractors giving us junk," Sturgis exclaimed, slamming his fist down on the control panel. "At least the older stuff worked, even if it fell below power specs."

"Well, not only are the contractors screwing us," McAllister said, "now I hear that Washington is sending us some big-wig from OMB to take a razor to our appropriations."

"OMB?" asked Tranh.

"Office of Management and Budget. It's the Congress' way of cutting the military even if the president gets appropriations passed for us. General Knolls' men have done a wonderful job to date in keeping our funds untouched even after S.A.C. and Missile Command were cut. But it's finally coming down on us now. He should be here today, from what I hear. He's flying in on one of their private OMB jets. Now that's a waste of money they don't seem to mind."

"Politics and war—a bad stew," said Tranh.

"Anyway," McAllister continued, "I'm scheduling more tests. If the ax is gonna fall, I want to try to direct it a bit. At least we can save the best."

Four men in khaki coveralls, Sturgis in the lead, walked down the long gray hallway to General Knolls' office. They saluted the guard at the door, and he opened it and leaned in. "Colonel Sturgis here to see you, sir."

They were let in and snapped to attention lined up in front of the whitehaired general, who was going over some reports. Without looking up he said, "At ease," then the general spent some more time perusing the documents on his desk. At last he sighed, took off his pince-nez reading glasses and looked up.

"I got a call from the local sheriff's office, if you can call Diablo Springs local, and he asked me if we're doing any funny experiments with lights and flying saucers. I laughed of course, but I knew immediately that it was *you* Sturgis, again. How many times have I told you not to go near County Road 4? And don't tell me it wasn't your bunch. Listen to these descriptions that couple and their kids gave the sheriff." The general picked up some papers and holding his pince-nez to his eyes read, "Martians with blinding lights and red antennae, floating over the ground. Eight ten-foot tall monsters with heads twice as large as human and no necks . . . Need I go on?"

Sturgis couldn't help but smirk as he said, "Eight. Well then it must have been Martians. There were only four of us on maneuvers last night."

"Don't get wise with me, Sturgis. Fortunately," he put the papers down again and paused. "Fortunately, I have a good rapport with the sheriff and this story won't go any further. He's just going to say he's investigating. I used the old dodge about robot crop-spraying machines. That got us by last time. Now . . . how about the firepower reports. Don't go into details but what happened?"

The general listened as Sturgis recounted the successful tests of the weaponry.

"The only glitch was the brightness of the blue screen seemed to go down about 50% on the way back. In combat, that could be serious."

"The battery? Could it have been that?" General Knolls

asked.

"No, it's in the computer. The light sensor maybe," Sturgis replied. "We should build in a command that could adjust screen light levels by voice command and not depend on the computer always knowing the right brightness to set the thing to. I think the dawn light confused it."

"Very well, go over all that with Dr. Van Patten. He'll be most interested. I'm overlooking you and your men screwing around this time, but the next time you take it in your mind to scare the hell out of tourists, it's forfeit of a month's pay. Get me? Dismissed, except *you*, Sturgis."

The three others snapped off stiff salutes and walked out.

"At ease Sturgis," the general said after they had left. "You and this project go back a long way, don't you? Don't we?"

"Yessir."

"You were an astronaut in training—a Distinguished Service Cross winner in the Cambodian incursion, in on the M.I.A. rescue attempts . . ."

"Yessir."

"You helped to develop the A-12 suits that the astronauts used in the Skylab Project?"

"Yessir."

"And you also get into more trouble than any fifty men on this base."

"If you say so sir."

"Don't play *coy* with me. Listen Sturgis, you pushed around an important contractor's main liaison man today. Why?"

"He's a creep sir. A . . ."

"So he's a creep. Did he do something to you?"

"He took issue with my loyalty, sir."

The general paused in rising from his chair. "Hmmm, well, we can't have that, can we? I know of the many sacrifices you've made."

"Yessir. So do I."

"But the reason you washed out as an astronaut and why we so luckily have the enormous resources of your knowledge for our C.A.D.S. project is the fact that your temper is uncontrollable, you're insubordinate, and you have a rebellious nature."

"Plus my smoking, sir. They don't allow astronauts to smoke and I find it hard to quit."

The general sighed. "You're a damned iconoclast, Sturgis, but we need you. However, the next time you manhandle anyone around here I'll for sure make your life very miserable indeed. Understand?"

"Yessir," replied Sturgis. He saluted and walked stiffly from the room.

He was the worst peacetime soldier you could ask for, thought General Knolls. Well, soldiers weren't for peacetime anyway. Sturgis was just the man who would make the difference when the chips were down . . . if I can just keep the bastard out of a court martial.

CHAPTER THREE

"Up periscope!" Admiral Vestok said. The 8 meter cylindrical viewing device rose from the top of the immense nuclear submarine *Peter the Great* and broke the surface of the sea above it. There, just 2,000 yards off was the American battleship *New Jersey*. Ripe for the pickings. And Vestok, in the radar-evading sub, would be the picker. He and his wolf pack of 10 nuclear subs hidden 1,000 feet below the water's surface. The Russians had been playing cat and mouse with the NATO fleet on maneuvers in the Adriatic. The foolish Americans had deployed nearly two-thirds of their Navy to cover the Jordanian war with Israel in the Middle East, which had conveniently heated up.

The west always reacted without consideration of the greater issue: global thermonuclear strategy, thought Vestok. The American President Armstrong truly believed that the nuclear war threat was very small. Vestok stared at the sitting duck, wishing he could fire. Soon. Soon enough. The orders would come through when the Soviet pre-strike plans were put into effect — when the American satellites were disabled and the Russian killer subs were all in place near their targets throughout the world . . . the U.S. Trident Class submarines that carried their own armada of nuclear death, and the cruise missile ships like the one before him.

The new cloaking device that blocked radar and sonar tracking was sometimes successful — sometimes not. But that was the way that the superpowers often played deadly games of tag out here in the depths of the oceans. American subs were frequently tailed and they frequently were hot on the trail of the Russians. But no games this time. At the given signal from Moscow U.S. subs would be fired upon — as would their entire world-wide fleet. It had been decided in the Politburo meeting two months before. They had all agreed it was now, or it would be too late.

Normally Admiral Vestok commanded the lead aircraft carrier of the fleet, the nuclear powered *Bulganin*. But now he was here under the sea while up on the deck of the *Bulganin*, was his double, waving to the American PB-109 spy planes that monitored the "exercises" of the Soviet Warsaw Bloc fleet in the North Atlantic. Other key personnel like Supreme Marshal Veloshnikov were also in secret locations directing the last preparations while their doubles were going through the all-is-normal routines. It was another Pearl Harbor, Vestok thought. The Americans were sleeping. Or, if not sleeping, at least dozing. The game was being won before it even began. The American forces were scattered, dealing with the countless brushfire wars that the Russian Empire had instigated — in Asia, the Middle East, Central America. Meanwhile Russian forces were moving into station. Final stations.

Vestok glanced at his watch. He felt tired — so much tension. "Down periscope," he called out, thinking that he could get some sleep and be fresh when his orders finally came. He looked about at his crew. These men are the best, he thought. This submarine the most survivable in the fleet — the Stalin Class nuclear *Peter the Great*. The Americans had nothing like it, yet to their satellites' probing eyes the subs appeared almost primitive with exposed rivets, lumbering along at less than 20 knots. They appeared to break down often. The Americans were in for a surprise. It went twice as fast as their intelligence reports indicated. Within days he would be entering New London Harbor in

Connecticut — and blasting their nuclear shipyard there with his atomic torpedoes. All his life he had trained for such a mission.

"Hold her steady as she goes at one-third speed. Increase depth to three thousand," Vestok said to the sub's chief officer.

"Yes, Admiral," said the sailor. He looked expectantly at his leader.

"Soon, Chernenkov, soon. The imperialists who have endeavored to condemn our motherland, and destroy communism will themselves be condemned and destroyed. The entire military is as one in this endeavor. There will be no slip-up, no foul-ups. We are prepared. There are shelters for the urban populations, who could not be moved lest they create suspicion. Our anti-ICBM defenses are in place, their spy satellites will soon be knocked out. The plan is perfect," he said, reassuring his mate.

The admiral began sifting through the computer-generated maps which depicted every mile of the world's ocean bottom terrain, and the last known locations of all U.S. ships and subs. The nation that strikes first with overwhelming superiority is doing the human race a favor, he thought. In any even attack-and-counter, the whole world would be destroyed. Better to have one clear victor, and better, if the war is inevitable, that the victor be the Soviet Union.

The admiral took off his cap and opened his collar. He lay down on his blankets, and soon snapped the reading light off and closed his eyes. Here I am, he thought, sleeping on the eve of Armageddon. He wondered if Supreme Marshal Veloshnikov, in charge of the US invasion, and General Petrin, and the premier himself could be practical and get some sleep. He doubted it. But he fell into a dreamless pit.

* * *

President Armstrong looked up as press secretary Richard Manning came in.

"Richard, how goes it?" the president asked, leaning back in his chair.

"Excellent, Mr. President. We're up five percent since the last fireside chat you gave on nationwide tv. The sweater-and-pipe image is working. Not to mention the increased hopes everyone has for a peace treaty before the election."

"Wonderful, and the negotiations?"

"Good news there too. Ambassador Dobrynin and Foreign Minister Trekian have given in on the aerial inspection plank of the draft treaty. And we've only agreed to cutting the initial overflights by twenty-five percent from our original proposals. We're getting an ironclad verifiable disarmament treaty, Mr. President."

The president sat up in his leather recliner, straightening his blue pin-stripe suit. "So I will be known in the history books as the president who brought not SALT or START, or those other partial steps like the Nuclear Test Ban Treaty in '91 — *I* will be the Great Peacemaker!"

"If the treaty is signed before the election," Manning said, "we can expect to carry every state, except Massachusetts of course, and perhaps the District of Columbia."

"It'll be the biggest runaway since Reagan in Eighty-four," grinned Armstrong. "That's good news. I don't like playing it close. I want a firm mandate. Richard?" The president's tan, square-jawed face looked suddenly apprehensive.

"Yes, Mr. President?"

"Are the Russians giving in too fast? Is there something hidden in their eagerness? Something we're not seeing?"

"They're hurting, that's all there is to it. Their grain yield is down again, their people are demanding more consumer goods and freedoms. It's just like we hoped. They have to moderate under the pressures of their economic limits. They know we can go on spending and spending far over

34

our abilities."

"Yes. It's exactly as I hoped," said the president. Yet there were lingering doubts. Something just didn't sit right in Armstrong's stomach.

The United States had over the years been subject to numerous intelligence failures — Pearl Harbor, Viet Nam, the Bay of Pigs, the surprise OPEC oil cutoff, the Lebanese terrorist bombing — all failures caused by a lack of accurate, timely intelligence. Damn, the president thought, I'd better make sure. After Richard left, he put in a call to CIA Director Stanford Quarterman and asked him to hurry over to the Oval Office. Within an hour, the tall, gaunt CIA director stood on the carpet in front of the president's desk.

"Stanford, are you sure that the Russians aren't up to something?"

"Well, our satellites don't see any unusual activity in the Soviet Union," Quarterman said, seating his large body in a nearby chair. "Our agents report no significant moves to cancel military leaves. The Red Army is on normal status, likewise their air force and navy. Aside from the winter maneuvers, which they've held for the last few years at about this time anyway, aside from that, nothing."

"Nothing? Nothing at all unusual over there? What about their key officers? Are they visible?"

"Yessir. Our man in the Kremlin has seen all of them in the last week, and he reports that their meetings aren't lasting any longer than normal."

"Any new weapons being tested, deployed?"

"No sir. Not that we've detected. They have the ABMs that are allowable under treaty, just as we have. No new defensive systems in place, although they've been doing a lot of research in Kazaskistan on those energy-beam weapons. Our reports are that they're not anywhere near operational."

"Thank you, Stanford, and thanks for coming over on such short notice."

"Anything up, sir?" Quarterman asked, rising.

"Not that I know of—just making sure." He grinned, looking up from his reclining leather seat. "Those Ruskies are in over their heads—they have to quit the arms race. Besides, the old guard is dead. The strict Marxist-Leninists have given way to a more practical breed in the Soviet hierarchy. Those new guys have never known war—and don't want to."

His disarmament advisor, Gridley, spoke up from the corner. "Why shouldn't we expect the USSR to make concessions, Mr. President? With their crop expectations, the protests of their dissidents, the unrest in their satellite states . . . Everything in these peace negotiations has been predictable."

"It just feels too good to be true!" Armstrong said softly.

"But Mr. President, it was *your* tough stance, the buildup of forces that has caused this result. You should be proud . . . and confident," Gridley said, rising and walking over to Armstrong. He took it slowly. The gray haired man had an old knee injury.

"But doesn't it strike you that it's all coming a bit too easily now?" the president asked. He fingered his aquamarine silk tie nervously. "I want a complete military briefing—the Joint Chiefs, the CIA, especially the CIA. I want to know the disposition and quality of their military. I haven't heard a thing from the Joint Chiefs since last month."

"They're evaluating the accuracy of the data, Mr. President," Quarterman added. "But Gridley's *probably* right on all he said."

"You mean there's some question that these reports I've been getting—poor training in the Soviet army, revolts, breakdowns of equipment, shortages of fuel, failures of new weapons systems—that's what JCS and CIA have been telling me—you mean to say it isn't all *verified*?"

"No, Mr. President, it's just that we may have to upscale

our estimates of their preparedness by twelve or fifteen percent . . ." Quarterman said.

"That's a hell of a lot, Stanford. I want a briefing at seven o'clock tonight. Fix it up. Full scale — top men from every intelligence department."

"Yes, Mr. President. I'll get to work on it immediately."

Alone again, the president sat silently for several minutes. Of course everything was going well, he thought. No cause for alarm. Yet something bothered him, something unnamable, hidden. Something that sent a secret shiver up his spine.

Vice President Arthur Williamson was on the phone at 3 p.m. He had been trying to see the president for three days. Damn, Armstrong was tired of the constant nitpicking from his VP. The president sighed and picked up the phone. He was always somewhat annoyed by Williamson, who wanted to have a constant hand in the policy making of the administration. Williamson hadn't even been his pick for the VP post. He had never liked the guy, even though he had nominated him for the position at the convention saying he was just the man for the job. Actually, Armstrong had settled for the Oklahoma Senator to help balance his ticket east-west. Armstrong knew he was weak in the west and the opposition party had a western Veep candidate. And that was that.

"What is it Art?" Armstrong said with fatigue as he allowed his secretary to put through the call.

"It's the peace talks, Mr. President. The concessions the other side has been making — it's very uncharacteristic of them. It flies in the face of . . ."

"I've just been through all this with my intelligence men, Art, and the consensus is, they're hurting, and they need this peace. *They* need it more than *we* do."

"I wish I could have been there, Charles," said the vice president. "Could you arrange that at the next discussion . . ."

"Sure, sure, sure. I just thought you'd be too busy packing for that Indonesian tour with your wife. Bring me back one of those bali-dancer statues, will you?" the president chuckled.

"Listen, Charles, I think, er, I believe we should think about putting our bombers on twenty-four hour alert," Williamson said nervously, knowing the president didn't want to hear suggestions from him.

"What?" Armstrong cried, his voice showing his annoyance. "What the hell kind of a signal would that be of our intentions? Haven't I built up the conventional forces budget by twenty percent? You know as well as I do that the nuclear thing is a standoff. It's the conventional army, and the airlifters to move them, that make the Russians nervous, keep them in line."

"You know I disagree with that, Mr. President . . ."

"It's the goddamned platform we ran on Art—you and I. It clearly stated we would build up conventional and rapid deployment forces to combat terrorism and the risk of war."

"I know what it said, but it didn't say we should lay down our nuclear shield."

"Hell, Art, we've been through this. That's my policy, and you're my vice president. I need you to back me up—there have been press reports that we're in disagreement, and I don't like them. They're coming from your office. We have to put up a united front for the peace negotiations, and we goddamned will, Art. Do you understand me?"

Arthur Williamson did not answer. What could he say? His office, the office of the vice president, was basically one of little significance as long as the president lived. A waiting game, possibly a step up—not even a guarantee of a nomination for the presidency after Armstrong's second term. At last he spoke up, but hesitantly.

"Just think about activating our bomber units for twenty-four hour flyaround. That's all I ask. Just our B-1 units. They couldn't even get off the ground—in the unlikely event . . ."

The president just sighed. "I'll think about it, Art. Good-bye." He hung up the phone without waiting for a final response.

That damned Williamson annoyed him more and more. If it came to a second term he was determined to drop that man, if possible. Did Williamson think he was a damned fool? Why have the high profile provocation of those bombers armed with nukes flying around during a peace conference? Aren't 2,000 cruise missiles, 6,000 Peacemaker ICBMs and 2,300 sea-launch MIRV missiles in Neptune class submarines enough to deter the Soviet Union?

Christ, he thought. Maybe just to placate Williamson, and perhaps his own nervous stomach, he *could* do something. Something short of provocative. That unit up by the Bering Sea — the Alamo Squadron — the newest of the fighter bomber bases. He could order them onto yellow alert status, right now, and when he met with Williamson tomorrow to see him off, he'd mention it.

He picked up the phone . . .

CHAPTER FOUR

They all sat slumped in armchairs somewhat the worse for wear — Sturgis, Tranh, Fenton, Billy, Rossiter, and Roberto. Rossiter was wolfing down a bag of Nachitos. They had gathered in the television room next to the mess hall to watch the 7:00 news. Dan Rather was reporting the day's events with a grim expression:

"The situation at the bargaining table *seems* to be improving. A missile decrease in Europe and a DMZ zone from the Black Sea to the Baltic has been agreed on, at least in preliminary negotiations. But there is disquieting news reported from Iran. Massive amounts of Soviet equipment and men have apparently been brought in, in violation of an understanding between the U.S. and Russia. Soviet divisions of missile-launching personnel have begun setting up weapons — intermediate range Farcon Rockets according to our sources. The Soviet Ambassador to West Germany was questioned today by our reporter in West Berlin about these alleged events. Go ahead, Neil Conyers, in Berlin."

"Right Dan, thank you. We are standing here with Anatoly Dzerzinsky and I will ask him directly. Mr. Dzerzinsky, is the Soviet Union using the occasion of the peace talks here to move offensive missiles and troops into Iran?"

"Mr. Conyers, we do not know how these rumors get

started, and we suggest perhaps that disruptive elements in the west who wish to scuttle the very substantive and mutually beneficial peace talks now in session have concocted these wild ideas. There is not a shred of truth to this nonsense."

"But *Das Stern Magazine* has published an alleged aerial photograph . . ."

"You hit it right on the head Mr. Conyers — *alleged*. This photograph is of our maneuvers in the Siberian area, not in Iran. And in either case, the missiles there are anti-aircraft IX-23, our SAM 32, as you designate them in the West."

"Well there you have it Dan. This is Neil — "

Sturgis turned to Billy seated next to him and snorted with disgust. "Bullshit. They're doing something, and the news media is letting them use their reporters to snow us."

"The big lie always works best," Macleish muttered. "Hilter was signing peace treaties the day before he invaded."

The report continued as Rather said, "Another dark cloud on the horizon is the show of force in East Berlin where Russian armored units drove up to the very borders of the wall and are maintaining a state of readiness. Observers in the west believe that this is a bargaining chip to encourage small concessions, and that the action has no particular military significance. However, the East Berlin forces now triple the capability of our multi-national force in West Germany, and they are more heavily armed, both conventionally and with tactical nuclear weapons."

"Terrific," said Billy Dixon. "And where the hell's the president and his 'braintrust' in all of this?"

As if to answer his question Rather said: "Reached for comment at the White House, President Armstrong said: 'We are in touch with our Soviet counterparts on these matters and there is no cause for alarm'."

Billy groaned as Tranh smirked, "That's what they said one hour before Ho Chi Minh's troops marched into Saigon."

"In other news, the tanker war between Iraq and Iran, supposedly now at peace, intensified, as Iranian terrorists used new Soviet Cruise-11 Exocet Missiles to destroy five supertankers. These attacks are seen as more significant than the land-based military developments, eliciting fears that the large oil spills could threaten much of the marine life in the Persian Gulf."

"The Reds are destroying the western pipeline of crude—using the Iranian terrorist ships to do it," Sturgis snapped bitterly.

"It's *your* president's obligation to stop it," Fenton said.

"Two of those tankers were under British flag. Where's *your* prime minister?" asked Roberto, cleaning a fingernail with his commando-knife point.

The six men sat dumbfounded as Rather reported that Ten Downing Street issued a "no-cause-for-alarm statement".

"Jesus," said Macleish, running a nervous hand through his red hair. "I sure hope they're doing something and are just saying that they're not."

"You give the west too much credit," said Tranh. "They're blowing it—the safety of the west—in exchange for hollow promises at the peace talks. Both the president and your prime minister, Fenton, are up for reelection and they wouldn't have a chance if they said things had turned for the worse after all that peace hoopla. They've got to play it down."

"Politics—it'll be the death of us," commented Billy.

"Maybe literally," Sturgis thought to himself.

CHAPTER FIVE

Charlie Krangle was a locomotive of a man, bulky, and with a head of steam that looked ready to go the distance. He was called "The Ax" around the Office of Management and Budget in Washington D.C., and he wielded one with deadly accuracy. His specialty, his desire, his *raison d'etre,* was to reduce military waste: read spending. He had worked for years to get to be number two man at O.M.B. – years of struggle, blind ambition, some would say less kindly. He hated the military. Perhaps it was the fact that he had tried to join the Marines when he was eighteen and had been turned down for obesity and hemorrhoids. Perhaps a psychiatrist would say that was the beginning. But whatever the reason, he was out to cut, cut, and cut some more. Somebody had to stop the military juggernaut from wasting so much money, and he had elected himself the one to do it.

Krangle steamed down the hallway to General Knolls' office, swinging his black leather briefcase filled to the brim with budget analyses and expenditure tables. My God, they had this Air Force Unit well hidden. Not just in physical terms – he didn't see a thing from his private jet until they were landing. He thought the plane was in the wrong place – descending on some godforsaken farm.

But they, meaning the Pentagon, also had it hidden in a jungle of paperwork—an appropriation here, a bit there—scattered throughout the budget for Fiscal 1996. It took a year to even find what the hell was being spent on the so-called Omega Project. He snorted as he turned the doorknob of the frosted glass door with the words *Commander, General Knolls* at the top.

Inside he was told to wait by the male secretary. A typical military type, he thought—glasses, acne, pecking away at a report in triplicate.

"I won't," Krangle said, pushing through a swinging wooden gate and opening the inner door.

General Knolls put on a phony smile and came around the desk excitedly. "Mr. Krangle? O.M.B.? Glad to see you."

He glad-handed the federal investigator and pointed him toward the naugahyde chair at the side of his desk.

"Cigar? Cigarette?—feel free."

"Thanks I will," Krangle said, flicking his lighter up at the Camel filter he took from a pack in his suit pocket.

"Well, I'm glad to see you . . ."

"Are you, General? You shouldn't be—this project . . ."

"Magnificent isn't it?" General Knolls winked. "Quite an illusion from the air."

"I'll say, but even more so from the ground—and in the budget. General, there's a three hundred percent cost overrun on this project and the total budget for the past four years is approaching a *billion*, I repeat *one billion* dollars."

"That much, eh?" Knolls said nervously. "I assure you the cost overruns aren't here. They're at the sub-subcontractor levels. See our suppliers about all that—defective, late, you name it."

"Yes, yes, but that's to be expected," Krangle said, irritated. "What I am questioning—could you clear off your desk a bit so we can lay this out?" he asked.

The general piled papers in his "in" box as Krangle opened his ominous black briefcase and extracted stacks of stapled reports.

"Look at this," he said accusingly, underlining in red a figure in the six-digit category for Arm Sling Mount. "$567,000 for an Arm Sling Mount? What the hell is that?" Krangle asked sarcastically.

The general put on his reading glasses and turned the papers toward him, studying them.

"Don't snow me, General," Krangle said softly as a warning.

"Well, this arm sling is what the weapon's firing tubes are mounted on on each C.A.D. device. The C.A.D.S. suits—as they are called. This is a very special mount—and see here—this figure for twenty-five modified suit weapon mounts—"

"General, aren't suit mounts little more than brackets?"

"Well, you can say that. But brackets that can move in thousandths of a second, that won't rust or snap. That—"

"And this here—in red, a seven-figure amount for visors—" He slammed the papers down on the desk. "I mean, come on now, General. We're not total idiots in D.C."

It went on and on like that. General Knolls was in full retreat but getting madder all the time. He was just seconds from taking a swing at Krangle when at last he snapped.

"National security isn't cheap, mister. Where were you when Viet Nam was going on? In grade school?"

"Kindergarten."

"Well I was *there* Mister—at Khe Sahn."

"I've heard it all before," said Krangle, sitting back and lighting another Camel. "I'm sure you were very brave. But this is 1997. It doesn't wash—another foolhardy wasteful project."

"A vital national security concern," Knolls protested.

"Whose purpose is to fight *after* a nuclear war," Krangle said, exhaling the smoke through his nostrils slowly. "General, *after* a nuclear war—isn't that the Omega Force's mission?"

"That and in case of limited nuclear action—maybe a Red satellite like Bulgaria nukes the oil fields—we go in and secure the area to safeguard our oil supply and prevent occupation of the fields."

"Pretty unlikely, don't you think? In fact wouldn't you say that the very idea of there being anyone or anything to fight with after a nuclear war is—ridiculous?"

"War is always pretty unlikely, sonny, and yet it happens. Men go insane and order the annihilation of millions. We just prepare, God help us, for the worse."

"If your unit was even known about, the Reds would be down our goddamned throats diplomatically," Krangle said nervously.

"What do you mean?" Knolls asked.

"If there was a leak that we even *had* such a unit as Omega Force it could jeopardize the peace talks. The president wants your project cut, Knolls, and I'm going to tell him I want it killed entirely. There will be something else for you to do I'm sure—at the Pentagon."

The general pressed the intercom switch instead of knocking Krangle's plump face into mush. "Dennis, get me Sturgis and Chief Scientist Walters on tie-in—tell them to come to my office—drop everything." He turned back to Krangle. "Before," the general said, "you start cutting, mister, you'd better take a look around."

"Be delighted," Krangle grinned, "with your permission, of course. They said I needed your permission."

"You've got it. You'll see what we do, and then you'll order an immediate dropping of further cutting ideas in this area."

"Oh, will I?"

"You'll tell the president we are vital, Krangle. *Vital*."

"We'll see—I don't doubt that you are sincere," he said, more softly now, "but the Reds wouldn't be pleased about an American *post*-nuclear holocaust brigade. It's political, not personal, General. We can't signal to the Russians that we're preparing for post-Armageddon and expect them to negotiate with us."

"Are the Reds running this damned country?" Knolls exploded. "Are they telling us we can't defend ourselves anymore?"

"It's not that."

"Well, mister, I never thought I'd see the day when some premier of Russia could say to the U.S. 'tsk tsk, please don't have any defense' and somebody in the White House would say 'oh, okay, we'll disarm if it pleases you'."

"You're distorting the situation."

Sturgis opened the door. Behind him was Chief Scientist Walters. They all shook hands.

"I want you two to show Krangle everything," Knolls said. "He has top security. Impress on him the necessity of our unit. Show him what we can do for the country. I want him to go back to the president and say, 'Mr. President, Omega isn't getting enough money.'"

The first place Krangle was taken to was the testing cavern. Let him see the firepower, Sturgis thought. That should impress him.

"With these suits," Sturgis said as he guided the servo-robot out and up the corridor toward the firing range, "the American ground force becomes the most powerful in the world."

"*Ground* force is supposed to be *the Army*," Krangle said slyly. "Aren't they spending enough without the Air Force getting in on the act?"

Sturgis sighed. "The C.A.D. suit came out of the con-

47

cept of the lunar walk suits — and the weaponry out of
Air Force labs. To turn it over to another service would
have slowed development."

"Nevertheless there is a strict separation of duties between services," Krangle said, looking at the array of futuristic control panels filling the walls of the test center.

"How about the Marines? They do everything," Sturgis
said, guiding the robot into the huge scarred firing range.

"I'm against that — strict division of duties is more eco-
nomical," Krangle replied.

"In any case," said Sturgis, "watch the monitor. The
robot will fire EB-11's — electroballs — into the boulder
field at the rear of the cavern."

Sturgis pushed the activation switch. Blinding light
flashes were muted by the red screen. They could see the
electroballs slam into the immense wall and rip out thou-
sand-ton chunks like plaster.

"More powerful than a TOW anti-tank missile," Sturgis
said proudly.

"Impressive, but a TOW is a lot cheaper. This is dupli-
cation of effort Sturgis — and money. Army military
should be doing this."

"It's part of the C.A.D.S. suit concept," Sturgis said.
"Come this way Mr. Krangle, I'll show you what I mean."

Sturgis led the OMB bureaucrat down a hall until they
emerged into an antiseptically clean, aluminum-walled
chamber filled with racks of the seven-foot tall black
C.A.D.S. suits, side by side, a sleeping army of giants.
One of the suits moved slowly toward them as a voice
came out over a speaker built into it, and one of the
giant arms snapped up in salute.

"Sir, Corporal Hayward, sir," the voice said.

"At ease, Hayward," Sturgis said to the arsenal-of-
death before him. "We're just showing one of our Washington friends what the C.A.D.S. are capable of. Mr.
Krangle, would you come over here and hold onto the

corporal's outstretched arm?"

Krangle, looking a little mortified, grabbed hold of the nearly four-foot long appendage bristling with hidden weaponry.

"Lift," Sturgis ordered. The C.A.D.S. suit operator hoisted the 250 pound-plus Krangle up until he was nearly three feet off the ground.

"Okay, okay," the OMB official called down.

"Down," Sturgis said and the arm quickly but gently lowered Krangle to the floor. "Now jump," Sturgis ordered.

"Well I can't go too high," Hayward said, "but—"

He pushed up slightly and with a single whooshing burst from his jet-pack, rose instantly 18 feet in the air, almost bumping into the ceiling. Then landed without a sound.

"Oh I got it," Krangle smirked. "You fly, you lift anything, you save women, kill dragons. You're knights in shining armor. I see what you guys are playing at now. You're using the taxpayer's bucks to create your own fantasyworld—where you can do any—"

Sturgis hit him just like that.

No one picked Krangle up.

Sturgis snarled between his teeth. "I've seen my friends die testing this suit. They weren't playing at being knights in shining armor, mister. Don't even *suggest* it. They were trying to, as archaic as it might sound to you—help their country survive."

Krangle wiped the blood from his cracked lower lip and shook his head a few times." Slowly he picked himself up.

"*You*. You dare *hit me*?"

Fenton grunted. "Watch it mister, he'll do it again."

"Get me out of here—I want to see a doctor. You hurt my nose. I'll sue your goddamned ass. I'll bust you down to—"

Sturgis was about to return the fat man to the floor but Fenton caught his arm.

"I don't think this pile of blubber in a pinstripe suit could take any more, Sturg. Let him go and sue you."

Sturgis relaxed his fist as the man bolted out the door. Walters said, "You shouldn't have done it, but I don't think it would have done any good not to. The man is a fool and he's against us plain and simple."

"I should have let him have an electro-ball," Sturgis only half-joked.

"Right up the you-know-what," Fenton said in Her Majesty's heartiest English.

Twenty minutes later Sturgis was confined to quarters — order of General Knolls. The best man in tactics, in knowledge about the suits. The most admired soldier on base, the morale builder, Sturgis. And the man was blowing it all by swinging at government officials. Damn, Knolls thought. I need him — but — he went too far this time.

Sturgis stayed in his room and stared half-hypnotized at the TV's continuing stories about waves of terrorist sabotage in the NATO countries that were beginning to hamper their maneuvers and causing real fear and political instability. The beginnings of sabotage/terrorism directed at military installations in the U.S. was also rumored, though the FBI reported there was no similar wave going on here. "But law-enforcement officers throughout the country support the theory," went on Dan Rather, "that many of the 'sleeper' Cuban agents who had come here in the Mariel boat evacuation 20 years ago were being investigated and that arrests have been made."

The news that seemed to get the most attention, however, was a Chinese panda's new twin cubs in the Washington Zoo. The public was invited to win a free trip to somewhere or other by entering a contest to name the new twins.

Sturgis turned off the TV, lay back on his canvas bunk and lit a Camel. He wondered about these sabotage attacks—so widespread. The press wasn't making much of them. But it was yet another sign that though the peace talks were supposedly going well—dark forces were swimming below the surface. His mind wandered to other things—peace, always the elusive peace for mankind. He lay there as his pit bull Excalibur, with what could hardly be called a kindly face, though it seemed so to Sturgis, sat patiently looking at his master. Sturgis reached over and petted the dog's head. He remembered the three of them together—he, Robin and Excalibur. At the farm. That old farmhouse on 50 acres of land he had bought in Virginia. The floors creaked, the roof leaked, skunks liked to mosey through the loose boards—

"Fix it," Robin had insisted. But it was a loss really, leaning as it did. So he built a "shelter house" on the side of a mountain. It took almost two years—in the summer, on weekends—but slowly they excavated and created a home built into solid bedrock. "Make a hell of a bombproof house with all the comforts of home," Sturgis said, christening it with a bottle of champagne.

She had been angry. Not at the inside living quarters, but at the fact that it looked like a bomb shelter.

"Modern architecture," he told her with that smile that could both charm and irritate her so much.

"Have it your way," she said. But that was the beginning of the loss of the dream.

He had tried to reason with her.

"Honey," he had said, "I know you don't believe me, but this is for you, for us. War is a distinct possibility. If things get better we'll build a new house here too—and give this up."

"I'll indulge your macho fantasies," she had told him

51

coldly, "as long as you leave a window in, and let me pick the curtains."

So he had and they had spent many of his leaves up there, wandering through the fields picking petals from the carpet of daisies. They talked about kids. She wanted them, soon. She had begged him to quit the military. But he wouldn't. He couldn't.

"Look at it this way, Dean, you could make five times as much working for a private firm developing—shit whatever the hell stuff you use in the military—electronics wasn't it?"

"Secret, honey, sorry."

"Shit. Anyway, wouldn't you make five times as much?"

"I like the military, I like the men, the morale, the patriotism. I'm old fashioned. My daddy raised me that way—a career soldier. In our blood since the Civil War. I'd rot away in some office stuffed with wheezing two-hundred-sixty-pound heart-attack candidates."

So it had gone like that for almost two years. But when the Omega project got off the ground there were fewer days of summer and winter vacation with her. She became cold and would angrily glare at him the few days he made it back to Baltimore each year. Their trips to the farm were shorter and increasingly bitter.

Then the divorce—the letter first, the uncontested separation papers in the mail at the PX. And then—a miracle—if having the second chance to love is a miracle.

They had a reconciliation at the Ronga-Lai Hotel in Key West a month ago; they had spent a week together, the sun setting on the blue lagoon outside their window each night, vibrant reds, and oranges, and yellows—the fireworks of nature. They'd never see eye-to-eye on peace and war, but there was that spark when her eyes met his. Those bottomless doe-like brown eyes. He reached for her. At first she half-fought him off.

"We're legally divorced," she said. "I don't know how you talked me into coming down here and going over everything with you again—what's the use?"

But he pulled her closer and said nothing.

"But we *can't*—we're—it's all over . . ." and with those words she plunged her mouth against his and her tongue entered his lips. He felt his passion for her—that he felt for no other woman and he pulled down the straps of her pinafore dress.

"No, no—" she pulled away, desperately trying to regain what she had already lost of herself, and failing.

He reached behind her and started undoing the snaps of the dress, never letting her go. She struggled in his arms, kicked at him and then stopped. Her lips stroked along his cheek and she started unbuttoning his stiff military shirt, and before she finished she had his exposed shoulder covered with kisses, moaning softly as he ripped the last few snaps of her dress off and pushed it to the floor. She stepped out of it—and she felt Dean's hands slide down her chilled back and into her thin applegreen underpants.

Moaning, she passionately kissed his shoulder and moved up to his neck. He knew her anatomy. His hands moved expertly, encouraging her to surrender and she did, letting her bra slip to the carpet, revealing her warm full breasts which pressed against his hairy bare chest and the cold dogtag he wore.

She was lifted in strong muscular arms and carried to the motel's wide bed and dropped there—and he was beside her—on her—over her—inside her. She had closed her eyes and started mumbling.

"Oh yes, oh yes, oh my love, my love," she whispered in his ear. "Yes, yes, darling . . . yes. You'll always be a part of me. It's the only—"

She was lost in a snowstorm of emotion, as was Dean. It was a new beginning for them. They were over their divorce like they had been over their stormy marriage.

They would marry again—and he would start thinking about leaving the military and working with assholes like the one he just punched out this morning. He sighed.

Maybe the loss of his temper this morning would get him thrown out. That would solve things—perhaps that's what he was hoping. If she'd have him back—they'd have kids—grow old together—at least until they started dropping the big ones.

They would abandon his bombshelter farm—and live in a prime target zone like New York—so they would be among the lucky dead when the war happened.

CHAPTER SIX

In the icy waters of the North Atlantic, at a depth of 450 feet over the mid-ocean mountain ridge, sat the USS *Shark*, a Neptune Class nuclear powered missile sub. It carried 20 multiple warhead 10-megaton nukes ready for launch within 60 seconds. It was on station, supposedly in a location undetectable by Red spy satellite or sonar ships. But the new Red spy satellites in the sky had deep eyes, deeper than western analysts imagined. From an altitude of 645 miles it was picking up traces of the heat put out by the two powerful atomic engines of the craft. A Russian killer submarine of the Iryunkin class — with atomic torpedoes, had been relayed the information and was approaching on a heading that would intercept the U.S. sub within one hour.

To the men aboard the USS *Shark* it was business as usual. Four hundred men were eating, enjoying the recreation and sun rooms, and tending to the smooth running of the ultra-modern craft. In the radar/sonar room, Lieutenant Ferris stared with boredom at the sweeping electromagnetic dial of his sonar. He had his earphones half off, draped below his ears. The damned things hurt with their sharp beeps. Instead he had a pair of Sony Walkman phones to his ears as he listened to "Hey You, Get Off of

My Cloud", an old song by the Rolling Stones, and one of his favorites.

He suddenly heard a louder beep increasing in rate and tone. Damn—another malfunction on the screen—appearing to be a rapidly approaching enemy sub. He pressed the Test button and hit three function keys in a lackadaisical way with his index finger. "Test Verification—Enemy sub at 5 miles and *closing*," appeared on his screen in green digital letters. Ferris dropped the candy bar he had been opening and signaled the captain on priority code.

"Captain Norstrom," he called. "Captain?"

At last the captain responded. "What the hell is it? I'm in the middle of a meeting."

"Ferris here sir—I've got a confirmed—and I wondered—"

The captain instantly hit the Emergency Scramble Alert and its ear-shattering drone rang throughout the ship. "Damn," Norstrom said as he bolted from his quarters. Another cat and mouse game with the Reds was about to begin. He had been in one on the *Shark* last year. But he thought that fun-and-games were over now that the talks were on. Apparently not!

Captain Norstrom made his way quickly up three decks to the sonar room. He double-checked the verification procedures, but it was true—they were being tailed.

He ordered all the water-tights sealed as the sub burst into defensive activity. The sailors had seen it all before, another of those damned games they had played under the polar ice last year with a small Polish mini-sub, obviously on a spying expedition, which had stumbled onto them. They hoped this wouldn't take too long—especially those late-shift sailors awakened from a sound sleep. Discarded *Playboy* magazines fluttered to the floors in the heat of the engine rooms and among the living quarters, now devoid of its fifty or so loungers.

The captain stared at the large sonar screen lit up with the red combat signals of the S-Section. "Did you run an ID?" he asked Ferris, who remained at the controls.

"Yessir," the lieutenant replied. "It's a Class A attack sub — nuclear — probably Russian, running radio silent. Appears to be on an intercept course with us, though like always I'm sure it's going to turn around soon."

"*Damn*," the captain bit his lip, and it started bleeding violet in the dim light. He dabbed it with a handkerchief. Class A. He had never encountered one before — a class designed to *kill* subs like his. Of course, that would mean all-out nuclear war — taking out 67 U.S. counter-strike sub-launched nukes would certainly touch off World War III. No, there was no chance of that happening — but the damned Reds could be out to force us into a deadly game of chicken — see our maneuver capabilities, photograph and analyze our defense/offense capabilities. It had to be that — it couldn't be . . . Couldn't.

"Get me that damned Red skipper on the phone," Captain Norstrom bellowed.

"Sir? That's against — regulations!"

"The commie asshole better be told that he's trespassing."

They tried in vain to contact the killer sub's captain. "Intercept in five minutes," Ferris said, keeping his eye on the increasingly loud beeps.

"Max speed, evasive tactics. Take her down to 5600," Norstrom commanded, now on the horn to the helm.

"Will do," said the smooth voice below, and suddenly the sub tilted. It was sort of like an entire office building tilting, but with little indication of motion, so smooth was its descent into the depths.

The captain stared nervously at the screen. "Well?"

"It's following sir, and gaining, say — at thirty knots per hour — "

"Electronic countermeasures."

"Yessir," Ferris contacted countermeasure station, where they had a few tricks of their own.

Blasts of aluminum foil emerged from a torpedo tube, designed to confuse Russian radar and sonar with a storm of electro-reflective materials.

"Get on the horn to ELF in Michigan, Derment," shouted Norstrom, "and tell them what's going on."

"They couldn't raise the ELF satellite relay today sir," Derment replied. "Interference."

"Is ELF-2 below the horizon at this time of day?" Norstrom asked Wooster, the communications officer.

Wooster paled. "No sir. It should be on contact right now — and it isn't. It's *dead* sir. What should I do?"

The captain felt a bead of sweat form and wiped his eyes.

"I'll tell you in a moment." At that moment, deep in his knotted guts, Norstrom knew they had entered the first stages of World War III. It would start like this — a satellite out, the Reds trying to destroy the counter-attack capabilities of the west. This sub was the best of the U.S. Counter-Attack Forces. Norstrom knew his duty.

"Activate missile banks."

"But sir . . ." Lieutenant Colonel Saperstein, in charge of nuclear crews and equipment, began. "We don't have auth . . ."

"Activate," Captain Norstrom yelled. He ripped open the orange-plastic sealed envelope once he got it out of the safe — and read the orders.

Firing coordinates for their missiles were — Leningrad, Moscow, Kiev, 20 other Red cities, Riga, Odessa. How many people, how many children, how . . .

"Prepare to fire while moving," Norstrom instructed the launch crews.

"Sir? The wash — it would — " Saperstein began.

"Destroy us. We're all *dead men* as of right now, — sorry . . ."

58

"I'm sorry too sir. Thank you." He turned to the moving blips.

The sub's missile command station suddenly grew so silent you could hear a pin drop as they sent the commands to the computer to bring up the dormant missiles to firing sequence.

"Set them for full-launch, fully armed. Bring the count down to ten seconds and hold."

But the trailing Red sub wasn't about to give them 10 more seconds to get their load of nukes off. The Russian commander gave the order to fire as they closed to within 1500 feet of the USS *Shark*. Two nuke torpedoes shot out from the forward launch tubes, ripping a foaming pathway 50 feet below the water line. Their laser-guided sighting system turned them slowly to the left as they ripped through the ocean like twin porpoises of bleak death.

The nuke torpedoes exploded in a hellfire, blasting a 60 by 50 foot hole in the mid-section and 400 screaming American sailors went down, into the depths. Around impacted sections, steel doors closed.

The captain ordered the remaining watertight doors sealed. Somehow they were alive. The controls were dead.

"*Jesus*," Norstrom muttered. He felt nauseous. They were descending rapidly. "Blow the ballast," he yelled as the hand of a sailor was chopped off by the slamming of a compartment door, sealing off the section he was in. Water was already waist high—the pipes were bursting.

"Ballast blown aft, not responding in—"

"Mayday! Mayday! Buoys to the surface—" The bump he heard told him that the radio transmitting red buoy had been ejected from the stern and was rising to the surface—they were in 9400 feet of water.

Captain Norstrom was shoulder high in the water now. The subdued red light of the combat lamps flickered and died. He was in total blackness. He could hear the coughing and screams for help of sailors floating about him, gasping at the air near the ceiling. He was going under, then pushed himself up. He was just a few inches from the ceiling. He felt terror, sharp heart-pounding terror for the first time in his life. They were going to die — all of them. And if they didn't, what would there be left to live for — now. He knew that while they sank like a bloated corpse to the bottom, up there the big war was about to begin. All those bombs, thousands upon thousands of them, each one equal to 1,000 times, 10,000 times the destructive power of the Hiroshima bomb. Damn, his kids, his wife, the countryside around their Colorado ranch, all would soon be, or already was charcoal, glowing with the grinning eyes of death. He felt liquid streaming down his face but could barely notice the tears, as he was neck high in water.

"Goddamn fucking bombs, why'd they ever invent them?" Norstrom screamed into the three-inch airspace above him.

Suddenly a hatchway shot open just to the side of him. A mangled head shot toward him, its eyes and teeth and tongue all ripped, trailing veins and flesh in a thin stream of blood behind it. The head came right at the captain, one twisted eye fixed on him, the teeth almost moving from the currents of the water, as if coming to life. It was Ferris! Behind it, a geyser of water shot into the control room quickly filling the last airpocket.

Captain Norstrom screamed. And when he opened his mouth again, he took in only water.

One-thousand miles above, 24 Russian Cosmoprobe 'astronomical' satellites changed orbits to be on impact paths with the U.S. spy satellites. They glided now through the depths of space, their laser eyes looking, searching for the targets they would soon find . . .

The Cosmoprobe satellites — supposedly peaceful astronomical instruments aimed at X-ray sources in far off space, were actually complex weapons of war—nuclear armed EMP devices—that once activated, would move out of orbit and intercept any object—like a U.S. spy satellite—and explode with immense radiation, enough to generate an electromagnetic pulse that could destroy all electronic equipment for 10 miles—and the resultant radiation spectrum would spread. That was the new advantage the Russians built into these EMP devices—EMP would spread and mimic a huge flare from the sun, setting off a spectacular aurora that would appear to be an unusual, though natural, occurrence.

When the Americans realized their eyes-in-the-sky were dead their scientists would conclude it had happened naturally. Or so the Kremlin's top strategists hoped. They needed time, just a little more, just hours—

President Armstrong was called ten minutes later and told the USS *Shark* had apparently sunk in the North Atlantic—with 432 men aboard.

"Was it—an attack?" he asked Admiral Turner.

"We don't know. The mayday buoy was deployed—they were in 9000 feet of water—they were in position on routine patrol and something happened but we don't know exactly what."

"Was there radiation leakage?"

"Probably, sir. It was carrying sixty-seven multiple warhead ICBMs—if there was an explosion . . ."

"Are any of our ships nearby?"

"Negative, sir. They are as you know all spread out throughout the North Atlantic on randomly selected computer determined positions to deter aggression."

The president thought a moment. "Turner, what is your assessment?"

"Can't give it sir. Normally I would have the Air Force

boys zoom in their lenses on their surveillance satellite Beta, which is over that area, for a close look-see."

"Why can't you do that? Wouldn't that show if there is a Red ship near the scene of the sinking?"

"That satellite has been knocked out. Some sort of solar flare, the tracking station says. It happens. Sometimes the interference lasts a few days—happened on the last shuttle flight to—"

"Then the Shark *could have been attacked and we wouldn't know?"*

"Yes," the admiral conceded. "We wouldn't know." Armstrong put down the phone and clicked on his intercom. "Mary, put me through to S.A.C."

He got on the line, "General Burke—put SAC on yellow alert—all leaves cancelled."

"Acknowledged, Mr. President! Acknowledged," Burke said. "A crisis?"

"I hope not. I hope to God this is all just a lot of bad, bad circumstance. But be ready to move!"

Next the president called Jerry, his aide-de-camp. "Jerry I want the entire crisis team," he thought a moment—"*and* the vice president in here, the Oval Office in a half hour. We've got a submarine down. It's one of our biggest—might have been taken out by the Reds."

"Holy shit," Jerry stuttered. "Will do, sir, but some are farther away—"

"Then get me those members of the team that can be here in a half hour. Get going."

"Yessir."

President Armstrong had his secretary run through the checklist of those to be notified—the Allies, the NATO commanders—of a potential crisis. She took care of it— with a team of aides who took over a phone room down the hall.

Armstrong went to the file, rolled it out and took out the *contingency envelope*—a carefully thought out response to a submarine attack. He tore it open.

Step One: Call the Russian president and inform him that you are aware that an American submarine has been destroyed and that—

He didn't finish reading it before he was on the steps of marble leading down to the Hotline Room, manned 24 hours a day by two Marine officers. They snapped to attention.

"At ease—put me through to the premier of the Soviet Union, son—"

"Sir, it's five a.m. there in Moscow."

"I'm aware of that. Put me through."

"Telex or voice?"

"Voice," the president said. "Picture if you have that."

"We don't sir, not at his house."

"Well then, get him on the phone."

The phone rang for five minutes before the premier's voice, overlaid by an interpreter's English—smooth, non-emotional, came on.

"What took you so long?"

"Shouldn't you be saying that you are sorry to be disturbing my sleep?" said the Russian premier.

"Normally I would—but it's you, Yuri, who are disturbing *my* sleep."

"Don't talk in riddles, Armstrong. What do you want?"

"You know, Mr. Premier. One of our submarines, the *Shark*, has met with disaster, and I suspect—"

"You suspect, you suspect—why is it when everything is improving, when the spirit of detente—"

"*I suspect*," overvoiced the president, "that your side has done something rather nasty to it."

"You are accusing the Soviet Union of damaging a submarine? Where? How?"

"In the Atlantic. This could be serious, Yuri. We will take the loss seriously if you have anything to do with it—and will respond," he looked at the contingency plans language and read, "appropriately."

"What makes you think we are responsible for this accident?"

"Our surveillance satellite over that area had a simultaneous accident — quite a coincidence, don't you think?"

The premier's voice rose, uneasy under the translator's bland translation. He was defensive, greatly agitated, upset, and shouted:

"I know nothing of this."

Then he seemed to stop — for a moment — then continued.

"Just a minute. I have a report just handed to me." Another pause. "Ah. Mr. Armstrong. The mystery is over. Would you like to hear?"

"By all means, Yuri, if you can explain — "

"I regret to say, Mr. President, that one of *your* stupid commanders has crashed his submarine into one of our undersea exploration vessels resulting in an inestimable loss of life — this matter will come up at the United Nations tomorrow — goodnight." Click.

The president was angry. But relieved. An accident — it had to be. His hands felt sweaty as he replaced the receiver — a terrible accident — probably their fault — but an accident.

His breathing steadied. He walked back to his office and called his wife.

"Honey, I'll have to be at the office for awhile. Nothing serious. I'll call you later."

"But dinner with the Peruvian — "

"Tell him I'm sorry — *have* to go — " he made a kiss and got off.

"Shit," he picked up the phone. "Mary, have my crisis staff assemble in conference room A. And I'll meet with *whoever* shows up Mary, get on the stick."

"Yessir."

Twenty minutes later they had all assembled in the

64

White House conference room — the Secretary of State, the top Pentagon brass, Admiral Turner, and the Security-1 Team. The admiral had the latest information.

"Mr. President, that 'accident' — do you trust the Soviet premier's response on this?"

"How do we know he's telling the truth?" asked the Secretary of Defense. "We have no independent verification. We must retaliate — take out one of their ships."

"This is the most serious provocation since the Cuban Missile Crisis in the '60s" shouted General Burns, the acerbic red-headed chief of the Army.

"Calm, gentlemen, calm," the president directed. They were seated around the long table in the middle of the conference room.

The vice president interrupted. "Mr. President, before we begin — the complete war room and facilities in the shelter below the White House is now completed, is it not?"

The president paled. Everyone was silent.

"You mean the *bomb shelter*?"

The vice president continued, "In the interests of precaution, Mr. President, perhaps we could adjourn for a moment and continue the meeting in the facilities prepared below — the bomb shelter. It has everything."

"Well, as a precaution," the president said, after a silence, "I don't see the harm."

They rose and began filing out. No one said a word as they strode down the hall with the Marine guard in the lead to the steel doors of the elevator.

It was a long ride down, the sinking sensation in the stomachs of the men increasing for about a minute, then levelling off. The ride was smooth and easy, but they could sense moving downward at an increasing rate. The president had been down only once, to inspect the enormous, impregnable facility.

"How deep is it sir?" CIA Director Quarterman asked,

breaking the silence.

"2345 feet."

"My God, we'll be in this elevator for the next ten minutes."

"No, it's a two minute ride. We're descending quite rapidly."

They were silent—and when the gravity increased and the pressure built under their feet for the last minute they knew they were arriving. The steel door slid open perfectly level with the smooth marble floor. The fluorescent lights of the hallway before them and the saluting Marine guards greeted them.

"Must be tough son," the president said to one of the guards. "Duty down here must be tough . . ."

"Yessir. No sir, I mean. Proud to serve, sir!"

"At ease, Marine," he said. They walked down the corridor, which was tastefully appointed with warm wallpaper featuring lilacs and roses. Here and there a Turner painting accented the decor.

"Looks like a museum," the secretary of state said.

"More like a mausoleum," whispered the president under his breath, then he looked back and said, "It feels clammy even though I know the air is as fresh as a mountain breeze in here. I just get the feel of being buried alive here." He shivered. That was why he had never been down here—except that once. There were many offices—but he and the Crisis Group headed directly for the conference room's oak doors, which were opened by two other Marine guards.

"How many hours a day are you down here, son?" the president asked one.

"On duty fourteen hours a day for six months—then six months leave—we sleep down here, eat here, sir."

"My God—make a note to have the schedule more rotated, Miss Ross." His secretary jotted something down.

They entered the room which had an artificial window

with lights behind it to make it appear as if the shade were merely drawn on an outdoor vista. Clever. And there was an elaborate cut-glass chandelier pouring friendly full-spectrum lighting down on the long oak conference table.

"Well gentlemen, be seated."

"Perhaps we need some water," suggested Stanford. Two waiters brought what they needed.

There was a defense communications technician standing to one side of an enormous blank wall.

"Watch this gentlemen," the president grinned. "Screen," he said.

The technician punched into his computer keyboard and the wall rolled up to reveal a complex array of status reports and grid maps depicting the world military situation including hourly updated placement of the entire Russian fleet.

The president scanned the monitor, conferred quietly with his aide-de-camp Jerry, then said aloud:

"The CIA and other intelligence says that there is no current evacuation of any Soviet cities. NORAD reports no Soviet bombers on its screens, nor any cruise missiles or ICBM's. Perhaps it was an unprecedented magnetic storm that knocked out our satellites. General Burns, how soon can your people send aloft a new spy satellite or two?"

Burns was already on the phone speaking softly and rapidly into it. "I'm talking to Vandenberg Base now sir, there's a TELOS satellite on the launch pad — we estimate we'll have a satellite in orbit in two hours tops and it will be at station over the Soviet Union in another hour after that. Three hours at least until spy satellite intelligence is restored."

"Then," said the president, "just in case, we'll all stay down here, but I think the crisis is manageable gentlemen, if the Soviets are lying about the sea incident —

Jerry, hand me the *contingency package* for Soviet Action against one of our nuclear missile subs—I left it there on top of the stress analysis report on the Russian premier's voice pattern—which came out negative, gentlemen. Ah, thanks Jerry. Gentlemen, we've already initiated Step One: Calling the premier on the hot line. Step Two is to go to Red Alert, send bombers aloft. That could be provocative . . . Step Three of the plan is to destroy one of *their* ships—not very imaginative—or better yet—to make it look like an accident just as they made our loss appear like an accident. Tit for tat. What do you say?"

"I disagree," said Williamson. "If it *was* an accident, why kill *more* people? If it *wasn't*, we'd better spend all our time on preparing for total war, rather than squandering it on managing a counter-incident at sea—scrap the contingency plan."

It was a consensus around the table that the vice president had something there. The president wrung his bony white hands a bit, but sighed and nodded. "Of course you're right on this one, Williamson. Good thinking."

"Sir," said the tech sergeant at the computer monitor. "Something is coming up on the screen. From NORAD on number two monitor."

They turned to the indicated screen. A dull glow spread across the map depicted there, the borders of the Soviet Union.

"What the hell is that?"

"NORAD reports it's an odd weather pattern—interfering with our radar in Turkey and the other border states."

"Is it that magnetic storm?"

"Not verifiable at this time, sir."

"Damn. Their bombers could be taking off at this minute. Their goddamned nuclear missiles too, Mr. President," screamed General Burns, "and we are fucking around here twiddling our thumbs."

"What would you do? Attack a weather pattern?"

asked the science advisor.

"Is that your opinion of what is going on?"

"Yes, Mr. President. It's possible — unlikely, but possible."

"Shit," said Burns, red faced and steaming.

"Keep the information coming, Sergeant."

"Yes, Mr. President."

They sat there staring at the screens. The president looked at his watch. Twenty minutes more and the new spy satellite goes up — another hour and a half until it reaches station. Sit tight. Just sit tight. His mouth felt dry as a bone.

In the Super Class Command Sub *The Lenin*, 1200 men maintained a fantastic undersea command center to carry out the war plans of the imminent invasion. Rows of technicians were constantly in touch with all ground, sea and air forces. This submarine, the brainchild of Supreme Marshal Voloshnikov had been the first to receive the triumphant news: It had begun. The U.S.S. *Shark* is down!

The glorious time had arrived! At last his policy of being first to attack — his master plan for surprise occupation of the west and then domination of the world in a Pax Soviet, would be carried out. Supreme Marshal Mikael Voloshnikov was told in person by the premier, speaking via radio from Moscow.

"It has begun and they are unaware of it. The plan is working," said the premier, elated. "General Petrin's Special Forces are aboard their paradrop planes on their way to Washington, D.C. The sand drops through the hourglass. The last few grains are slipping down."

Voloshnikov smiled, put down the phone, and poured himself a vodka while his mind drifted to the upcoming battle in Washington.

Petrin's Gray Suits, as they were called, would be in the thick of the action. General Voloshnikov himself had years ago given the go-ahead to this brainchild of one of his best men, General Petrin. They were the special-weapons armored anti-radiation suited troopers who would jump into Washington—which hopefully would not be totally destroyed for it was targeted with neutron bombs.

Voloshnikov strode triumphantly, dressed in his full dress officer's uniform with medal-filled jacket, up the marble staircase to the second level of the submarine attack-control base. More than a submarine, *The Lenin* was a veritable high-tech mansion under the sea. And it was his. The largest, best submarine ever built. His to rule. His to wreak destruction with.

He had always hated the United States. Raised in a strict Marxist family, sent to Soviet special gifted grammar and high schools, he had been well-indoctrinated to do so. But the really personal hatred began in Viet Nam, when he had been an advisor there, and the U.S. B-52s, in a surprise raid on Hanoi, had killed his wife and two children. From then on, he filled the years with a burning hate, watching as war grew closer.

This plan—code named Gagarin after the first man in space, was Voloshnikov's from the beginning. Twenty years of planning, of developing marvels like Petrin's Gray Suits, and this marvelous undersea command post, which was now headed toward the United States' east coast. Twice as big as the largest U.S. sub, *The Lenin* could stay self-sufficient for two years, move at 45 knots through the sea, and carry a mighty nuclear arsenal. The ship spent most of its time in hiding under the polar ice cap.

Voloshnikov, clad comfortably in a soft silk shirt and French-tailored trousers beneath his formal high-shouldered gold bedecked uniform, his hair dyed a pleasing brown, with just a touch of gray at the temple, was a striking figure. His brown eyes burned with the intensity of youth possessed, even though he was 59 years of age. He could never get used to the silence, the stability of this submarine — its nuclear twin propellers made no noise, the lighting was almost like daylight, it had none of the cramped feeling of a submarine at all. The rooms were spacious and had drapes along one wall with dim light behind them — false daylight. Every comfort — including women — was provided, though of course they were not the wives of the men, but rather the special service KGB trained relief women, that aside from their technical duties — ECM and communications — had been trained to perform the necessary services. The weary sailors might keep their morale up in the years the submarine would spend undersea. Voloshnikov, boarded *The Lenin* in the ice-clogged harbor of Murmansk, while his double took the train to Moscow. The double would appear on the parade reviewing stand, to keep suspicions down in the west. The first day in the sub, the real marshal had made use of a green-eyed full-bodied nymph named Natalya. She was the most beautiful of the choice KGB squad. The best.

He now walked down a red velvet carpet, saluted by every officer and sailor he passed, and entered the oak doors of the Naval War Command Center. There he sat down in the command chair and watched the vivid display of deep sea life before him. They were at 12,000 feet as a precaution, but rising to get better communications with the surface. How real the screen looked, like a giant window out into the water. Bizarre marine life passed by silently — glowing squid, huge multi-eyed monstrosities made of nothing but claws and mouths. He put on the earphones and listened with satisfaction at the reports pouring in. They were all good. The U.S. submarine fleet had sustained massive damage — and more missiles were on the way.

The Russians had expected to lose a few Soviet nuclear subs. Five or six perhaps of small ships carrying satellite country flags. But now, even this might be avoided. He glanced at his watch. One-half hour into the attack and all was well.

He could feel his powerful heart pounding. This was the sweetest revenge, this final onslaught on the capitalists of the west, the nation that had destroyed the family he had cherished. He was closing the port view and instead of fishes a computer map display appeared. It showed all the blue — the American ship positions, red for the Soviet ships of war.

The American ships were turning yellow all over the seas, indicating nuke hits. The red dots of the Russian subs and the green lights of their carriers were all still there —

"What's that?" said Voloshnikov. He leaned forward. No! It couldn't be! They couldn't have gotten the submarine *Peter the Great*! He heard the shaking voice of the commanding officer:

"It is gone — weep comrades, weep. Imperialist America has destroyed our beloved *Peter the Great*!"

This shook Voloshnikov. Perhaps an American officer had acted without orders from Washington. He watched the screen, and nothing else changed from red to blue. He eased back in the chair's soft velvet. A loss — tragic, he thought, but nothing like what was happening on the American side! The Americans still don't know!

He continued watching the silent battle. A forty-foot square table in the submarine command center had an instantaneous read-out showing the positions of all ships relayed down from the Soviet satellites, which were specially shielded from the attack-satellite bursts of damaging radiation, unlike the U.S. satellites.

From these heavenly vantage points, the Soviet Navy could be seen tagging the U.S. fleet. In this phase only the undersea forces were moving against their counterparts, but soon the surface ships would engage as well, when the undersea war was won.

This command submarine stayed well away from those fights, deep within the Arctic Ocean, and yet it maintained a constant stream of give and take with the commanders of the Soviet ships.

Voloshnikov was well-pleased with this command room's functioning and told the technicians to keep about their work, ignoring his presence.

Then he strode down the corridor to the next huge room and the different theatre of the war displayed there. The giant world map grid with the blinking, slowly moving positions of the Red air force. The few blue lights aloft—American fighters and bombers, were routine. The U.S. bombers were not in the air, still they were unaware of the happenings throughout the world. It was as the Americans would say, a turkey shoot.

He spent some time gleefully watching the screen, and then he went to the third room, as yet barely active. It showed a map of the United States and the 500 principal targets there still glowed blue, untouched by the missiles and bombs that would very soon burn away most of the U.S. population.

The screen was slowly lit up—the west, the east, and then the central U.S., where the heaviest missile attack would be—the U.S. Minuteman and Peacemaker missile bases. Those deep silos would take the biggest hits, hopefully, before they discharged their missiles into the air to retaliate for the surprise attack. All was quiet on this map—for now.

He went back to the Naval Theatre Room and watched the U.S. fleet being attacked, in visuals from the high-flying Soviet observation planes, as well as the digital read-outs from the computers. Everywhere the blue lights signifying U.S. carriers were turning yellow — read destroyed. It was going well, very well. If only the premier remains steadfast and gives no hint that the strange phenomena affecting the world's radiation levels and communications was anything other than a weird natural phenomena caused by solar flares.

And he knew that the premier was succeeding. He was the cleverest man who had ever ruled Russia, Lenin aside. He would give them the time they needed.

With Admiral Vestok and his flagship *Peter the Great* gone, the sea war was now in the hands of Vice Admiral Kuznetsov. And the new flagship — also a submarine — was the *Odessa*. Would there be less competence at those crucial moments in the early phase of the war? No, it didn't appear so. Kuznetsov was continuing the relentless pounding of the U.S. fleet, destroying those most dangerous of all U.S. vessels, the Neptune subs. The Neptunes had dozens of SLBMs on them — submarine launched ballistic missiles — that could hit Soviet targets. They *had* to be destroyed, and quickly. And looking at the number of yellow lights that came on replacing the U.S. blues, it was working as well under the command of young Kuznetsov as it had been under the veteran Vestok.

Voloshnikov felt his pulse rising. He himself would soon be sitting in the Ground Forces room, and directing the invasion forces now on their way in the huge troop landers from their battle stations off the American east coast. There would be instantaneous decisions of the utmost gravity to be made. Things that one can't anticipate as well as the inevitabilities of ship movements, speeds. He would need all his faculties and need them for several days without sleep. He was glad he had the nap. Who knows when the next chance for sleep would be? Perhaps after landing in North America, as a conquering general. Yes, a conqueror of the despicable mongrel race of

Americans.

General Petrin's Ilyusin-65 transport jet was poised for flight. Petrin sat and watched the hirsute hand of the flight engineer click all the situation switches and prepare the huge transport, now filled with Gray Suits, for the flight. A ten-thousand mile flight from this remote Siberian base to Washington—a Washington that should be a radioactive deserted city filled with bloated black bodies when they parachuted down.

He looked at his watch—the radar blotting devices should be on now along the Soviet border. Just before he took off he heard the exultant voice of his communications officer on his earpiece.

"Their satellites are dead. The EMP explosions from our killer satellites have worked and the Americans are swallowing the magnetic storm theory."

So, he thought, part one is going well. The U.S. subs with the nuclear missiles on them will now be picked off and we will take off under maximum invisibility, with the American spy satellites out of order and the cloaking devices making their ground radar ineffective. That's part two—once our bombers—and this troop transport and the six behind it—are just off the coast of America, the missiles will be launched. They will hit and destroy all the targets they can—five to a target—every major city, all military installations. Ten missiles apiece on the American ICBM silos and air bases. Then our bombers come in in waves and destroy what's left; and in the last maneuver of the brief deadly war, my men jump into Washington and seize it intact. For Washington will be hit with neutron devices not H-bombs. It will serve as our capital and if we can get President Armstrong to sign the peace document—on television and we broadcast his surrender—the peaceful occupation can begin without much interference

75

from the remaining U.S. forces.

It *would work*. Part one and two were already successful. Why not the whole package? Why not even the sixth element, the laser defenses of the Soviet Union, the secret installations around the expected targets—that will blast U.S. missiles and bombers from the sky, assuming they don't get an enormous number off the ground—a big assumption dependent on complete surprise. Well, it was too late now for questions. The die had been cast.

The immense six-engine jet transport rolled down the fog-covered runway without lights on and took off, destination: U.S.A.

"Onward to victory, comrades," Petrin shouted, lowering the face visor on his helmet and adjusting the oxygen rich mixture inside the plastic shield. America. In just hours they would be landing in a ravaged land, setting up a headquarters in the secured perimeter of Dulles Air Base near Washington.

There would be a month at most of work, suppressing the resistance, occupying the breadbasket of the world—the American midwest, teaching the surviving Americans to serve their distant masters. Russia would be like ancient Rome, he thought, bringing peace by the sword, making the whole world its colonies, its slave states, to do its bidding. It was the fate of the Motherland to rule the world, Voloshnikov had said. Now Petrin believed him.

"Sir," said Jerry, "we have a report on the telex from the Navy." The president just sat facing the wall, deep in thought.

"Here let me see that sonny," said Admiral Turner, snatching the sheet of paper from the messenger's hand. "Holy shit! Mr. President! There are Soviet ships and submarines *shadowing* all our carriers out in the seas—all over the world, the reports are the same—"

A drop of oily sweat rolled down the president's nose. He wiped it.

"Could it be *their* contingency plan? There has been damage—severe damage, the premier said, to *their* ship that collided with the *Shark*. Perhaps they are just being cautious—they perhaps suspect us of being up to tricks—"

"Bull," shouted Turner. "*Nuke 'em*! Nuke them now! Before they get their licks in." The admiral's face was growing red as an apple.

Another sheet of paper was ripped from the telex and handed to Jerry who read it aloud.

"A PBY-11 recon plane returned to Quantico with its tail half shot off. It reports incredible battles going on in the North Atlantic. There was so much smoke, it has to be the fleet, sir. Massive debris. The PBY fired upon by carrier based MIGs, sir. No national markings on them. They said all communications with ships at sea is impossible, a jamming effect. And the pilot says he saw a lifeboat—with U.S. markings—being fired on by the same sort of unmarked jets."

The president spoke softly. "Jerry, get me the red attache case from the safe." They all paled. The red case. The codes—changed daily—that would release all the ICBMs and cruise missiles, and send our S.A.C. bombers aloft.

The president dug down into his shirt, unbuttoning the collar and sending his red-striped tie askew. He found the chain with the key at the end.

Jerry put the red attache case in front of him. He took the key and placed it in the lock.

"It stays there, gentlemen, until I remove it, and the crisis is over, or until I turn it and open the case and read out the codes to our launch facilities. Pray, gentlemen, that this key isn't turned in the next three hours."

They all sat silently, the only sound being the telex machine.

Finally the secretary of state rose and leaned on white knuckles pressed to the table.

"Gentlemen, before we think about unleashing Armageddon, I suggest we call the Russian premier again and inform him about these unmarked planes of Soviet MIG design. Maybe one of his admirals has lost his marbles and the premier—maybe he'll stop whatever the hell he's pulling off."

The president nodded. They all agreed. The president picked up the red phone in front of him. A few minutes later the premier's voice, again overlaid by the bland interpreter, came on the line.

"Mr. President?" The premier said. "What is going on?"

The president told the premier that he would consider any moves on the U.S. fleet as an attack on the United States to be met with total nuclear retaliation—the first time in history since the Cuban missile crisis that that threat was ever used.

"I see," said the Russian. Turner whispered in the president's ear: "Make sure the voice-stress thing is on. I know the bastard is lying."

Turner met the Soviet premier—a jolly man, outwardly, with white hair, a bit bent with age, yet tall—six foot three and well built. They had talked at a party—he noticed the Russian drank Perrier, not vodka—sly bastard.

"Too bad we don't have video so we could see the bastard," Turner said. "Then I could look at his eyes and tell you he's lying for sure."

The premier's voice, overlaid by a translator's calm tones, came on after a long pause.

"I assure you, Mr. Armstrong, there are no Soviet—er—maneuvers near your ships—anywhere. You are misinformed. All our planes bear markings, and are on

78

routine—"

"And I assure you, Mr. Premier, something is up out there, and we know it involves hostile actions. And desist immediately or we will retaliate massively with our complete nuclear arsenal."

"I don't understand what you are saying, Mr. President," came the reply. "Your equipment must be malfunctioning. There is no attack. Soviet ships, planes and soldiers are in place. It's your computers, your *generals. They* might be trying to instigate war between our nations."

The president glanced at the generals. They all shook their heads.

"I have consulted with all my experts, Mr. Premier. Our reports are accurate. Desist immediately. If I don't hear that your forces are breaking off in fifteen minutes, I will be forced to take unprecedented action."

There was another long pause, then the dry voice shaking with emotion.

"You shame yourself, President Armstrong—I do not wish war. I tell you your reports are madness. Why do you lie to Misha? Aren't we friends? Have not we visited one another's home? Did I not give your child a puppy dog? Are we to—"

The president signalled to cut off the broadcast.

"The premier is stonewalling us. That is the only conclusion." He looked at the screens. Still no communications to update the positions of the ships in the U.S. fleet. Last known Soviet positions projected on the giant situation map before them shown as red dots near the U.S. blue ones. The electronic red dots—versions of the death approaching the U.S.

The president looked at his watch. "Fourteen minutes more, if we don't hear that our fleet is safe."

Three of the generals nodded—two dissented.

"Launch *now!*" demanded Air Force General Abrams.

79

"You have to launch!" he yelled, leaping forward. A nearby Marine restrained him.

"No," said the president. "We give them time."

"How much time can we safely give them, Mr. President?"

The president sighed. "If anyone wants to start World War III now instead of giving this situation *a little time*, raise your hands." He was red-faced, livid with anger.

No one raised their hand.

"Well if you put it that way," said General Burns.

"I *do* put it that way," said the president. "We wait, until we're sure it's an attack. Our ground radar will give us enough time to launch most of the ICBMs even if the satellite eyes are out. The Russians can't be madmen. They know that. And whatever is happening, if they are attacking, they will be dead thirty minutes after we launch—and I will launch, I assure you gentlemen, if their missiles come over the pole at us."

"What if they have some defense against our missiles?" asked Williamson. "The possibility exists that they have made some sort of breakthrough in defensive weapons against our missiles, and are launching a surprise attack based on that capability to defend themselves."

The president turned to his science advisor, white haired Gridley, who shook his head.

"Unlikely. We're ahead on that score. What does CIA say?" he asked.

Quarterman was white faced. "My latest information is in agreement with Gridley. There is no new anti-missile system in Russia. That's virtually assured."

"Then we wait *a few damned minutes*. We can't start a war when it isn't clear if we are under attack or not. Remember the computer foulups of the late 1980s, when the SAC computer insisted that we were under attack and Reagan gave the red alert signal and sent all our bombers scrambling? No one to this day, outside of a handful of people knows about that fiasco. Thank God he didn't launch the missiles—it turned out, as you are all aware, that the computer was reading the Soviet satellites in orbit as Soviet missiles headed our way."

Turner sighed. "I take back what I said. It could be some sort of terrorist activity during a solar flare. I can't believe Russia has a way to prevent us from hitting back."

The crisis team stared at the one man who would make the final decision and the ominous brief case that would set it off.

"Then we sweat this one out," the president concluded. "If anyone knows a prayer, please say it . . . Supreme Court ruling or no Supreme Court ruling."

CHAPTER SEVEN

General Knolls had all his men assembled in the main briefing hall at Omega Base. The air was chilled with the news updates coming in by the minute. Men, even hardened vets, walked around with moist eyes. Knolls called for order and addressed his troops.

"C.A.D.S. Troopers, I've had a call into Strategic Center for a half hour — something's up, but when I ask what, they say 'hold for orders', and they're still holding. I've exceeded my orders by assembling you here and telling you this."

Sturgis, in the second row, smiled. Now *the general* was disobeying orders.

"Anyway," continued Knolls, "I want this unit ready to move out on short notice. All scheduled training is cancelled. I want all suits combat ready, all equipment checked and loaded on our special vehicles — Rhinos and Tri-wheels. I want the Rhinos charged and the suit batteries replaced with new ones, even if they're only one-hour old — and I want this to start the minute you leave here.

"I don't think we'll be hit in the initial attack — no one, I hope to God — knows we're more than a tree farm. If we are hit, probably it will happen before we can do anything. There's no use thinking about that. The first I hear

82

of any definite attack, we move out, orders or no orders. I know I can depend on you men."

He looked down somberly, then added, "Any questions?"

Fenton stood up. "Can't you tell us any more, sir? Are there planes in the air? Are our bombers, fighters up?"

"Negative, but I do know, Sergeant, there's a major crisis."

The general was handed a sheet of paper. He read it quickly, then put up his hand asking for silence.

"Gentlemen, one of our subs has been destroyed—possibly deliberately—the USS *Shark*. The president has been in conference with the Soviet premier and has not received assurances to his satisfaction that it was an accident." Knolls suddenly looked old, grim. "Then—" Rossiter blurted out, "it's war . . ."

"It's *not war yet* damnit," he exploded from the tension. "But we're on the brink of it—this is how it would start. I don't like what's happening on our side. Decisive steps to maximize our position should have been taken by now—orders sent out—and nothing is happening at SAC. They should be *up*."

Sturgis balled his fists in his coveralls. The jerkoffs in the Pentagon and the Capitol are fools, he thought. They should have all the planes in the air, the silo doors blown and open just in case. The cruise missiles, with the charges activated that could destroy them in flight if it were a false alarm, should be on their way to the Soviet Union. They were wasting *time* in Washington talking to the Red bastards when there was *no time*. While they stall us, they grow closer and closer with their goddamned claws around our throats.

The mental image of an atomic bomb's mushrooming cloud flashed in his mind—then the thought of Robin, his wife. She *was* his wife; even if they were divorced. She was in a big city—Baltimore. She would die, instantly. If only she were out here in Diablo Springs, where some of the other men's wives were. Out here in the western desert next to no targets, unless the Reds were on to the fact that White Sands wasn't raising trees after all . . .

Robin, he pushed the thought of her blue eyes blinded by the nuclear fireball out of his mind, only to be replaced by the mental picture of her skin bursting into flames on the side facing the blast — like the Hiroshima pictures he had seen.

General Knolls continued:

"The crisis could simmer down, but it doesn't look good, so I want all of you men to plan a move out — get the Rhinos charged up — "

"Sir?" interrupted Laird Van Patten, the project scientist, "only three of the Rhinos have power. The contractor delivered the wrong — "

"What!"

"The contractor delivered a defective set of batteries — and we're waiting for replacements. And even then — "

The general sighed in disbelief. "All right Van Patten, how many Rhino all-terrain amphibious vehicles do we have?"

"We have six sir, but not all ready — with the N-3 charger that can refuel the batteries of the other Rhinos. I suppose I can scavenge two and make four operate fully . . ."

"Armaments?"

"Full array on those four, sir — 55mm twin guns ready to fire, the howitzer cannon, mortar, four ground-to-air missiles on each."

"How about the Tri-wheelers?"

"Out of two hundred possible we have one hundred in parts and about thirty malfunctioning — about seventy are combat ready."

"Get thirty more together. I want at least one hundred of them operative by tomorrow. Sturgis?"

"Yessir?"

"I want your men to be ready for intensive briefing tonight — no absence, all on alert — in equipment rooms or in their barracks when off duty. Have them help refit the Tri-wheels that need work — and get those damned suits charged. Rossiter's a whiz with the suits, get him on it."

Knolls pulled down a series of large maps side by side on a wide panel showing in detail the terrain of the U.S.

"Now, I don't know what kind of deployment we're going to be asked to execute, but I'll bet it's going to focus on the east, though we can't discount moves toward California or Arizona. I figure the Pentagon will surely give us word soon. It might be hours, or a week — but this crisis, if it fades, will just precipitate another one. I want you all to be familiar with off-the-road conditions everywhere. You four men," he said, picking out Lieutenant Glenner, Colonel Sturgis, Colonel Moyers, and Major Dawkins, "are going to lead the force in twenty-five-man teams."

"Off-the-road?" mumbled Rossiter, the going-to-fat puffy-faced tech sergeant who re-upped recently and hadn't been on the project for more than six months. Sturgis fumed. Rossiter was a damned good tech, but a sloppy soldier. And Rossiter had the uncanny knack of saying the wrong thing at just a crucial time. Like now. Rossiter continued, "I mean, sir, I expect I'll be in Colonel Sturgis' group as usual and they — they ride *too fast* off the road . . ."

Sturgis frowned. "We're going off the road for certain, Rossiter. You'll have to get used to the bouncing. Takes weight off."

That brought a few laughs.

Sturgis hoped he could keep him out of trouble and override any foolish mistakes that Rossiter might make. Once he had seen Rossiter demolish a brand new jeep by accident while pointing directions for a visiting dignitary before de-activating his C.A.D.S. suit weapon tube!

"Anyway," the general continued, "off-the-road conditions as well as on-road maps should be consulted."

Knolls looked grim. "If the United States is hit by a nuclear attack, the roads will be filled with civilian cars—and a big mess of wreckage shortly thereafter. No, we built these Rhinos and Tri-wheels for off-the-road travel for just this purpose. In any nuked zone, the roads will be hell-choked with refugees."

There was a murmur from some of the men in Second Company—the men who would serve under Lieutenant Glenner—who was only 26, but Earley stood up and said, "I suppose you men have all known me for the duration. Lieutenant Glenner will have my expert guidance in technical matters, and of course as commander of 2-Omega, he will make all the tactical decisions in accordance with sound military strategy."

Earley's speech quieted the men down.

"Now," Knolls said, turning to the terrain maps with the roads minimized as thin red lines, "get familiar with the move-out to the east, or the west—Sturgis, know every hill toward Amarillo, first off. I believe that's where Omega-1 will be deployed. And you Glenner, Earley, get to know the south through the Nogales . . ."

The briefing session went on for hours. At the end Sturgis came up to General Knolls—something had been gnawing at his gut.

"General, I want a three-day pass," he said brusquely.

"You've got to be *kidding*, Sturgis. *All* leaves are cancelled—*finito*!"

"General, I've got something I have to do. Tranh can ready the men as well as—"

"Dismissed Sturgis. Let's not hear such an insane request again. You get your man Rossiter on the suits—

86

watch him."

Sturgis saluted and left. He was at a crisis. He wanted to obey, and knew the gravity of the situation. Yet Robin was filling his mind like a vision. What a fool he had been! They *had* to be together—now that it looked like *the end*, he wanted only to be with her.

He went to his room and the pit bull wagged his short tail and licked at his face.

"Easy boy, I've got a lot of quick thinking to do."

He sat on his bunk and lit a Camel. He leaned against the concrete and brick wall.

What's more important: Robin or the military? It always comes down to that. Well, I always said it was the military and she always said goodbye. Now, in the crunch—she's in that city back east and probably about to get nuked. Baltimore, with its naval targets, is high on the priority list of the Reds. And here I am playing games out in the middle of the fucking desert . . .

It was 2 a.m. in Baltimore. He decided to call her—tell her to get to the farm—the shelter survival camp retreat of theirs in the Virginia mountains.

He strode to the hall pay phone next to the coke machine. He knew they were all monitored, that his ass was on the line, but he didn't care. Sturgis had a little trick up his sleeve. He had found the override code in General Knolls' office a few disciplinary calls back. When the general left him alone for a second. "Never leave Sturgis alone near classified documents," his psychological report had cautioned. "The man is a natural investigator and highly inquisitive."

The colonel smiled, put the code through, and dialed Robin's number. The operator in Las Cruces came on and asked if he wanted person-to-person or station-to-station. "Only Robin Adler," he said. She lived with her roommate, a vegetarian teacher named Barbara—a nice sort, and it helped cut expenses. Then a recording came on as the call was interrupted, "Unauthorized use of mili . . ."

"Code 23-333-56-AS-1," he said loudly. The PBX operator put him through immediately. For every lock there is a key. Sturgis knew that and he always made sure he had his keys.

The phone rang eight times before a sleepy voice, the voice he loved, came on the phone.

"Hello? Hello?"

"This is Dean."

"Dean! Are you on leave? Where are you?"

"Never mind. I'm *going* to be there. Not in Baltimore, at the farm. And I'll be there by the time *you* get there."

A slight pause. "I haven't heard from you in a month."

"I'm sorry — this was a long stint — no communications. But I want you to go to the farm."

"Can't we meet in — "

"No, at the farm."

Pause. "Sturg? Is everything okay?"

He paused. What could he say. "Have you read the papers?"

"The peace talks?"

"No, the — never mind. Get some supplies — the usual things we take up there. It's stocked with all the essentials. Just bring what you need for the trip — take Barbara if you — "

"She's away visiting her folks in Cadaigua, New York — you know, near Rochester?"

"Then just get out of bed now and start packing up. *Now.* Don't take too much time — but don't drive too fast either."

"Sturg!" she yelled. "What's going on? No words of love, only some insistence that I get myself out of bed and into the van. *Oh shit, Oh no!* Sturg — is it?"

"Maybe not — no use taking chances — don't tell anyone else."

"Can you get in trouble for this call?"

"Don't worry about it—I have my ways to avoid that. Besides, it won't matter much. I'll be there. *You be there*. Of course I love you. More than anything—especially now—I've decided it's you, only you who matter. Meet me, do it. Love me?"

"Love you, Sturg—but I don't believe it. *Can't* believe that it's finally happening—"

He sighed. "Baby, if you love me, get in the van and go to the farm. I hope to God it's in shape."

"It's in fine shape Sturg, it even has a new battery. I drove it when I took some of my students—Oh shit, how can I leave my class—the kids—"

"Baby. Just get in the van. Don't call anyone, don't say anything. If someone asks where you're going in the middle of the night say your mother has an appendectomy or something. Now I've got to go," he said, hearing some stirring down the hall. Two of Rossiter's men, grumbling to each other, were heading down the hall to the Coke machine.

"Look, I've really got to go, I love you more than anything."

"And I love you."

"You'll be there?"

"By tomorrow afternoon—earlier maybe—maybe a little late—but I'll be there—go, go now."

He hung up. Cold sweat was pouring down his back. He had done it. He had. Now for phase two, which would be a trick in itself. But he knew the base, the personnel, and he wasn't expected to do any such thing. He had the advantage—most of the men trusted him, and they wouldn't be surprised if he was walking around, inspecting things on the camouflaged runway, late at night. If something happened, before he could pull it off he might have to shoot.

He had the pellet gun in his room, and the gas cartridges—illegal ammo, but he had had it all these years since the MIA raids—good stuff. Came in handy then, and he sure as hell didn't want to take out his own buddies to do what he had to do. Not when he could just put them to sleep for a few minutes.

Grim-faced, he loaded the forty-five with the gas-cartridge bullets and checked the mechanism—clean. Good. He reholstered it and walked out his door. *The Rebel*, as they called him, was about to be his most rebellious. If World War III didn't break out, it would be a court martial for him. If it did, what did it matter? Robin. Robin. Each step made him say her name. Cold boots on hot concrete, like the walk down the last mile . . .

Sturgis knew what he was doing, he was being the troublemaker again. They all, including him, had thought he had put that reputation behind him—aside from throwing an occasional punch at a Washington big-wig. Now he saw that he would forever be the *rebel*. Until they shot him, or until one of his wild reckless departures from the accepted norm of military behavior led him to his death. But he had his own concept of values—his own way of doing things.

He walked those icy night steps in the dark, the cool breeze blowing the loose khaki shirt he had thrown on, and feeling the heavy holster on his hips. Toward the camouflaged airfield he moved. His walk was smooth and quiet like the night, like the breeze itself.

CHAPTER EIGHT

Sturgis walked quickly past the security guards at several checkpoints inside the compound. He saluted, his ever-present cigarette hung from his teeth, and they let him pass without a second thought. Goddamn Sturgis was always out poking around the suits or something. Besides they couldn't read his mind, know what he was thinking. Sturgis made his way up the concrete plank that led to the outside and brushed by a set of thick camouflage netting made to appear like dark green vines that overhung the central farmhouse of the installation. He headed over to the similarly camouflaged airfield with large strips of netting hung high on posts a good thirty feet above the ground, with infrared jamming grid built in, in case of any prying eyes high above searching for the heat trail of jets.

"You're out late," chief mechanic Saunders said, pulling himself out from under the wheel of Krangle's OMB Delta-wing jet.

"Quite a vehicle for one fund cutter, *par excellence*," Saunders said, wiping a grease coated sleeve across his equally grimy face. "It sure is a beauty, Sturg. The civvie version of a Lockheed Eagle II—they made just fifty of them as super-maneuverable airlift to be used in rapid deploy missions. This one's got all the equipment, the speed, the radar jamming devices—everything. With a few machine guns and missile launchers you could take the damn thing up against a squadron of MIGs."

"And it flies too," Sturgis asked with a thin grin.

"Ready for takeoff. I heard you got into some sort of scuffle with Mr. OMB himself this afternoon. He's being treated in the infirmary here, overnight I guess—seems he hurt his nose."

"Dangerous wound—much better to be hospitalized and avoid any permanent damage," Sturgis smirked.

"Say, Saunders," he continued, "you don't happen to have the key to get in there and get the whole shebang going, do you?" Sturgis struggled to conceal his tension.

"Matter of fact I do, I was checking out a faulty readout on the oil pressure in the cockpit. They left the keys. But Sturgis what the hell do—"

Suddenly the mechanic saw a strange look in Sturgis' eyes. He knew the man had killed, knew of his determination, and had never wanted to be on the receiving end of those burning dark-blue eyes.

"I don't want to hurt you," Sturgis said softly as he slowly lifted his 7.2mm automatic. "And I'm sure I won't have to, now will I, Saunders? You and me go back a long way."

"Hey Sturg, I sure as hell ain't gonna get in *your* way," the mechanic said, pulling back a few feet and holding out his hands to show he wasn't going to go for anything. "But what the hell you got in mind, man? I never figured you for no traitor—or deserter—"

"It's personal," Sturgis said, softly, "but I swear to you it in no way endangers the security of the U.S.—just my own career—a few loose ends."

"It's no good, Sturgis," Saunders sad softly. "They ain't just gonna bust you on this one—they're gonna put you away, for a long time, man."

"They may. The way I figure it pal, the whole damned show is about to go kablam. So I don't think there's going to be much putting-away done around here anymore. Anyway, that's my problem. Now, if you'll just turn around I'm going to tie you up. Don't want you getting involved in this thing."

"Sure, Sturg—anything you say," Saunders said, turning around and putting his hands behind his back. Sturgis walked over to the mechanic and raised the butt of his auto-fire 7.2mm a foot above the man's neck. "Sorry, I ain't got no rope," he said as he brought the pistol down in a swift arc just below the base of the skull. Saunders slumped to the cold ground like a sack of potatoes. Sturgis hoped he hadn't hurt the man, just put him out for 15 or 20 minutes. Be better for him to have a big lump on his head anyway—otherwise they might just start throwing people in the stockade and asking questions later. He pulled Saunders about a hundred feet away, laying him against a stack of camouflage netting and taking the keys from his pocket, he headed back to the Delta-wing jet.

He jumped up the aluminum ladder two steps at a time. He snapped the cabin lights on the second he entered. The door was of a different design than on military transport, but he managed to figure it out, and closed it tightly behind him.

Sturgis kept his gun at the ready just in case—but there wasn't a soul in the jet as he made his way down the aisle, plush seats on each side, capable of holding up to twelve people—but in this case carrying a load of one. Someone should complain to their congressman, the colonel thought with a cynical smile. If there's anything left in a week, maybe I will. He lowered himself into the pilot's seat and flipped on the "ready" switches on the control panel. Everything was ready to go. Fuel—full, batteries, charged, computer readouts signalled all systems go.

"Well, there's no time like the present, eh chum," Sturgis muttered to his invisible co-pilot as he turned the ignition switch on. The jet roared to life, trembling for a few seconds and then settling down as the two jet engines caught fully. He didn't have much time, he knew, as he pictured General Knolls scrambling out of bed, the security guards rushing outside. Sturgis, who had been trained in the flying of just about every aircraft in the world at one time or another, including a captured MIG 30, turned the control levers as he squeezed a little more juice into the engines. The Eagle-II jet shot forward and skidded around a full 180 degrees, the back tires peeling off a layer of rubber on the concrete runway. He shot sideways across a grass lane and hit the end of the main runway, a 50-foot wide blacktopped road that disappeared beneath the camouflage nets far in the distance. Usually rows of amber lights were turned on each side of the runway, but tonight all was dark, as no air-traffic was due.

Behind the jet, lights suddenly snapped on as guards came running out yelling, their rifles snapping up in quick arcs trying to get a bead on the jet. Sturgis didn't wait around to see the target practice. He slammed the accelerator rod forward as far as it would go, keeping the wheel dead straight so he wouldn't veer off the darkened runway. The Eagle-II sent out a bright stream of flames and shot forward as if propelled from a cannon. Sturgis was slammed far back into the pilot's seat from the acceleration. The netting and poles on each side of the pathway were just a gray blur shaking violently from the shock waves of the Eagle II passing by. Sturgis knew he had only a few seconds to make his move, and there would be no room for error. Once the camouflage netting ended, there was but 200 yards of flat terrain before reaching a ravine that dropped down nearly 100 feet. He gazed up through the curved cockpit window searching for stars so he'd know he was out. Suddenly, like a time-elapse photograph, he saw a blurred ocean of lights in the sky. He pulled the jet up sharply, rising at an almost 70 degree angle and glancing down, he saw the wide ravine right there. He didn't let himself think about how close he had just come. He was alive—so fuck it.

He rose to an altitude of 15,000 feet and headed the Eagle toward Virginia. He knew the specs of the new model plane and that it had an almost double storage capacity for fuel, giving it a range of nearly 4,000 miles. That would be a hell of a lot more than he would need.

"Just get me to Virginia, old pal," Sturgis said, patting his instrument panel. He made it a point to become personally acquainted with any machine that his life depended on. Once he broke through a few desultory clouds the sky was clear as an ocean of diamonds. He looked out over the ground far below, the twinkling lights of a lone car out in the middle of nowhere, little towns and villages, flickering indications of life. It was beautiful up here. He loved to fly, and somehow never got jaded or bored with being up. It always put a certain tingle up his spine—the power, the speed, feeling almost like a god as he stared down at the little world below. How fragile it looked. Like the tiniest of dollhouses that could be smashed with a single swipe.

His earphones suddenly burst into life as General Knolls' screaming voice came floating through the radio.

"Sturgis! Goddamnit Sturgis! I know you can hear me. I don't know what the hell you think you're doing but turn that plane around right now and I'll see what I can do about saving you from a firing squad. Sturgis, Sturgis! Do you hear me? Come in!"

Sturgis took the phones off and laid them down over the arm of his pilot's seat. There was nothing to say.

He leveled the jet off at 20,000 and put her on autopilot. He leaned back in the seat, relaxing for the first time since he took off. Knolls would send out an all-points to the Air Force scramble squads. But this baby was as fast as anything they had, and Sturgis had a few tricks up his sleeve. He kept a sharp eye on the radar screen which indicated some air traffic but nothing heading his way. Robin — he kept seeing her face superimposed over the night sky. Her impossibly blue eyes, her summer wheat blonde hair. God, she was beautiful. He had been a fool to almost destroy the only worthwhile relationship he had ever had. The only woman he had ever really loved. And now that he had her again a nightmare made of nuclear energy was threatening to take it all away. He couldn't lose her. Let the whole damned world rot in its death-riddled juices. He and she — they would live. He glanced down at the readouts on the panel, elapsed distance 400 miles. Good, at this rate he'd actually reach Virginia by —

Suddenly a brilliant flash lit the horizon. A towering funnel of whirling white reached high into the night sky like a pillar from hell. Through the tinted cockpit windshield his eyes were protected from the piercing light. But he knew what it was instantly. The thing that mankind had been trying to prevent since the day Hiroshima had lit up the world with a new horror. Damn — the fucking bastards had actually done it — had started World War III. He watched with horrified fascination as the writhing white-orange maelstrom ballooned out in all directions, twisting sheets of star-hot flame, burning, melting, sending everything that it touched into an eternal hell of nothingness. He was far enough away from the nuke blast, about 30 miles, to hope that he was safe. Though within seconds shock waves from the explosion shook the jet, vibrating it as if it were in a blender. Then it passed and the glow suddenly faded from white to darker orange as the mushroom cloud rose out of the ruins, reaching up toward the very heavens as if it wished to destroy them too.

Then another blast far to the east. This one he could only see the dim glow of, it must have been several hundred miles off. And even at that distance it was almost too bright to watch, as its all-consuming destructive energies took out God knew how many lives, how many men, women, children—dogs, cats—every goddamned thing it could touch. He felt the evil of the A-bomb blast. The pure darkness of death destroying all that was good. It was hell—hell on earth—and man had done it to himself. He could picture the devastation. He had seen enough films on the impact and the aftermath.

"Damn damn damn," he muttered to himself. Then he thought of Robin—of her sweet flesh seared to a powder that he could never touch again. No—it couldn't be. She couldn't die. He would feel it, he knew, if she was gone. And somehow he felt her presence far off. If she had listened to him and left immediately she would have a chance. The second blast dimmed slightly and even from the great distance he could see a second mushroom-shaped funnel rise up thousands of feet into the darkness, illuminating the clouds above with the dark light of megadeath.

He felt torn as he had never been before. The picture of Robin—alone, maybe wounded, and his duty to his country tore at him as if he were pulled in two. He had been a career military man for more years than he could remember and though he had always had problems in fitting into the regulated life, still he had been good at what he did. And now his country needed him, more than ever. God knew what was going to happen now. But Robin needed him too. He argued violently in his mind, seething inside like a volcano ready to explode with emotion. Damn. Damn, he had never felt so confused in his entire life. At last he made a decision, gritted his jaws and turned the jet at a sharp angle, making a 180 degree turn. His country would have to come first—for right now. If he left, ran, he could never live with himself. With the country devastated by atomic attack, the army probably shattered, he and his men of the Omega team might be the only force, with their C.A.D.S. suits, that could make a difference. Robin would have to wait. But he would find her and be with her again, though it might take days, weeks . . . They would be reunited.

With tears in his eyes, wishing he was dead, he steered the plane back around, getting a final glimpse of the two towering shafts of gray smoke, and headed back toward White Sands. When he got within a hundred miles, he radioed in to the C.A.D.S. base to get the lights on the runway. Takeoff he could manage in the dark, but landing, no way.

Sergeant McKinnis, the flight controller, sounded surprised to hear Sturgis' voice, but made no mention of the stolen Eagle II. In no time he was cleared for landing and came down sharply toward the two rows of lights beneath the camouflage netting. He came in smoothly, threw the twin engines into reverse and skidded to an abrupt stop. There was a greeting committee awaiting him: five security guards, their rifles aimed at chest level. They looked sheepish, their eyes hardly able to meet Sturgis' as he came out the door and stepped onto the runway.

"Sorry, Sturg," Flanners, head of the base police unit said. "Wish I didn't have to be the one, but under orders of General Knolls, you're under arrest."

"Don't worry about it, pal," Sturgis said with a lopsided grin. "I'm the one who fucked up. But listen, fellas," Sturgis said, eyeing the carbines leveled at him, "do you think we could dispense with the hardware? If I was going to try to escape, I wouldn't have come back."

The men looked nervously at Flanners who nodded and they let the rifles fall.

They marched Sturgis inside the compound and into the stockade. Every one of the guards and prison officials who saw him could barely make eye contact. To them Sturgis was one of the best damned men on the whole base. They all knew how much he had contributed to the project and respected him perhaps more than anyone in the place. He was led into one of 10 cells, only two of which were occupied—by men who had been drinking while on duty. Flanners closed the cell door behind him.

"I—I'm sor—" Flanners began.

"Skip it," Sturgis cut him off. "Just make sure I get orange juice with my crumpets in the morning."

Flanners smiled and walked off.

It felt strange to be behind bars, trapped. Not that Sturgis hadn't spent a few days in the hoosegow on numerous occasions around the world—for drinking, fighting, you name it. But that had all been years ago before he had done at least a little maturing. He lay down on the cold wooden bunk and folded his arms, unable to banish the thoughts of Robin that swirled through his mind like a hurricane. He had only been in the cell for a few minutes when he heard a commotion down the corridor. General Knolls came bustling up to the bars with three of his top staff trailing behind him. The general stared hard at Sturgis through the steel, his eyes blazing with fury.

"Open up, open up," he said impatiently to Flanners, who whipped out the key and opened the door. Knolls walked inside and looked down at Sturgis who couldn't help but grin at the pure fury in those pale gray eyes.

"Well, are you going to shoot me?" he asked without shifting from the bunk.

"If we weren't at war, I'd do it myself," the general replied somberly. "But as I assume you know—and that's why you came back—*it's here*. The shooting match has begun—and is over already. We took heavy losses,

Sturgis. Very heavy. Somehow the Reds were able to disable much of our spy satellite equipment and take out nearly half our submarine fleet in a single stroke. The reports we're getting in from around the country are bad. Very bad. I don't know what the hell's going to happen next. But we're members of the country's armed services, and by God we're going to do every damned thing we can to save what's left."

Knolls looked down for a second, his own inner turmoil evident on his stony face. Then he looked up straight at Sturgis.

"I need you—we need you. You're the best damned fighter here. If it was peacetime I'd throw the key away. But it's not, and all the rules have gone out the window. But grow up, man. There's too much at stake for these damned impulsive adventures of yours. I don't know where you were heading or what you had in mind. And I don't care. You came back. And that's enough for me. So get up and get your ass in gear. I want you to do a run-through for all C.A.D.S. combat personnel with less than three months training in the suit. The real stuff, Sturgis—how to survive—how to kill as ruthlessly and efficiently as possible. I'm waiting for orders to move out. If there's anybody out there to give orders anymore."

CHAPTER NINE

Christmas Eve, 1997

In New York City, as part of the spirit of detente, the Moscow circus was in town. And a grand circus it was, epic in its spectacle and costumes. The KGB operative, Yaslov, who watched his flock of performers—especially Petrovski, the lion tamer—who he suspected of counter-revolutionary tendencies—was happy that not one performer had defected this time. And tomorrow they would be heading back to Russia. He puffed a cigarette, leaning back against one of the big crates that the lions had been transported in. The show had gone extremely well. The reviews from the local papers had praised the beauty of the pageantry and the great skills of the Russian acrobats. The entire affair had been a plus for American-Soviet relations, and a feather in his cap for preventing any defections.

Now they were busy packing up in the emptied stadium amidst the roars of the beasts. The smell of sawdust and dung was exhilarating to these circus people but not to him. He stared at one of the giant black bears in its cage. My God, how does Yevtoshevik handle him, Yaslov thought. He makes him wear that silly hat, do those tricks. Surely the man has gypsy blood, for that inferior race did retain the ability to control animals. That was it. It defied Marxist scientific logic. It had to be the bloodline.

And beautiful Marina—he had hoped she would sleep with him on this trip, enticed by his privileges, his wealth and position in the Party. But no, she, the aerialist, with the most stunning body he had ever seen, had taken up with Petrovski. He would have to do something to make life miserable for that man when they returned home, he decided.

They were stowing the last of the costumes into their crates when Yaslov dimly heard sirens outside—a warbling shrill sound. Just a test, no doubt. But a minute later a man came running down the aisle—Meshnekov, his assistant.

"It's *real*, Comrade, people are taking cover. The radio says there are missiles coming. It . . . it's nuclear war!"

Yaslov slumped against the crate. "This is no sick capitalist joke?"

Meshnekov shook his head. He was weeping against his will. "We will die here—with these Americans. Our own bombs will—"

"Perhaps we should take shelter—a sub-basement."

"Sub-basement!" a voice laughed. It was Petrovski who had heard the noise and come around. "So it is war?"

Meshnekov shook his head. "My wife, my children. Perhaps Russia will win and they'll be safe. They're in Leningrad."

Marina also came over, still clad in her low-cut corsette with sequins. "What do we do, Misha?" she pleaded to her tall blond Petrovski. "The animals. What can we do?"

"What can we do?" her lover answered, laughing heartily, "we die friends, that's what we do. We are so lucky to be here in this fair city of New York, right in the heart of one of the best targets for a nuclear bomb on earth. Let us have a few last drinks, and kisses—yes, kisses for all of you so you'll know you are loved when the bomb falls."

He began running around with a bottle pouring stiff

drinks of vodka, not caring if he spilled healthy portions with each serving. Petrovski kissed each after he poured, on both cheeks—even the KGB operative Yaslov who pushed him and the glass away.

"Ha, Yaslov of the beloved KGB—now I can tell you—I *hate* the motherland and its stupid egotistical rulers. They are *idiots! Marx* was an *idiot! Lenin* a *pimp*—yes a *pimp*—now I can say it."

Yaslov took out a little black notebook and started writing. "This will mean your confinement, Petrovski, never to travel again." Then he stopped and burst into tears. "Petrovski—is it really—the—end?"

Petrovski put his arms around the KGB operative. "It's all over. The nonsense is over now, Yaslov. Here—" He handed the KGB man a drink which he downed in one huge gulp.

Marina walked over and hugged Petrovski. "Ah, you have been such a good lover. I have been so lucky to have you."

Petrovski kissed her cheek, and then raised his glass.

"A toast," he said. "To all the Americans who die with us, to our foolish leaders, to Mao and Hitler, to Presidents Washington and Armstrong, let us drink—"

They all shouted, "Nastrovya" and downed their vodkas. Even the bears and lions were growling and jumping around in their cages.

"Ah, the animals know the end is near—see?" Petrovski laughed.

Vanya, the trapeze artist, and Anatalia, her death-defying partner, walked over. They had a bottle of champagne.

"Shall we open it?" Vanya asked. "It's French—not Russian. Dom Perignon. I was saving it for the right time and—"

"Of course open it," Petrovski chuckled. "Let's all have a drink—to this America—which will soon be gone."

103

"Not to America," Vaslov protested. "They have undoubtedly started this war—"

"To the Americans," laughed Vanya, ignoring him. "Long may they live. Remember comrade, we're on their side of the missile exchange now. We'd *better* root for them—to shoot down *our* missiles."

"Not a chance," said the KGB operative. "Our technology will be more effective than theirs. Our homeland will be safe—but we are in danger. I suggest you desist in this insane party atmosphere and do the logical thing and take cover. Cage the animals—in case of a nuclear explosion nearby—there is still a chance we will survive. This stadium is concrete, steel. We have some warning time and you are all wasting it on this—insanity."

"It is *you*, darling, who act insane," Vanya laughed. "Don't you see if this is a war we are as good as dead right now? Do you believe in an after life?"

"Certainly not. I am an atheist," Yaslov said bitterly.

"Then I suggest you get your drinking done in *this* life, comrade. If there is a heaven, all us bolsheviks are not likely to make it in—and angels don't drink."

"To a short sweet life of capitalist decadence," Petrovski toasted. They all clinked glasses for the last time.

"It has been ten minutes since the sirens began wailing," Petrovski said. "It has been a great party and I expect it will—"

Suddenly there was a flash as bright as the light of the sun as a 20-megaton warhead went off a thousand feet up, almost directly above them. In a 10,000th of a second, a temperature of 18,000,000 degrees evaporated everything for a distance of nearly two miles. Petrovski, Vaslov, the entire circus was disintegrated into super-hot atoms flying off in all directions—as was the entire island of Manhattan. The Empire State, the U.N., the World Trade Center—all were blown into a fine black powder which filled the skies in a tornado of darkness. The fire storms swept out in burning waves of white flame, heading off toward the other four boroughs of the city, toward New Jersey and the suburbs. They burned every living thing, every building and factory they passed, leaving a wasteland of devastation. By the time the rising mushroom cloud had begun to form above the fiery graveyard of Manhattan 5,000,000 people were dead. In ten seconds, more people had been killed from this one blast than all the troops America had lost in battle in its entire history.

A crater nearly two miles wide and 1,000 feet deep stood in the middle of the rubble that was once Manhattan as water from the rivers that bounded the island poured in from both sides sending up a storm of super-heated steam. Where once had stood the greatest city on the face of the earth — now was nothing. Nothing but death.

Emma Johnston was watching TV in Scarsdale, some 15 miles north of New York City when the shock wave hit her. Her dress erupted into flame as blisters from the heat bubbled across her body like the outbreak of some dread disease. Her hair caught fire, burning with a pungent odor as she slammed her hands to her skull in agony. She screamed in unimaginable pain as her body was consumed. The windows suddenly flew in, shattering into a million pieces of flying shrapnel. She sank to the floor, her body impregnated with shards of glass, blood pouring from every part of her mangled flesh. Her son was riding his tricycle when the heat wave hit. He continued to ride it for a few seconds screaming until he keeled over, his skin a dark brown color. The infant was more fortunate. It was on the porch lying in the bassinet and was instantly cremated.

* * *

The old America was gone—and a new America was being spawned. A twisted mutilated landscape filled with immense craters, roaring mushroom pillars, clouds of gray and black fallout spreading their filth through the skies. An America of blinded, bleeding people writhing in agony, each in his own personal hell. First New York, the flash, the molten steaming crater giving up its huge mass into the sky as a cloud of radioactive death. Then Pittsburgh, Detroit, Omaha, and the ICBM-silo-filled areas of Idaho, Montana, Wyoming . . .

Monuments and mountains alike fell beneath the unstoppable atomic onslaught. Whole forests burst into incendiary hells, uncontrolled fire storms roared through the suburbs of Chicago, Atlanta, Kansas City—sucking in all the oxygen so those who weren't burned to death suffocated, their eyes bulging from their red faces.

Everywhere a new terrain was taking shape. Where there once were forests and rushing streams now were hundreds of thousands of acres of smoldering black-ashed trees, shorn of life. Instead of pleasant rolling hills carpeted with flowers, now there appeared fissured and eroded soil with crystallized topsoil reflecting the dull glow of yet another nuclear flash in some distant region.

Out on the roads and highways speeding cars careened and crashed into one another as their terror-stricken drivers drove toward the countryside in vain attempts to escape. Burning heaps of multi-car collisions on the nation's freeways continued to claim new victims as, driving through the impenetrable smoke of the fallout and fire storms with their headlights on, more cars ploughed into the piles of flaming metal.

The lone motorcyclist, the mountainman with a rifle slung over his back, the rugged survivalist, the country folk huddled in their shelters and shacks in the mountain valleys—these were the new Americans. The far away, the few, the self-sufficient, the wretched outcasts of the modern world. They saw the flashes, the false dawns at every corner of the compass and few didn't know what had happened. Then they loaded their guns and waited. They counted their supplies and pooled their resources in meetings lit by Coleman lamps in countless general stores. The old way was gone. The city folk — those who survived — would become human waves over the next few days and weeks, seeking refuge, food, supplies. And they would have to be shot dead in their tracks — picked off by these country folks so they couldn't spread the destruction and disease, so they wouldn't consume the precious remaining supplies. A thousand small towns were getting ready to defend themselves against the other America — the old America — that was dying.

In Washington D.C., President Armstrong and his advisors sat stunned as they watched a computerized situation map of the U.S. in their bunker deep underground. Red dots were lighting up like a pinball machine.

"What was that?" asked the president.

"Sir," choked out a technician at the board, "New York has been hit by three thermonuclear devices." They watched as Omaha and Dallas flared and went out.

"*Now* will you launch?" yelled General Burns. The president held the key in his command suitcase. He stared glassy eyed at the situation map.

"How the hell are their missiles getting through without being picked up on radar?"

"Mr. President, we're receiving reports from Houston Center — all our radar has been hit by electro-magnetic pulses from the blasts and rendered inoperative — they won't advise on —"

The Houston light went on — red, flared to a dull orange

and went out.

"Sir? I've lost contact — I — my family — lives — *lived* in —" the technician started weeping.

President Armstrong was having trouble with the suitcase, his hand was trembling violently from the sight of his nation torn to shreds.

"General, should I do this?" President Armstrong asked softly.

"You have to — the only way to cut our losses, sir," Burns replied firmly.

The president opened the briefcase and took out the launch codes. He picked up the white phone to Colorado SAC Headquarters. "This is the Commander-in-Chief — Code Apple, dog, baker, 345-AS-213. Authorization OZ-X345."

Next, the general took the phone. "This is General Burns. Be damned quick about this, Charlie. You only have minutes."

President Armstrong put his head down on the cool perfectly smooth wood. He pushed away his secretary's hands of consolation on his shoulders. They all sat motionless as the president cried quietly. At last, General Burns, trying to hide his look of disgust said, "Try to pull yourself together, sir — in case —"

"In case," the president said, his eyes red, "in case there are some Americans left alive. They'll need me — need us . . . I'm sorry. I — I. I know I seem weak in this dark hour, but as president it was up to me to defend the security of our country — and — I've failed."

They all looked down at the floor. No one could dispute his words.

At an icy wind-blown field in Colorado the scramble order came to the 232nd tactical wing — 25 fighter-bombers, FB-25s with cruise missiles suspended under their wings. The pilots ran from their quarters and entered their planes, crawling up the cold metal ladders, checking out their craft, as they had practiced for years.

"This is not a drill, I repeat, this is not a drill," the voice of their base commander came over their earphones. "The bastards have done it. America is already in flames and many of our missiles have already been destroyed. You boys may be the only ones left for all I know." He paused, as the pilots revved up their engines and wheeled out onto the runway. "God be with you—and give the Reds some presents they won't forget. I may not be seeing any of you again—so good luck and—and—" his voice cracked. "You're the bravest bunch of bastards I've worked with. Good luck."

Colonel Williams was the first in line. He shot down the blacktop like a bat out of hell, banking sharply to the right the moment he left the ground. His fate lay in the Soviet Union, over Murmansk, his naval-port target. Whether he would be able to fire his cruise missiles and wheel around in the polar sky to head back didn't matter much. This base was a number-one priority target; it wouldn't be here when he got back. As he soared northward he decided what he would do. In his imagination he had run through this eventuality a dozen times, and he had carefully planned his course of action. He would drop his load and then head back to the Maine shoreline and parachute down onto a beach near his vacation home. He would wait for Jackie, his wife, and his four-year old Freddy. But now that it was all *real* he laughed at his naïvete. He'd never make it back, that was obvious. He would fire his cruise missiles and then point the jet straight down and accelerate into the icecap. He didn't want to survive. *It was over*. For him, for his family, for all of them.

* * *

Frantic crews in the deep missile silos of Utah and Nevada rushed through firing sequences, turning keys and pushing buttons to unlock and unleash the weapons they controlled. The concrete covers of the silos blasted into the sky as multiple-warhead ICBMs rose from their holes deep underground. But they never made it, as incoming Soviet missiles, each 20 megatons, vaporized them into craters. The maps that the Cuban intelligence officers had sent to Russia had been accurate. Those Cubans, agents hidden among the half-million that came over in the Mariel boatlift, had done their jobs well. Now they sat in Havana smoking big cigars and listening to Fidel's speech broadcast on the interrupted music festival. Cuban armies were already on landing ships headed toward Florida. A new sort of boatlift—that of a conquering army—was enroute.

Beyond the Arctic Circle, huge doors in the snowbanks opened to reveal their secrets. The American planes taxiing down the underground runway toward the howling winds outside were MIG-29s. Exact copies, rivet for rivet, of the sleek delta-winged Russian fighter-bomber. Russian counter measures—electronics, missiles, even their radar—were designed to avoid interfering with *friendly* aircraft, This super-secret U.S. forward base had 36 of these planes, flown by the best pilots the U.S. had.

Lieutenant Neil Warton, squadron leader of the "Deception Squadron" as it was called, knew that this was no exercise, since a blizzard was completely socking in the base. It was real. They'd never risk these planes and men for an exercise in weather like this.

The winds were wild and buffeting as he roared out onto the short runway and his afterburner blasted him into the night sky, dark but clear. He soon saw the glint of moonlight on metal to his right and left—his wingmen. They were maintaining radio silence and flying without lights. Then came their orders—a thin burst of radio activity—a compacted direct message from S.A.C. in Colorado. He fed it into the slow-playback of his computer and pressed the button. He didn't like what he heard.

"This is S.A.C. Command. A-1. Situation A-1. Proceed to designated targets in the Soviet Union, maximum speed."

War! World War Three! He took the bearing designated in the secret orders he now ripped open and watched as the sun crept up on the horizon like a bloody ball.

He descended to a gut-wrenching fifty feet over the Arctic icefields, his 35 companions spread out behind him. The bastards would pay. These MIGs would get past their defenses and deal the crushing blow. There would be hell to pay in the Soviet Union in minutes. He looked at his fuel gauges. At this speed, 2,235 knots, the jet was gobbling fuel at 1,200 gallons a minute. There would be no return flight. He grimly pressed the sets of switches that armed the twin nuclear bombs slung under his wings.

There was a sudden buzzing sound in his earphones, as they entered Red airspace. He shot over a startled Russian trapper removing an animal from a trap. The heat of his exhaust seared the snow, tore up the tundra, throwing the man from his feet and bursting his eardrums. Lieutenant Warton moved the control stick slightly to the left to avoid some high rolling hills. Over that ridge was a series of frozen lakes, and then, far in the distance, the city of Leningrad. A city that would die in eight minutes.

In the scattered boroughs of imperial Leningrad, amongst the stately old whitewashed buildings dating back centuries, frantic Soviet workers at facilities designated Searchlight Stations were at work. They rolled back the huge domes above the structures, no easy task as the snows were piled five-feet high. The crews wheeled the "search-lights" into place and plugged in the main switches as technicians maneuvered the dials to the appropriate setting for "low strike jets."

Searchlights. That's what they appeared to be to U.S. spy satellites high above, that's what the signs said outside the crumbling buildings. But they weren't. There was the gleam of ruby-colored glass pulsing with energy that yearned to be unbound inside those gleaming arrays of silver tubes. They rose up on their hydraulic lifts into positions aimed by advanced computers. For these "searchlights" were the secret defense of Russia's population centers and military bases—Laser weapons for air defense.

The workers had been told earlier in the day that the U.S. was known to be preparing an all-out attack on the mother-land and they were called upon to give every effort to save their nation and their lives. Bewildered, some wondered if it was to be a *surprise* attack, how the Soviet Union was aware of this surprise. But they were told that the KGB had heroically penetrated the White House communications center and decoded the fatal commands. Because of the KGB's heroic brilliance, Russia would be saved.

A hundred domes were opened throughout Russia, the snows sifting in with the cold as the giant arrays of laser weapons pointed skyward, waiting.

Neil Warton saw the first flash of doom slash the sky with a blinding stream of light-energy as he swooped down toward the center of Leningrad.

"My God—what was that," he gasped. Another blast of energy filled the sky; then another. He saw his right wingman's plane disintegrate alongside him, melted into glowing fragments by the beams. Lasers, he realized as he tried to veer sharply. But the computer was locked onto

112

him. He reached for the bomb release button and as he pressed it his MIG disintegrated in the incredible heat of the beam.

Down below the red technicians cheered. The sky was filled with flaming U.S. planes. Their defense was working. Then . . . the blast of a thermonuclear weapon exploding thrust them into silence. In a split second the heat wave slammed into their installation, turning the laser's open dome into a crematorium for the 100 technicians inside. Leningrad was no more . . .

CHAPTER TEN

There was doom in the air on the cold blustery streets of Washington D.C. The sun was sliding down below the Washington Monument and the sirens were wailing a mournful cry that echoed down Pennsylvania Avenue. Pigeons dotted the steps of the Lincoln Memorial, sitting on the great man's head, pecking at bits of bread that were stuck in the cold blown snow. Empty cars stood deserted everywhere.

A lone man walked down the middle of Michigan Ave NW, bundled up against the cold. He was 76 years old and he had cancer—inoperable cancer—in his gut. They had said he only had a few weeks, but now it looked like he wouldn't get to die on his own. It was just as well, he thought. He didn't relish wasting away in some hospital. The chemotherapy had left him weak and he walked slowly, supported by a cane. He was a black man, and his great-great grandfather had been a slave here in Washington, one of the slaves of George Washington, whom the president had emancipated upon his death. Frank Jessup thought about the three-quarters of a century he had lived here—his childhood running around in the streets of the slums, dropping out of high school, his wife, Sarah, who had died 10 years before. They had had two kids who had gone on to college, and then got jobs out west and lost touch. No one had visited him in the hospital. He remembered the depression, the recessions, years of little or no work, living in his rooming house, looking out the window. Freezing cold in the winter, roasting in the summer heat. He remembered the assassination of Martin Luther King, of President Kennedy and his brother Bobby. And now—the cancer—and the sirens.

The black man paused in front of the White House. Even the guards were gone at the huge gate. Inside on the lawn the Christmas tree was lit up brilliantly. Red and blue and white bulbs. It was a real beauty this year, taller than ever.

The night before Christmas and all through the house not a creature was stirring—

The old man laughed to himself into his scarf and then coughed a bit, spitting up blood. The pain in his gut was intensifying again. Great, he thought. Which will get me first, the cancer or this war that's supposed to be going on?

The sirens had been warbling for nearly half an hour. He laughed. Sirens—and all those fools taking cover. A policeman had tried to hustle him off the street into the subways, but he had said, "I'm old. I don't want to die like a rat in a sewer."

The young black cop had looked in his eyes and said "Suit yourself mister," and gone back into the subway entrance he was in charge of. The funny thing was—and it *was* funny—the people were lined up into the street to buy a token to get in. Even in World War III they had to buy a token to get in!

He laughed and started coughing again and continued his way down Pennsylvania Avenue. It seemed so peaceful, he thought. So peaceful out here. More so than he had ever seen it. Like a dream. A soft, sweet billowing dream. He closed his eyes, enjoying the thought.

Suddenly there was a brilliant flash directly above. A flash that he could see through his closed eyes, as bright as day. Ah, here it is, he thought for a fraction of a second. I'm gone—

The neutron explosion bathed all of Washington in its deadly rays as it exploded at 10,000 feet, high enough to saturate the metropolitan area of the District of Columbia with radiation, yet only set fire to the buildings directly under it—slums on the east side of the Capitol area. The remainder of the physical structures of the city remained intact.

The black man was knocked down as the shock wave hit, his face smashed on the pavement. A windstorm whipped the snows into a frenzy as lampposts and cars toppled end over end. He opened his heart to God, to take him into the sweet peace of heaven. He felt an unbearable heat sear clear through his body. Then he felt nothing.

One-thousand feet below him, the president felt a slight tremble. "Is it—" he asked.

The technicians shook their heads. "Much too faint—it—wait a minute—there's radiation above—but only a slight shockwave registered. Sir, it must be a neutron explosion. Deadly to life but not to structures except in the immediate blast area. Anyone in the open will die in a few hours, more or less—"

A stunned silence swept the room.

"My wife, my—" The president looked down, closed his eyes, squeezing them hard.

Williamson said softly, "We must go on . . ." Armstrong opened his eyes, nodded slowly.

"My God, why didn't they destroy the city?" Armstrong asked.

The consensus of his staff was that the Reds probably

wanted Washington intact for their occupation capital.

"And maybe," said Vice-President Williamson, "they want *you*, Mr. President—alive—if possible. They know about this shelter—though not, I hope, its exact location or depth. If they can get you on nationwide TV or radio, and have you *surrender*, it would make their occupation of America much easier."

"Occupation?"

General Abrams spoke up. "In a matter of days, maybe hours, they will be here. As soon as the radiation dies down sufficiently for an airborne attack, paratroopers, lots of them, I imagine."

They stared at the big screen map of the U.S. before them. Almost all the blue lights depicting cities and green lights depicting military installations had flared red and died. Washington was the only yellow light—depicting "radiation-weapon" attack rather than thermonuclear destruction.

"My God," said the president, looking at the computer printout he was handed of casualty estimates. "One hundred twenty million people have died, in the last hour. My God . . ."

He buried his head in his hands, mumbling "One hundred twenty million . . . one hundred twenty million . . ."

"Sir," a communications technician said, rushing over, "we've lost all communications with the surface, local and long distance."

Many of the war room screens were dead, and the light bulbs above were dimmer and flickering slightly. The auxiliary electric generator had cut on. It would last for days, as would the air supply. They were sealed off from the surface.

"Perhaps we should blow the detonators on the elevator shaft," General Abrams said, "in case Russian troops try to get at us. It could be only a matter of hours if it *was* a neutron bomb that hit us upstairs. N-radiation won't last

117

long, it dissipates quickly."

"But if you blow the shaft how will we get out?" Armstrong asked nervously.

"The emergency tunnel — it winds up near the Potomac, where there are several powerboats hidden. We could try an escape in a few days. We could even retreat back if the radiation level looks too high." Abrams was trying to keep cool but his voice cracked under the reality of their situation.

The president took a deep breath and ordered, "Blow the detonation charges in the shelter elevator shaft, seal us in here — and them out."

Then disaster struck. What the neutron device had done on the surface had merely created a shudder in the bomb-proof survival headquarters under the White House. But a careless mistake — or a saboteur — had caused a misplacement of the charges that were to be detonated to close off the main elevator shaft. The firing button was pushed and all hell broke loose.

The president and his crisis crew were thrown from their seats as the room went dark. The war screens shattered, raining down glass and electronic debris on all of them. The technicians slumped in their chairs, their dead bodies covered with blood and equipment.

There was silence for a few seconds after the explosion, then screaming and moaning sounds filled the air. Williamson — who wasn't seriously injured — crawled about, taking a cigarette lighter and surveying the scene. The president lay unconscious under some beams that pinned his chest.

"Help me," Williamson shouted. "The president — I don't know — help! Help me!"

CHAPTER ELEVEN

In a sleek 787 jetliner dubbed Air Force Three, 30,000 feet over Kansas, a man with a neatly trimmed beard, acting president of the United States Walter Christian, looked down on the black clouds below glowing a dim orange. A lump formed in his throat. Twenty-four hours ago he was the secretary of state, but today, by reason of the president and vice president being presumed dead or captured, he was president — by rule of succession. He had just been sworn in via radio by Supreme Court Judge Thurston Morris. Now he sat in his flying command post reviewing the bad news as it came in over the scramble networks from still-existing military strongholds, which were scant and far between.

By act of Congress this third plane had been added to Air Force One and Two as emergency command posts. It had incredible range and flying time capabilities thanks to its fuel-efficient engines. Nursed along at minimum cruising speed it could stay up four days. Still, in a few days it would have to try and land, and that would be the end for him. Reports indicated that jet landing fields simply did not exist anymore in the U.S. They'd have to ditch. It was his duty to be commander-in-chief till then. And damned if he wouldn't do everything to hold off the total collapse of the U.S.

Air Force Three was outfitted as a total communications center, filled to the brim with advanced electronic equipment including ECM (electronics counter-measures) and sophisticated weapons systems manned by crack Air Force crews. So far they had not been approached or fired at, and the channels they were using for sending and receiving were "burst-capacity." The messages would be stored up and then transmitted in code in a millisecond, too short a time to be detected. A whole hour's conversation in a millionth of a second. Still, the Reds, according to reports, were already sending in an armada of planes, detection equipment, and paratroopers dropping everywhere around the nation. There was no doubt as to who had won the war—they had. Their attack had been devastating—nearly the entire U.S. east of the Mississippi was in shambles. West of the great river, the country's ABM defense network, which had only been partially completed, had stopped a large number of the Russian missiles. Even there, however, many major cities—Los Angeles, Dallas, Houston, San Francisco—had been wiped off the face of the earth.

Some U.S. missiles—S.A.C. estimated 20 to 30 hits—mostly secondary targets—had killed 20 to 30 million of their citizens—mostly civilians in the cities who had no control over the reigns of Red power but were pawns in this nuclear nightmare age.

The nation that recovers first is the one that really wins, Christian thought. The fact that they dropped so many—645 (at last count) atomic explosions in the U.S.—would give the Reds a heavy dose of their own radiation as the radiation clouds drifted around the earth. Never mind the people the war had already killed—three to four times that number would die in the next few weeks and months. The ecosphere—the system of life on earth—plants, animal, insect—very possibly would never recover. All the theoretical evidence indicated that the clouds would stay thick over the northern hemisphere for at least a year. A nuclear winter, keeping summer temperatures as low as winters, in the USSR, the U.S., Europe, Japan. No harvest this year—maybe no harvest *ever.*

Why? Why had they made this insane move? But Christian knew the answer. Because they feared it would happen sooner or later, and the sooner *they* struck, the better they would fare. The U.S. was recovering from a long period of neglect of the defenses of the nation; in another few years the U.S. might well have been vastly superior, its defensive systems totally in place.

There were those in the U.S. who had advocated first strike in the 1980s, when America was superior, when the Reds couldn't shoot down our bombers or destroy our missiles. Saner heads had prevailed then. But now, the Russians, caught up in their own paranoia, on this Christmas Eve 1997, had done the unthinkable. Didn't the dumbest leaders in the world know that the radiation from a full exchange would kill *them* as well as *us*? Insanity. Perhaps the human race was meant to extinguish itself from the start. The species that would end all species.

Perhaps up there in the dark sky above him, filled with flaming stars, there were beings who would not destroy themselves. They were the rightful inheritors of God's firmament—not aggression-prone man, descended from the fierce carnivorous apes . . .

Christian felt a tap on his shoulder. It was General Farrell. Farrell's deeply tanned face was heavy with etched lines, his eyes red. "Message about Bermuda, Mr.—President." In the slight pause he had almost said Mr. Secretary.

"What is it?" Christian asked.

"Bermuda is gone, sir," he looked down. "Sorry."

The president said nothing. His wife and two children

121

had been vacationing in Bermuda. He just looked at the watch on his wrist—a gift from her—the only thing left now. "And your family?" he asked Farrell. "Where were—are they?"

"They were in New York."

"I'm sorry."

"Thank you, sir . . . There's also a message from Omega Force."

"What's that?" Christian asked.

"Sir, it's a top secret Air Force Base in White Sands, New Mexico," General Farrell answered. Christian, seeing the man was exhausted, asked him to be seated facing him on the sofa outside the communications section of the aircraft.

"From what little I know of it," Farrell continued, "they've apparently been developing some sort of super-combat suit. I know it sounds incredible—but supposedly the damned things can fly and are equipped with arsenals of weaponry. I don't know if the things are jokes or not, but we've been unable to reach any organized military forces at all. The Omega Unit has offered their services."

"Jesus Christ, Farrell, so many have died already. It seems like a fruitless move to send more into battle. Anyhow, what the hell could one unit do against a Soviet invasion?"

"I hadn't brought it up, sir," Farrell said, "because we're not sure it's true, but one of our other communications jets that got aloft says they got a message from the underground command center in Washington, that the president is *still alive*. The message was garbled and only lasted a few seconds but—"

Christian put his hands over his eyes and leaned back. He didn't want to send more men to their death, but if Armstrong really was alive, he might well be able to organize what remained of the country's defense. It was a slim chance, but there was nothing left to lose. Christian couldn't bear the weight of responsibility—having to decide America's future. And wouldn't have to. One thing was for sure—this plane would go down in a few days.

"All right, let's use them. If they're crazy enough to want to go out there and get killed—then let 'em. Can we make contact again?"

"Yessir. We're scrambling code on an unused frequency and bouncing it off one of the communication satellites that the Reds missed. They're waiting for a reply from you right now."

"General Farrell, put me through to them," Christian said, rising wearily from the brown leather couch.

He was patched quickly through to Omega base and after a few seconds General Knolls' voice came over a speaker.

"This is General Knolls sir, commander of the Omega Squad. I've been told that you are now Acting Commander-in-Chief, and as such, my men and I await your orders."

"Washington was hit," Christian said, "but we have reason to believe that the president and some of his staff were able to get into the bunkers beneath the city. We've also received word that the Russians are already landing an invasion force on the east coast and parachuting men into D.C. If you want to do something, rescue him and whoever else is there. If they're gone, so is America. If you can save them, we might have a chance. I know it's an almost suicidal mission, across thousands of miles of radioactive land that will soon be teeming with Reds, but—"

"We'll do it, sir," Knolls replied through the scrambler. "And with great honor. It will take me twenty-four hours to assemble the force. And I can assure you that every man will want to volunteer for this mission."

"God be with you," Christian said softly.

"God be with you too, Mr. President. Out."

"This Knolls, Farrell, can he do it?" Christian asked.

"If anyone can, Mr. President, Knolls and his men will do it. We served together. He's one of the toughest bastards around."

"How log till we have to go down?" Christian asked, suddenly conscious of the jet as it vibrated for a few seconds from an air pocket.

"Fifty-six hours, give or take—"

"Well is there anything else I should know about?"

"Yes. Fourteen of our bombers have returned. The entire B-1 fleet is gone, but 14 RB-71 stratobombers have landed in Mexico and are refueling for another nuke strike on Russia if you give the word. A secret A-bomb stockpile in Yucatan is being loaded on right now."

"Their targets?" Christian asked.

"East European satellite cities—Krakow, Dresden—"

"Dresden again?" He remembered the holocaust of World War II.

"Yes—and Brest. Soviet seaports—factory cities . . . "

"How many of our bombers will get through?"

"Five or ten, Mr. President—"

He thought for a moment. "Okay, but hit *military* targets. The seaports, hit the seaports—keep them from coming over here by boat. And order all our remaining forces to destroy all the airports in the U.S. that aren't already blown up—top priority. We've got to make it hard for them to get massive numbers over here to occupy us. That's more important right now than revenge."

"Wise decision, Mr. President. I—I'm glad *you're* the one—left—"

"Thank you, Charles. I wish I wasn't. I'll be honest. I wish I had died with my family. But my wish will come true soon enough—we're all dead men—"

CHAPTER TWELVE

General Knolls called a meeting within the hour in the mess hall, the only room large enough to hold nearly every man in the White Sands facility except those on vital support duties. The men and women gathered, sitting down at the long formica tables where they had their meals. The usually cheerful faces were on this night filled with pain and sadness. Every one of them had lost loved ones, and they knew what dark fate had befallen their country. In a strange way they felt guilty. After all, they were still alive, even in comfort, with food and supplies to last indefinitely, as the base from the start had been seen as necessarily having to be self-contained and had loaded up an underground warehouse full of supplies. They spoke in hushed tones — the technicians, the back-up personnel and the C.A.D.S. teams themselves, those 200 who were trained in the use of the death machines. They sat facing each other across the bare tables exchanging every bit of information they had gathered with one another. Rumors were rampant — that the Reds had already taken over Washington, that Russian troops were already sweeping across the country killing every person they found — even that the blasts had tilted the axis of the earth by several degrees, possibly sending it in a spin into the sun. They were desperate for the truth, but no one knew what it was.

"Attention," a voice suddenly boomed out from the front of the fluorescent lit hall. Nearly 800 military and civilian personnel rose as General Knolls walked in his usual erect military bearing into the room.

"At ease, at ease," Knolls said, waving his hands for them all to be seated. He stood up on a chair and then onto a serving table at the front of the mess hall. "Forgive me this somewhat unorthodox podium," Knolls continued, managing to muster a slight grin, "but from now on we'll have to use whatever we can find. Now I know you're all wondering just what the hell is going on out there, and I hate to be the one to tell you—but it's bad. Very bad. The Reds launched an all-out strike on us and blasted this beautiful country to bits. Apparently they were able to incapacitate many of our spy satellites and radar systems so they got their warheads in on us while they were able to stop most of our counterstrike." The men and women in the room looked on transfixed. Sturgis sat at the table directly in front of Knolls, looking at him with stone cold eyes.

"Now I'm not going to play any games with you or give you all a speech about how things aren't that bad and everything will work out in the end. Because it won't. We're close to finished. I know it and you should too. There won't be any secrets between us. I can assure you of that. I know you all have families out there and you're worried sick about them. Well, so am I. We're in the same boat together and I know it's hard but we all have to do our best to bone up and work together."

"Work together for what?" a voice cried out from the back of the room. It was Kreogh, the well-known scientist and the cynic around the post. Some of the personnel seated near him gave the aging, always disheveled man hard looks.

"No—he's right," General Knolls said above the murmur of disapproval at the question. "It's a legitimate thing to ask. And until a few hours ago I wouldn't have had an answer. But Acting-President Walter Christian contacted us from his flying command ship and asked if we would undertake a mission. A mission, ladies and gentlemen, that could alter the very destiny of our nation—Lord knows—the world. The president is apparently alive, hidden in a bunker deep beneath Washington. And we've been asked to go and get him the hell out of there before the Reds move in. As I'm sure you can imagine, the survival of President Armstrong could be a profound morale booster for every American who's still alive. And his loss—well it's obvious. The Reds are already moving in, we know, to try and capture him. They understand the importance of taking him prisoner. For the office of president is more than just a single man—it's a symbol. A message to all Americans that the nation relies on—that there is hope. That perhaps even at this late stage of the game something can be done to resurrect America and throw the damned Russians all the way back to the Baltic Sea."

The assembled personnel rose as one and hooted and hollered, slamming their hands down on the tables. It was the first time they had smiled all day. Not just because Armstrong was still alive—but because they were being asked to carry out perhaps the most important action conceivable—the freeing of the living, breathing symbol of all that America represented—embodied in one man.

"Good—good. I'm glad to see there's still some life left in all of you," Knolls said, rubbing his long pale hands together. "Now I told Christian that we would undertake the rescue of the president post-haste, and would do it with honor. I don't want to sound melodramatic, but this military trek across the continent may well be the most

127

important event of our nation's history—ranking up there with Paul Revere's ride, Sherman's march across Georgia, and Patton's drive across France. And those are the details in a nutshell." Knolls paused for a moment and looked over his staff. He felt prouder at that moment as he looked at their hopeful upturned faces then he had ever felt in his life. Out of the most tragic disasters, the most overpowering odds, men and women rise to their heights of human potential and courage.

"Now are there any questions before we go on with the exact method of operation?" Hands shot up all over the room, wanting to know just how much of the country had been destroyed, what cities, what armed forces were left. Knolls filled them in with every bit of information he had, patiently answering each and every question.

At last there were no more hands and Knolls said, "I'm going to turn the meeting over to Colonel Sturgis who will be in charge of the operation. Thank you for all that you've done to help make this base run so smoothly and for all the work you've put into the development of the C.A.D.S. suit. After all these years at least we can feel proud that the suit will at last be put into use. The brains, hearts and energy of every one of you is in those suits—and, well, I just want to give you my personal thanks in this most terrible of times for all that you've done."

With that, Knolls stepped down off the table and Sturgis rose and jumped up onto it.

"I'll be brief," he said, his ever present Camel dangling from his lips. His tanned hardened face looked even stonier than usual as he looked out over the crowd. But his mind kept wanting to head to thoughts of Robin and he had to push them down, be hard on himself just to keep going.

"Operation Snatch is the designation for this mission. We're going to get the president and whoever hell else is still in that bunker from right under the noses of the Reds. They're protected inside concrete walls and steel doors. It will take the Russians days to get in. We've got to move fast. The strike force will consist of one hundred men. General Knolls and I both feel that we can use only half the two-hundred-man force, in case of disaster. We've got to have something left for whatever else comes down the pike. There will be four squads of twenty-five men each, traveling in parallel lines one hundred miles apart, each equipped with twenty-four Tri-wheelers and a Rhino. As Walter Christian said, when he spoke with General Knolls, this could well be a suicide mission. So I'm only going to ask for volunteers."

Two-hundred hands shot up from the assembled C.A.D.S. team which was seated at the front of the mess hall. Sturgis formed a grim smile. "Thanks for your vote of confidence. I'll pick those men who I think have become the most proficient in the use of the C.A.D.S. You will be notified within two hours. And we leave in the morning. So get your beauty sleep—and pray. Pray real hard."

CHAPTER THIRTEEN

The waters of Long Island Sound, off New London, Connecticut were rough, tipped with teeth of gnawing foam that slapped up against the shoreline in large dark waves. Above them sea gulls flew, their wings outstretched catching the updrafts and then suddenly shooting down into the water as they spotted the quick flash of a fish rising to the surface. An idyllic scene, pretty as a postcard except for the fleet of landing craft with large red stars painted on them that were coming in to shore from cruisers, battleships, and two aircraft carriers several miles offshore. The Russian invasion of America had begun.

New London was famous for its seashore beauty, but that wasn't what the Reds were interested in. For the small city had become one of America's largest naval bases with a virtual armada anchored at its many docks, and one of the most modern ship-building facilities in the world. The Russians had wanted to get the Electric Boat Yard at the head of the long estuary that now lay before them, and they had dropped two low-yield neutron bombs over the peaceful town, killing nearly 75% of its inhabitants within hours. But the town and ships themselves had been barely scratched other than a few singed rooftops and some old wooden houses that had caught fire. The American fighting ships just sat there, dead in the water. Most of their crews dead, their electronics knocked out, they hadn't sailed. Death leaves many spoils for the victor, and these were too sweet to pass up. Besides, Russian intelligence reports indicated that there was virtually no organized military force to oppose them.

Admiral Kozinsky watched with binoculars from the bridge of the aircraft carrier *Stalin* as the waves of rectangular landing boats surged onward leaving long white furrows of foam behind them. He was in a good mood and, unusual for him, smiling frequently at his underlings who stood around him with earphones on ready to receive the first reports from the attack. This would be the first beachhead in America, Kozinsky thought, a bull of a man with shoulders as wide as a table. It would be an indication of just how the invasion of America would proceed. It would be a good omen to the brass back in Moscow for the taking of New London to come easily. For although they were atheists, Kozinsky knew that the general staff was a very superstitious bunch, and quick to panic when things didn't go right. But there would be no problems today, not with nearly 20,000 heavily armed commandos about to hit the beach.

He jumped for a moment as the harsh sound of helicopter engines suddenly jarred his daydreams of conquest, from below him on the nearly 1,000 foot long deck of the carrier. Ah, the paratroopers were taking off. They would be dropped in the back and the center of town, just in case. The plan had been in the works for nearly two years, and even Kozinsky, a man who knew caution was the word in Russian battle plans, had to admit that they might well have overdone this particular event. After all—who could be there waiting? Who would dare.

* * *

Major Krezhnov was in the first craft to hit the white sandy shore and he leaped out into the foot-deep water — wanting to be the very first man to hit American soil. A photographer along for the occasion snapped away as Krezhnov waded through the seaweed-filled water and hit the beach. Behind him, hordes of commandos, the best and toughest of the Russian armed forces, splashed onto the ground, their Kalashnikovs with fixed bayonets at the ready. They were smiling, joking with one another, moving at a medium pace. This would be a great day for Mother Russia, and for all of them. A day that would see them bedecked with medals. A day when the superiority of communism would shout its power from the quaint rooftops of New London.

They marched across the wide beach covered with driftwood and the rotting corpses of a few old dinghies and within minutes hit the wide road that skirted the shorefront edge of the town. In the distance they could see the flotilla of the U.S. boats waiting, bobbing in the rough waters, moving ever so slightly up and down. A few mangy looking dogs, their fur singed with burns from the neutron blast, looked out at them from beneath the mossy wharfs, their watery eyes red, their tails hung between their legs as they waited tiredly to die from the results of their radiation doses. The Red troops formed into brigades and marching in columns, descended onto the town, bringing their own version of hell to whatever inhabitants still remained — Russian style. For their orders were clear: every American still alive must be eliminated. There would be no prisoners, no mercy. The town must be cleansed as surely and efficiently as a festering wound. And when the cells of Americans who still remained were eliminated, then the Reds would have a whole new fleet to add to their naval power. Major Krezhnov moved to the front of the march, his chest puffed up with air like a mating gamecock. The official photographer ran yards ahead of him, snapping away every second as the major struck heroic poses, and moved his head slightly to the right so the left profile would be picked up. That was really his most handsome side. And after all, if these pictures were going to go down in history, he might as well look as good as he could. A few thousand years from now, his descendants would look at his firm jaw, his clear eyes, and know—this was a man—a soldier, a hero.

"They're coming! I see 'em now. They're just hitting the beachroad," Grant Smathers said to the other Americans grouped behind him on the third floor of what had been Grant's General Hardware Store. He peered through his binoculars as the magnitude of the Russian invasion became terribly clear. "And there's a fucking shitload of 'em too."

He pulled suddenly back from the wood-frame window as he saw the officer in charge of the lead column look up at the windows and rooftops in front of him. Smathers sat down on the creaking wide board floor and glanced around at the people who sat there waiting. It was pitiful—there was no question about it. There were 15 of them in this room, some of the few who still lived after the neutron blast. If you could call them all living. The 15 men and women in the storage room, filled with rifles and ammunition—and Grant himself—hadn't escaped the ravages of the blast. Their hair was already beginning to fall out, their skin a pasty white covered with small festering red and purple sores that oozed a slow stream of greasy pus. They could barely move, and even the weight of their weapons, cradled in their arms and across their laps, gave painful reminders that their bodies were disintegrating—rotting away. For the effects of a neutron bomb are most insidious and horrible to those unfortunate recipients of its killing energies. Designed to kill people—not damage property, the neutron bomb emits a storm of deadly gamma radiation which can travel through walls, stone, even steel without damaging it. It searches out living things—creatures with cells, and then bombards them with an invisible hail of the gamma rays. Those who are not severely burned instantly by the radiation find themselves over the next few days slowly losing their flesh, their teeth, their minds. For the gamma rays attack directly at the center of every cell, destroying its control center, the nucleus, and making the cellular network incapable of functioning. The once strong and protective blood and bone and brain cells begin to disintegrate from the inside out. With their nuclei gone, the cells lose their function, the electrical bond that holds them together, and they just—fall apart. Death is quick, usually within weeks at most, but not sweet. For dying from radiation is perhaps one of the most painful ways to go—and worse, those who are dying are totally and fully aware of every gut wrenching second as they see their own beings deteriorate into liquidy sacks of nonfunctioning flesh.

And yet . . . if they were going to die they wanted to take as many Russians with them as they could. The survivors of the blast had met two days before in the local school gymnasium—all 2,347 of them out of an original population of nearly 300,000. It had been a grim meeting as they came in to the high school, their hair burned off, limping, vomiting. But they came from every part of New London—store owners, housewives, sailors, technicians from the shipyards, a few cops, and the children, those pitifully few who were left. They came and they wept and they mourned the deaths of their loved ones, of their town, the passing of an era from relative comfort into hell. And after their tears could flow no more they angrily decided to fight back.

"I know them Reds will be coming," one of the few

134

naval officers still left alive, Lieutenant Harris, said grimly, his once spotless blue uniform now filled with holes. "That's why they dropped a neutron bomb instead of one of their big boys," he said, addressing the crowd from the platform at the front of the gymnasium — once the home of basketball games and laughter — now the scene of a nightmare.

"What the hell can we do?" Alice Parsons shouted up. "It's all over. We might as well just dig our own graves and jump in. You know, I know, we *all* know we're going to die. Can't you feel it inside you? Feel your body coming apart at the seams, feel your mind dissolving?"

"Yes, I feel it," Harris answered softly. "I feel everything you do. And I'm not going to play games with you. We are going to die, every last one of us. But Jesus, let's go out fighting — like Americans. Let's make our death mean something in this hellhole of a world the Russian bastards have created. Let's at least take some of them with us. Let them know that taking over America isn't going to come easy. What the hell have we got to lose? I'd rather go out with a bullet in my chest than dissolving like a bowl of overcooked porridge on the floor."

After a loud and lengthy debate, it had been decided. They, the dying people of New London, would fight. Would try to give some little bit of meaning to their demise. Doctor Harrigan, the only M.D. still alive, managed to scrape up a truckload of medical supplies from the local hospital and he handed out stimulants and morphine to all those present, so they could keep going. Then they had formulated their defensive plans, as rifles and pistols were handed out to the assemblage. They would conduct a guerrilla war against the Reds when they entered New London. Would fight them from every rooftop, every alley. The dying but proud citizens of New London would make the Reds remember the day they came to conquer for a long, long time.

* * *

"What quaint streets," Major Krezhnov said with a grin as he led his men into the winding streets of the town. "I think I'll take that building there," he said, pointing to the town hall, "as my headquarters. Yes, I rather like it — the domed roof, the — " His words were cut off as a hail of bullets dug into the front ranks of the lead battalion. The commandos dove for cover as Krezhnov looked around in confusion. Suddenly the official photographer took a slug in the center of his skull and his brains splattered out across the major's clean uniform.

"What the — " Krezhnov said, still standing as pieces of white hot metal whistled by his ear.

"Down man, damnit," his second-in-command Narpov said, grabbing the major around the legs and dropping to the ground with him.

"Why they're — they're shooting at us," Krezhnov said incredulously.

From throughout the town the dying citizens of New London poured out a hail of lead on every Red they could sight up. The Russians in the lead ranks dropped like flies, littering the pavements with oozing red corpses. They pulled back to cover and regrouped as Krezhnov sent out orders over his walkie-talkie. The Russian battalions spread out through the town, moving forward on their bellies, darting from corner to corner, trying to find their hidden attackers. But the Americans had hidden themselves well — shooting down from windows, from cellars, getting as many Reds as they could, and then fleeing through back doors to another sniper site. As tired as their decomposing bodies felt, they were filled with an exhilaration at doing something, at making a difference.

The Reds advanced in fierce hand-to-hand fighting, losing five, even ten men for every American they at last found and killed. But it was slow, deadly slow, as they moved only 10 or 20 yards an hour. From the town hall third-story windows, Major Krezhnov watched the street fighting as he sent out frantic commands for the support of ships' guns. It was not good — not good at all, the major thought, picturing what the chiefs of staff would say back in Moscow. How, they would ask him — how the hell a few rabble dying of radiation could inflict such heavy casualties on trained Russian fighters? He heard Admiral Kozinsky countermand his order for shelling, on the crackling radio.

"Look out," Grant Smathers yelled over to the other window where Frances McCullough was firing her pump-action shotgun. A Red sniper perched on a roof across the street aimed and fired and Frances, two days before the mother of four, exploded backwards from the window, her guts hanging out of her stomach. Grant sighted up on the Red and fired. The sniper screamed as the bullet entered his right eye and he stood up screaming and crashed through the glass to the street below.

"Bastard," Grant muttered as he rushed over to Frances who lay in a pool of her own blood. He cradled her head.

"You did good Mrs. McCullough, real good. You got five of them."

"I'm going, Grant," the once beautiful woman said. "And you know what — I'm glad." Her eyes closed as her head fell to the side. Grant felt the tears rush to his eyes but pushed them down again. There was no time for emotion now — just death. He rushed back to the window and opened up on the crawling troops below, hitting three of them in the back. They stopped moving. But the rest of the squad, nearly 50 of them, raised their rifles and let loose with a steel spray that slammed into the white-washed wooden walls of the building ripping the boards to splinters. Grant felt a slug rip into his shoulder and he winced with pain. There were too many now—they'd get him in a second. He rose and rushed down the rickety wooden stairs and out the back door. Quickly he dashed through backyards, almost strangling himself on a clothesline filled with laundry hung before the bombs hit. Baby's clothes, t-shirts, with no one left to wear them. All around him Grant could hear the firefights coming from every part of town. Good, we're doing it, goddamnit, he thought, as he rushed through the door of a weathered old building, to the second floor.

Two men inside turned in a flash, their rifles aimed at him. "It's just me boys," Grant said, mustering a thin smile. "I came to join the fun." Clint Crayton and Greg Chin let their Winchester 30-30's fall from their target.

"Should announce yourself next time, buddy," Chin said, "or you might get a slug meant for a Red."

"Ain't gonna be a next time. When this party's over, the festivities end."

"I love guys who are optimistic," Clint said, twisting back around in the window frame just in time to catch sight of ten Reds running crouched over through the backyards littered with overturned tricycles, dolls, and toys. The three men let loose with a welcoming committee of hot lead and the Reds tumbled face forward, riddled with the American-made ammo.

Suddenly they heard the sounds of heavy vehicles approaching.

"What the hell is that?" chin asked nervously. But they didn't have long to find out as three tanks came lumbering down the center of Main Street three blocks away.

"Where the fuck did they get them?" Clint asked, his jaw opening wide.

"Don't matter where they got 'em—they got 'em," Chin said, sighting up the observation man on the lead tank. He fired and the Russian slumped over the turret, dead.

The three immense K-12 tanks swiveled their cannon toward the fire and began blasting away. The shells tore into the lower level of the woodframe, blasting truck-sized craters in the walls. On the top floor, the three American fighters were knocked off their feet as the ceiling collapsed on them. Grant rose shakily to his feet and looked around as the dust settled. Chin and Clint were motionless, huge beams covering their bloody bodies.

"Damn," Grant muttered, wiping the plaster dust from his face. He crawled back to the window and raised his rifle. It was a futile gesture, he knew, but he wanted to end his last second behind the trigger. The tanks opened up again, this time missing the house and hitting the 250-year-old Colonial home to the right, which erupted in a volcanic explosion. Grant sighted up on two commandos riding on the back of the lead tank and fired, pumping the lever of his 30-30. They both fell backwards, tumbling off the metal death machine in bloody heaps.

"Well I guess that's about it," Grant whispered, looking up at the blue sky one last time.

Suddenly he heard the high-pitched sound of motorcycles—a lot of them. Down Main Street they came, 20 of them, driven by the surviving teenagers of New London. They screamed out rebel war cries as they came, shooting over the rubble at 60 miles per hour. The tanks saw them too and slowly turned their immense 120mm cannon to make quick work of the approaching foe. But the teens wouldn't be slaughtered quite that easily. They had made gasoline bombs, molotov cocktails—as the Russians who had invented them called them. Each teen, wearing black leather jacket and boots, carried a satchel of the gas bombs—milk bottles filled with the remaining store of the gas from the local stations.

"Hit 'em," Chris Megan, the leader of the group, screamed out as the bikes took evasive action and then roared up to the tanks. Keeping one hand on their handlebars the teens whipped out bottles and lit the gas-soaked rag stuck in the end with the glowing ash of the cigars they had tightly clamped in their jaws. The rags caught fire and the bikers streamed by the tanks, heaving their deadly load. The bottles hit the sides of the tanks, and exploded into a violent eruption of flame. Bullets can't penetrate two-inches of steel, but fire-heat can. It poured through the breathing holes, through the machine-gun sighting slit, and consumed the men inside. The bikers screeched to a stop just yards on the other side of the burning tanks as they heard the screams of the dying Reds inside, rising even above the roar of the battle.

"Come on man, we got more work to do," Megan yelled out and the bikers tore off, heaving their loads of fiery death at every Russian head they saw.

Grant watched with a broad smile on his face from the window. He had never felt prouder in his life than at that moment. They were good kids—damned good kids. He was sorry he had ever yelled at a one of them—every face of the cyclers he knew. The tanks suddenly erupted as the fire made contact with their munitions stores and exploded. Burning shrapnel shot in every direction, setting half the block on fire. Grant felt a stinging pain in his throat and reached up. Blood covered his hand as a piece of the exploding tank shrapnel had nearly severed his jugular. But he was ready to die now. He leaned forward on the window ledge, his body slowly losing strength. But his dying eyes saw the flames spreading off igniting the old wooden houses on the block. Yes, fire—we will cleanse the city with fire—leave them nothing. He slumped forward, his body dead, his vacant eyes reflecting the flames that shot up everywhere.

At the shipyards and docks, the few remaining naval

personnel could hear the battle going on several miles off, could see the clouds of smoke beginning to rise above the once picturesque town. The Reds were closing in, as tanks and infantry came shooting down the long wharves to capture what remained of the American fleet on the East Coast. But they weren't going to get it—not by a long shot. The 30 or so surviving military men had spent the last few days setting charges in every one of the battleships and destroyers; and in two nearly completed nuke subs that sat in the huge Electric Boat drydocks. Charges were placed among each ship's munitions supply so when they went . . . But the men, now deciding things democratically as there were not enough officers left among them, had decided to wait until the last possible moment so they could bring a whole legion of Russian souls with them on their trip to hell.

From the bridge of the missile cruiser *Darrell*, Ensign Nader watched the approaching Russians. They scurried along the wide docks like so many rats searching out food. Closer and closer they came, thousands of them until they were almost upon the gangplank. "Now's as good a time as any," Nader said softly over his ship-to-ship radio. "Bye-bye boys, it's been fun."

With that he closed his eyes and pressed a button in front of him. The entire U.S. fleet docked in New London exploded with a thunderous roar that could be felt for miles. Twenty ships went up, at once, every bullet, every cannon shell, every missile, in a living hell of fire and twisted metal. Every Russian troop within a half mile was gone, disappeared into nothingness. The ships burned wildly and quickly sank, twisted shells, into the dark waters. Now there was nothing.

Major Krezhnov watched the fires from the wide curving windows of the domed top floor of the town hall. His face grew pale, his lips dry as sand. The entire town was aflame now, brisk winds from the ocean sweeping the fire from street to street. It was a disaster. By the end of the day there wouldn't be a thing left here. Not a blade of grass, not a building would be left standing. The major kept gulping, his eyes unable to believe the devastation below. Everywhere his men lay dying, his tanks blasted to steel carcasses by these crazy Americans. The sky above the town was filled with thick smoke that stretched for miles as thousands of fires joined together, sending funnels of blackness into the heavens.

He was still alive, though God knew how many of his force remained. But the major knew he would be better off dead. When he returned to Moscow there would be no mercy. Not for this fiasco. He would be court-martialed and then . . . Major Krezhnov took his Turganev 7.2mm revolver from its holster. Slowly, ever so slowly, he raised it to his head. A single shot went off—heard by no one in the midst of the living hell that was New London, Connecticut.

CHAPTER FOURTEEN

The sky was as dark as the blackest nightmare as the C.A.D.S. teams rode up the steep ramps from the hidden exit of the underground Omega base. One at a time they shot up the concrete and out into the new world that awaited them, their bikes roaring with 600 horsepower of energy, their immense black suits of destruction covering their bodies in protective cocoons. And it looked like they would need some protection, each man could see through his super-hardened bulletproof visor as he pulled his bike to a stop on the sandy parking lot just east of the aboveground "Agricultural Station".

The men breathed deeply, many of them fighting back tears as they looked at the post-nuclear world. The air was filled with a thick grit, a million little particles floating everywhere, creating a smoky haze that almost seemed to glow. But it was the sky itself above that sent shivers down their spines. It was a blackness they had never known existed. So dark it seemed almost solid and within its darkness filled with a million million undulating currents of browns and greys, all twisting together like an endless pit of snakes. The wind howled past them, slamming into their heavy bikes. And even within the armored suits strapped down to the Tri-wheelers they could feel the angry gusts smash against them again and again like fists that wanted to kill.

Something was different. Every man could feel it — not through the advanced sensory mechanisms of the suit, but in his guts and soul. The world had changed. The cloudless impenetrable sky was charged with fury and death. It was as if the earth were filled with hatred at man for what he had done to it. From within the sheets of blackness, one behind another they could hear aching rumblings that bellowed down shaking the very ground on which their Tri-bikes stood. Every few seconds a shrieking flash of blinding energy — God even knew if it was lightning — came careening jaggedly down to earth, exploding whatever it touched and sending it up into the foul darkness.

Where was the moon, the stars? They scarcely dared wonder as more and more of the roaring bikes poured from the tunneled earth up into the world of a billion deaths. The presence of evil was palpable, even through the suits. No material could protect against what man had done to his own species and his world. It was as if the very legions of hell had been unleashed and now danced through the skies in a maddened frenzy of unseeable shadows, reaching down to consume all that remained. The winds howling in a deafening roar above them almost seemed to be made up of the choruses of the dead — singing, screaming out their songs of blood and destruction. The eerie, ghostlike sounds went right through their suits and into their nervous systems, into their bones, planting seeds of terror in every one of them.

"All right, snap to," Sturgis ordered through his helmet mike as he rode up the ramp, the last one to leave. A sliding steel door descended smoothly behind him, blocking off the concrete-walled underground bunker with a two-foot slab of leaded metal. He steered his bike up to the assembled team, nearly a hundred strong, split up in

144

four separate units. He saw their helmets all pointed up at the sky as he spoke and glanced up. Yeah, he saw what they were looking at; it wasn't pretty.

He stopped in front of them as they looked back down again. "Look, I'm not going to give you all a whole bunch of pep talks. We've had enough of those in the last few days to last everybody a lifetime. Okay, we're out here—it looks like shit. It's going to look worse. The death and ugliness you're all going to be forced to witness over the next few weeks will be enough to try the strongest man's soul. But as bad as it is, we're all that remains from it getting even worse. Understand? And if all seems just too horrible to go on, then you might as well commit suicide right here and now. Just hold your hand to your head and turn your wrist to the right. You all know how to do it. 'Cause every other man on your team will depend on you—stake his life on you. So anyone that's not up to it—get out now."

Sturgis waited for long seconds. "All right then, let's go. And boys—whether we win or lose, whether even one of us comes out of this thing alive, let's let the Reds know they've had a fight—something they'll remember for a long, long time."

Sturgis wheeled around suddenly, his back tires sending up a spray of crumbling gray soot that coated the normally yellow-sanded desert, and shot over to the lead of his own unit. All his usual crew were there—Tranh, Roberto, Billy Dixon, Fenton, handling the Rhino—and even Rossiter. Sturgis didn't know if the almost obese man was up for the trip, but he had trained hard and had technical expertise in C.A.D.S. suit maintenance. Rossiter volunteered, and Sturgis was damned if he wouldn't let the bumbling but well-liked man give it a try.

"Let's go," he said, reaching the front of the 24-man team. Their bikes puffed out little streams of blue smoke in the frigid air as they pulled in behind him, spaced about 20 feet apart. The long line of the wide, squat bikes with their steel-stud impregnated 4-foot high back tires and single foot-high forward wheel, appeared to be leaning forward, about to pounce, a pack of steel panthers ready to strike.

They shot forward out past the wire mesh gate that surrounded the base, out into the dark desert, whipping with sheets of sand. It was as if they were going into the jaws of hell itself as Sturgis' team headed onto the northernmost route that the four teams would take toward Washington, spaced a hundred miles apart. On his radar grid, at the lower right quadrant of the computerized visor, Sturgis could see the other three teams head off, each to their own fate, colored blips on the grid map, their lines stretching out nearly 20 miles. They were all able men, and brave. They had trained as hard as one could. It was in the hands of God now—if he was still around.

Sturgis' thoughts slowly died down as he settled into the bumpy ride through the night. The twin super-beams of his bike penetrated the twisting sand and dust storms ahead. By a complex inter-penetration of sodium, ruby and normal-spectrum lightwaves, the beam was able to tear through the moving darkness like a spear, lighting the way. The men behind him kept their beams on low, just enough to see the man ahead and the road around them. They roared with precision, rock-steady, down the tarmac road, a fleet of mortals daring to enter into what surely was the domain of dark gods and demons.

Sturgis switched his visor from mode to mode, testing his various perception systems. In Infrared he could see the shimmering blue outlines of cactuses, and small scrub brush that dotted the flat prairie. An occasional hawk or jack-rabbit would dart by every mile or so, their heat-sensed bodies showing up clearly on the screen. He switched to Radar-dead-ahead, scouting for any vehicles, but could find nothing for at least the next 5 miles. Cautious at first, as Sturgis got used to the terrain and the darkness, he slowly increased speed from a slow 25–30mph up to 45 and then, after an hour or so, up to 60. He wanted to ease them all into the real thing. Once the darkness lifted — if it ever did — he'd take them up to their optimism cruising speed of 100–125mph.

Sturgis' computerized defensive and information gathering systems kept a steady read-out in green moving letters at the bottom of his visor. Everything from outside temperature to probability of rain to life-support functions and position of the entire crew were constantly fed to him. It was up to Sturgis to pay attention to what he wanted, though the C.A.D.S. Early Warning Functions would call his attention to any emergency situation with a warning tone and larger, impossible to ignore, letters. The radiation readings were fairly low outside thus far, but Sturgis knew that would change. Nothing big had gone off really close. But when he looked straight up at the black pit of a sky for a second, and commanded the computer "Give Rad reading on visual focus". The readout read: "Radiation levels within cloud formations up to 1,000 RADS. Radioactive elements within include: uranium, strontium, plutonium, zelium, krypton — "

"Cease function," Sturgis commanded, getting the general idea. The readout instantly stopped and was replaced by the regular flow of data, moving like little green ants at the bottom of the visor. Those clouds were radioactive hells, dense amalgamations of highly lethal particulate matter circling the world again and again, embracing it in a tightening grip of atomic death. Sturgis suddenly had a vision of the earth totally dying, every bit of life on it and those bands of radiation coalescing into huge circles like the rings of Saturn, glowing green and red and blue — for all the universe to see. *Don't stop here — the idiotic highest species has destroyed itself and made the planet uninhabitable for any life form — off limits.*

They rode through the night, their bodies getting adjusted to the slung back positions they drove in on the Tri-wheelers. Moving at increasingly high speed, their suited bodies just inches above the ground, they had the sensation of almost flying as the world spun by below in a blur that they could reach out and touch. With the dawn sun trying its best to throw a little light back on the earth's affairs, they were able to see a little better. But not much. The sky turned from black to somber gray. The dust still hung in thick swirling sheets all around them and turned a sickly brownish red by the few pale rays of sun that reached them. Far above, the omnipresent fallout clouds writhed like things alive, stretching as far as the eye could see, a vast crawling pit of death. They could hardly stand to look up — and kept their eyes dead ahead, sinking into an almost meditative trance as the desert landscape slowly turned to more wooded land, and more bodies as well.

They had only come across a few lone corpses at first, sighting the first one after about two hours' drive, at the edge of the road. A car filled with a family of dead, their faces a dripping putty of blistered flesh. But as they went on, passing towns along the route, the dead increased geometrically, until they were a common sight.

Now in the dim light of what passed for day, the dead seemed to stare back at them, as if they were parading just for the rows of corpses on each side of the road. Sturgis got a prickly feeling down the edge of his spine as he swore the things were about to clap their bony hands together. But of course they weren't. The dead stayed dead.

It seemed cold enough out there to begin snowing, yet instead a driven icy rain began to pound away at their suits and Tri-bikes. It started as a light drizzle and slowly rows of heavy black cumulus clouds rolled in low overhead, bringing a heavy torrential downpour.

Sturgis didn't like the looks of it.

"Sounds like it's hailing," said Fenton from the Rhino, watching the wide forward color video screen of the ATV.

Slugs of ice a quarter-inch wide began slamming against the men and bouncing off the tough outer layers of their suits.

"Christ," Sturgis muttered, "what next?"

"Reminds me of the New Hebrides," continued Fenton over the mike. "I was there once, guarding the Queen on . . ."

"Shhhh!" Sturgis answered back. "Do you hear *that?*"

Fenton listened over the rumble of the Rhino and Tribikes. Despite the noise, he could hear a strange whooshing sound.

"Yeah," he answered, thin lipped. "What do you make of it? These crazy winds?"

"I hope to God it's only *wind*," said Sturgis eyeing the blackness above swirling ever closer to them.

Ice balls began hammering down in apple-sized chunks, buffeting the men and their bikes. Sturgis called out to his men on the helmet radio. "I'm going to slow it down a bit—visibility's lousy. If anyone sees some hills, some sort of rock cover, cliffs, anything *strong*—let me know. We might be in for a blow . . ."

The clouds grew more and more ominous, taking on a purplish tint. Even through the suits, the men could feel a strange sensation—changes in the air. Sergeant McGowan, who had grown up on the western wind belt said, "Sir, these are *tornado* clouds. That quicksilver look on the horizon, the strange feel in the air, the ice-balls. I've been through a few of these back home in Oklahoma. It's twister weather. Maybe several brewing up. We'd better find some shelter. The wind and lightning can get fierce even if the twisters miss us."

Sturgis scanned the orange-black clouds swirling on the horizon and the flat plain ahead.

"We might have to dig shelter, though where I can't imagine.

Then they saw it, or rather *them*. On the eastern horizon. First six, then eight, then ten funnel clouds; black swirling furies. And beneath them dusty spirals of debris lifting thousands of feet into the sky.

"Never saw anything like that," Sturgis said. "Twisters in December could only have been spawned by the nuke explosions."

They were moving right at them, like a set of dancing dervishes lined up for the kill.

"Let's head south," Sturgis said. On the south horizon he saw a highway lined with a few houses. "Maybe those houses over there have storm cellars."

"But what about the equipment?" McGown asked over the radio.

"We're dead men without the equipment," Sturgis agreed, "but let's get to those houses."

It was a good two miles or so, and they were quickly set upon by the immense howling freight-train-like first tornado. The first twister, the smallest of them, was upon them like a predator. It was the kind that sets down just for a second, does its havoc, and jumps away again. It caught them in the open field. They had spread out — each man driving his Tri-bike 50 feet apart, on Sturgis' orders. If some would die, at least others would survive.

The whole radius of this baby was less than 200 feet, but it got McGowan, the one guy who had lived with the twisters all his life. He was suddenly swirling and spinning up into the blackness. They heard screams as he and his Tri-bike flew overhead in an insane ballet of death.

"Help, God help me!" the disembodied voice of McGowan cried out over the suit radio.

"McGowan, don't panic," Sturgis screamed back. "Use your jetpack! Use the thrusters. Don't fight the wind, go with it. Get out the *side* of the twister."

150

McGowan's voice was full of static now. He was already far away.

"I'm firing Sturgis, I'm *firing* the jets. I think — *crackle crackle* — I think — *crackle* — I — I'm getting out of the — *crackle* —"

They watched the twister rip off to the north and then just for a second saw the brief flare, like a match being ignited in a huge black room. McGowan's jetpack was activated. Then there was nothing.

"Get moving," Sturgis yelled as another funnel blackened the horizon. It was tearing in their direction and it was wider and blacker than the little baby that had taken McGowan away. The Tri-bikes, their tires bouncing madly on the corrugated ploughed field, roared toward the farmhouse and barn. Sturgis was praying that the farmhouse — a large sprawling white-shingled one — had an underground shelter for the men. And that the barn might somehow protect the Tri-bikes and Rhino.

The funnel cloud was nearly upon them now, the roar so deafening that nothing else could be heard. The gray daytime sky was now dark green, turning to black.

Sturgis screamed on his helmet mike, "Get the vehicles into the barn!" Fenton smashed the Rhino right into the barn door and it splintered like balsa wood. No time for amenities, not with a 500mph funnel bearing down on them. The Tri-bikes filled the space quickly. The whole barn was trembling. It offered little protection, Sturgis realized; what the hell could they do to prevent the bikes from sailing away if the barn went?

He suddenly had an idea — the steel tow cables. "Quick men. Get out the cables and wire all the equipment together. Run the cable through the handlebars and through the Rhino's two small windows."

They tied the whole assemblage of vehicles together in a tight circle — over 15 tons of weight. In a matter of minutes they were done. Then they double-timed it to the farmhouse a hundred feet off. Sturgis ripped the door off its hinges, and the black-suited figures filed in.

"Over here," Sturgis said, "quick, roll up this rug. Sometimes there's a cellar underneath." They shone their strobes on the bare, wooden floor. "Nothing, damn it," snapped Sturgis.

"Aren't we safe in here?" asked the rawest recruit of the C.A.D.S. team, Jimmy Bowen. He was wildeyed inside his helmet. He had just seen his best friend torn up into the air and carried away to his death, as if some giant had grabbed McGowan and casually thrown his life away.

"Steady son, steady," said Fenton, fixing his eyes on the 20-year-old youngster.

"*All* of you, get a grip on yourselves," said Sturgis. "We're *not* safe in here. This house is like a toy compared to the power of those winds."

"What do we do?" Bowen asked, ignoring the "sir" in his fear.

"We *hope* the twisters miss us," Sturgis said, "and we keep *looking* for a cellar door. There has to be a cellar somewhere."

The glass in the porch window of the house exploded outward. The roar was like jet planes bearing down on them. Nothing except the ferocity of the twister's screams could be heard. They had their strobes on, eerily lighting the dusty interior as the whole house shook violently. The walls gave up their pictures of farmers at their chores, which flew through the air like things possessed.

"Open the windows," yelled Sturgis, but no one could even hear him. He ran over to the largest window and smashed it with a single punch. The others caught on, and did the same with the other windows. Sturgis knew that what often destroys a house in a tornado is an explosion of the *higher* pressure air *inside* the house into the extremely *low* pressure of the tornado. If they weren't in the direct path of the tornado, perhaps the house would survive.

A gust of wind threw debris from the farm yard against the outer walls of the house. Threshers, branches, pieces of metal, loose rusting tools, all hit the house like some giant's fist pounding away, demanding entrance.

"This ain't gonna work," Sturgis yelled. "We've got to find the cellar."

They all fanned out and soon Tranh found a trap door. The storm cellar. They rushed down the steep musky stairs into a stone basement. The whole house was groaning now, like a wounded bull elephant. It could give at any second.

A nuclear-blast spawned twister 300 yards wide was nearly overhead. "That's all of us!" Fenton said as he slammed the door shut. They stood there, surrounded by shelves of clinking belljars filled with jams and preserves.

"Well, at least there's plenty of chow if we get trapped down here," Rossiter said enthusiastically, reaching out to look at a jar of the richly colored preserves. Even Sturgis laughed aloud along with the others, as the words broke the electronic tension and fear in their guts.

There was an enormous crash above. "The roof," muttered Tranh. "Shit."

Then came a rumble that shook them to their bones as an avalanche of dust fell through the bending floor boards above them. The house had collapsed on them, Sturgis realized. That might be good, he thought to himself. They could dig out easily with the power in their suits. It might just keep them all alive, to be buried away from the howling winds.

Sturgis was more worried about the equipment than his own life. If the cables didn't hold the Rhino and Tri-bikes, or if the funnel were strong enough to lift all the vehicles right into the air . . . He licked his lips in real fear. Their entire mission could be ended at the very start by a *damned tornado*. The whole future of the United

States might depend on an old barn and a steel cable.

There seemed to be a loud rumble again. "Another twister," whispered Dixon. Sturgis nodded grimly. This one was even fiercer than the last. Canned fruits fell from the cellar shelves, crashing to the floor, as some of the boards above snapped and rained down on them. Even the stone walls around them seemed to buckle, making a terrible crunching sound like teeth grinding together. Sturgis had never felt so helpless before the awesome power of nature.

Suddenly the oceanic roar above turned to a deep rumbling and then thunder boomed out, and the sharp cracks of lightning. Sturgis felt a surge of hope. It could mean that the storm was becoming a funnel-less thunder cloud.

Sure enough, within seconds water was dripping through the cracks above. And there was relative silence between the thunderclaps.

"Time to dig out men. Let's all say a prayer for our equipment, and for McGowan's soul. He helped us get to safety, but he didn't make it himself."

They simply pushed together, and all the debris moved away. There was no house above—just a junkyard of debris. And heavy rains pouring down like a thousand waterfalls. It was still dark but Sturgis saw instantly that the barn had collapsed. They all ran over, nearly slipping in the mud, and found the piles of collapsed wood and beams had covered their tied-together vehicles. They spent almost an hour carefully removing what had been the barn, trying not to cause any additional damage to their vehicles underneath.

The damage was slight, considering. Just one Tri-bike totalled. A few of the others had sustained minor damage—mostly scratches and dents. The rugged Rhino was okay. By the time they got started again the sky actually began growing a little brighter and an orange-yellow setting sun appeared low on the western horizon. For the first time since the war began, it actually looked like a sun, a life-giving star trying to burn its way through the radioactive swamp above. A large shimmering rainbow suddenly formed to the east, arching up above them. It seemed a message of hope to the men of the C.A.D.S. team who had seen only deathly grays and blacks thus far in the New America.

"Goodbye McGowan," Sturgis muttered by way of a prayer into the throat mike so the other men could hear him. "And God rest your fighting soul wherever the hell you are."

He hit the accelerator.

CHAPTER FIFTEEN

They drove on and on, through the flat lands of New Mexico, and reached the outskirts of Peakesville, Texas, some 260 miles from base, just before dawn.

Burned and twisted pines along the hills surrounding Peakesville lifted naked black branches to a sky boiling with orange-edged black clouds. The sky to the west seemed made of stone — slate smooth — but here it was active as a nightmare. Gust of icy wind like the hand of a giant slammed against the men's Tri-wheelers, buffeting them about. The low valley below — a shopping mall, a twisted ribbon of highway with a few abandoned cars on it, their doors still wide open as if whoever owned them had just fled — was full of what Sturgis at first thought were white birds.

"Max 30," he said to the suit computer and the "birds" turned out to be flying newspapers, twisting in the dust devils. There was no sign of life at all, the huge flat parking lot in the front of the J. C. Penney department store was newly marked with brilliant white lines indicating places for cars to park. In front of the store a yellow sign ordered NO PARKING FIRE LANE. The windows held signs saying AFTER CHRISTMAS SALE — 40% OFF. The window was shattered and sheets and designer pillow cases were blowing in the wind, the mannequins like frozen naked bodies. Probably someone needing warm clothes did that. Maybe there was a hunting jacket display. Perhaps some poor soul was still in the Woolco down there, living on candy bars and canned food.

"Okay men, let's bypass this valley and keep to the ridge," Sturgis said. He didn't want to go down there. He had once stopped at that mall to buy a present for Robin when it was a live thing, not a place of death.

The air grew strangely colder as dawn broke. The sick pale ball of a distant sun seen dimly through the desolate gray clouds overhead did not do anything to warm it. The desert breeze, cold before, but bearable, had turned into something harsher, and whipped at them now in frigid eddies, clawing at them, slamming against their Tri-bikes. Sturgis, though insulated by his suit, instinctively hunched his shoulders and gritted his teeth. It was as though the frigid emptiness of the prairie was rushing in to straighten out whatever illusions they had about things being normal. There was no hint out here that the war had happened—only yucca, the scrub pines, the endless strip of black asphalt. But the dark gray sky, unwavering in its opaque bleakness, was proof that things *had* changed. It wasn't black but more like a blanket of dust, of charcoal—the charred remains of a billion living things, now circling the earth in a shroud of death.

"Nuclear winter," the words went through Sturgis' head, sending a shiver up his spine. He remembered reading the predictions, made in the mid-1980s, that if even one percent of the world's nuclear arsenal was used in a war it would mean the beginning of a nuclear winter. A blanket of darkness would cover the earth making temperatures plunge and vegetation die as the life-giving rays of the sun were cut off. It was Carl Sagan, Sturgis remembered, who had put forth the concept. And according to him, it would be a winter from which the earth would never recover. There would be no spring as the earth's entire ecosystem fell into a dark pit of no return. The ground would become cold and hard, lifeless. And as the precious oxygen that the plants and trees produced disappeared, the entire earth would die. Every single living thing, every animal, every flower, every insect and microbe would become nothing more than fossilized remains as the planet grew as cold as space itself, resembling after a few centuries, its sister, the mottled moon.

Sturgis looked up at the sky. Well, it wasn't black yet, but it sure as hell was gray—the pallor of a dead man. He'd have to worry about it all later, when the president was rescued, when Robin was safe. He doubted he would even live long enough to see if all that happened anyway.

The team roared onward, toward the east. The hard sharp edge of the horizon ahead was like a knife to his eyes. Why go on, the wheels of his machine seemed to say as they whined in a cacophony on the macadam below his Tri-bike. *Why go on—Why go on—Why go on?*

He'd smoked his last Camel five miles back. They had plenty of food from the base depot, but the goddamned cigarette deliveries had been late. Now they'd never come. He'd have to stop at the next store and grab a few cartons. He knew he'd need them.

Several miles down the highway they came upon the wreckage of a fifty-car pile-up, bodies dangling from every window. They saw a circle of corpses facing each other all holding guns. They had shot one another. They lay there in a mass like Jonestown—a suicide pact realized.

A father, a mother, five kids, an old man, maybe a grandfather or uncle. They had shot each other in the head. Sturgis could picture it—they had survived the wreckage but were out in the cold without food or transportation, without hope—freezing perhaps. And they knew what had happened to the world. The father knew what a young girl of perhaps 12 or 13 would be worth and he had decided for them. He knew she would be raped, mutilated. So instead he had put a bullet through all of them and then killed himself. Right next to the pile-up—nearly 50 cars and trucks—now nothing but wreckage. It must have burned for days.

"Let's not mess with it, men," Sturgis said. "We'll go around. Nothing for us here except sadness."

"Shouldn't we bury them?" Billy asked. "It ain't right."

"Can we bury all of America?" Sturgis replied. "Where do we start? Where do we stop?" Were all the buzzards dead also, he wondered. Where were the birds of prey? Scared off by the blaze, or extinct already?

They headed off, driving nearly another 300 miles, long after the sun had sunk from the sky and the moon had vainly tried to pierce the dark radioactive blanket that now covered the earth. Everywhere along the highway they passed bodies—the decaying corpses of people, animals, even whole flocks of birds that looked as if they had fallen from the sky like stones. The men of the C.A.D.S. team glanced nervously through their visors as they passed the carnage along the road. They had seen death before, but never like this, death like a river on each side. A bomb must have gone off nearby and the heat and radiation had killed all living things. It was unnerving—even for these combat men who liked to think of themselves as tough. It seemed a bad omen. Was the whole damned country like this—a sea of rotting carcasses? They sat almost flat back on their Tri-wheelers, ensconced in their immense C.A.D.S. suits, making them appear to almost be giants, their visors reflecting the headlights of the bikes around them. But inside the awesome suits of ultimate destruction, they were men, and they felt fear.

At last Sturgis called them to a halt. They'd been riding for nearly 20 hours. The men wearily got off their bikes in a clearing by the side of the road and took off their suits. They set up a couple of pellet stoves and threw some food on.

"Where's Fenton?" Sturgis asked Rossiter as they sat on logs eating the army chow. Rossiter looked around.

"I don't kn—" he began. Then, suddenly, they heard the Rhino's door opening, sliding on its smooth metal track. Out stepped the Englishman, in kilts, a heavy English lambswool sweater, and the black beret of the Queen's Guard on. He was blowing into the long mouthpiece of his bagpipe of green plaid, filling its bellows up. A plaintive mournful sound echoed through the pitch-black starless night, the eerie strains of "Silent Night." Christmas—they had never celebrated it. There hadn't been time, what with a few mitigating circumstances— like World War III. They listened, their forks suspended in midair beneath their mouths as the deep spine-tingling notes echoed through the surrounding trees and up into the impenetrable night.

They all started singing along, and passed a few hidden scotch bottles around, as Fenton played on. There were tears in nearly every man's eyes. This had been some Christmas—the U.S. ravaged and twisted by nuclear Armageddon, the very air radioactive like the hand of death at their throats. But it just made them sing louder— louder—*raging* against the death, the anti-life of the swollen misshapen plains that once had been fertile wheat fields, and the homes of millions of citizens.

"Silent night, holy night, all is calm, all is—"

Sturgis was thinking of Robin. Two Christmases ago, the night they had danced their hearts out in Danceteria in New York City. Then they spent the night at the Plaza Hotel making love—looking at the skyline and the stars . . . It had been so—beautiful—and now . . .

Fenton played on, looking like some apparition in his kilts, as Roberto stood up, quite drunk, and began a

160

speech in Spanish and then read a poem by Garcia Lorca. Something about "Cultivate the white rose of love . . ."

"Merry Christmas Sturg," said Tranh, clinking his scotch bottle against Sturgis' metal cup.

"Yeah," replied Sturgis, looking around at the twisted darkened trees and flattened cremated crops, and the abandoned tractor off in the distance. "Merry Christmas to you too, old buddy."

They rose early to a sun grimly trying to force its way through the sooty skies. The constant gray darkness above was already getting to be pretty depressing. It was as if a rain of death was always about to fall, but never quite did. The heavy skies were oppressive, as if they were being crushed beneath a weight of the angry heavens. They all silently prayed that the sun would somehow burst through—give them even a glimmer of hope in this new dark world. They suited up, squeezing into their seven-foot high C.A.D.S. suits, sealing them tight and slamming the visors closed over their faces. Inside them they at least felt less vulnerable—more like gods, less like mortal, feeling men.

They drove for hours, the fleet of Tri-wheelers tearing down the highway at speeds up to 100 mph. They had to make good time now because later, Sturgis knew, things would get a lot worse. He took the lead, with two lines of bikes trailing behind. Fenton took up the rear in the huge oval-shaped Rhino, its four hemispheric wheels looking like immense black balloons as they spun over the blacktop. In their wide low-slung vehicles, with their C.A.D.S. suits on, the team looked as if they had just arrived from another planet. And the bands of ragged people walking forlornly along the sides of roads they occasionally passed looked up with a mixture of shock and sheer amazement at the futuristic armada.

They came over a rise in eastern Oklahoma and saw a burning town. As they approached it, they saw cars moving, dead ahead, filled with heavily armed men.

Two old Buicks with metal shields with slits cut in them drove down the road toward the Omega Force, firing streams of machine gun fire. Bullets ricocheted off the armor of the C.A.D.S. suits as Sturgis screamed out to halt through his helmet radio.

Then he called out over the P.A. system of the helmet which amplified his voice tenfold. "We're Americans. Not Russians. Americans. Cease your fire!"

The automobiles pulled up about 50 yards off and stopped firing. A man stepped out of the lead car holding a white flag. He was a bearded and greasy looking man wearing a makeshift army uniform with a wide white belt and branches for camouflage strapped to his helmet. He walked with a limp, supporting himself on a rifle. As he drew closer the C.A.D.S. team inhaled the pungent smell of urine and chewing tobacco. He approached Sturgis, who lifted his visor so the man could see his face. He knew they all looked pretty ominous in their full regalia.

"Americans, huh? Well, you are something else, man— you astronauts or something?" the man asked.

"Air Force special unit," Sturgis answered. He didn't like the way the other grubby members of the party were following the man with rifles at the ready.

"Well I'm Renquist," the man said, sneering. "Generalissimo Renquist, and I have the pleasure of running this here free territory. There ain't no U.S. anymore, nor no U.S. Air Force either—so give us your weapons and get out of those diving suits, or you're all dead men—"

Sturgis put his visor back down. "I should warn you— we have some pretty powerful weapons at our disposal," he said to the man. Then he raised his arm and blasted a

162

dead elm tree with an electroball as the would-be attackers hit the dirt, the tree exploding into flaming splinters.

"Hey, just kiddin', man," Renquist said, rising from the highway. "You guys can *join us*. We got a nice outfit—the 'All-Caucasian Army'. We got food, women, anything else you want—share and share alike. In our camp we've been training for years for this. First how to build fallout shelters, how to knife-fight, terror tactics against Red troops, marksmanship, even ammunition production. We've learned crossbow, woodcutting, meat preservation, wilderness survival—the lot. Mister, you and your U.S. Air Force don't have any authority here, but you join us with those big guns and we'll give you any of our precious supplies you want. I might add that this here's a nice low-radiation town."

"Well, since we have some black and Puerto Rican members among our party," Sturgis said coldly, "I don't know how welcome they'd be in this 'all-caucasian' army of yours."

"No niggers, Mister. No spics, no nothing if it's anything but white," the man smirked.

"I see," Sturgis said. He stepped forward in disgust at what America was already sinking into and slammed the leader square in the jaw. The man fell to the ground and should have been knocked unconscious from the force of Sturgis' punch. But he sat there glaring up. Sturgis knew the guy was tough. He wiped the blood from his cracked lower lip and stood back up in a half crouch.

"So that's the way it's gonna be huh? Boys," he said to the men behind him, "cover me in case these astro-boys make a move."

The men weren't anxious to, after having seen Sturgis' demonstration, but they raised their guns. Sturgis could have laughed—a few M-16's. Then he saw a bazooka—that could do some damage. He spoke through the suit P.A.

"We're not spoiling for a fight. We want to see the town authorities—the real mayor, the town council—and then we'll talk to you again. Otherwise, we'll wipe you and your men out like flies right now. Understand?"

"Yeah," Renquist said disgustedly. "They're in the town hall, been holed up for days, afraid of us. We deposed them two days ago. They ain't men—didn't even fight for their town or women or anything. We're the ones you want to join. You'll see . . ."

Renquist turned his back and started walking away as Sturgis mounted up on his Tri-wheeler. Suddenly he saw the leader of the All-Caucasian Army run toward the two armored Buicks ahead, yelling to his men to open up.

Renquist jumped behind a wrecked car by the side of the road and the rag-tag army started shooting. The Omega Force sat still in their Tri-bikes awaiting Sturgis' orders. Their first combat test—they felt both frightened and exhilarated as bullets whistled all around them. At last they'd find out after all these years of preparation and training if the damned suits worked. And if they didn't, they would all be dead men.

"Should I let them have a round?" Fenton asked from the Rhino as he slowly swiveled the turret of the 150mm cannon in the direction of the flaming guns. Bullets whistled off toward the woods from direct hits on Sturgis' suit. He saw a whole damned mini-army of men in what seemed to be somewhat-the-worse-for-wear National Guard uniforms, advancing.

"Hell yes. Maybe they're blind or stupid or something but they're our enemies—even if they are wearing militia uniforms," he said through the suit walkie-talkie. "Omega—use Plan C—Deploy!!"

His men spread out on both sides of the road and opened up with their weapons. A hail of 55mm bullets tore into the advancing force, ripping into flesh. Sturgis could see from the insane grins and wide eyes of the attackers that they were on some kind of drugs. They looked fanatical as they came pouring down the road by the hundreds, firing rifles, pistols, shotguns at the Omega Team.

But the shots merely ricocheted off the C.A.D.S. suits. Then a mortar hidden in the woods blasted a hole in the road several yards behind Sturgis, sending Billy flying end-over-end and smashing the suit of one of his men behind him, leaving him a bloody pulp.

The Omega Team was pouring out a deadly stream of 55mm's and electroballs, turning the attackers into red sprays of blood and flesh. But there were so damned many of them—marching down the road, firing from trees, from behind numerous wrecked cars just off each side of the highway. As many as they took out, more seemed to take their place.

Fenton was having trouble with the Rhino's short-barrel 150mm cannon. "Fire Fenton, *Fire!*" Sturgis yelled, still on external. Fenton suddenly let loose with a barrage of cannon fire, demolishing the car barriers where the heavy artillery was coming from, sending twisted metal flying into the air with bits of singed flesh. Billy was back on his feet and slammed his jet pack into jump mode. He rose off the ground as he poured flames from his liquid plastic fire unit down on the attackers. Screams erupted like the choirs of hell as they burst into flame. He poured down fire for a full 30 seconds, cremating them. They fell like crumpled pieces of charred beef.

Suddenly he stopped and dropped back to the road. There was total and complete silence for a few seconds as the burnt men smoldered in pungent flames for hundreds of yards. Then the ear-piercing wails of women—half naked things running from the woods toward the pieces of flesh that used to be men.

Sturgis, seeing them to be unarmed, opened his visor and walked toward them. He approached the nearest woman. "They fired first, we had no choice," he said.

"Bastard!" she screamed, beating on his suit. He let her until she had it all out.

"What the hell were your men doing?" Sturgis asked, not feeling great about the slaughter. "Didn't they see our colors? Didn't they hear me warn them about our fire power?"

"We—my husband was part of the Renquist Army. We joined him to defend ourselves from the *other* warlords and their gangs. We held the town against them—they were dressed in uniforms with U.S. flags too, like you, but they raped and murdered everyone they could get their hands on. The U.S. is no more and since there was no government, we took matters in our own hands."

"*We* represent the government—or at least we're still under its command."

"You mean there *is* a president? A congress? The war hasn't destroyed everything?"

Sturgis fudged a bit but said, "Yes". These people needed some hope, to carry on. "Now, we're going to let you go, tell all your people there *is* an America and those who live like savages will die. Those who keep the flame of hope going will live. Our only hope is for Americans to not sink into barbarism. Otherwise the Reds *will* win without even having to fire a shot. Now take what remains of your 'army'," Sturgis said, looking around at the dazed and wounded members of the caucasian army who had survived the assault as they slowly rose from the ground, "and get the hell out of here. I know you have to survive—but not by preying on your weaker fellow man. *We* are the law now, and others like us. Tell your people that—tell everyone you see. The Omega Force will be back and we don't take kindly to murderers. Understand?"

"Yes," the woman said, suddenly spotting her husband, bleeding but still alive. She ran over to him and helped him to his feet. Sturgis stood, nearly seven-feet tall in his C.A.D.S. suit watching as the walking wounded dragged themselves off and disappeared into the woods.

It hadn't been as total a slaughter as he had at first thought. Nearly half the attackers still lived, but they would remember this day for a long time, and perhaps, just perhaps, the lesson would do some good.

"Damage? Casualties?" Sturgis asked Tranh as he turned back to his squad.

"One man, Tech Sergeant Jones, sir, and his suit and Tri-bike—he took a direct hit from a mortar. He's dead."

"A good man," Sturgis said. He felt personally responsible. "I should have known better—should have opened up immediately."

"Yeah, I know," said Tranh. "It's tough to make those decisions. It's like Nam all over again, only a thousand times worse." He put his suited hand on Sturgis' back. "You had to hold fire—we've never fired on Americans before. It's not a good feeling."

Billy came over, adjusting the flame-thrower nozzle.

"Fast thinking," Sturgis said. "You saved a lot of our boys' lives."

"Well, I can't say that I feel great about it," Dixon replied. "But but we had no fucking choice. As my father used to say, if you're ready to kill, be ready to die!"

Roberto and Fenton joined the group standing at the front of the motionless Tri-wheelers.

"I guess it was bound to happen," Sturgis said, surveying the grim scene, "given the circumstances, and the lack of any central direction. It seems to be a breakdown in society already. The strongest—the meanest—will survive. And God help us all."

Suddenly they saw a crowd approaching, unarmed men and women in suits and ties and dresses—dressed for talking, not for war.

The town mayor, a ruddy faced man with a lariat tie

walked forward. "Welcome, welcome to Wellstown, Oklahoma, friends. I am glad to see that there is some law and order left. We were hostages to Renquist and his gang, who took over everything and used this town as his base. Now the hell is over. Those are pretty strange suits you're wearing, something for the radiation I suppose."

He shook Sturgis' immense gloved hand. "Why don't you all come into town? I thank you for what you've done," continued the trembling mayor, "but there are more—another gang of cutthroats in the town—a rival bunch. The ones you killed were bad but the others . . . come, come see for yourself."

"All right. But we can't stay long. We have a mission of vital importance." He told his men to stay put and to check their suits for damage.

The mayor led Sturgis and his inner group to the gymnasium building of the old grammar school. It had a lattice-work above, for holding gym equipment and to support the roof—and there were nearly a hundred bodies hung there, flies buzzing around them as they swung by their necks on ropes that dangled from the ceiling.

"Who did this?" Sturgis asked with disgust.

"These are victims of the gangs," the mayor replied, "Renquist's and the others. They did this to the people who resisted their whims, who—who tried to fight back. They took many of the children—girls mostly. These are the parents who went down to their end of town to try to get their kids back. They confiscated all the weapons too—searched everywhere—and most of our food, except what we managed to hide. We are starving slowly, though we share."

The group walked back outside as others came out to see Sturgis and his men—bedraggled sad people who were once the proud citizens of Wellstown, Oklahoma.

"We can pay you if you help destroy them, and rescue

our children—" the mayor said, desperation evident on his sunken face.

"We're Americans mister, you don't have to pay us," Roberto said, pulling a knife from his belt and balancing it on his palm. "I will personally cut the throats of anyone who hurts a child. When my sister was molested in the South Bronx several years ago, I had the pleasure of wreaking my revenge. They gave me a year in jail for that, but it was worth it."

"Nevertheless, we'll pay you," the mayor said nervously. "Please—please take anything you want—as payment. If you don't help us, I don't know what will happen." He seemed near tears.

"We'll discuss that later," Sturgis said. "First we have to clean out your vermin. Where are they?"

"Down in the warehouse at the far end of town. There's a sign 'Acme Auto'."

"I want to see maps of this town," Sturgis said. "Do you have any?"

The mayor and his disheveled friends led Sturgis to the city hall and showed them the town blueprints.

"They call themselves the Atomic Lords—they have all sorts of equipment—even a tank."

"Leave it to us," Sturgis replied. "My men are experts at infiltration. We'll take these scum out and get your children back—if they're still alive."

A woman spoke up from the crowd surrounding them. "Please, my daughter Jessica—she's only eight years old and the leader of the faction, named Duke Marley, took her for his use. They're sick. Psychotic. Their motto is 'we get ours before we die' or something like that. They wanted the town's girls, they had the guns trained on us. They said they wanted them just as hostages but we hear these horrible screams and—and—" she burst into tears, "but everytime we go in they shoot, and we don't have any weapons—they made sure of that—you've seen the

169

gym."

"We'll take care of it," said Sturgis. "You remember the routine," he asked Tranh, "we used it at the Saigon Embassy—the last time?"

"Yeah, kill the guards silently, go in and wipe 'em out fast."

"That's it," Sturgis said with a razor-thin grin. "The B plan for a single-story building."

They looked over a blueprint of the warehouse and the mayor pointed out where he believed the children to be.

"We can't promise some of them won't—" Sturgis left the end of the sentence dangling.

"We understand," said the mayor. "But they'll all die for sure if something isn't done."

Sturgis and his men moved out, spreading through the town. Roberto and Fenton took off to the left flank, moving through a series of abandoned stores. On the right were Sturgis and Billy. Tranh moved down the edge of the street darting from shadow to shadow.

"Listen to the little girl scream when I put this hot poker to her," One-Eyed Jackson said as he approached the tied-up quivering 13-year-old with a glowing piece of iron in his hand.

"Yeah—beautiful," replied Duke, the leader of the Atomic Lords, half drooling the whiskey he guzzled. "It's like 42nd Street."

He stood grinning as Jackson touched the smoking steel to the tender flesh. Screams echoed through the warehouse. The other captured children sat along the concrete wall, hands tied behind their backs, eyes wide with horror as they watched the grisly scene. For they knew they would be next. The gang had already gone through five of their young captives—the bodies lay sprawled, covered with a sheen of red at the far end of the warehouse where they had been dumped after no more screams could be elicited from them—after tortured bodies could take no more, their hearts stopped beating.

Other members of the gang watched from atop crates, lying on the floor, stoned out of their minds on liquor and drugs taken from the town pharmacy. They hardly knew where they were anymore—only mutilation and death could pique their interest. They watched through half-opened eyes as Jackson had his fun with the young blond girl. She screamed good—really good, awakening them momentarily from their stupors.

The C.A.D.S. Team came down the street, moving carefully. They stole through the shadows like fish through the sea darting from patch of darkness to patch of darkness, concealing themselves with whatever cover they could find. With all the lights in the town now extinguished, even in their immense suits they were able to remain hidden as they drew closer and closer to the gang's headquarters. They had to be careful, not so much for themselves, but for the children. If the gang had enough warning they might well do in the whole bunch. Sturgis didn't want that on his conscience.

Sturgis, with Billy just behind him, flipped his visor to infrared mode. The world became alive with dancing, shimmering pools of light—heat left from the daytime, the movement of a few rats scampering from basement to basement in search of food. Before his eyes, imaged on the visor, was a dayglow scene of life which thought it was hidden. Within the infrared mode, he shifted to telescopic view and scanned the windows of the surrounding buildings and the warehouse itself as they drew closer. He could hear Tranh some 10 or 20 yards off as he came down the street, his eyes darting back and forth looking for trouble. Sturgis and Tranh had been through this kind

171

of gut-wrenching scene before—several times in fact—in Viet Nam where they had helped rescue captured airborne troops right from out of the clutches of the Viet Cong. They knew what to expect for the Cong were a much more cunning and dangerous foe than a gang of misfits could ever be.

Suddenly Sturgis saw movement from one of the windows in the three-story house across the street. The curtain moved quickly and the long barrel of a pump shotgun poked through ready to draw blood. But Sturgis was faster. He raised his arm and mouthed the words, "Dart-Fire Two." With the barest of whispers, two steel shafts with needle tips shot from a hidden firing tube beneath his right arm. They sliced through the air and up toward the window in a split second, ripping two almost invisible holes through the fabric. Sturgis heard a sputtering gurgle, and then a body, the two eight-inch darts embedded nearly all the way into the gangman's chest, fell forward through the window frame spinning end-over-end, and slammed into the street below. One down—God knew how many to go, Sturgis thought, moving forward.

"Strike," he heard Tranh whisper over the suit radio. They approached the main door to the warehouse, a large corrugated steel square that sat half open. Billy and Sturgis emerged from the shadows on each side of the door as Tranh walked toward it.

Sturgis spoke into his helmet mike. "Fenton, Roberto—where are you?" There was a bit of static, probably from the radiation in the air, Sturgis thought, as the replies crackled through his earphones.

"Coming up in back," Fenton said in his crisp clipped dialect. "Took out two of 'em already. Can see one more guard just inside back door. Await further instructions."

"Wait a second," Sturgis answered. He looked right toward the warehouse wall and said "Mode Blue—Structure directly ahead."

"Checking," the computer flashed onto the inside of the visor. "Computation time — 2.7 seconds." Suddenly the visual mode that Sturgis had requested — the number of enemy forces in the closed structure — flashed on the screen in the visor. A grid map of the warehouse appeared in bright blue lines depicting walls and the two floors and within the grid bright red dots representing living homo sapiens. The entire three-dimensional image revolved slowly before Sturgis' eyes, creating an almost holographic image, so that he could see the enemy placement from all possible angles.

"Precisely 73 enemy in the structure," the words moved in a quick line across the bottom of the visor. "Humans in grid juncture 3/11 are all below the weight of 90 pounds — 13 of them. Remaining humans armed with pistols, pump shotguns, automatic rifles, hand grenades, two cannon." Sturgis linked in the others to his visor cap and instantly they were all able to see the glowing outlines of the warehouse's internal structure and the whereabouts of the Atomic Lords and their prisoners, the children.

"Okay boys, we're going in. Watch out for that middle room where the kids are. Go, go, go!" Sturgis, Tranh and Billy Dixon came through — tearing through the nearly 30-foot wide loading door, their infrared modes scanning the darkened front end of the warehouse and instantly picking up the heat-pools of the guards lounging on crates, sleeping on bare mattresses strewn around the place. Two guards just on the inside of the door looked up startled from their game of cards as three black-clad visions of death were suddenly upon them. Sturgis let loose with a quick spray of the 'iron icepicks' which caught men at head level, piercing their faces with bloody quivers, right through the eyes. They groaned, trying to catch the gushing pulp of their faces in their outstretched hands, and crumbled forward, slamming onto the cold concrete.

"Move, move," Sturgis intoned through the visor mike. "Split up—take 'em out." Billy headed off to the right and Tranh to the left as Sturgis tore down the middle of the crate-filled warehouse in great leaping strides. Suddenly two men jumped down from high boxes, landing right in front of him, their shotguns raising in a blurred arc toward his face. Without breaking stride, Sturgis chambered his arms and punched forward, shooting the huge magnasynth gloves out like pistons. With the muscular-enhancement system (MES) of the suit's computer working along with his every movement, the punches were amplified nearly a hundred-fold. His fists smashed into their chests and then continued right through, sending out a blasting spray of red shattered fragments of bone. The men scarcely had time to scream. The broken bodies flew backwards like bowling pins and slammed into a row of barrels, sending them flying.

The gang closed in from everywhere upon hearing the ruckus, firing wildly with everything they had, their eyes wide in drug-crazed excitement, their mouths screaming out curses and mindless howls of violent rage. Their cover had been broken, Sturgis thought to himself as nearly a dozen of them charged straight toward him from ahead. He raised his right arm and turned the wrist slightly to the left. A spray of teflon-coated 55mm machine gun bullets cut down the 12 like a scythe mowing grass—only this grass screamed and shot out fountains of blood as it died. Sturgis suddenly heard a noise and saw a fork lift swerve from around a large crate and head right toward Tranh.

"Tranh!" Sturgis screamed out over the suit mike. "Jump!" Without a moment's hesitation, the Vietnamese commando was in the air as the lift ripped into the empty air below him. In his arc over the vehicle, Tranh aimed his left arm down—"E-Ball—Fire," he said. A small shining ball, crackling with blue electricity tore down into the driver's seat of the fork lift blowing the machine and the thing that had been steering it into red dust. Tranh came down some 30 feet ahead, landing on the cushioned-feet of the suit.

"Thanks," he whispered back to Sturgis, without turning, as another gang member drew a bead on him from behind a pile of canvas bags just yards ahead. Tranh raised his arm but the shotgun exploded toward him first. The x-shaped pattern of shot caught him from less than 10 feet away. He felt the jolt shudder through the suit, which absorbed most of the kinetic energy through a computerized spring-recoil shock system. The pellets dented the outer protective layer of the suit and then ricocheted back in all directions, unable to penetrate the C.A.D.S. armor—composed of an alloy of nearly 35 different irons and plastics, nearly three times stronger than the protective coating of the space shuttle.

The shotgun-firer looked on in disbelieving horror as the black-suited astronaut or whatever the hell it was, commando looked down at him through an impenetrable tinted helmet. The monstrous suited figure seemed to almost shake his head slightly back and forth, as if saying "no". Then the impossibly big arm pointed at him and released a streaking ball of lightning that slammed dead into the top of his head blowing everything above the ankles into a moist powder that swirled around like a mini dust storm.

So the damned suits really could take a blast from a twelve gauge pointblank and survive. Tranh had seen all the tests performed on the suit back at White Sands, but he'd never actually been *inside* it when it happened. He couldn't say he really liked the feeling, but, on the other hand he was still around to talk about it. He heard a sudden motion behind a stack of building lumber and spoke the single word "jump" into the mouthpiece. His suit took off straight up, nearly reaching the 30-foot high steel-ribbed ceiling. Not a moment too soon, he could see as he looked down and watched one of the Atomic Lords swing a bazooka up and let loose with a round right where he had been standing. The shell tore 80 feet across the floor and into the other wall of the warehouse sending out a deafening roar as half the wall for a space of about 20 feet collapsed into dusty bricks and twisted sheet metal. Almost directly overhead, Tranh decided to save ammo and test another feature of the suit he was curious about.

"Down," he said to the suit and the C.A.D.S. unit dropped straight down atop the bazooka man. The Vietnamese heard a kind of squishing sound beneath him when he landed, as the full weight of the suit crushed his attacker into pulp. Tranh didn't look down at his handiwork.

Sturgis continued forward, his right arm held up straight as he scanned from side to side for more attacks. Shots pinged off the top of his suit and helmet, someone firing from above. He looked up and caught the orange and purple shimmering infrared face of the sniper. "Jump," Sturgis commanded and the C.A.D.S. suit jumped off the concrete, straight up, until he was level with the second story platform which ringed the warehouse. As the sniper raised his "poodle-puncher" to strike again, Sturgis struck first, letting loose with a hail of 55mm death-dealers. The bullets slammed into the low wooden sides of the platform and through them. The Atomic Lords had one less murderer in their ranks as the body stood bolt upright and tumbled through the plywood side and down to the concrete floor where the skull cracked open like a coconut. Sturgis checked the grid map again for a bare second, the image superimposed over the lower portion of the visor. There—the children should be in that room off to the right.

176

He came right at the near wall of the room and putting both fists out strode into the place at full speed. The sheetrock and 2x4s crumbled into splinters and chalky white dust as he walked through the jagged opening and into a storm of bullets.

Sturgis could see instantly that the children were there—and still alive, tied up along one wall. Although from the remains of the poor creature they had just been playing with, spread out in a bloody mess on top of a plywood table, the bastards had done their evil already. The five butchers fired at the plasti-armor coated avenging angel-of-death that stood before them, looking at them with sheerest hate through his glistening impenetrable visor. Slowly Sturgis raised his hand, one finger pointed forward, like Michelangelo's "Creation"—only this finger wasn't bringing life—but death.

"Fire," Sturgis said cold as ice into the suit mike. The computer sent the signal to the suit's firing mechanism in a millionth of a second. In another millionth of a second the ball-firing charge was struck. It took almost a tenth of a second before the buzzing sphere of super concentrated high explosive, guided by electromagnetic tracking slammed into the center of the attackers. The explosion left nothing that Sturgis could recognize as man after the smoke cleared. He turned and started toward the whimpering children.

"Hold it, spaceman," a voice screamed out from the far end of the room, by a boarded up window. The man held one of the children in the crook of his arm, a knife at the young girl's pale white throat. "You move and she's dead, man."

"You've killed enough, friend," Sturgis intoned through the suit's P.A. system. His voice came eerily out of a hidden speaker with a resonant other-worldly quality.

"Who the hell are you fucking guys anyway—Russians?"

"Sorry pal, no such luck," Sturgis replied. "We're Americans, just like you. Air Force Commandos."

"Air Force Commandos, big shit—right. I'm supposed to beg for mercy? Well, I'm Duke—Duke Marley. I run things around here."

"Used to, Marley. Used to run things," Sturgis intoned in a ghostly whisper over the mike. He started forward, slowly raising his arm.

"I told you not to move," Marley screamed. He ripped the long sharp blade of his hunting knife clear across the 12-year-old girl's throat, severing the vocal cords and jugular, nearly slicing the whole left side of her neck in half. He pushed the choking bleeding thing forward and grabbed down for another girl crawling the floor below him. The slit-throat girl was just feet away from Sturgis staring up at him with the most horrifying expression he had ever seen. Her hands were over her throat which the C.A.D.S. leader could see right into. Within a second the girl was completely saturated in her own blood then she toppled over at Sturgis' feet, her eyes rolling heavenward like white eggs in their sockets.

Even Sturgis, who thought he had seen death in just about every hideous form it could take, felt himself sickened by this foul deed. Marley wasn't human, he was an animal of the lowest order. Although no animal would ever do something like that to its own kind, only the human-animal.

"You want more—you'll get more," Marley screamed, holding the knife blade at another throat. But the 10-year old girl he had grabbed somehow managed to lunge forward with her jaw and bite Marley on the wrist. The gang leader yelled in pain and pulled the knife back for a split second. The kid dove to the ground as Marley reached for her, but that was all the time Sturgis needed. In a blur of motion he ripped his arm up and screamed "Fire!"

The E-ball tore across the 50 feet separating them like a lightning bolt searching for a tree, crackling with a violent electrical energy. It hit Duke Marley squarely in the pelvis and exploded in a blinding roar. Pieces of flesh, fingers, and sharp glass-like fragments of bone spat out in all directions from the red mouth of doom.

At the other end of the warehouse, Sturgis suddenly heard a fierce firefight, which just as quickly was over. He checked the room he was in, turning quickly around as he spoke over the mike.

"Status reports—" The rest of the team told him they had taken out everything in their part of the warehouse. It was over. Sturgis walked slowly over toward the children who huddled together, trying to bury their heads so as not to take in any more of the nightmarish violence.

"It's okay now, kids," Sturgis said, in as soft a tone as he could muster, through the P.A. system. "You're free, you can see your parents again, can go home." One by one they looked up to see the towering figure with helmet above them. But children care less about the looks of things and more about the intentions of people. They knew Sturgis was good. Slowly they all raised their heads and looked nervously around.

"Are you a spaceman?" the bravest of the lot nervously asked the giant in black. She said, "I'll bet you're an E.T.!"

"It's a long story kid," Sturgis said, bending down on one knee and untying the knots of the ropes that bound the young prisoners. "I was a spaceman, but got bounced for drinking, fighting, and—ah—forget it. Yeah sure. I'm a spaceman, kid. Sent here by my Uncle Sam—just to save the lot of you."

"Really?" the children asked wide-eyed, their faces almost smiling.

"Really," Sturgis said, as the other C.A.D.S.-suited members of the team appeared in the doorway. "And

179

these are my space buddies." Might as well give them something to remember, Sturgis thought as he released the last of them. Something to tell their grandchildren. He suddenly realized these were days of legend again — as in the distant past. Days when giants walked the earth.

CHAPTER SIXTEEN

Outside of Gary Indiana, the Cragmoor Sanitarium for the Criminally Insane was buffeted by the shock wave of the twin 40-megaton blasts that destroyed Chicago and West Chicago. The sanitarium, a 16-story structure, was of thick brick construction with Victorian overtones — blocks of concrete forming buttresses to its walls and fortifying it far beyond the need to resist lake-generated thunderstorms. It was for that reason that the institution, though all the glass was blown out on the northeast face, survived intact. But a huge crack was opened in the walls and parts of them — on the upper three floors — came crashing down, exposing the cells inside — the wards for the most dangerous of the state-committed insane: Ward D.

The doctors and nurses who were on duty the night of the nuclear attack largely survived, though some were sliced up by bits of flying glass. They had the common sense to avoid the fallout over the next three days, and stayed under cover in the deepest recesses of basements, leaving many of the patients locked in their cells without food or light or heat. But the blast also ripped open many of the cells. The D-Ward patients ran amok, climbing down improvised ladders to the other floors, finding

181

food, drugs, weapons. They took over, making the institution above the basement entirely theirs. And through a shift in the wind, no heavy fallout encased the eerie Victorian building in the first few days. When the doctors and nurses at last ventured forth, they heard the animallike snarls and moans of the aroused army of the insane. They were quickly grabbed as they emerged from the basement and taken to the lecture auditorium. There, they were tied, struggling wildly, into the seats and the whole scene lit by candlelight became *theater*. Theater of the mad, the psychotic, the schizophrenic. On stage the patients, under the leadership of a patient named Carl Stranger, a five-time serial murderer, were treated to a lecture. He stood on an upended chair wearing a doctor's green uniform and a stethoscope around his neck. His eyes were red like the licking flames of hell itself. He stared up at them with undisguised glee.

"You see, you see, now you listen to me, like a good audience. I am in control here, am I not?"

Snarls and shrieks echoed from out of the dark from the freed patients holding sticks—some bloodied in the struggle—and axes with crimson-edged blades that waved in the air like worms coming out of the earth in a rainstorm.

"See? They have elected me, to teach *you* patients how to treat *us* doctors." He let out a maniacal laugh that made the imprisoned staff's hair stand on end.

"But *you* are the patients—*we* are the doctors," Supervising psychiatrist Caruthers shouted from his confining seat.

"*Not anymore! We* are the sane and *you* are the insane patients who must be treated. I can prove it. *Prove it!*"

The masses of laughing, screaming captors jabbed at the tied doctor with sticks. "*Prove it, prove it, prove it,*" they shouted in unison.

Carl said, "*The facts:* They, the so-called sane ones,

have destroyed the world—not us! They call us insane, for we kill a few—but they kill billions and they are called sane. Now, we the sane will treat those now proven insane."

"*Proven proven proven,*" shouted Stella-the-Axe along with all the other ex-patients who now ruled. "*Proven proven proven,*" shouted Walter the Waxer—named for the way he constantly walked around with a rag under his shoe, sliding about, waxing the floors until they were shiny as a mirror.

"Furthermore," continued Carl, who they all knew had a university degree—he was a doctor—though not of medicine, of something else even better before they took him away for the murders in West Chicago, "Furthermore," he shouted, "we the sane have decided to benefit you all with the treatment you need—drugs, electroshock, to purge your bodies of the evil that you have done to the world. Perhaps heat treatments first—since you have given your atomic heat therapy to the entire planet." Carl laughed again, his eyes opening wide.

"*Heat treatment, heat treatment,*" the patients shouted.

The doctors and nurses, their hands tied behind their backs, were lifted one-by-one and forced to hop up the stairs in their bindings, where they were lined up on the candlelit stage, lit by a thousand little wax candles procured from God only knew where.

"Yes, you are to be sorted out—each will be given the specific treatment you need," Carl said as he lifted the sullen face of Caruthers, who was now gagged as well as trussed. "Ah, a manic-schizo-arbitrary complex! I think this man needs enemas. Do you concur my fellow surgeons?"

The 'doctors' paraded around him shouting, "hot enemas, hot enemas," and dragged Caruthers away.

Head nurse Johnson came next. "Ah," Carl said, "this one needs the ice-cube bath—and then electroshock her . . ."

"*Electroshock*," the masses shouted, the word echoed back as they danced around in their torn white gowns, their hair matted, their flesh covered with sores. "They must be treated for their crimes. They must be treated like they treated the world—burned, raped, cut, disfigured, shocked, shocked, hurt hurt hurt . . ."

"*Hurt hurt hurt*," the patient-doctors yelled, dancing around the stage, raising their makeshift weapons like war banners.

"What treatment exactly do they need doctor?" asked a woman with glue in her hair holding it straight up. Hair decorated with hypodermic needles that poked out from everywhere.

"The same therapy they gave the earth. They must be treated like they treated the earth. And *how did* they treat the earth?" Carl asked with all his newly found regal majesty, as he wrapped red library-drapes about his body. "Now come on—suggestions, suggestions, doctors. We must confer, confer—"

One ex-patient timidly asked, "Rape them?"

"Good, good—any other suggestions?" Stranger asked as he strode back and forth on the stage, the staff standing terrified behind him.

"Burn them," a voice screamed out. "Burn them till they're well done!"

"Tear them, strip them," shouted another. They were all getting into the spirit of the thing, Carl noted with approval, as he adjusted the crown on his head; a bowler covered with tied-together pill bottles. The pills rattled every time his head nodded yes or no.

"Come on, more suggestions, more suggestions for the treatment of these insane people. We must make the treatment fit the disease. Think—*think*!"

"Feed them to each other," a fat bald thing screamed out. "Slice them up into itty-bitty pieces and make them

184

eat from china bowls."

"Electro-shock them," a tall, naked man smeared with blood from his self-inflicted chest wounds shouted.

"*Electroshock, electroshock, electroshock,*" a chant began.

"Fine, fine. Good idea," said Carl. "But we must fix the electricity first—who is an engineer?"

Everyone raised their hands. Carl frowned. "*Really* now, if you want to be engineers—you can't be doctors and nurses."

All the hands went down except one.

Within a few hours all the patients had been tied naked in the cold unheated treatment rooms. Crude signs were scrawled on the front of each door. Caruthers was shackled in the Hot Room where a small fire of furniture pieces on a sheet-metal slab was heating various scalpels and iron rods ripped from the cracked walls.

Nurse Johnson was in the Sex-therapy Room, tied and shackled face down on an operating table. An eager line of male inmates waited outside for their five minutes with the screaming, abused woman.

In the Cold Bath Room, more ice water was poured over the body of nurse Greer, who lay naked and shivering—her large breasts the only things aside from her head that showed above the blanket of ice cubes that covered her.

In the Enema Room were the two doctors who had administered the shock therapy to *him*. Carl wanted to return the experience but the electricity didn't work. The scientifically inclined patients were trying to start up the emergency diesel generator so the Shock Therapy room could be used, but this would have to do until then; an appetizer, as it were. The doctors screamed as a powerful jet of hot soapy water was shot into their anuses by the laughing female ex-patient now called 'Therapist X'. Therapist X had dyed her hair green and covered her face and skin with interesting pieces of wall paper and fabric she felt looked decorative. The old styles of the sane world were out now, you could do what you wanted to dress up. She wore sets of surgical gowns to keep warm — but her enema-therapy patients who were trussed up like the pigs they were, wore nothing. She increased the pressure of the manually operated pump to maximum, providing load after load of water until the doctors were ready to burst.

Carl, the King (as he now designated himself), called a meeting in the lecture hall. It was darker and gloomier as many of the candles had burned out. There were fewer "patients" tied in the seats, and they looked in pretty bad shape.

"Doctors, nurses," Carl the King said, "and distinguished patients too. I've called this meeting to report the excellent success of our treatment program. Many patients have died — but of course this is to be expected, for they were suffering from Terminal Insanity. Did not their kind destroy the city to the north? Did they not fill the sky with the black clouds? They were all hopeless anyway . . . And yet out of the goodness of our hearts we are treating them, giving them our precious time — and without charge — not reimbursed by Blue Cross *or* Medicaid! We must, however, persevere."

"*What we do now*?" shouted Helgate Hefty. "Do we finish 'em off?"

"No. We lock these up in the morgue room with the ones who are already dead. I'll put a barrier — with your help — across the door so they'll they there until they adjust to the smell. And maybe they will eat the bodies when they get hungry. It will be a new kind of therapy — Cannibal Therapy. "Yes," Stranger said proudly, "I think I've developed a new cure — Cannibal Therapy. That's *good* isn't it?"

"*Cannibal Therapy*," they all yelled. One woman was

carrying a head on her lap. "Nurse Johnson's head — well, it fell off," she said when Carl looked at her disapprovingly. "They come off, sometimes," she said, slightly embarrassed.

"*So it is,*" Carl said, turning his attention back to the crowd of the insane. "We have to move out. Helga says that the ambulances start up real nice and they are full of gasoline. We must go — pack some picnic lunches, doctors and nurses. It's boring in here, let's go — out — let's go out."

"*Let's go out, let's go out,*" they took up the chant and marched with Carl the King in the lead to the garage underneath the asylum.

The patients got into the ambulances. They couldn't understand why these worked when all the cars they tried outside — Buicks, Toyotas with sun roofs — didn't work. They didn't know that the electro-magnetic pulses generated by the nuke blasts had destroyed their electronic ignitions. But the ambulances — three old trucklike state vehicles kept deep in the underground garage — worked fine, having not been damaged by the EMP. The insane ones poured into the ambulances' rear doors as Carl the King directed them with a stick that still dripped the entrails of Dr. Caruthers.

"This way, this way to the new world, ladies and gentlemen. Step right up, step right up and see the world," he shouted like a carnival barker. The insane ones covered themselves with warpaint-like stripes of smeared color on their faces, wearing every sort of costume imaginable. One had two trousers — one for a shirt, with the legs dangling below his hands and a slit in the seat of the pants from which protruded his head. For this he got many compliments — for after all, wasn't the world topsy-turvy? They boarded the vehicles and the ambulances snorted out their exhaust into the beams of moonlight shooting down from the sky. At last they were all packed in — with lots of goodies including fresh meat cut from the "new" patients.

They headed out onto the road holding their bloodied axes and electrical generators with electroshock headsets, their jabbing sticks, and sharpened forks and knives. Their mission: go out and purge and cure that nation that had been part of the insane world that had called itself sane.

Carl stood on the running board of the lead ambulance holding onto the mirror strut shouting *"We go to cleanse, to cure the minds of the diseased,"* and with that the trucks roared off, driven none too steadily by laughing, grimacing ex-inmates who foamed at the mouth with excitement.

"To cure, to cure — we go to cure the world . . ."

CHAPTER SEVENTEEN

Days earlier. Robin, alerted by Sturgis' call, didn't know whether to listen to him or not. She let the phone sit in the cradle, staring straight ahead. Suppose there was going to be a war? Wouldn't it be better to stay here in the city, teaching the kids, giving them comfort as they all were vaporized together? Why live and suffer? She had read all about post-war survival possibilities — cancers, radiation diseases, plague, starvation, cannibalism, the complete and total breakdown of civilization. The end of nature itself — no more trees, insects, plants, crops — slowly but inevitably certain death. Why go through it all? But *his* face kept spinning around behind her closed eyes. She wanted to be with him. If Dean lived she would live too, and face whatever horrors the new world had to offer at his side. She packed up the Ford Bronco RV with everything she could stuff into it and headed out of Baltimore in light traffic at 6 am the day before Christmas. She had some Christmas presents packed in the back, not really believing it would happen. It had to be just more survivalist paranoia — like the kind that had made Sturgis turn his small farm into a fortress and fallout shelter complete with all the necessities for holding out for several years after the apocalypse. Not that it couldn't happen, she thought; it just wouldn't! No, she knew it wouldn't. But she'd play the fool—drive hundreds of miles to the farm, turn around and come back.

She was 55 miles out and on a country road when she was nearly blinded by a white flash in her rear-view mirror. She quickly looked away, silently praying that it wasn't what she knew it to be. When she looked anxiously back, she saw the horrible orange-black cloud—a mushroom cloud forming over Baltimore like a shroud of death. She was flooring the accelerator a mile further on when the shockwave hit. It was like a hurricane, 80 mph winds tearing down loose branches and rocking the big vehicle. But she kept going and going, tears falling from her eyes. Many drivers had stopped their cars and were nearly blocking the way, standing in the road gazing back at the writhing cloud. Many of them had heard word leaked from a friend—that something was going on. And those friends had told one friend. Little did she know there was a colossal tie-up an hour behind her, as a half-million people had begun fleeing the city, caught crawling along the interstate in their cars, when the bombs fell. Ten of thousands were cremated, blown thousands of feet along the road like so many ants on an anthill in which dynamite had been placed. Maybe they were better off dying instantly. She felt suddenly guilty being out here, safe for the moment. Then swarms of private planes all heading east—over the ocean, and south, to Central America, droned overhead. The rich, who also had found out about the imminent disaster, in their Lear Jets and Comanches.

Suddenly the car began sputtering. God, she thought, had she put in the wrong gas at the last filling station? The damned thing didn't work anymore on low-test. It rolled and coughed to a stop. She checked the fuel gauge, frantically turning the starter over, but the battery was dead. Oh God—the EMP—electromagnetic pulse. She remembered Sturgis saying that all vehicles would be knocked out. Her digital watch was out too, showing only dashes. My God—every power supply in the whole area must be gone—even the hospitals.

Suddenly she felt something at her shoulder. With a start she turned. Someone was poking her with a shotgun.

"Have a little breakdown, did you, Miss?" a fat, half-drunk man asked. He had dripping chewing tobacco on his red plaid shirt and his breath stank. She tried the coy approach.

"Yeah," she smiled. "Perhaps you could give me a hand?" Her eyes darted about the tree-lined road. Deserted.

He backed up a bit, looked at her up and down and seemed pleased with what he saw. "You step out, real slow-like." She did.

"You ain't from around here are you? No, too pretty, and those tight jeans—not good for field work. No, you're good for only one thing. You're one of those sexy city girlies—how old you is anyway?"

"Now look," she said, turning to face him squarely, "I don't know who you are or what you are but that gun is pointing right at me and I don't like it."

"And it's gonna keep pointing at you while you undress nice and sexy like—you hear me?"

"Don't," she said. "Don't do it. You're still a man—not a goddamn animal."

"Ain't no men left now, just us animals. And I reckon that things like the law ain't around either nowadays, Ma'am. I'm going to sample your merchandise right now and if you're *real real* good to me, I won't kill you. I'll just take you to my little ol' place, my farmhouse, and I might even feed you every day if you're nice to me and my two brothers. *Now undress*! And be quick."

He pulled back the hammer of the big 30-30. Robin started unbuttoning her khaki shirt, tears streaming down her cheeks.

"That's it lady, nice and slow like." His eyes widened as her ample breasts appeared — she had no bra on.

"Well I thought you was one of them lib ladies from the big city. Man, I never had me no lib woman — do you do it in the rear? Don't matter if you ever did, you're gonna now — "

She had stopped undressing — she had to do something. He'd kill her anyway, or there'd be months and maybe years of imprisonment and sex with him and his brothers — and then she'd die. She had to make a move now. She tried to remember her karate lessons with Master Okadawa. It was only a YWCA course. But she had dutifully gone six days a week for a year, and had gotten leaner and trimmer. She still did her Katas each day, along with her yoga. He stepped forward a bit to poke her with the barrel of the gun. "I said get to undressing agai — "

This was her chance. A gun was useless at close distance. Karate-trained reflexes moved into action, and she was amazed how easily she deflected the barrel. It exploded with fury, both barrels, blew holes into the side of her Ford. Her ears were ringing when she threw a star block, then another and a short sudden kick to his right knee made something crack as he crumpled to the ground, then she delivered a left roundhouse kick with her hobnail navy-issue paratrooper boots that split his head wide open like a cantaloupe. He fell shuddering and spitting blood through his gasping mouth. She stood there stunned, numb. Then she put on her blouse again, and not looking at him, she picked up the gun. It could come in handy — there were more ammo and rifles at the farm. She couldn't stand the thought of going through his pockets. He was clearly dead, already growing pale.

She tried the car once more — but it was dead — forever.

With a sigh she took her backpack and filled it carefully — vitamins, a book, her warmest clothes, a knife, and some silly things she couldn't bear to part with. She looked at the Christmas presents in the back of the car all neatly wrapped with little bows and bright paper. It was all so absurd now. There would be no Christmas. Maybe never be a Christmas again. She felt her eyes start to fill with moisture again and clamped them tightly shut. She couldn't keep bursting into tears every time she felt bad. She thought of Dean, what he would say and do. She could picture his face, his mouth moving. "Be tough, baby, the soft will all be dead meat when the proverbial shit hits the fan." She had had many arguments with him about the prospects of war and peace, about the kind of world she wanted to live in. She had always thought him too hard, too cynical in his views. But God help them all, everything he had predicted had come to pass. And now only the tough *would* survive. She didn't even know for sure that she wanted to live in this violent and dark new world. But what was her alternative — to lie down by her dead car and join it. No, it was equally ridiculous. She had been thrust into survival almost unwillingly by Sturgis' phone call. Now she would have to do her best.

She headed through the low hills, moving away from the road. She wasn't in the mood to run into more 'animals.' The next few days were hard on her. She had camped out with Dean in the past, but city living seemed to soften the body up fast. But her basically strong frame responded quickly to the hiking and though she ached like the devil, by the second day she felt much stronger. In a way it was wonderful being in the thick forests, rabbits and deer scampering around her. The lush smell of moist foliage filling her nostrils like an intoxicating perfume. One would hardly know in here that a nuclear war had just devastated America. She hiked until the sun set each evening and then camped, cooking cans of food she had brought with her over a small fire. Surprisingly, it kept above freezing, sometimes over 40°.

She walked for nearly six days, using a compass, although she knew the general area from previous outings with Dean.

At last she reached the outer edge of the 50-acre farm. She drew back the chain, fastened it again and walked down the dirt road for nearly a mile until she came to the product of Sturgis' and her three years hard work. At one side of a clearing stood 'the Farmstead', half burrowed into a cliff face, looking much like an old Indian rock shelter which it had started out as. Sturgis had stripped a farmhouse that came with the land, scavenging materials for the semi-cave home. She wondered if he would be there, but as soon as she unlocked the steel door she could see that he wasn't. She hoped against hope that he would come soon.

Robin walked through the large four-room dwelling. Though she had feared the place would be crude and covered with dust when Sturgis began building it, he had ended up creating a lovely finely finished dwelling with oak floors and wood paneling on all the walls. Well-water from underground was pumped up with the self-contained generator and heating units—the place was a virtual fortress. Its four large windows had steel shutters that could be closed from inside, making the place impenetrable. She flipped on the light switches and track lighting units illuminated all four rooms. She threw her stuff on the living-room couch and checked the kitchen. Thank God Sturgis had been so sure things were going to get bad. She had berated him in the past for his doomsday prophecies, but now she was glad for his preparations.

There were supplies for a long time, and weapons also. Lots of people who made it out of the cities would be looking for food, medical supplies, weapons in the days and weeks to come. She'd have to be—God help her—prepared. But she knew that the first thing for her to do was to seal off the place and decontaminate herself. She'd have to wait three or four days at least for the worst fallout to settle. Those who stayed out of doors these next few weeks, if they were under the settling dust, would die slow, horrible deaths from radiation. Then, perhaps, if the winds were favorable, she could come out again. If . . . if . . .

Taking a shower of pure mountain water—freezing cold so as not to waste fuel, was her next order of business. She showered well, for nearly half an hour, to wipe off traces of radiation she knew must be there. Then she sealed herself in like a mummy in a cold dark tomb for the next 72 hours. She heard occasional noises outside. But whether they were animals, the wind, or people, she couldn't tell, and she didn't try to find out. "Never, never answer a knock—unless it's my code—3, 4, plus 2," Dean had told her. She was starting to believe that every damned thing that he had told her was advice she should heed. The farm had been their vacation home for the past four years. She always frowned when he got into his survivalist lore, but now, she realized, it would be life or death for her. And all those things she had reluctantly absorbed became law for her now. She fell asleep for nearly 20 hours after the exhausting trek. When she got up it was dawn outside. She ate and turned the TV-set on but got nothing—just a hiss on all the channels. She turned on the radio and at last found a station in Wichita still broadcasting a frantic civil-defense bulletin that pretty much just said that all was lost.

"Reports from around the country point to a massive first strike by the Soviet Union," the report stated. "Although this has not been positively confirmed. At least— we repeat—at *least* 325 cities have been hit, and there are reports of waves of Russian troop-ships arriving off the east and west coasts, as yet also unconfirmed. Reports, I repeat, are sketchy. The radiation level here in Wichita, which has held steady at twice normal for three days, is now rising, nearly doubling every hour. We are operating on emergency generators at 1230 kilocycles on the AM dial and we hope—static-static-static—" She listened for an hour without hearing anything, and then went and looked at herself for a long time in the lighted cosmetics application mirror she had insisted Sturgis install in the bathroom. She checked her skin, her eyes carefully for any kind of radiation damage. She couldn't find any. Her cheeks were still smooth as ivory, though she knew radiation damage could take weeks, months to develop. Best not to think about it. If she was dead—she was already dead. If not—she'd find out soon enough. She began brushing her hair.

Suddenly she felt as if she were about to go mad—staring at herself in the mirror—wondering, wondering . . . She ran to the record player and put on *Phil Ochs' Greatest Hits* and listened to him sing "My car, a car, my kingdom for a car." When it was over, she listened to Pink Floyd's *The Wall* and smoked a joint. Maybe she should take all those Deximils in the bathroom and overdose herself and get out of this nightmare. Love—love for Dean was making her stay alive. She had to fight the feeling in her gut of sheer terror and panic and wanting to find an escape, a way out. But she wasn't at all convinced that this life was all there was. There might be reincarnation, as the Buddhists believed, and suicide would bring a lower birth. The half of her which believed in spiritual things, the better half she decided, would not let her do such a thing. It was the side that had made her march in peace demonstrations, actively supporting a nuclear freeze, that was positive, life affirming. And yet did that help bring on this war? She refused to believe that

196

working for peace causes war, something that Sturgis in his cynicism sometimes suggested. No, *she* had done what she could, as *he* had done what he thought would stop war. "Being prepared is insurance," he had always said. Well, if the U.S. was prepared, it sure as hell didn't look it. So much for preparedness.

She had read a paper by a senator once that stated the failure of 'intelligence'—spying he meant—would be the cause of World War III. Did that bring on the war—The CIA fucking up? Making a miscalculation? Was President Armstrong responsible? No, the people responsible, directly—were those who launched the attack. Armstrong wouldn't. It *must have been* the Soviets. Were they still alive over there? Yet she didn't put it past the U.S. military to have launched first; or perhaps they goaded the Reds into the war. She didn't trust the news media. Who would ever know if *we* or *they* started it—it didn't matter, did it? The "aggressive ape" theory of Ardrey had proven true, hadn't it? That man had never really evolved beyond the emotional level of his distant ancestors, the aggressive apes.

"It's sad but true, baby," Sturgis had said to her. "Though we like to think of ourselves as civilized and we don't *look* like our caveman great-grandfathers, inside where it counts, man is a vicious, greedy, ornery son-of-a-bitch who would just as soon smash you in the face and take everything you've got. It's not like I want it to be that way, but it is! If you look around you, what do you see? I'll tell you what—the world's mad. Stark raving lunatics, operating at the emotional level of an angry six-year-old. A planet of children who hold in their sweaty little hands the power to wipe this planet right out of the skies. What do I think? It sucks, but it's true. Man is his own worst enemy, he carries the sword—and he stabs himself with it. He is the killer and the victim, one and the same."

"Oh God," Robin screamed out, lying face down on the bed holding a pillow between her arms and squeezing it tight. It was all so fucking depressing. Trying to keep an optimistic mood in a post-nuclear world. Sure everything's okay. We'll just sweep up the ashes, replace a few broken windows and good-as-new!

She fell weeping on the bed as *Brown Sugar* by the Rolling Stones came on. She got up and began dancing around the room, the joint in her mouth. Dancing, closing her eyes and spinning around, losing herself in her own little world. Then she fell asleep without knowing when and slept for about ten hours. When she awoke she couldn't remember where she was for a second. Then, slowly feeling the unfamiliar coarse bedding, she remembered, and muttered, "Oh God." With great effort she rose and made some coffee. She turned on the radio again and there was nothing. Nothing! She tried shortwave — picking up lots of languages she didn't understand. Then, suddenly, a clearly Russian-accented voice speaking English came across.

"The Liberation Forces have won a decisive victory over the war-mongering capitalist rulers of America. The liberation of the United States, and the freeing of the workers has begun. The temporary president, General Voloshinsky, of the United States announced that the attack by the United States leadership and its imperialist allies on Russia has been soundly smashed and the Soviet Union and its heroic allies have begun the peaceful cleanup of the damage caused by the fascist military powers upon the people of United Soviet States of America."

The hairs on the back of her neck stood up as a rippling chill rushed through her spine. She turned on the television and saw a color picture a bit out of focus and beaming a Russian face in front of a wide map of the world. "Yes, listeners out there in Free American territory, the glorious victory won just days ago is now being consolidated, with the working classes, the black, Hispanic, and Third-World oppressed classes of the United States helping to mop up the last traces of the fascist military clique which caused this terrible war. President Voloshinsky, acting as interim president until a new truly democratic election under the auspices of the Communist Party can take place in the near future, had good news indeed for the struggling masses of—"

A tear formed in her eyes—America—defeated, destroyed, occupied. Its farms, factories, cities wiped off the face of the earth forever. A radioactive cloud hanging over it killing everything in its shadow.

"—just a few more days now, and those workers and fighting minorities will be able to come out of their shelters and aid in the rebuilding of a Communist America, as they have all wished and hoped for, for so long."

Robin burst into laughter. It was all so stupid, what they were doing. No one would buy that crap. Maybe it went over back in the U.S.S.R., but it gave her brief comfort to hear them making such asses of themselves.

"Food and clothing and medical aid," the announcer continued, "will be passed out by our victorious armies as they move to reestablish order in the liberated areas. A new day has dawned on America, my fellow proletarians. And it won't be long until all is a communist utopia." The announcer smiled and the broadcast ceased, to the waving of the Russian flag and the playing of the Communist Internationale, sung in English, "Arise ye prisoners of starvation, throw off your chains . . ."

My God, a nightmare—it has to be a nightmare. She turned the unpleasant hiss of the TV off but left the video on in case something else came on.

The call letters broadcast were those of WKET in Kingsley, West Virginia, a station she remembered for *Hee-Haw* and the *Andy Griffith Show* reruns and lot of

Grand Ol' Opry shows. Was there any resistance? Did the president really surrender already? Lies, of course. All lies that we surrendered, just like the other nonsense about 'freeing' us. Propaganda — tacky, absurd propaganda.

She opened a can of chili and heated it up for her breakfast. She was ravenous and devoured it in quick bites, not caring any more, as in her health-food days, that it had preservatives, coloring and 25 additives that she would have been repulsed by a week ago. It tasted wonderful. The pantry was immensely stocked — dried fruits and meats, everything conceivable in non-perishable form. All that they needed was a steady supply of uncontaminated water, and the artesian well that the water in the rock shelter was drawn from supplied an ample source of that precious liquid that Sturgis made sure was immune to radiation poisoning for years to come. They were set, but whether the farm would be the start of a new life or an imprisoning tomb in a dead world remained to be seen.

"Please come to me," she whispered. "Oh Dean, *please* come."

CHAPTER EIGHTEEN

It was midnight when the sky started to blaze to the north—and a tower of flame rose into the night. Sturgis ordered the Omega Team to stop as he brought his Tri-wheeler to a halt at the edge of an abutment.

"Could it be a city burning?" asked Tranh. "At this late date I thought they'd all be burned out."

"I suppose some sort of fire could have started again," Sturgis answered, using macro/visual mode for a closer look. But the smoke created an impenetrable haze. "The weather's been dry and the temperature is above freezing—maybe some trapped natural gas—or maybe, God knows, it's been burning since the attack."

They looked at a map that flashed onto their visors depicting the mid-western U.S. "We can get a better look from that low hill over there," Sturgis said. "There's some sort of fire tower on top that looks out over the whole city."

Sturgis told the men to wait, and taking Tranh and Slater, the man right behind him in the convoy, they reached the 100-foot high tower and climbed to the top. "This is higher than we could get with jump mode," Tranh said. Ten miles away, they saw the source of the blaze that lit up the sky in red and orange and sickly green curtains of fire. It was definitely the city of Muskogee. "Maybe the Russians have landed there," Tranh said. "Could be paratroopers—haven't seen any sign of regular army or mechanized divisions so far, but they must be moving in somewhere."

"We'd better get a closer look," Sturgis said. "We're ahead of schedule and I don't want to have to make a 30-mile detour."

They notified Billy on super-scramble where they were going, and started making their way down the other side of the wooded hills toward the blazing city. In a half hour of traveling along a small county road filled with deserted cars they were able to see the wavering silhouette of the engulfed city—the straight lines of streets dissecting the gutted buildings which poured forth their reaching hands of flame. Nowhere did they see a soul, and strangely the geiger counter readings flashed onto their visors every 30 seconds stayed almost inactive. A ghost city burning until it *was* nothing—nothing but ashes to join the ocean of ashes that blew across the land.

They made their way to the edge of town, when they suddenly heard a strange chanting chorus coming from several blocks away. They turned the corner and saw them—long lines of moaning men, singing out a slow Gregorian chant-like drone as they stumbled forward, each holding a whip, or stick, or chains, and beating one another on the backs, over and over. At least 200 of them, walking in a line like death-incarnate, one behind another. Their torn black and gray robes were spattered with blood, their eyes mad, fanatical.

They scarcely looked up at Sturgis and his men, their eyes glued to the back ahead of them which they smashed at again and again. One of them fell and was trampled over by everyone in line, his bloody corpse painting their bare feet a bright red. Some had pieces of plate glass

202

buried in their thighs or jammed into their eye sockets, others had razor blades in their mouths. They seemed immune to pain, yet they groaned at each bite of the whips, each painful step. Sturgis and his men watched as the procession came right past them.

"*Penance, penance, Oh Lord*," screamed a black-robed preacher holding a Bible, leading the parade of Flagellants. "We offer you our pain, oh Lord, in hope of a better life in the hereafter."

"*Amen*," the host yelled in raspy voices, and passed on. They didn't care about activities in this world anymore, not even startling apparitions like the Omega Force.

"Followers, heed not those black devils, for they are sent by Satan, verily, I say, to mislead you. Look to the sky—to our Lord's coming. For is it not in *this* book, the *Bible*, in the *chapter of Revelations*, that predicted this day?"

The crowd called out, "Verily."

"And did it not say in *this book* that the guilty shall be punished, and the faithful saved in *these* days?"

"*Verily!*"

Sturgis listened for a bit, smiling grimly. Less than a week and the goddamned country was already back in the Middle Ages. Where would they be in 10 years? He and his men did look like devils from hell, he supposed, in their shiny black suits with the gleaming red strobes flickering on their helmets.

The "preacher" went on. "This is the Great Apocalypse that was spoken of in the Bible, when the seven seals were broken and the sky opened and the beasts rose from the oceans and liquid fire burned the unworthy and sinful. Yet, the true believers of God, the God that can do anything in this universe, were saved. Shall not these true believers in Him be saved?"

"*Verily*," they shouted.

"Then we march onward to *glory!*" He led his flock of

penitents along the endless road that circled the city just out of reach of the flames and they flailed themselves for their sins, begging for forgiveness with each slashing stroke that bit into them.

"And it is our duty," the preacher intoned, "to imitate the Lord in all ways. We must be scourged as *He* was. Yes, only in this way, in the religious ecstasy of chastisement," he told his flock, "we can hope to enter the World of Paradise that awaits us. Look up and see the glory. See the glory that is to come." The preacher's disciples followed him, believing, *knowing* him to be divinely inspired, for did he not speak the tongues, babbling in strange godlike languages, frothing at the mouth in angelic madness? Did not this minister preach the only way to salvation? Had not the end come as predicted, and were not they the *true* believers, who destroyed their own flesh as Jesus had done. Would they not rise into heaven at any moment now?

They marched onward, each step with a simultaneous crack of the whips and the scourging chains on their backs, running with red blood.

"God answer us," they yelled in unison after each blow. But *He* had to test their devotion mightily, this God, and they had to march on and on into the black night, until *He* came to take them in his bloody arms.

"God answer us . . . God answer us . . ."

"God of our fathers save us," the preacher screamed, hitting himself in the side of the head with a stick.

"Amen," the Flagellants screamed back in unison.

"Grant us entrance to your heaven."

"Amen."

"I know you brought your righteous rage down among us to destroy the evil modern world that worships Mammon."

"Amen."

"We scourge ourselves to show our repentance."

"*Amen.*"

And so it went, as the sky rumbled with sudden thunder that brought not rain, but snow. White snow for the very first time.

"*A sign, a sign,*" he yelled. "*Hallelujah.*"

"*Hallelujah,*" the crowd called as they waited for the sky to open, for angels to lift them up.

They waited for long exultant moments, their arms outstretched, their eyes closed in ecstasy. But as neither God nor his flock of angels descended after five minutes, the black-robed, black-bearded preacher rose from his bended knees and, holding the disintegrating Bible in his hand, yelled out, "Not yet. It is not yet time for our Lord to deliver us. He speaks to me. He tells me that we have not punished ourselves nearly enough to take upon our shoulders the sins of the world. *More,*" he screamed out, his red eyes wide as saucers. "We must hurt ourselves *more.*"

They all rose and began circling the burning city again, hitting one another even harder and faster. The blood flowed like rivers into the ash-covered streets beneath their feet.

Sturgis and his men cut between the line to get in and get a closer look at the city. It would save them six or seven hours if they could cut through the center. The line held up as the seven-foot giants paraded through them — more visions from hell — and started toward the burning city.

"Stop, non-believers," the preacher cried out. "Those who enter the city of the damned shall be damned themselves. The Red Death walks the streets, cloaked in robes the color of blood. All he touches die."

Sturgis continued forward, ignoring the Flagellant's leader.

"What the hell does he mean, Red death?" Tranh asked over the helmet radio.

"Maybe the advance Russian Commando Forces," Sturgis replied. "Weapons ready, men." He glanced over at Rossiter, a doubt in his mind. Rossiter was clumsy, had to learn to be careful—and fast.

"Weapons, Mister?" Sturgis double checked. Rossiter sometimes misloaded. "Yes sir. Firing mode on, sir. E-balls, machine gun, operation mode, sir."

Sturgis laughed. "Good, and you don't need quite so many 'sirs' Rossiter. Just once in awhile will suffice."

"Yes sir," 'Fatty' Rossiter barked back.

They moved carefully down the main street, which was nearly burnt out. Rossiter was the first to spot something—a car all battered and charred in the front. "Oklahoma—the Proud State" the license plate read. The old Dodge lay overturned in a ditch on the side of the road. The windshield was smashed and it was filled with bullet holes. Rossiter looked inside.

"My God, look inside," he called. "There's somebody still alive," the fat C.A.D.S. member shouted. Sturgis stopped him from opening the door. But just then Pvt. Trager, one of the youngest team members, tore it off its hinges with his muscular-amplification mode. There was a ghastly smell inside which Trager could smell as he had left his visor slightly ajar. Trager reached in and pulled a groaning half-naked man with a bullet wound in his shoulder out of the front seat. A woman lay dead on the seat beside him. Both of them had red spots all over their faces and body.

The man suddenly struggled with Trager.

"No ha *hahahahahahaha*. You are the ones. The black ones that come from the rocks to eat my flesh and my brains."

"Trager!" Sturgis yelled, "pull your helmet shut."

As Trager's hand rose to the lever, the man suddenly vomited green slime all over the helmet and suit. Then he twitched violently, fell to the street, and was still.

Sturgis rushed over to Trager. "Did he get you?"

"I'm afraid so sir. I had my visor open. Sometimes the air-conditioning doesn't . . ."

"See the doc when we get back to the squadron," Sturgis said. "I hope . . ."

"Look," Tranh said, pointing to a sign just ahead.

Sturgis read it and gasped.

'WARNING RED DEATH PLAGUE AREA AHEAD' Just that, no more, no less.

They watched the city flicker and waver in the orange heat for a few seconds, then they turned around.

"What kind of a plague is Red Death?" Trager asked nervously.

"They — the people who wrote the sign probably didn't know," said Sturgis, lying.

"Maybe no one knows," Tranh spoke up. "I've done some reading on atomic mutations and there is a good chance that a new mutated virus or germ could arise out of all this fallout and rotting bodies."

A new disease. The Red Death. "Maybe they named it after the Reds. They brought it on us," Sturgis said half out loud.

"One thing," said Tranh, "if it is a new disease, then there's probably no vaccine against it. No way to stop its spread — except . . ."

"Except," Sturgis said grimly, "barricading off any town or city where it breaks out and burning that city with all its inhabitants inside. That might be what's happened here."

They scouted ahead and soon saw that because the center of town had burned first, it was already passable, at least for their vehicles. With their helmets and suits sealed tight, the air purification system of the suit which included sterilization of every drop of oxygen they breathed by a super high-temperature laser beam, would make them impervious to microbes. But as for

Trager . . .

By the time they returned to the waiting Omega Team, Trager already had the shakes and was vomiting. Sturgis isolated him from the others, telling them to seal everything tight. Lieutenant Boone, who doubled as the squad doctor, told Sturgis, "I think gamma globulin might help. It's worth a try." He injected Trager, who was too weak to stand.

But nothing worked. Within an hour, Trager's face was mottled with dime-sized bright red spots that seemed to grow by the minute. They took off his helmet as he kept screaming he couldn't breathe. His entire face soon swelled up, grotesque, like a misshapen balloon. Then his tongue grew so large it filled his mouth and he could barely breathe. Suddenly he began twitching and jerking violently, like a puppet on the end of the strings of a madman. His arm would flail around in the air and then smash to the ground, his legs kicking at an invisible enemy. Then they saw his stomach start heaving and stepped back. Thick waves of dark green bile swept out of his mouth as if pouring out his very guts. Then, mercifully, he was still.

The others stood a few feet away watching, filled with revulsion. Death was all around them, behind every shadow, in every hand, reaching, reaching for every one of them. Suddenly the presence of death was palpable to each man as it had never been before. They could see its aura in the skies, in the burning eyes of the Flagellants, in Trager's mottled red flesh, in the dying flames of a dying city. Death was with them now. It was their constant companion. It would ride alongside them every second now, waiting to pounce, waiting for their one mistake, their one slip, like Trager's slightly ajar visor.

"Should we bury him?" Fenton asked Sturgis.

"Cremate him. Those germs or whatever the fuck they are, can't be allowed to fester, and release their venom somewhere in the future." Billy Dixon walked over, and with a grimace that no one could see, poured a rain of Liquid Plastic Fire over the body until there was nothing left.

CHAPTER NINETEEN

1500 miles to the east, the few surviving American forces in the nation's capital were using the reflecting pools of the Washington Monument as a mass grave. It was already filled to the edges with bodies — civilians, soldiers, every body the special unit led by Sergeant Rip McKuen could find; and already the corpses were rotting, swelling. The job had to be done. The next threat was disease — cholera, typhoid . . . plague. When the pools were completely filled, gasoline would be poured in and the bodies burned. The job was revolting to the men who performed it.

The radiation meters had gone off the scale and many soldiers looked stunned and numb. One came up and said to McKuen, "We're walking dead men."

"Do your duty, G.I.," McKuen said softly. "We're all dead men. Me too."

"Yessir. But . . ."

"Do your duty. There's nothing else anyway."

The next dumpster of bodies had arrived from the northern part of D.C. The men shoveled and pitchforked them into the reflecting pools, now red rivers of blood.

In the dim red-brown glow of the day turning twilight, McKuen suddenly heard someone on a roof yell out.

"*Paratroopers*. Dropping everywhere!"

The sergeant stared up into the murky sky and saw the Red planes flying a mile up. Red Tupolov airliners, with the rear door open, *Aeroflot* airliners pressed into paratroop service. They had always been equipped for a swift change-over—out go the seats, in go the troops. Now Red commandos were hitting the silk by the thousands, tens of thousands.

The sergeant stared around at his men. "Line up," he yelled to his unit. They stood frozen. He fired his M-16. "I said *line up*!"

They moved into rank—forty-one men. From around the city anti-aircraft batteries, those on trucks that had been sheltered, damned few at that, began opening up. He saw a few streaking Rapier missiles and a few hand-held Red-Eyes going up. Two of them hit their targets. But there were plenty of planes to replace them. The first of the paratroopers dropped to the ground just blocks away.

"Spread out," McKuen yelled. "Get them in the sky if you can. Use each round carefully. Pick them off like pigeons before they hit. Everyone of you is a sniper now. You're on your own. This is our country, *not* theirs. Do every goddamned thing you can to hurt them. There's no surrender."

The men rushed off, each to his destiny. One soldier stayed behind. He looked at McKuen impassively as the sergeant walked up to him. He picked up the man's fallen rifle and handed it to him and said, "Get moving soldier. Don't make me shoot you."

"It's useless, Sergeant. Why bother? They've won."

"Are you kidding soldier? This is just the first battle.

Do you realize that our guys are in Moscow right now?" he lied. "We're taking care of business over there. Now we've got to hold on. Protect the president until the Reds are forced to retreat. And it won't be long. I guarantee you soldier, we're going to win this one."

The man brightened up. "It's not over?"

"Not by a long shot, G.I. Get going. Die a hero. Make your life mean something."

The soldier slapped his ammo belt. "I'll get a whole slew of 'em, sir."

"That's the spirit," McKuen grinned.

"Sergeant," the soldier hesitated.

"Yes?"

"Thanks." The trooper ran off to his dying duty as the paratroopers filled the skies with their billowing chutes. The sergeant scrambled into his jeep and took off toward the Smithsonian Institute ruins. A top floor there would give his M-16 with superscope a good sweep of this plaza below. He might get 30, 40, even 50 of them before . . .

He floored the accelerator and winced in pain as the jeep flew over a bump; nausea crept through his guts. His vision blurred. He was slowly dying from the radiation. The bastards. He drove like a maniac, like a man possessed, toward the tall marble structures ahead.

What the hell. He screeched to a halt. An American, a civilian, wearing just a tee-shirt that said *State University at Binghamton*, came frantically waving at him from a building doorway. He was holding an old .30-30 hunting rifle with scope. The sergeant looked in his eyes. They had seen death. The civilian said nothing, just stood there huffing.

"Want to see some action against the Reds?" McKuen asked.

"Better believe it, chum."

"Then hop in and get ready for the Battle of the Little

The paratroopers dropped all over Washington, like flies descending on a freshly dead corpse. They hit the ground and quickly wrapped up their chutes and, under the barking orders of their squad commanders, assembled into battle formations. They were armed to the teeth with Kalashnikovs, bayonet-fixed, tripod mounted 55mm machine guns, flamethrowers and belts filled with grenades. They came down in the streets, atop roofs and occasionally landing right on the Pentagon, the Capitol Rotunda, or amidst the barren cherry trees along the Potomac. All of America's most famous monuments became landing pads for the Russian invaders. America was theirs now, the relics of the past might as well be destroyed, so that the new Socialist America could start fresh, with new symbols, a new history.

When all the commandos had regrouped, the second wave of transport planes flew over D.C., this time dropping heavy equipment attached to three, four, even five immense chutes. Trucks, jeeps, armored vehicles, even tanks dropped down from the dark skies into open fields and the wide avenues of the capital. The terrified surviving inhabitants of the city peered through their sooty windows, scarcely daring to look for fear of being spotted. They grabbed their few weapons, some only a butcher knife or baseball bat and waited to die. The tanks quickly assembled and began grinding down the streets of Washington, formations of flak-jacketed special commando units taking up their rear. Their morale was high—from all that their officers had told them, America was as good as gone. Theirs was merely a mopping-up operation, with lots of medals for everyone when the Capitol was taken. They looked around curiously at the great marble building they had only seen in books and magazines. America—it was supposedly the most powerful nation in the history of the earth, and yet, here they were, foot soldiers from Mother Russia marching where no foreign troops had marched before.

At first there was just token opposition, a few shots fired here and there. A barrage of tank cannon and 55mm slugs took care of that. But as the commando units swept deeper into the city the resistance began opening up on them in larger concentrations. Grenades came flying down from rooftops. Garbage cans filled with kerosene or gasoline pushed down onto slow-moving tanks engulfing them in flames. The Reds began bogging down, their troops getting a little more nervous, frightened as they saw their comrades fall around them.

"On, push on," their officers screamed, waving their Turganev service revolvers wildly in the air at their reticent charges. But the counter-fire only grew in intensity until they were pinned down everywhere, snipers firing at them from every opening, every window.

Before long, the Reds were in the battle of their lives as citizens of Washington put up fierce resistance. All over occupied Washington, the American irregulars were moving in from neighboring less-radioactive zones. They had holed up there until the radiation died down, and now came in groups of five or six, armed with shotguns, hunting rifles, a few handguns. America had over 100,000,000 weapons in private hands before the apocalyptic attack. Now those who could wield those guns and saw the Reds moving in were fired up with patriotism. Overcoming their shock at the war, and with a devil-may-care attitude of those who were soon to die anyway, they moved forward in small bands picking off the Reds everywhere they tried to push forward. A few at a time, a constant harassment. Helicopter gunships had to be diverted in order to get one or two American guerilla snipers, and the continuing landings were slowed down. Soviet forces began slipping out of their schedule of occupation. The commando teams all met unexpected opposition from armed teens, housewives, police officers. Anywhere there was a building standing there were Americans standing too, holding smoking weapons directed at the Red enemy . . .

McKuen and the college kid kept firing from a window on the top floor of the Smithsonian Institute. Behind them stood several space capsules from the first manned missions in space, *Apollo, Gemini*, and a replica of Neil Armstrong and "Buzz" Aldrin standing in their shiny white and aluminum colored space suits holding an American flag and planting it on the surface of a fake moon landscape. America's tribute to greatness, the statues, had been knocked over on their sides by the N-bomb blasts. The space capsules were pocked with shrapnel hits, their once smooth surfaces heavily dented. The emergency lights, four days after the neutron bomb, were still partly functioning, though weak. Sergeant McKuen had found his way to the front windows and knocked a little hole in one when he couldn't get it open, being careful not to expose his rifle barrel. The M-16 had good range, but he wished he had a long-range weapon. He was using up too much ammo. Still, as the paratroopers had been falling in the square immediately in front of the building he and the college kid were able to pick them off like flies, with a flyswatter made of lead.

Hold Washington—an impossible task with probably only a few thousand armed soldiers and civilians still capable of functioning. He had seen the makeshift hospitals set up along the sidewalks, whole blocks filled with the soon-to-be dead, their bodies bleeding, blackened like charcoal. The casualties had been immense. His little radiation-film indicator had turned opaque. He was a dead man, already he had the dry heaves. He

215

hadn't eaten except for a few bites two days earlier which he had promptly heaved up again. And he was so thirsty, all the time, filling his dehydrated body with canteen after canteen of water. But he sure as hell was going to take as many of the Red bastards with him as he could. He saw a unit crawling forward toward the Institute on their bellies and let loose a full clip hitting three or four of them. But their officer spotted the bursts of fire from the shattered fourth story window.

A Red bazooka team rushed forward, setting the tubular weapons on the edge of an overturned car and fired up at the snipers. The shell shot forward and slammed into the Institute just yards below the sergeant's window and blasted a chunk right out of the building. McKuen ducked inside, grabbing the college kid. They ran to another floor and opened up again, but McKuen spotted demolition teams — that's probably what they were — with wires and satchels hanging from their shoulders, running toward the Institute. So they were going to blow the whole damned thing up. After several minutes the teams ran out again. McKuen picked off two, but the one carrying the spool of wire leading into the building made it back to cover. McKuen had an idea. He grabbed the kid.

"Time to die, friend."

"I'm ready," the civvy smiled.

They ran down the stairs and came flying through the door. The Reds hadn't expected that. The two Americans ran forward laughing as only those who know they are about to die, and no longer care, can. They managed to get six or seven of the demo-guys before the Russian officer pushed the plunger of a small box and set off a volcanic explosion. It blasted one whole side of the Institute into a storm of concrete fragments and dust. The sergeant and the college kid felt a hot wave lift them from behind like giant hands and throw them through the air. That was the last thing they ever felt in this life.

The first Russian to reach the roof of the White House pulled down the burnt ragged American flag and hoisted the red flag with hammer-and-sickle over the seat of the United States' government. Suddenly he was cut down by long-range sniper fire. And the flag itself was shot off its lanyards by hundreds of bullets migrating through the misty radioactive air. The hunters in the Hilton Hotel windows blocks away put down their scoped rifles and cheered. They opened the last bottle of whiskey, which they had not let themselves drink until they had something to celebrate.

Suddenly there was a noise in the hall, just as the hunters gulped down the burning scotch. They reached for their rifles as a Red advance team kicked down the door and opened up with a fusillade of automatic fire from three Russian burpguns. The Americans' bodies were instantly dissected into bloody pieces of meat. The leader of the killer team, Orvonsky, took out his communicator and reported the mission accomplished. He wanted to get the hell out of there. Something in the room had a lot of radiation in it. He swept the suite with a mini-geiger counter. Shit—it was the bodies. The Americans themselves were giving off lethal doses of rads. There were rumors spreading in the Russian ranks that the Americans—who all knew they were dying—did impossible, insane, heroic things—throwing themselves in wave after wave at troops and tanks, already winning astonishing victories by sheer determination and by bravery beyond belief. Like these two, shooting down the Russian flag. Their act had rallied the American resistance in the streets below. Now they would fight on for days; it was insane.

The Russians ran back down the stairs, leaving the scene of their first killing ever. Their training had helped

217

them not to think—just plunge their bayonets. *Kill* any Americans—for men, women, even children, were attacking their comrades throughout Washington. They came out into an ambush, met by half a dozen women with kitchen cleavers and long knives.

"Mother," yelled the commando leader as his head was cleaved in half. The women buried their weapons in Russian flesh, hacking away until the Reds were unrecognizable as human.

CHAPTER TWENTY

The C.A.D.S. team drove their Tri-bikes all night through a cold forbidding land of burned trees and blackened earth. There had been an immense fire here, a plains fire that must have lit up the sky for a hundred miles and blazed for a week. It had just burned itself out, leaving nothing that resembled the old heartland of America. Here and there Sturgis saw collapsed charred farmhouses, burned out cars, some with charred skeletons inside. But no life. No life at all, in this once fruitful and ripe land. Everywhere was the same mile after mile of utter desolation. The rad meter was clicking away so furiously that if there *had* been any life around it wouldn't last very long.

They could only hope that the radiation at this high level didn't reach all the way to Washington D.C. If it did, all was lost. If the radiation was like this all over the east, there was no hope for America, no hope at all. Sturgis decided that if the rad meter remained at 300 roentgens for another day, they would have to turn back, because there would be no sense in going forward. For one thing, the radiation was so high that they were getting some exposure even inside their "rad proof" suits. They would be dead men if this kept up. And dead men can't rescue a president—nor would there be anyone but corpses to rescue.

A heavy rain began to move in and soon the rad meter readings started dropping back to "high" but "safe"— (within the scope of the suits' protection.)

The rain was so heavy at times that they used their suit radar to guide their Tri-bikes—the visors set on forward radar, capable of detecting any object larger than six inches in diameter. The view through the R-mode gave them an eerie image of the world—shimmering burnt trees outlined in green, an occasional wrecked car, looking almost whole through the bounced-back radio waves. The computer within the helmet interpreted each object in readable visual figures for the C.A.D.S.-suited warriors, rather than merely showing the traditional blips on a screen. That was one of the ingenious features of the visor—it could use all the traditional electro-magnetic radio and energy spectrums used for detection, but could then reassemble the images for human perception modes. The men were symbiotically linked up to energies beyond the normal ability of humanity to comprehend—receptors of an invisible rainbow.

The Rhino, with its superior radar, was in the lead to guard against any crevasses or other unforseen danger. But it was just a barren flatness ahead, stretching endlessly before them. If the mud weren't so deep, they could be making good progress here, could have made up for some of the time they had lost. But even the big tires of the Tri-wheelers sank almost a foot into the slippery surface.

The rain turned to a light flurry of snow by dawn. They hadn't heard any jets, thank God. But each mile east meant more danger from the air. This was Red airspace now. They'd best remember that.

The cartography-computer in the lead Rhino said they were near a town called Driverville. "It's a small town nestled between two hills," Fenton reported over his radio. "According to the map, it's a mile or two ahead—though in this bleakness it might be a little hard to find."

"Well there *are* some rolling hills ahead on my radar," Sturgis answered. "We'll see if there's still a Driverville out there soon enough. If there is, let's hope it has some provisions, and not just bodies."

They moved onward. Soon they were ascending a blackened hill, the sun above was just a yellow smudge but it made viewing the terrain with the naked eye possible once again as the rain and sleet slowly diminished.

Sturgis slowed his Tri-wheeler as he came to the top of the hill. Down in the valley it was very misty but using the visor he could see a steeple, a white church steeple.

"There—*look*," said Roberto, standing next to him. "A whole damned town—all white shingles and carefully laid out streets—like a fucking storybook village—untouched."

"Just as sweet as a Currier-and-Ives postcard," Sturgis replied.

"And low rad," Fenton added from inside the Rhino, sweeping the rod of the geiger-probe forward.

"Wait here," said Sturgis, "I'm going to take a quick look. If all's well, I'll signal."

He got back into his Tri-wheeler and headed down a small asphalt road bearing a sign that read "County 18." Sturgis rolled down street after street. No signs of life, not even any bodies. All was neat and tidy.

"They probably ran out of food and headed someplace," Sturgis called back on his radio. "There's lots of firewood piled up in the yards, though. We can stop and wash up. I don't know about you guys, but it's starting to get a little funky in here. We can recharge our batteries too, from the Rhino's atomic generator."

The C.A.D.S. team came down the hill eagerly, joining Sturgis who picked out two large houses a hundred feet apart for their base. Sturgis and Fenton pried open the lock of the three-story Cape Codder and stepped inside. It was neat and filled with antique wood furniture.

"How about dragging some wood inside and getting that fireplace started," said Fenton, his breath making clouds of frost. "It's cold as hell without a suit on." Fenton, who had been riding in the Rhino, was the only one of the team without a suit on, as the Rhino was temperature and environment controlled.

"Okay. It seems safe enough. And we've been up all night," Sturgis said. "We'll divide up. Those who want to stay up the first sleep-shift take this house. The rest of us, including *me*—I'm dog tired—will move over into that white shingle ranch house." He pointed out the second building. "We'll sleep in shifts."

"Right," said Fenton. The men quickly divided up—12 to the Cape Codder, the rest to sleep in the white shingle house.

Roberto and Sturgis were in the small bedroom on the first floor of the smaller house. It had two short beds and lots of kids' toys in it. A pang went through Sturgis' gut. The kids must be dead somewhere, their flesh burned to a crisp.

"Goodnight," he said to Roberto. "The chronometer is set for six hours. Hope they don't party too loud over there."

Sturgis immediately fell asleep on the soft sheets, dreaming all sorts of unpleasant things.

Carl Stranger, the leader of the Ward D Inmates, pointed to a town ahead. They were on the crest of a burned hill, and cold and hungry. Their ambulances and other commandeered vehicles were all abandoned now, from breakdowns or lack of fuel. They had already walked the last 30 miles or so in the cold snow, abandoning much of their equipment. They were half-frozen and very hungry. Their guns, stolen from the armory, they still carried tightly under their arms or slung over their shoulders.

"*A town! We will have food, drugs, ammunition!*" Carl yelled as he topped the rise and saw the pleasant steeple-dotted village below. A typical picture postcard town with a sheath of snow, a few church steeples, a small main street, the houses neat. Only, two chimneys had smoke coming from their tops. Americana cloaked in white, except there was no movement on Main Street—no cars, no trucks, no pedestrians, no kids with sleds running back home as a crescent moon rose in the east.

When Stranger looked down through his cracked 7 x 50 binoculars, he was pleased. There were people down there that they could give the *Treatment* to. The *Treatment* that they *needed* to be cured. Like his followers had cured the doctors and nurses at the asylum. The way of pain, the eternal cure.

"Let's go," he shouted to his followers.

"The Treatment, the Treatment," they chanted, marching in cadence down the hillside. The snow wasn't more than a few inches deep and they slid down, laughing like children playing on the slope. Carl quieted them up after they were halfway down, screeching, "*You idiots*—keep *quiet*. Our patients might be sleeping—we have to sneak up on them. In their madness—they might not want the Treatment."

"I don't want to shut up," Stella-the-Axe screamed.

"Then *keep quiet*," Carl snarled.

"Okay. I'll keep quiet, but I won't shut up. Goddamn it!"

They continued stealthily now, the 16 escaped patients. Carl told them to spread out around a big white two-story house that had smoke rising from its chimney. There was singing inside, a whole group of men's voices.

223

Outside were the strangest vehicles Carl had ever seen. Giant tricycles, they looked like, parked every which way outside the house. He heard the words:

"Off we go, into the wild blue yonder . . .
Climbing high, into the sun . . .
Off we go . . ."

The Air Force Theme—how cute. A song fest. The men inside *definitely* needed treatment. They had to be insane, to sing that song when the world had been blown up by the *Air Force*!

Carl winked at his right hand man Walter-the-Waxer in the neon glow of the half-moon. Carl pried open first a screen door and then the wooden door inside.

Walter had finally forsaken his mop for an M-16 at the armory they had pillaged three days ago—an armory full of rotting corpses. Carl hadn't liked that place—nobody to cure. Still, they had fun with the bodies for a while, until they got bored. He was glad that here were new patients to cure at last.

The women-with-glue-in-her-hair, (Carl still didn't know her real name so he called her "Glue"), had been good at the killing-treatments so far. He called her in a whisper: "Glue, strip off your clothes and enter the room next to the singers." She smiled and quickly stripped down. She walked into the unlit foyer next to the room where the singers were. The room looked strange, filled with black suits propped like statues against the walls of what must have been a library for it was filled with books. Books to burn later, books that talked nonsense and made her head hurt. She *hated* books.

"Go into the next room," Carl said over her shoulder. She strode naked into the next room while some of the others poked at the strange spacesuits. The singing stopped abruptly.

Fenton stood up and smiled. "Well, will you look at *that*! A naked— There's life in this town after all!"

Fenton was quite drunk, as were the others. They were seated before the roaring fireplace. They were in their overalls, warm and relaxed. They had been singing for hours now—and drinking.

"A pretty lady," said Tranh, "but don't you think we'd better see who she's with . . . ?"

There was a mad scramble as the other escapees burst into the room, brandishing rifles and pistols, drooling as they chanted *"More patients to treat"* over and over.

The Electrician, who had done such a good job using electro-shock on the insane doctors and nurses at the sanitarium—crawled around on the floor inspecting the electric sockets as the C.A.D.S. team members stood, their hands raised to the ceiling.

"Lots of plugs," he said, "but they're dead."

Fenton watched grimly. They had been idiots for leaving the guns—and the suits—in the library. You're never safe—never—without your gun nearby, he realized perhaps too late. He looked the madmen and women over. What the hell did they want? They looked—*insane* . . .

"Who are you people?" Fenton asked angrily. "Why are you holding guns on us? We're Americans. United States Air Force, on official business."

"Who are we? Us? We're the doctors, here to cure you insane people," Carl shouted.

"What do you mean?"

"We escaped from the *Sane* Asylum, where they keep the small-time killers. You big-time killers are *our* patients now. We, the sane, will judge you and treat you. And it will be a very painful series of treatments!"

"Treatments, treatments," yelled Axe Lady, jumping around on the Karistan.

Electrician went over and turned on the 27″ color TV "No picture or sound," he said glumly. "I thought *He-*

Man or *Masters of the Universe* might . . ."

"*Shut up,*" said the Axe Lady. "Shut up, shut up."

"You fellas astronauts?" asked Carl, cheerfully.

"Why would you think that?" asked Fenton.

Carl hit him hard in the stomach, but the Englishman only winced.

"Stupid. You have a bunch of spacesuits in the other room. So of course you're astronauts. It's elementary."

"*Elementary, elementary,*" they started to chant.

"Now, I'll ask you one time, where's your spaceship if you're astronauts. Are you guys escaping—maybe to the moon, and having a party first? That's it, isn't it, big boy? You were splitting for the goddamn *moon,* leaving all of us behind to rot; well, you ain't going. We'll find out where your spaceship is and take it to the moon ourselves, right?"

"*Right, right, right, right,*" they yelled in unison.

"Now where's the fucking spaceship—before I get mad," Stranger said.

Fenton didn't utter a word. The Electrician smiled. "We can use the broken glass . . . they take off their clothes, then we . . ."

"No! First we find out who is in the other building over there," said Carl. "You all keep singing. I don't like it when you stop, big boy," Carl snarled as he dragged one of the suits over and started inspecting it.

Fenton licked sweat from his lips. "You don't want to mess with those spacesuits—they're dangerous."

"We'll see about that—Glue-lady, Electrician—cover these guys, and the rest of us will get into the space suits. Carl the King and all of you are going to the moon, soon, goons." He half sang the weird plan. Helga was the first to crawl into one. Carl put the helmet on her and laughed at the sight of her inside.

"All kinda funny knobs in here," she called out.

Carl was the last to put the helmet on. God it was cool

in here — and warm too, depending on where you pressed the buttons.

"Air-conditioned spacesuits," he yelled over the microphone automatically linking him up to nearly a dozen of the others. "You all ready to go to the moon?" he laughed maniacally.

"Ready to *go*," they yelled back.

"The spaceship must be behind the other house with the chimney smoke. We'll go over there and get it!"

"Get it, get it" they yelled into their suit mikes.

They walked into the other room with ungainly movements. It seemed easy somehow. Carl was surprised he felt so light despite the suit's bulk and weight. And more surprised when he reached for the doorknob and it ripped out in his gloved hand.

"These spacesuits make you super strong" he yelled.

"Strong, strong," they chanted as they headed to the next house.

Fenton was beside himself with rage. These madmen had done what a thousand miles of bandits and renegade troops hadn't. They'd gotten the C.A.D.S. suits! All because *he* let his guard down for a few minutes. "Heaven help us now," he muttered under his breath. He had to warn Sturgis and the others somehow, otherwise everyone's blood would be on him; an entire C.A.D.S. squad wiped out because he hadn't paid close enough attention to the house that was supposed to be a guarded quarters. After all, what could get you out here in the middle of nowhere? But that was always when death struck, when you least expected it.

"Hey you," he screamed over to one of the madmen who had been left behind to guard them, their hands tied behind their backs as they sat around the floor in a tight circle. One of the escapees walked cautiously over to

Fenton.

"Yeah, mister. What the hell do you want?"

"You know you got the ugliest face I've ever seen?" Fenton growled up at the bald-headed obese creature who stared back down at him. "And you're so fat—you look like a big fat piece of pasty white turd. Don't he boys," Fenton said, laughing and looking around at his fellow captives. They saw what direction he was heading and laughed loudly along.

The escapee, a four-time rapist and murderer before he was finally caught and put into the Cragmore Asylum, was growing enraged, his face turning beet red as the prisoners, and even some of his fellow guards, chuckled at the comments.

"And you know what else," Fenton said, lowering his voice to a whisper. "I think you're a queer too—a fucking fairy who . . ."

"Say what you want about the way I look mister," the obese-thing screamed out, nearly foaming at the mouth in fury, "but I ain't no goddamned queer . . . I'm a rapist." With that he aimed the old rifle he was carrying at Fenton and pulled the trigger.

Carl Stranger was having the time of his life inside the C.A.D.S. suit as he headed toward the second house. He was trying to understand all the little blips and printouts on the visor, realizing that they were some kind of sensing devices. Suddenly a shape stood in his way. It was Mary-the-Therapist with her arms upraised.

"Stop. I want to be in a suit too. You left me. They always leave me. I—I," she burst into tears and collapsed into Stranger's arms.

"There, there," the King of the Madmen said, stroking her face. He pulled her tightly against the suit to comfort her and heard a sudden cracking sound. He held her out at arm's length and looked at her. She was dead, trails of blood seeping from her nostrils and eyes. He had crushed her!

"Hey, be careful with these things," he said over the mike. "They kill." He let the body go and it fell to the ground in a heap. Suddenly he heard a shot from behind him. The prisoners. Those in the second house would be alerted. They had to move fast.

"Charge," Stranger screamed. "Kill everyone in the house." Like an invading army from outer space the dozen lunatics moved forward on barely steady legs as they tried to manipulate the immense futuristic battle-suits.

In the other house, Sturgis stirred from his sleep hearing the faint gunshot. Something was wrong! Fenton would never . . . He jumped from the bed and looked out the window.

My God, he thought, rubbing his eyes, those figures in the suits, *waddling* this way couldn't be his men. *Then who the hell was inside those suits?*

He shook awake. *"Men, get up! Get suited. Trouble."* They were into their suits within 30 seconds. They hit the jet packs and smashed right through the bedroom's wide picture window into the air.

"Let's jump over to the other house and see what's happening. Get our men out if they're in trouble," Sturgis said.

"But what about these people in the suits?" Roberto asked. "If they know how to use them . . ."

"Got to get the men safe first," Sturgis ordered. *"Go!"* They jetted down to the back door of the first house and he blasted through the doors using an E-ball.

Sturgis came bounding into the living room at full speed as the armed mental patients swung their weapons up.

"Helmet Light—Maximum intensity," Sturgis screamed

into his mike. A small strip of metal moved down two inches near the top of his helmet and a tube of glass an inch thick and a foot long suddenly burst into brilliant light, illuminating the entire room with blinding intensity. The guards threw their hands to their eyes, dropping their weapons as they cried out *"Blinded—He blinded us!"*

The C.A.D.S. leader rushed over to lightly wounded Fenton, untying him. "What the hell happened?"

"God—I'm sorry," the Englishman blurted out. "We were relaxing and I—It was my fault—mine . . ."

"Well, we'll sort out the blame later. Take care of these guys here," he said, pointing to the lunatics who rolled on the floor screaming. "I've got a goddamned C.A.D.S. suited mini-army to deal with out there."

"Maybe we can reason with them," Roberto said as he and Sturgis swooped down in front of Carl and his cohorts.

"Let's talk," Sturgis yelled on the P.A. microphone as he walked toward the group on the snow-covered lawn. He didn't want to destroy the suits—but if he had to he would—before they could learn how to use the weapons systems.

"Talk," yelled Carl the King. "We are sane, you need treatment—take off your spacesuits. Only *we* are going to the moon. Show us your spaceship, and we'll let you go . . .

They don't know there are weapons in the suits yet . . . Sturgis realized.

"Let's *all* take off the suits and talk. I'm sure we can work this thing out . . ."

"No dice," Carl the King screamed. "The suits stay on!"

"Why not be friends?" Sturgis asked. "You are Americans, we are Americans. The Russians have destroyed our country. We need your help."

"The *insane* have destroyed the world! We are the sane now, and we will judge you," said Carl, his voice amplified to painful levels by his badly-adjusted mike level.

"Would you like me to show you how we fly?" Sturgis asked.

"Yes yes yes yes," chanted the escapees, spread out across the lawn, awesome and frightening in the C.A.D.S. suits.

"You see," said Sturgis, "we don't use a spaceship. We can fly anywhere with these suits."

"I don't believe you," said Carl the King.

"I'll show you. See that button on the left side of the utility belt? The red one that says Active Flight?"

If he could get them up in the air and get them to exhaust their jet packs, they would fall and kill themselves.

"Yes. I see it." said Carl. "So what?"

"Well," said Sturgis, hoping to hell the guy didn't think too well or too fast, "just push those buttons — all of you, then up we go — the little blue button next to it lets you down." The first thing that Sturgis said was true, the second wasn't. The blue button was emergency maximum jet function. It would propel someone who pushed it in mid-air up another 100-200 feet and probably burn out all the fuel pack, leaving them high and dry.

"I don't believe you," said Carl the King. "What do these other buttons do?" He pressed one and said "Hey! This makes you see like a telescope does!"

Soon they were all giggling. "Why I can see the hill — far away," said Axe Lady.

"Now or never," Sturgis said under his breath. "The red button is much more interesting — it makes you fly. I'll show you." He lightly pressed his flight button. "See?" He coasted up easily, hanging about 20 feet off the ground.

"Now you try it," Sturgis yelled down.

Carl did, and laughed. The flight was easy to control, he found, by just shifting his weight. The other mad men and women did the same.

"Now hit the blue button and go down," Sturgis said.

Carl pushed it and cried out in panic as he shot straight up, spinning end-over-end.

"Where'd he go?" yelled the others. "Where where?"

"He's going to the moon, and so are we. Don't be left behind!" said Sturgis, and shot up above them.

"Wheeee, fun," said Axe Lady as she and the others joined in. Within seconds, they were hundreds of feet up spinning out of control. Panic made them hit all the buttons. Machine gun bullets and electroballs went firing this way and that, barely missing other suits. One mad man pointed his index finger at his face and twisted his wrist.

"Scratch one more suit," Sturgis thought grimly as he watched from the side. The whole thing was like a mad circus 200 feet up in the air, with the whole mad crew twisting and turning in mid-air trying to regain their balance.

The screaming mental patients flew this way and that, completely out of control. Two of them collided and spiralled down to earth. Another pointed straight down and hit his emergency power button, rocketing him straight into the ground with such velocity he exploded on impact.

Sturgis' heart bumped. "Christ, another suit destroyed."

"Stop stop, stop . . . No fun no fun!" yelled Electrician as he flew by sideways firing by accident his suit's 55mm guns, catching Sturgis in the chest. The bullets bounced harmlessly off. "Thank God they weren't electro-balls," Sturgis muttered to himself.

The constant and high drain of fuel made the suits begin giving out. They started falling. Sturgis, careful to control his own fuel expenditure, watched them drop one by one. He snagged Carl's suit on the way down and

232

eased him slowly down, harmless and squirming.

"You tricked us, you killed us!" Carl yelled.

"I'm saving you, pal. Your own mistake, fooling around with things you don't understand."

They assessed the damages quickly. While the people in the fallen suits were probably dead, most suits appeared to have withstood the impact and they could probably be used again. Two of the suits were beyond repair.

"Now," Sturgis said, undoing the outer seams of the insane leader's suit. "It's your turn to be locked up."

Sturgis shoved Carl the King and the other six remaining insanos into the garage behind the second house and locked the heavy door. The C.A.D.S. team went back and took the dead bodies out of the suits. Seven had died from the impact.

"What do we do with the living? Execute them?" asked Fenton.

"No," said Sturgis, looking into the sky as a meteor charged brightly across the horizon. "They should be locked away in an asylum, but the whole world is an asylum now. In a way, they're right. Who can say who is crazier, the sane people who blew this planet to hell, or them? We've disarmed them, we'll just leave them. They'll be able to break down that wooden door eventually. From now on we'll move more cautiously. *Always* guards, no matter how safe it seems."

The entire team suited up and headed off into the glowing green dawn as a garage filled with schizophrenics performed a "treatment" on Carl the King, who, they believed, had betrayed and misled them. His screams rang out for nearly a mile, even through the wooden walls of the garage—though there was no one to hear them.

CHAPTER TWENTY-ONE

"Major Turkov, your interrogation room is prepared," the KGB major's underling, Sergeant Sharonsky said. "The female resistance fighter is already in there, ready to be questioned by you."

"And to be taught a lesson, to be taught *fear*. The American people must yield to their Soviet conquerors. That is why Moscow called an expert like myself here all the way from Afghanistan to run this intelligence and counter-espionage unit."

"That is so, Major," Sharonsky saluted. "We understand you are a master of such matters. I await further orders." He clicked his boot heels together and left the room.

Turkov took off his black leather gloves and put on the protective eye goggles which he had been holding. He was exhausted, having only received his orders 24 hours earlier in Kabul. A special jet had flown him as its only passenger to Washington. The commando teams were running into trouble. The resistance had been much better trained and equipped than Russian intelligence had any idea it would be. Thousands of the first waves of Red paratrooper units had been shot to ribbons. The taking of D.C. had slowed to a crawl. Unknown to all their field agents, the Americans—the Army or CIA—*someone* had obviously been training and building up a cadre of fighters for just such an eventuality. They had to have headquarters, a general staff, somewhere nearby. And Turkov would find out where. He had interrogated, a euphemism for 'tortured,' hundreds of fanatical Muslim "Freedom Fighters" in Afghanistan. They had all been tough—faces like beaten metal, lean hard bodies of sinew—but as tough as they were, every one of them had talked. Eventually. He was bone-weary from the non-stop flight, but anxious to begin his work. He was in a very advantageous position. In Afghanistan there had been no room for promotion—the military hierarchy was sealed in place—tight as a tomb. But here, there was much opportunity for advancement.

He was anxious to interrogate this resistance woman, a very young woman, and to find out just how many were in the group she came from, what help had they received from the American forces scattered in the nearby Virginia mountains. And he was anxious to have his own sick brand of fun.

He entered through the steel door of the inter-room and shut it with a loud ominous slam behind him. Sergeant Sharonsky sat at his desk just outside the room and studied reports. But he listened. It was so silent in there. He had seen the men prepare the room hours ago, bringing in implements of torture, and he shuddered. He did not like this kind of thing. But the Americans must be taught a lesson, and the man to do it was the Iron Major of Afghanistan, Major Turkov. The Afghanis called him the Mad White Demon. The sergeant listened. Still silence. When would it begin?

In the room was only a blazing fire and the victim. An iron bucket was glowing softly yellow and red with long metal rods sticking in the coals. Along the wall were whips to slice, scalpels to cut, and tongs to squeeze. A raven-haired girl looked at the man who entered with a mixture of fear and bravado in her eyes. Ellen Tracy from Brooklyn, New York. She had been visiting her aunt in Washington when the bombs hit. Somehow she had survived and somehow she had suddenly found herself handed a pistol and fighting alongside a motley band of dying but courageous Americans. They had taken out scores of Reds—even knocked out two tanks with that favorite American drink, gasoline-filled soda bottles—when the Reds had caught up with them. She had heard a loud crack, blacked out, and when she came to, had found herself tied, hanging by numb wrists here.

The officer approached her. He was wearing his crisply pressed black KGB uniform with red lightning bolts on each collar, his eyes glowing red in the light from the heated brazier that held the torture implements. She was young, he saw, very young, perhaps nineteen—well built. She said nothing, turning her face to the side and pretending not to see him at all. As if her stillness would save her, he thought—as if it would lessen the pain that she would soon bear. She wasn't naked but had a hospital-style one-piece robe of coarse gray material on. The only clothes they were allowed to wear.

He walked over to her and ripped it off in an instant. She was spread open wide, standing upright with her wrists bound tightly above to a pipe and a pole between her ankles keeping her legs wide apart on the concrete floor. She was very short, five feet tall perhaps, and the only thing she had on now were the flat black shoes prisoners were given. But she couldn't even kick at him, as both feet were also chained to rings in the floor. He knew she had been standing like that, practically hanging there, for hours. He wanted her to wait that long to increase her fear, her readiness to feel the pain he so loved to inflict. She whimpered now that she was naked. She hadn't a mark on her yet. Was she a virgin as well? He could see

236

that instantly as he probed her with his finger—quite a resistance in there—that must be broken.

He removed his hand of ice from between her legs as she opened her tearful eyes and whispered, "Please, please . . . I know I fought you. But I have a right to defend my country. If you're going to kill me, do it. But don't hurt me. I've done nothing to deserve it."

Her eyes boiled over with tears. But her pleas only aroused his desire to hurt her even more.

His mouth worked into a grin, a solid wide grin. He pulled back her head by her long black tresses. She groaned, still not meeting his eyes. He stared at her firm young body, so pale, so luminous in the red fire of the coals. Her lips trembled. Her body was strong and healthy, only recently did she lack of food and sleep and warmth. She would be used up and cast away before the radiation ate at her beauty. He stepped backward, his gaze never leaving her, and reached for the red-hot rod in the brazier. He held it with a rag around his hand to keep the heat from singeing his palm. It was a poker, for a fireplace, and its tip glowed white hot . . . crude, and yet the crudest implements of pain seemed to instill the most fear and sensation in their victims.

With the new-fangled electronic torture devices, the victim didn't even know what was going on. But with the implements of old, one could see the poker glowing red hot, could smell the coals, and one's own flesh burning up in sizzling pungent smoke. A multi-sensory experience—the major liked to think of it as an art. And he had had years to work out the application of pain into a fine art.

He came toward the girl who was screaming now, writhing against the chains that held her solidly in place. Her lips framed a desperate *No, no, no,* as he grinned and moved the poker around under her eyes in slow circles.

237

"Now tell me—where are your leaders? What unit of the Resistance are you in? What is your strength?" he asked in broken English.

"I don't know what you're talking about," the pretty teenager croaked back, her throat barely moving from fear. "I'm not in any resistance. I just met these guys yesterday. They gave me a gun and . . ."

"Please, please. Let us not play games here. May I introduce myself? I am Major Turkov, of the Soviet KGB. You may have heard of us. Now you are mine, to do whatever I wish with. If you tell me all you know, I may just let you live. Now again—tell me about your underground forces."

"I swear to *God* mister," Ellen whimpered. "If there is an underground, I ain't part of it. I never even touched a gun before yesterday. There are people all over the city, fighting. Even old ladies and kids. We just—just—felt like we had to do something. I swear. I . . ."

"Have it your way then," the major snarled, growing bored. "Perhaps after some fun, you'll change your mind."

He laughed softly. His other hand unzipped his pants and found his engorged member. He pressed the poker down on the top of her left breast where it sizzled a black mark.

Fainted, already. He was disappointed. He stepped back and removed the poker, pleased at the mark he had made. These Americans were so plump and appealing and the burn looked so much more striking against their white flesh than those scrawny Afghani women he had last year—in that bitter, dusty, primitive land. Kabul, where he had learned how to make pain, how to have pain serve your desires, the pain that made women his. Completely his, forever.

She was slowly reviving and groaning aloud. He stepped forward again after exchanging the poker for the

238

tongs, and he bent to inspect her perfect creamy-white thigh as she screamed for mercy.

In three days she was released. She was silent, her face flaccid, her eyes unseeing, like those of a corpse. She stumbled out of Red headquarters and walked slowly toward her dead aunt's house, not even knowing where she was going, or who she was. Turkov had let her go after he had his fun. He was convinced that, whether or not there even was a resistance, she wasn't part of it. There was *no way* she could have kept anything from him after the things he did to her. Now what he wanted was for the other Americans *to see* what had been done to her. She would be an example of what would happen to all of them now that Major Turkov of Afghanistan was here to enforce the martial law and crush the rag-tag resistance. They would soon surrender now, Turkov thought as he watched her stagger around a bend and disappear. After what he had done to her body, her mind, they would come in and lay down their arms. Fear—the conqueror's ally, the force that could rule the mind without having to fire a bullet. Fear . . .

His reply came three days later. It was a bomb that nearly destroyed the building, hidden in a horse-drawn food wagon. He lost both his arms—and more. A hundred American school children were lined up and shot in reprisal the next day. He saw to that. But he had no hand to torture with any more—and no balls either.

CHAPTER TWENTY-TWO

The Omega Force made good time in the next two days, with St. Louis and the Mississippi River just ahead. Almost halfway to D.C. — then the relatively flat lands of the midwest where they'd made excellent time and, Sturgis knew, start coming in contact with more Reds. They had to; the Russian forces must be coming in from each coast, establishing supply routes rather than risk a drop in the center of the country where they'd be cut off. Thank God the Russian military mind was cautious. It would give them time — time to reorganize, to strike back. Although he scarcely dared to believe it, somewhere in Sturgis' mind was the growing possibility that *they* might actually be able to make a difference. Their suits had worked up to promise so far. They'd been under fire, and used their weaponry. They'd need thousands more — men and suits. But where there had been only darkness in his thoughts the dimmest of lights began burning. Hope springs eternal in the human heart — even after nuclear war.

As they approached the outskirts of St. Louis, decaying bodies began littering the sides of the road, first just a few dozen, then scores, hundreds, until there were bodies everywhere like billboards-for-death along each side of the Interstate. Many of these corpses were in advanced states of decomposure. Their burnt flesh had withered and shriveled away to a dark leathery consistency that gave off a sharp nauseating odor. Their stomachs, inner organs, and faces had all been long eaten away by the food chain of nature's predators who had themselves survived the blast—mice, bugs, rats, and the billion billion bacteria that feed on the dead. The eyes had long been taken as the most delectable of treats by whatever scavenger had arrived first. As they passed, Sturgis kept glancing over into those missing eyes—into darkness, madness, the dividing line between him and them. Many of the bodies had frozen in place carrying out some pitiful gesture in their last moments—reaching as if for water or food, arms extended back toward the road. Perhaps someone with water or food had been passing. Or praying, bony fingers with just a spray of flesh still atop them, clasped so tightly together that no man could now pry them apart—*Take me oh Lord into thy merciful heaven—away from this merciless earth.*

And amidst the dead, and already rotting, were still the living, if one dared call them that. Eyes staring straight ahead, chests moving every 30 or 40 seconds. They sat or lay against the dead bodies of their fellows, using them for blankets and shelter—and waited—waited for the inevitable. A *thing* raised one hand out with pitiful hopelessness as Sturgis and the Omega Team cycled slowly by, careful not to run over any of the outstretched arms or legs that dangled out onto the highway. When the nukes came, Sturgis thought, steeling himself against the horrendous sight of so many of his fellow creatures in such agony—every goddamn person in St. Louis and its environs must have hightailed it out to the major roadways. As if they could escape the writhing red and orange twisting screaming deathwinds of the hydrogen bombs. That's what made atomic weapons different from any weaponry that had ever existed before, Sturgis thought with disgust as the sides of the road became blanketed with bodies. There was no place to hide. No cave, no basement, no ditch, foxhole. You could pull your blankets over your head, or lock yourself inside a 10-foot thick steel bank vault. And it would get you. Those 10-megaton and 20-megaton monsters that spewed out 10,000 or 100,000 times the energy of Hiroshima or Nagasaki, making those first atomic bombs look like puffs of smoke from a cap gun. No, these bombs had the genius of exploding atoms on their side, they didn't have to search—they just found their victims. And they had found all the fleeing masses on the roads—had reached out for nearly 20 miles—the flatlands and highways giving them direct routes to send their heat and winds and radiation at the millions of ants that scampered for cover toward the horizon.

And Sturgis could see that none of the ants had escaped. Not a one. The suit's external mikes only amplified the whispered moans for "water." Everywhere they could hear the call "water—please God, just a sip of water." But Sturgis knew they couldn't stop—couldn't help one of them. They had a mission—more important than any of these *already* dead creatures. To save the president and whatever in hell was left of the government of the United States. Everything else was of no import. Still, Sturgis felt his guts churning as they coldly rode by in their big bikes, with quarts of water in canteens on each one. He knew the men were depressed about it.

Suddenly he clicked on his suit mike that linked him up to the rest of the team via helmet radios. "Boys, I know some of you less hardbitten ones think I should do something to help these suffering people. But we can't. Look. Look on each side. How many are there? A hundred every hundred feet? A thousand? They're all dead—nothing can save them. The thing I didn't teach when I

242

taught you how to use the C.A.D.S suits, fire them, almost fly the damned things, is what war is *really* like. It's like this. Nothing romantic, nothing heroic, no beautiful 'bombs-bursting-in-air'—it's all bullshit. Death is a monster, an all-consuming wretched thing that leaves what was beautiful *ugly*, what was singing, *screaming*. This is it—moaning faces, hands reaching out. Get used to it—you'll see more and more of it. And we can't do one fucking thing about it. If you want to get angry, get angry at the fools who set this whole damned shooting match in motion—get angry at me. But we got to keep riding—like stones."

And it did get worse, as they came up to the edges of St. Louis itself, once a sprawling city of over one million, now with a few half-melted steel frames of the gigantic Arch still standing, the outer facades stripped clean by the howling winds, leaving the blackened beams, reaching up 15, 20 stories, naked, swinging slowly back and forth in the wind, groaning out piercing shrill screams of metal ripping apart from metal.

The bodies grew ever thicker, clogging the streets in some places from end to end. The terror-stricken masses had run from their offices, their apartments. This must have been the only section not at first affected by fire-storm effect. So everyone had crowded here in this flat area—perhaps a park. But the fire-storm had reached here too, in the end, pitting man against man for the little bit of air and coolness. Eventually all had suffocated, or broiled, or were crushed by others trampling them into pulp. It was like a freak show—a circus of the myriad grotesque creations of death's artistic hand—that awful moment of megadeath.

"Slow down, Omega Squad," Sturgis growled over the mike. "We're going to have to ride over them—they're all dead anyway. I just checked them with my rad-meter—hot. Nothing alive for blocks ahead, other than bugs and vermin. So if you're gonna puke, keep on your helmet."

He edged ahead first onto the pile of dead that carpeted the park directly ahead. Piles of shrunken bodies one on another, rising several feet off the ground like a rug of cold flesh. The big front wheel of the Tri-bike easily caught hold of the outer edges of the corpse carpet with its deeply treaded tires, designed to be able to grip just about anything. The big bike moved through the carnage, giving Sturgis a strange sensation as the bike shifted around as corpses beneath it slipped slightly and rearranged themselves under the weight. Like riding on a waterbed of flesh.

Suddenly he noticed motion in the bodies, almost as if something was moving just beneath the surface of the dried up stringy flesh, creating little waves that undulated along arms and legs.

"Jesus," he muttered to himself as he commanded the visor to move to magnifying mode x10. What was just a brownish tinge to the flesh, became clear through magnification as—cockroaches. Thousands, millions of them. He turned his head to another brown wave. An army of roaches was crawling through the mouths, the eyes, the opened chests and stomachs of the uncountable corpses. They had moved right out of the collapsed buildings as soon as the dust settled—and right into these dead people, Sturgis thought. Living inside the bodies, eating the flesh, laying their eggs. Roaches—the inheritors of earth. Rad-proof. They scrambled away as the Tri-bikes rode over their fleshy living quarters, streaming out from each side of the trail of bikes like brown waves pushing up by a ship. They spread out to the right and left until the Rhino, the last vehicle in the force had passed, and then the waves closed back in again, continuing their feasts where they had left off.

The Omega Force reached the halfway mark through the center of the city, which had taken a nearly direct hit from about 5,000 feet up. There was no crater to speak of, but the buildings, the people who had been here, were now just a fine dust — black as the darkest dream — powder that clung to the outsides of the suits and the Tri-wheeler's engines. Sturgis checked the radiation counter readout on the lower portion of his visor — 150 rads — high. Their suits would protect them for awhile but they couldn't take hours of this high exposure. He scanned ahead putting the visor on Telescopic and Macro Views. The blocks ahead of them on the other side of the mile-wide circle of black dust, was all that lay between them and the Mississippi. Once that was crossed . . . Sturgis sighted far ahead until he caught the dark rolling waters of the Mississippi on his screen. There she was — the legendary river. Even a few A-bombs couldn't destroy her — just boil away a few million gallons — which were quickly replaced. He felt a secret joy in his heart that the river *was* still there. The Reds couldn't take every one of America's wonders.

"We're almost there men," he spoke to the rest of the team, moving nervously across the solid packed corpses beneath their wheels. Though one could have scarcely imagined that anything was left in these mummified monstrosities as the bikes rolled over them. The men dared not look down.

Sturgis pulled his field of vision back from the river and scouted the blocks ahead that stood in their way. More bodies of course, and more movement beneath the rotting flesh. But these motions were quick, violent.

"Telescope x20," he ordered the computerized visor. Instantly, the screen zoomed up on the jerking slabs of human flesh. Filthy dark shapes loomed into view — their mangy fur coated with dried sheets of scarlet blood, their toothy mouths ripping chunks of the dead pink and brown and black meat, butchering them apart. Sturgis gulped involuntarily — *the rats* were everywhere ahead, moving like a covering of matted gray fur across the thousands of bodies moldering in the grave below them. Roaches and rats, Sturgis thought darkly. That's what the anti-war scientists had always said. When the big ones get dropped, bye-bye homo sapiens, hello cockroach and rat! God knows, maybe they'd do better with the planet than man had done. He just didn't want to be around to *see* it.

"There's trouble ahead," Sturgis said briskly over the suit mike. "Rats. Lots of them, living among the corpses."

They were just coming out of the blackened central core of the atomic devastation to the once proud city of St. Louis and into the garbage dump of flesh.

"Valves closed on everyone," Sturgis commanded. "And make damned sure you're sealed up tight. Get one rat inside and forget it. I'm sure these things are rabid and carrying a mutated disease or two to boot."

The rest of the crew quickly scanned themselves, making sure all the ziplocks, plastic tabs, and clamps were tightly closed. They rose up onto the second obstacle course of the dead, Sturgis in the lead. The rats closest to the vehicles froze in midstride, their dark ears perked toward the noise. They pulled back slightly as Sturgis approached, but they seemed unafraid. They stood on hind legs and hissed at the lead bike, their nearly 3/4" long curved fangs glistening white against their filth-spattered bodies. Sturgis didn't like the looks of it. Rats were usually much more cautious than this. These were actually challenging him. Maybe they knew that they'd won, and weren't in the mood to take any more guff from mankind. They knew it was their world now and the banquet of bodies was proof. They would feed on the dead of the old world, and from their furtive and unclean ways, a new race would be born.

"Not quite yet," Sturgis thought to himself, snapping out of an unpleasant daydream with huge rats growing human babies for food; of roaches, a hundred times bigger, their writhing mandibles wrapping around human skulls. "Not fucking yet," he mumbled out loud. "Firing a few path-clearers for us," Sturgis said over the mike as the convoy wobbled across the sea of ex-humanity, surrounded on every side by thousands of hissing, snapping rats. He raised his right arm and commanded "Electroball, Fire." Within a fraction of a second, one of the pulsing blue fist-sized globes shot out of its hidden tube and flew two-hundred feet ahead, exploding out a minitornado of human and rat flesh. Then the second, hitting another hundred feet ahead, with the same result. They rode into the carnage, a red mist of blood still hanging in the air, coating their suits like the fine drops of a rainstorm.

But although the immediate path had been cleared, the rats were growing more aggressive by the second, banding together in large concentrations on each side of the line of vehicles.

"I don't think they liked that," Tranh radioed up to Sturgis, three bikes behind him. As if to confirm his words, the hordes of angry rodents suddenly charged in from both flanks. They hit into the bikes and their C.A.D.S-suited drivers in a dizzying storm of leaping, flying, gray and black bodies, endless rows of teeth slashing at their arms and bodies, teeth cracking against their visors. Every man in the unit was covered with the twisting biting things.

"Don't fire," Sturgis screamed over the mike. "You'll hit the person in front of you. Just keep going. They can't get through to you."

"Can't see, can't see," several of the drivers yelled desperately back. "Covered with the damned things."

Although the rats couldn't actually penetrate the suits, if they had bitten on them for the next hundred years, they could inundate the humans. They came in sheer numbers, body after body joining in the pile, trying to drag the ever-slower Tri-bikes to a stop, as dead rat bodies were sucked into the turning wheels and ground out the other end in a red gruel.

"Don't leave your bike," Sturgis ordered, "or . . . "

But Billy had already stepped from the seat, rats hanging onto every square inch of his body. He hit his power-assist jets, and took off straight in the air about 50 feet. The rats flew off from the acceleration and tumbled back down to the moving landscape of brown and black below.

"Sturgis?" Billy yelled through his mike, "these suits of ours rated to withstand LPF fire?"

"For maybe a minute—no longer," Sturgis shouted back, himself slowed now almost to a crawl as a solid wave of the clawing vermin filled his vision. "*Go ahead* man—do your thing—it's our only chance."

"Hang on boys," Billy broadcast to the team. "It's marshmallow time."

He hovered over the force which had slowed to a trifling pace and aimed his right arm down. "Flame on," he commanded the attack system computer. Instantly a stream of brilliant white flame shot out, as if from his gloved fingertips, and poured down over the convoy. The rats were ignited instantly by the flames themselves or the burning stream of liquid plastic that caught onto fur and claws and burned down until there was nothing left. The dark imprisoning net of vermin was suddenly afire, a thousand foot-long meteor, leaping from the suits in mortal agony, diving into their own ranks and setting others on fire. Within seconds the C.A.D.S. unit had been cleansed of the wretched creatures.

"Billy—burn a path ahead of us—all the way to the river. I'll have Chalmers, the bike in front of yours, tie his cable and pull yours."

"Will do Sturg," Dixon replied in his slow southern drawl. He set down for a moment among the glowing fires of rodent flesh beneath him and then jumped up, leaning slightly forward. Though the suits could hover, their fuel was quickly used up, so they had been instructed to keep to jumping rather than actual flying. But reality doesn't pay much heed to the things that are theorized about it. Billy flew thirty feet above the undulating bodies below him, filled to the bursting point with rats and their broods of shrieking young. He let loose with a spray, adjusting the nozzle to about a 20-foot width when it reached the ground. The rats burst into flames everywhere along the path, creating a river of fire that suddenly developed 20,000 channels as the howling rodents tore into the bodies everywhere around them. It felt like he was on a magic carpet, Billy thought, bemused, as he floated in slow motion a hundred-feet ahead of the Omega Squad, burning their way to freedom.

Sturgis shot through the flaming bodies ahead. He knew the tires and the engine were built to take fire, but for how long? They would have to speed up on this highway of flaming fur that Billy was building for them.

"Speed up, everyone. Billy, move faster—don't worry about getting all of them. We'll be right behind you."

He turned the accelerator a quarter stroke and the Tri-wheeler shot ahead up to about 40mph. The flaming bodies squashed beneath the huge spinning wheels, but even though flames licked up at him from below, Sturgis couldn't feel even a rise in temperature inside the controlled suit.

They followed the blazing trail for nearly 20 minutes, at last reaching the waterfront, and a series of rickety, half-burnt docks. The team pulled right up to the water's edge atop a long, concrete roadway that ran along the river. They screeched to a halt as Billy at last touched down.

"That was close," he said to Sturgis, setting down just in front of the still bike. "My fuel gauge reads empty."

"Fuel well spent, my friend," Sturgis said, rising from his Tri-wheeler. The C.A.D.S. suits and bikes as well were coated with matted fur, flecks of rat flesh, and blood. It was a mess. Sturgis turned and looked back. Behind them was a smoking trail of death. Carnage, Sturgis knew, that was already being consumed by those unharmed rodents — eating their flaming brethren while they still lived. But the rats were no longer interested in them anyway. Not one followed in their tracks. Unlike humans, they had short memories.

CHAPTER TWENTY-THREE

Sturgis stood on the edge of the concrete roadway and unloading dock looking out over the Mississippi. He had never actually seen her before except from a high flying jet. She looked majestic, almost awesome, her millions upon millions of gallons collected from the hills flowing with rainwater from the central portion of the country, moving 2,350 miles from Lake Itasca in Minnesota all the way to the Gulf of Mexico and then spitting it all back out again. Sung about in songs, written about in myriad books, the country's most celebrated river conjured up images of the Deep South, of paddleboats, of boys on rafts, of powdered faces of young southern belles sipping mint juleps.

But today the river looked cold, angry, to Sturgis as he snapped open his visor. Thank God for another low-rad reading. The river looked wide, filled with ripping currents that slammed into one another, fighting with watery hands. Sturgis saw a bobbing pink thing several hundred yards out, and pulled the visor back down to get a better look. The Telescopic Mode of the visual sensors went into action and the floating thing came into view. It was a woman or what had once been a woman. And what had looked pink now was a ghastly purplish white, as the bloated, bursting flesh of the woman slid quickly down-river, buffeted about by the four and five foot high waves. Sturgis caught a sudden motion near her head and glanced up. From within the black mouth two glowing orange eyes peered out. He almost jerked back with a start at the gruesome sight, but kept his vision on the corpse's head. A forked tongue suddenly lashed out from between her lips followed several seconds later by the rounded light brown skull of a water moccasin. Christ, Sturgis thought, the damned thing was hitching a ride. The head peeked quickly out, perhaps sensing in some animal instinct that it was being watched—even though from afar. It came out between the shriveled woman's lips several inches, the darting eyes jerking back and forth. But, seeing nothing, it just as quickly pulled back in like a snail into its shell and hid. Then a wave took it and shot the corpse from view.

Sturgis watched for several minutes, trying to get a sense of the currents and eddies, the way the river was moving. He had sent one of the men to check the bridge five miles up-river and the report back had been as he feared. It was out—just a few jagged support beams still standing. "Wasn't hardly a sign of that damned thing," Lyons, the scout, had told Sturgis. "Must have gone down in pieces that the river just swallowed up."

So they'd have to ford the damned thing, somehow. Well, he couldn't say he was surprised. He had assumed things would be bad. As Tranh had once said to him when they were captured by a band of VC, "Hope for the best, prepare for the worst." That advice had never failed to prove accurate.

He watched as more bobbing bodies came into view, moving swiftly down the river—a tree, some random clothing whipping around as if in a washing machine, and the corpse of an immense bloated cow, its ballooned-out flesh making it appear nearly double its already large bulk. The udders had swollen to the size of tires yet still refused to burst. The outer flesh of the damned thing was stronger than its innards—thick leathery hide that would probably explode out in the next day or two as the build-up of gases became too powerful—and cow's guts and rotting steaks would fly through the air. Great—he'd miss that barbecue.

He pointed his arm straight out so it was aimed at the center of the river. "Rad-reading," he commanded the suit's computer. In a second the readout appeared at the bottom of the visor, small glowing letters moving rapidly by: "Radiation count averages to 2.3 rads to 5.6. Acceptable level for human tolerance. Within C.A.D.S suits exposure up to two hours no detectable exposure."

"All right men, we're going to have to cross the damned water ourselves," Sturgis said, turning around and addressing the team. The men had desuited and were stretching their aching bodies. Hour after hour inside the immense C.A.D.S suit took its toll. Now, walking around even in their warm army fatigues, they felt almost naked.

"Cross that?" Rossiter asked, his big belly half falling out of his khaki pants. "Don't look too friendly. And I can't swim."

"No, we're not going to do any swimming, at least I hope not," Sturgis laughed. "No, the thing that separates man from the duck is the raft. We'll build some."

Sturgis quickly set the men to work tearing up lengths of logs from the pier that were not waterlogged and still in one piece. They dragged the wood piece by piece to the edge of the concrete unloading dock where they laid them side by side. Sturgis and Tranh, who had made similar rafts from bamboo stalks years before, supervised the tying of the ropes—500 pound-test cable from the emergency supply storage panel in their Tri-bikes, just behind the seat. The ropes were woven back and forth among the logs, constantly being wetted down and stretched, and then tightened up again so that when they hit the water they wouldn't suddenly expand and come loose. There was nothing like sitting in the middle of a raging river with the raft beneath your feet turning into a mass of twisting logs. Sturgis had been through that particular scene as well. That's why he had the men pull the ropes again and again, constantly rearranging the logs, much to their torn hands' discomfort.

It took nearly a day to get the three makeshift craft assembled, but at last the final knot was tied and the team pulled back to admire their handiwork.

"I know they don't look like much," Sturgis said as he walked around the 20 X 20 foot tightly bound foot-thick logs, weatherbeaten and knotted, "but I swear to you, they'll go."

"Yeah right," Roberto said, eying the crude vessels suspiciously. He had his own memory of a raft—that he and three friends had made and took for a quick spin in the East River when he was a young teenager. That had come apart within minutes under the constant buffeting of the strong East River currents. The four Puerto Rican youths had hung on for dear life as not a one could swim. And only the fortuitous entrance of a patrolling police boat had saved their asses.

"Tell me, these suits of ours," Roberto asked Sturgis, "they got those emergency blow-raft things? You know, that pop out if something goes wrong?"

"Sorry pal," Sturgis said with a grin. "That's in the newer model—it wasn't ready yet." As it was once again growing dark with a thick cloud cover moving in from the north, Sturgis decided to camp right on the dock for the night and get moving first thing in the morning. They'd need to be rested, there couldn't be any mistakes. During the night, small bands of rats moved in, smelling the odors of the food the squad had eaten. But the two guards sent them scurrying with a few quick blasts of

LPF—and they didn't pay a second visit.

The sun rose like a soggy cotton ball trying to rub through the brownish haze that now hung constantly over them, miles up, like an old unwashed blanket. They rose quickly and after having some coffee, heated over a small electric stove attached to one of the Tri-bike batteries, they suited up and prepared to launch the rafts.

Keeping a long rope attached to the end of each raft at one end and tied to a large steel mooring post on the other, they heaved the craft one at a time into the rushing water some ten feet below. The first hit the water with a gargantuan splash, landing almost flat on its stomach. It bounced around for a few seconds as if getting used to the waters and then settled down, bobbing evenly up and down with not a log moving out of place.

"Looks good," Fenton yelled out, leaning over the edge. "She's holding."

Utilizing the power of their suits, moving the rafts was fairly easy, a task that could have taken hours was done in seconds. The second and slightly larger raft hit the water sideways, and dove down almost thirty feet on its edge, disappearing completely beneath the river. The men's eyes opened wide in shock, but almost instantly the thing shot back up out of the water, 5 feet into the air, and then flopped over on its side and was still. The third was dumped as well and Sturgis jumped down onto it, testing the buoyance and slickness. He jumped up and down inside his suit, his hand on the Super Thrust button just in case. But all three held, even under his pumping steel boots. They'd have to take the chance.

The three log rafts were pulled alongside the loading dock several hundred yards, to a long concrete ramp that slanted right down into the water. The men drove their bikes on, one at a time, filling up all three with little room to spare. Then the Rhino moved down to the water's edge.

The Rhino—a marvel of computerized high-tech equipment incorporated into a rugged battlewagon. Aside from being equipped with a virtual armory of weapons, the heavily armored oval-shaped vehicle standing 15 feet high on its four eight-foot in diameter black tires, could also be turned at least temporarily into a water vehicle. The thick grooved treads on the completely spherical wheels could be used to push the Rhino like paddlewheels. Primitive, but it worked.

"You got her all sealed up tight?" Sturgis asked Fenton, seated inside the oddly shaped craft. Since its design was based on the vehicle that NASA had used on the moon, it was hardly surprising that it didn't quite look as if it was meant for this earth.

"Sealed tight as a tomb," Fenton answered cheerfully.

"And you're positive you're clear about the water-mode functions of the controls?" Sturgis asked nervously. He knew Fenton was as good as they came in the use of the Rhino. He had been training on the damned thing for nearly eight months, on loan from her Majesty's Special Forces—to bring them back one and instruct in its usage. The war had changed all that.

"I'm clear, I'm clear," Fenton said in mock anger as Sturgis asked him for the third time in the last five minutes. "Now let me get out there—and as you Yanks say, do my thing."

Sturgis had half a mind to steer the blasted contraption himself. But he knew he couldn't worry about every man's capabilities in his unit. Besides, he had a bigger responsibility to the unit itself, and to the president. Still, as one of the designers of the Rhino who had helped along in every one of the modifications, and as someone who had put thousands of hours inside the claustrophobic tank, Sturgis couldn't help but wish he was inside it.

Fenton drove the Rhino down to the water and with the hatch open on top just in case the worst happened, he slowly headed out into the quickly moving currents. With its bottom air-tight, and the very design of the craft made to keep its weight centered and low, the Rhino took to the water like a fish. Fenton tested the controls, pushing the wheels forward at a slow speed. The grooved treads worked, catching the liquid and paddling the Rhino along at a good clip. Fenton put her in reverse and then turned the thing, only the top five feet of the ovular body still above the water line.

"Works like a charm," he broadcast to Sturgis over the mike. "Let's get going."

"So — we'll do it one raft at a time. You have any problems at all, you're to head right back here. Don't be a hero. Okay my limey friend?"

"Heros went out with Benedict Arnold — or was it Nathan Hale? I never could get your American myths quite sorted out in my head."

Fenton backed the Rhino up until it was just touching the first raft in line. The men on it tied the cable he electronically fed out of the back of the Rhino centerpoint on the bow of their long raft. They tested everything again and then Fenton slowly started forward.

The first 50 feet or so were easy going. The Rhino pulled its load along without any slipping or jerks. But as soon as they hit the first wild ripping currents of the river things got a little hairier. The back end of the Rhino tilted around to the side under the force of the current as the spinning tires dug deep into the water straining the craft ahead. But the raft, also caught by the river's pull, began swinging slowly around straight into the flow. Within seconds the Rhino was also pulled back around by the stern end and dragged back by its log load.

"Angle it, *angle it*!" Sturgis yelled out from shore as the makeshift ferry struggled under his watchful eyes. "You can't go straight against the river, so go into her at a slower angle. You might have to go upriver a ways."

257

"I hear you Sturg. Will do. The Rhino itself feels secure and she's pulling like a damn locomotive."

Fenton turned the craft away from the near shore and started slicing at a 45 degree angle into the Mississippi. They were still pushed down, but at the same time Fenton was able to slowly chug his way across, getting over about a hundred feet for every hundred they were sucked down river. The men on the raft held onto the sides of their Triwheelers for dear life. They stood in their seats as far from the edges of the raft as possible, telling dirty jokes to one another to keep their spirits up. If there was trouble they had a chance to rocket up—maybe—but once they were in the water, they'd be dragged down as surely as if concrete blocks were tied to their ankles. Every slap of the river's waves against the fragile craft brought that fact squarely to their attention.

But Fenton's turtle-like chugging at just the right angle-of-attack brought them, within ten minutes, to the other shore where they quickly debarked riding their bikes onto the gravel.

"That'll be one hundred bucks apiece boys, in cash," Fenton barked over the helmet radio as they untied the raft, "seeing as how this is the only ferryboat for, oh, say five thousand miles give or take a few."

"Do you take credit cards?" Roberto asked, happy to be on land again.

"Bank of London, ole boy. I'll collect in a few minutes." The Rhino headed back across, now nearly a mile and a half down river from the team waiting on the other side. But without the heavy load he found the return trip easy and virtually steamed across.

"Say, I'm rather getting to like this," the Englishman said as he pulled up to the second raft, edging the Rhino in backwards as surely as an acne'd teenager in a parking lot. "Father was in locomotives, you know," he grunted out over the radio so the whole team could hear, as they

258

drove their bikes carefully aboard. "I guess it runs in my blood."

Sturgis was glad for Fenton's mindless rantings. It took the men's minds off the real danger they faced. Sturgis knew he should make more of an effort at joking with them, trying to relieve their fears. But somehow he wasn't up to it. He had his own problems—like Robin. Sometimes he wondered if he was even cut out for this leader stuff. He had felt most happy when out in the field on his own—or with one man who was his equal. No one else to worry about. He sighed deeply watching from the causeway above as the last of the Tri's lurched up onto the raft and was tied down.

Again the Rhino headed out, Fenton this time immediately heading into the right angle for cutting through the currents. Within seconds he was pumping comfortably across the two-mile wide expanse of churning brown water. They made it nearly to the center when Fenton spotted a strange whirling current just ahead of the Rhino. But when he glanced back, it seemed to be gone. Suddenly he felt a spinning motion as the world outside began revolving around him. They were caught—trapped inside a whirlpool. Fenton's head emerged from the hatchway at the top of the Rhino. He and the Rhino were caught dead center in a wide funnel of water, turning them like a record, around and around. They were up on the cresting edge of the circle, but in the center the water grew dark and seemed to be sucking everything that came near it—straight down. Fenton put the Rhino into a higher gear and floored the accelerator, sending the wheels spinning. But the force of the whirlpool was too great, and slowly, inexorably, they were drawn down and toward the dark eye of the grinding spout.

Suddenly the walls of the funnel seemed to rise around them as the raft was tilted almost sideways, now pulling the Rhino backward with it. Three of the Tri-bikes were snapped from their ties around the logs and were flung through water, their suited drivers still inside them. Every man in the unit could hear their desperate screams as they landed right in the black funnel at the center of the spout and were instantly sucked down. The cries lasted for nearly a minute and then ceased.

"Jesus Christ," Sturgis muttered to himself as he watched the disaster unfolding through his visor, a mile away back on the dock. "Throw it in reverse," he screamed through the mike. "Fenton, put her in reverse and then give her every bit of power you can," Sturgis ordered. He waited long seconds, growing almost pale as he feared the worst. But suddenly the Englishman's voice sprang into his ears.

"Trying, Sturgis. It's bad out here."

Sturgis watched as the foaming water around the spinning wheels stopped. Fenton was flipping the engage switch. The raft, now pulling the Rhino, was angled almost upright now as it slid down the water walls into the waiting drain below. There couldn't be more than seconds left before the whole raft and everything on board would be lost. Fenton eased up then suddenly floored it. The craft shot backwards slamming into the raft. The force of the Rhino was now going *with* the spiraling current and the extra energy lifted the raft right up the side of the wall of water, pushing it over the top like a surfboard. The Rhino followed seconds later, the huge spherical wheels clawing at the top of the 15-foot high crests around the funnel. They splashed down on the outer edge of the thing as it moved off, whipping through the water at wild angles, as if searching for something to replace the prize that had just escaped from its jaws.

Fenton slammed the Rhino back into forward and took off, once again dragging the raft just behind the all-consuming spiral. He breathed out once they were past it and the rest of the journey was uneventful—except three more

260

men and bikes were gone—and they hadn't even faced the Reds yet. Fenton unloaded the men and then wearily turned the craft around and headed once more toward the western bank. The strain was starting to wear him down.

"What the hell happened out there," Sturgis asked as Fenton pulled up to shore and the remaining Tri-wheelers were loaded aboard the raft.

"Don't ask me—this big goddamned water funnel just snuck up on us out of nowhere and . . ."

"Shit. At this rate there'll be none of us left to get the president," Sturgis exploded.

"Did my best," Fenton replied, somewhat offended. "It's not like you can do that much when a million gallons of water starts pulling you down."

"Yeah. Sorry," Sturgis said over the suit mike. "The strain's getting to all of us."

Sturgis had never even heard of water funnels like that in the Mississippi or any river for that matter. Whirlpools usually occurred only in ocean waters. But God knows what the bombs had done—created more water cascading into her, opened new channels along the edges. Something had been tampered with—the river that had once given life to America was now a source of death as well. An enemy in her very belly.

"Well, let's go," Sturgis said, the last one on the raft as he tied himself down. "Move upstream from that whirlpool if you can, this trip."

At last they were all on the other side, drying themselves and their equipment from the somewhat violent crossing. Sturgis had a strange look on his face as he walked over to Tranh and asked him to take a walk. They had gone only about thirty yards when Sturgis lifted his face visor and told Tranh to switch all his C.A.D.S. suit's communications systems off for a moment.

261

"I've got to talk to you about something," Sturgis said with as soft a tone as the Vietnamese had ever heard. "In private. Don't want anyone listening in." The two men walked over a low rise to make sure they were out of any of the team's aural pick-up capabilities. Sturgis found a relatively flat-topped rock and sat down on it. He looked up at Tranh who stood next to him, waiting.

"Man—I've got problems," the C.A.D.S. leader at last blurted out, his eyes fixed on the blackish-tinted soil below him as if he could barely face his long-time friend. "Mental problems," he added cryptically.

"Yeah, I know pal," Tranh said softly. "It's hard out here. We thought we'd seen some bad stuff over there in 'Nam, but this is turning out to make that look like a romp through Disneyland."

"No—no, it's not the bodies or the blood, or any of that. It's—it's. Tranh—my heart—my brain—they feel like they're being torn apart. I want to find Robin—got to find her, but I can't leave the team here. I guess it's a problem men have faced since the first fucking war back in the Stone Age. Blood versus love. And *I'm* supposed to be the tough guy here—the guy with no feelings who can just go on and on forever. But I'm telling you, man, it's starting to eat me up alive. I see her face in my dreams, nightmares I should call them—because—because in my gut I know she's still alive. But I don't know for how long . . ."

"Once we get the president and his staff out of D.C. and back to White Sands, maybe then you could come looking for her," Tranh said, trying to find a solution.

"I don't think I can wait that long, pal," Sturgis said, putting his hands over his face as if he were in real mental anguish. "I—I've decided—that once we've got the president—and we're safely out of D.C.—say fifty—seventy-five miles, I'm splitting, man. I'm going to find her." He looked up at the Vietnamese with plaintive eyes, as if seeking the man who was his closest friend's approval. But Tranh only looked his usual cool neutral self.

"Sturg, I am your friend but I can't advise you on something like this. I'm sure you're already aware you would face a court martial and all that bull when—if—you get back. And knowing you—that's not the problem."

"No—it's leaving the men. I'm responsible for them whether I want to be or not. But Tranh—I'm also a man—with a woman I love. It's not like I can call her up and find out if things are okay. It's a whole new ball game now. Every man for himself. And if you love someone, you damned well better make sure they're going to survive, because I know there's no one else to help her but me."

"I can't, I can't—" the Vietnamese struggled to find the right words for the first time since he and Sturgis had been friends.

"I'm not really asking for your advice," Sturgis said with a quick smile, not wanting to put his friend in the same painful mental state he was in. "I guess I just had to tell someone—a confession as it were. Anyway—I'm going to do it. Once I know that we're out of danger—I'm heading for the farm—and Robin. I—I want you to take over for me. I can't face the men—so tell them after I'm gone. We can link up some kind of emergency signal system between our suits—so if things get hot you can let me know—and I swear whatever is happening—I'll get back."

"All right Sturgis," the Vietnamese-American answered. He didn't like it, but he knew once Sturgis' mind was made up all the minions of hell itself couldn't change it.

CHAPTER TWENTY-FOUR

Admiral Voloshnikov rubbed his hands together as he stared at the naval screen in the control room of his submarine. It depicted total Soviet victory at sea. He moved into the Air Theatre center, where his second in command Sterzinski saluted, and reported:

"Your brilliant tactics have worked. The Soviet bomber force has discharged its duty and the American cities and ICB bases are nothing but craters now—as are the naval ports, for the most part. The crippling blow has been delivered. Soon, the coup de grace—paratroop forces are about to seal off President Armstrong. We know that he is still alive in an underground bunker. We've monitored their sub-frequency radio messages to S.A.C., before we knocked out Colorado, that is."

"Excellent," Voloshnikov declared. "And within two days Petrin's Raiders—the Gray Suits—will be well into Washington. But now, adjourn to the banquet prepared in the main dining area. Your subordinates will carry out the monitoring of further developments for a time."

"But," Sterzinski began to protest.

"Sasha, this is the time to *celebrate*. The exhilarating defeat of the United States and her mongrel allies has occurred. Come." He wrapped an arm around the stiff-collared officer, a sharp contrast to himself in his casual slacks and silk shirt and stylish haircut.

They entered the plush Blue Room of the sub—the heavy blue drapery giving it its name. It was modeled after the famous Rainbow salon of the Tsar's summer mansion.

That had been Voloshnikov's idea, the banquet also. These northern Russians (he was Georgian) never knew how or when to have a good time. They were seated by a midshipman serving as a waiter and ordered drinks to start. Mazursky dancers began doing handstands and wild cossack steps as they sprinted around the open central portion of the dining area.

Voloshnikov clapped his hands loudly together in time to the music, and, after several drinks, went out and joined them for a minute before returning red-faced and sweating to the table. Soon, the most sumptuous banquet ever held on a naval vessel, of that he was sure, was served on four long tables against the back wall. The dancers continued their antics accompanied by spirited music from the balalaika orchestra off to the side. Voloshnikov wished the room could have been bigger—but at 20 × 30 meters it was the largest submarine-room ever created—a marvel of engineering and pressure resistance. In the center of the 560 meter long Soviet submarine, the banquet hall had been turned into a virtual Roman triumph, as the extent of the victory became known throughout the ship. It seemed as if they were in the Kremlin itself, not countless fathoms under the Atlantic.

"Eat, eat," he said, laughing as one set of waiters filled cups from steaming samovars full of aromatic teas, and another set poured vodka—straight—into crystal glasses. "The American fools drink mixed drinks and have terrible stomach problems," Voloshnikov stated. "Only the pure air of the steppes for us, and the pure straight vodka of life—eh, Sasha?"

His assistant could only smile broadly at each of the admiral's pronouncements.

The music grew louder and the general looked around in trembling ecstasy. It was rampant bourgeois. No—make that *capitalistic* excess! A banquet that the eyes of everyone present ran over with lust—pyramids of champagne glasses, mounds of paté, and bleeding slabs of beef. Slices of tender veal piled a foot high on silver platters, whole bins of pastries, oozing goblets of sauces, bowls of caviar. He ordered the frenzied waiters to bring him everything, including dessert, all at once. They obeyed.

"Sasha, Sasha!" admonished Voloshnikov looking at his almost motionless, soused underling. "Are you insane? Eat—eat. There is more where this came from." He rose and toasted to the tables filled with naval, army, and air-force brass, and their female "secretaries." Coarse laughter and conversation slowly died down as Voloshnikov banged with a serving spoon on the table.

"To the defeat of America, to the victory of the great and proud Soviet peoples, to the premier, and most of all—to victory."

They drank their glasses full of burning vodka down, then slammed their glasses against the wall, shattering them. Voloshnikov settled down to a feast.

Once he had been in New York's 21 Club, and they had made him wait for a table. He laughed. Now that waiter and the maitre-d, who didn't think Soviet diplomats more important than Charlton Heston, seating him before them, were all vaporized along with their wives, children, and stupid American cats—a creature he detested. Good riddance. The American mongrel race—Irish, Italian, Hispanic, Blacks—and their stupid, idiotic television-and-car culture finally dead. A race without real tradition or culture—just TV dinners and Wall Street stock manipulators. A culture of infinite sexual perversions shown even on their television screens where even young children could watch it all. He had seen one porno video once—disgusting. A race of filthy-minded capitalist swine. Better they were wiped from the face of the earth, and that the children—those still alive—would grow up to be communist pioneers in the new world.

America had a few things he liked—Disneyworld, the Niagara Falls. He wondered if the falls still fell or if they had been leveled off into a swirling rapids by the heat of the blast that took out Toronto and Rome, New York, site of a large U.S. Air Base. He smiled—they'd never gotten those B1s off the ground in Rome—nor almost anywhere else on the North American continent. It was a devastating blow, and a complete surprise. He thought of the medals that would be given out at the Kremlin soon, a river, a sea of medals for everyone. And the parade. *That* would be the parade of parades. That would stretch on for days, as the conquering generals and admirals of the Russian occupying forces came home to receive their accolades. "To the Russian soldier *Sasha*," Voloshnikov sputtered through drunken lips to the already unconscious Sterzinski. "The greatest fighting man in the world!"

CHAPTER TWENTY-FIVE

They came up from the Gulf of Mexico blazing a trail of destruction. Five hundred men strong, they wore American army uniforms, but were Cubans. Part of Castro's elite overseas force, sent into the U.S. two days after the bombs had struck, under the Russian code name "Trojan Horse." They were a part of a plan to attack the U.S. from within—a Fifth Column. When the word was given, Russian, East European, and Cuban agents already in the U.S. began to sabotage every military and governmental facility in sight. As Russian regular forces drove in from the east coast, meeting increasingly heavy and surprising resistance at every foot along the way, the attackers *from within* began carrying out their dirty work. They bombed military bases, police stations, national guard units, as well as destroying certain select power stations, bridges, airports and railroads. The intent: stopping the Americans from using them, while doing minimal damage to property so that Russian troops, once in total control, could begin resurrecting facilities for their own use. They struck from everywhere, disguised as anything from police to bands of war-survivors wearing tattered clothes. They came out of nowhere, carried out their destruction, and faded back into the surrounding devastation. Normally, American citizens would have seen them and reported them. But these were not normal times. What few police or military authorities were left were in shambles, with many of their men dead or wounded, their bases and equipment not in working order, and their communications with other forces virtually non existent. It was every man and every thing for itself in this post-war world and the Fifth Column forces were more than willing to take every advantage of that fact.

The "Che Guevera Squadron" had left Cuba in two heavily armored fishing boats just 12 hours after the bombs struck. Even from the Communist island they could see the glow in the sky far north in southern Florida—dim orange hemispheres that seemed to rise up miles above the earth as if lighting the scenes of devastation below. They were all the toughest, most ruthless of the Cuban special forces. Their scarred faces and blood-christened hands did not ask questions—but just killed. For Castro was a clever man. He had three ways of dealing with his incorrigibles, his criminals: 1, shoot them, 2, send them to America on leaking fishing boats where they could cause their own mayhem on capitalism, and 3, take the absolute meanest and most psychotic of the lot and turn them into killers-for-the-state. These were the men of the Che Brigade—murderers, rapists, destroyers of everything they had laid their hands on. And now they were to be turned loose on the already reeling citizenry of the U.S.

They had landed on luxurious Miami's sandy shores in the still hours of the morning, wading through the low waves loaded down with equipment. The people who had come to sleep along the beach were quickly disposed of. Once fully ashore with their supplies and vehicles the 500-man brigade began a long march north, destroying everything they could in their path. It was like Sherman's march through Georgia which had left the South in ruination and flames—only now it was Spanish-speaking butchers who sought only to bring down the United States of America. The small national guard units they came to at the northern limit of Miami looked on in utter confusion as what appeared to be a large detachment of regular U.S. Army troops in full battle gear marched right up to their checkpoint.

"Howdy," the Cuban lieutenant in the lead jeep said, a toothpick poking from between twisted front teeth.

"Where the hell you guys come from?" the sergeant in charge of the blockade asked.

"You guessed it," Lieutenant Salizar, the leader of the Cuban forces smirked—"Hell." He snapped up his automatic Kalashnikov II with cut-off 12-inch barrel and let off a long burst that sliced the sergeant in two. Behind Salizar the rest of his forces opened up, concentrating all their firepower on the dozen or so American reservists who died where they stood, unable to even raise their weapons.

Salizar was Cuban born, but educated in America through high school, at which point, bitter about his dismal chances of getting anywhere and the desolated ghetto in which he lived, he returned to Cuba to see if things were any different. Castro loved those who returned to his island outpost from the U.S. Once he was sure they weren't agents they were welcomed with open arms, given apartments and stipends from the government. Salizar had spent his first three years back in Cuba going from school to school, factory to agricultural commune, giving speeches on how awful America was, and how wonderful, of course, Cuba was. A regular paradise for the workers. But even *he* became bored of it all after a while and managed to get himself put into a more challenging line of work—murder. He had excelled, joining Castro's all-purpose death squads—equally capable of being used overseas in Angola, N.caragua, and El Salvador, as well as in Cuba itself.

Salizar glanced over at his second-in-command, Ramon Cordoza. "Think we will have fun here?" he laughed, his gold-filled cavities sparkling like myriad fires from his opened jaws.

"For me," Ramon answered, through a roughly cut beard reminiscent of Che's, "the fun begins when we get the women." He put his hand on his groin. "I will start repopulating this country with Cubans all by myself."

He threw his dark head back sharply as some of the killer force standing near the lead jeep grinned at the macho words.

"For me," Salizar replied, throwing the armored vehicle back into gear and shooting forward, "I take my fun where I find it. There is a pleasure in taking a woman it is true—but there's even more intense pleasure when I take a life, or many lives. It is total domination on my part—and total surrender on theirs. No Ramon, for me, there is nothing finer than looking over a field of dead that I have slain and knowing that because of me they no longer exist."

Ramon gave out with a nervous laugh at his leader's words and looked straight ahead as the jeep crashed through the thin wooden barricade that blocked the interstate.

Both men quickly had their wishes fulfilled—for there were women aplenty and disorganized resistance at each new community. The Cubans played it the same at every stop, pulling right up to whatever barricade had been erected, and bringing their forces right up the unsuspecting defenders.

271

Lieutenant Salizar joked reassuringly, sitting in the jeep telling them in his Bronx-tinged accent that they no longer had anything to fear, that the "GI's" had come to take care of biz. The moment the guards relaxed and lowered their weapons the Cuban battalion would open up with everything they had leaving ponds of hot blood where there had once been living men. Then they made their way into the town or base taking what they wanted, raping the women and then killing them or not as their mood dictated. There were no rules that these killers had to follow — not from Castro, nor from Salizar, nor from their own non-existent consciences. So anything went. They left a trail of corpses and screams all the way through the south.

The C.A.D.S. team thundered down the straight flat highway of eastern Kentucky like a herd of metal buffalo, unafraid, unstoppable. They were making the best time of their trek east to date, with the four-lane interstate free of rubble for 40 to 50 miles at a stretch. Sturgis looked down at the green digital readout on the speedometer of the Tri-wheeler control panel — miniaturized and filled with enough dials, arrows, and computerized three-dimensional images of the road a mile ahead to make a spaceship proud. His trained eyes instantly took in the nearly 50 instrumentation readings. His oil temperature was up but nothing to worry about. Tires could use a few more pounds of air — but he'd wait until they stopped. His main concern was time. They'd been on the road for nearly seven days now and still were at least two to three days outside of Washington. And Sturgis had no way of knowing whether the president — whether anyone — was even still alive there. All this effort perhaps for nothing. Maybe they would reach the bunker and find nothing but half-melted skeletons, grinning at them, mocking them for their wasted efforts. Ahh—got to banish such thoughts from my head, Sturgis muttered to himself as he quickly scanned the radar readout of the next few miles of road—clear as the day it was built.

With the wind whistling through his helmet, the visor half-up, allowing Sturgis to breathe in the cool, refreshing air, he almost felt, dare he say it—good. If there hadn't just been a nuclear war, if his heart wasn't aching in worry over Robin—he could just relax and enjoy the ride as he lay almost straight backwards in this throbbing Tri-wheeler, only inches from the ground, the road moving below him in a blur. At least the sky seemed to be opening a little, brightening after a week of gray. The sun was actually burning through, as if making little holes of fire through the ceiling of slowly twisting clouds. He checked his reverse radar—18 blips followed right behind him, in rock steady courses ten feet apart. He suddenly felt a surge of affection for them. Every damned one of them believed in his heart that he would not come back from this mission. And Sturgis had the same sort of premonition himself. And yet, not a man had complained, or shown even the slightest trace of cowardice. Sturgis had been in many battles, many wars, in his life, and he swore that this was the finest team he had ever worked with. Perhaps it was the knowledge that things were so bad. After all, there wasn't a hell of a lot more to lose. Except their lives. And they seemed more than willing to make that final sacrifice if it could help even one iota. He would be proud to die with them. If a man has to go, let it be with other men whose eyes don't flinch when death comes calling.

He saw a yellow line bisect the road and a large metal sign off the side, coated with a fine black powder but still legible—"WELCOME TO THE COAL MINING STATE OF WEST VIRGINIA".

"We're on our way, men," Sturgis said over the helmet

mike. "If the interstate stays clear, we should be at rendezvous in 24 hours." They all let out muffled cheers into their mikes, in a long spread-out line behind him. "So nobody get a flat or an appendix attack—all right?" A few chuckles could be heard over the suit radio. But life doesn't accede to the desires of men—rather the opposite. The C.A.D.S. team had gone on another 20 miles or so when a printout flashed across the bottom of Sturgis' visor.

"Picking up radio distress signal on 26.7 megahertz."

"Hook me in," Sturgis commanded the suit. There was a buzzing static as the computer zeroed in on the signal. Suddenly he heard it—a man's voice—desperate, terrified.

"Anyone, anyone out there—we're being attacked by men wearing U.S. Army uniforms. They're massacring everyone. I repeat—anyone out there? This is Carterville, West Virginia. Please help—"

Sturgis suddenly heard what sounded like the sound of voices behind the man transmitting the pleas. Then the unmistakable crack of automatic gunfire.

"What the hell is this?" a foreign accented voice spoke out as Sturgis listened. "Whoever is out there," the voice continued, "it is all over for this town. But there will be more, many more."

The ominous threat was followed by coarse laughter and then the line went instantly dead as if a wire had been suddenly pulled.

"Fenton," Sturgis said over the suit radio, "check maps of West Virginia. a town called Carterville. We anywhere near there?"

Fenton quickly keyed the requested data into the Rhino's computer. The large vehicle had among other special features a detailed map of the entire country, with literally every little town, village, stream and back road in its data banks. Within seconds a close-up map of western

274

West Virginia sprang onto his control monitor.

"Got it here, Sturgis," Fenton said from the Rhino, which tore along at the rear of the fleet of Tri-bikes. "We're about ten miles west of it, maybe five miles north. We'll be passing the exit in about four miles. According to the maps, there's a two lane asphalt road that leads right into the town. Population is about five thousand — no military bases or large industry. What do you think?"

"I think we're going to take a quick detour," Sturgis replied. He knew they couldn't police the entire country, but on the other hand they couldn't turn down such a desperate cry for help. God knew what was going on there.

"Can we afford the time?" asked Fenton's concerned voice over the radio.

"Yes. If we don't dawdle. We're ahead of schedule for rendezvous, and it wouldn't do to get there too far ahead of the other C.A.D.S. squads."

The column veered off onto the exit. Ideally, this is how the C.A.D.S. force should be used — not just to fight the Reds, but to become a roving police force, Sturgis thought, dispensing justice where it was needed. What was it they had called them — Texas Rangers — men who would ride into the jaws of hell with just their horse and a six-gun?

Perhaps the C.A.D.S. team was the twentieth century version of the Rangers — with 100,000 times their firepower. Perhaps if a few lessons were taught to those who revelled in their savagery, the word would get around. You can choose to be a barbarian, a murderer, but there are men out there, roving the nuclear wastelands, giants clothed in metal who appear out of nowhere and avenge those too weak or outnumbered to fight their own battles.

"Yes" Sturgis said to himself under his breath as he straightened the Tri-wheeler out from the long curving exit ramp and opened up down the two-laner leading to Carterville. Yes, there would have to be such men, fighting the forces of nihilism itself. In his years in counter-insurgency, Sturgis had traveled around the globe and had seen man at his worst, his most double-dealing and ruthless. And he had even doubted his own work — for many times the U.S. was carrying out Machiavellian conspiracies that rivaled the worst that the Reds had done. But he had closed his eyes and done his job. But now the battle was pure. Those who preyed on the wounded America and her surviving citizens would die — when he found them. There would be no doubts, no hesitations this time.

"We're going in, men," Sturgis spat into his helmet mike. "I don't know what the hell we're going to find, but be ready for anything. Don't let your concentration down for a second."

Ahead Sturgis could see the rooftops of Carterville, some two miles up the road. "Macro-view," he commanded the C.A.D.S. computer. The image on the lower portion of his visor shot forward as if his eyes were being shot from a cannon. The rooftops came into clear focus as if he were just feet away. He could barely catch the movement of men and vehicles between two rows of houses. But the attacking force, whatever it was, was probably spread out throughout the town. "Mode Blue," he told the suit, as he slowed the Tri-wheeler a notch. The C.A.D.S. manual gave the definition of Mode Blue as "Deployment of enemy troops and equipment within five-mile radius," but what it meant to Sturgis was you could see where the fuck the enemy was hiding. The telescopic view of the town projected onto the lower third of the visor like a movie screen instantly disappeared and was replaced by a three-dimensional grid-map filled with blue and red dots. It was hard for Sturgis to see any pattern at first as the streaming blips looked like so many anthills. But what the computer gave, it could also interpret.

"Number of men and vehicles?" Sturgis asked quickly, as he halted the fleet of Tri-wheelers just before a turn in the road that would bring them into direct visual contact.

"Force of 510 men," the computer printed out in a moving green line, just above the radar grid. "Other (EST.) humans in town—2,089 dead, 1,573 in critical state of life continuation, 2,112 alive. Two jeeps, 20 motorcycles, 2 light tanks—all in functioning condition."

Sturgis whistled between his teeth. Jesus, they had a goddamn mini-army in there. He couldn't believe that a real army unit could turn rotten so quickly—not all the men. And no warlord, however power mad, could have assembled that many men and equipment this fast.

"Optimum attack mode," he asked the C.A.D.S. computer, something he had scoffed at in the past. After all, if a fighting man of his many years experience couldn't figure out how to mount a damned attack—but already things were a lot more complicated than he had figured on. Within two seconds, the options, calculated by the data banks which were stored with enough information on warfare and attack/defense strategies to fill the Library of Congress scrolled along on the lower quadrant: Option one—Destroy entire town and force from distance. Probability of successful total destruction—90.7%."

"Great," Sturgis muttered back under his breath. "So we'll just kill everyone—kids, dogs. Logic at its peak."

"Option two—Full scale attack from all flanks of main force camped in central square. Search and destroy remaining forces. Probability of successful elimination of enemy force—83.3%."

"Out," Sturgis said simply—the only word he had to

utter for the computer to cease its last command. He'd do things his own way after all. The computer didn't have tricks up its electronic sleeves—but he did.

"Tranh, Fenton, Dixon, Roberto—each of you take a quarter of the team. Two teams will come in on bikes from each side of town—the other two will come in from the north and south by air. We'll hit 'em every which way—and fast. But first—*I'm* going to take a little mosey down there and see just what the hell is going on."

"Sturgis—don't be cra . . ." Fenton began.

"I'm in command, pal—I make the decisions. I'll leave you all wired in to my audio. When and if the shit hits the fan—and I'm sure it will, please do come running. I'll give you all five minutes to position yourselves and then I'm going in."

Sturgis walked down the Main Street of Carterville at a slow, easy gait. His huge armored arms hung loosely at his sides, ready to deal death in a second. The street was coated with a yellowish powder, residue from a distant nuke blast, and a small cloud of the dust hung in the air behind Sturgis as he walked, making it almost appear as if he was walking out of a mist. All his sensors were on maximum—radar, defensive-weapon, firing detectors, super auditory—enabling him to hear a crack of a branch or the click of a trigger from hundreds of feet away. He felt exhilarated, every nerve, every sense at peak function. He saw the killers ahead, both visually, through the visor, and at the bottom of his screen—their blips on the still-displayed radar grid. So maybe he was a Texas Ranger, a gun fighter. And this was High Noon.

Salizar saw him suddenly appear about 100 feet away. He and Ramon had brought two young girls they had found in hiding out for the rest of the men to enjoy. He did a double take for a second and then realizing he was in front of a hundred of his men gathered around the jeep, laughed contemptuously.

"Well what have we here?" Salizar said loudly, pointing at the apparition. His men turned around and quickly raised their 7.2mm pistols and Kalshnikov's muzzles, still hot from murder in the afternoon. "A spaceman. Isn't that nice boys? A spaceman from the U.S. of A. has come to pay us a visit."

The men all laughed at the strange thing that came toward them, sure that it was some sort of radiation armor and that whatever crazy Yanqui inside was fool enough to come into their storm of terror was about to die a very painful death.

Sturgis stopped 50 feet from the jeep and the assembled soldiers. He could see right away that they were not Americans—thank God for that. The faces looked Latin American and mean, faces you wouldn't want to look up in a dark alley and see. He raised one of the immense gloved hands straight up, palm forward, in the universal symbol of greeting.

"I come in peace," Sturgis' voice suddenly blasted out into the street from the mini-amplifiers hidden in his suit. "To all those who live in peace."

The soldiers looked momentarily frightened by the booming words that echoed back and forth along the ruined stores of what had once been Main Street. Many had grown up in the rural parts of Cuba—provinces where the old ways still held sway—voodoo, demons . . . They smiled broadly trying to hide their fear from one another and themselves, but their eyes beheld the giant armored man all in black who spoke with the voice of a god.

"He comes in peace," Salizar screamed out laughing, sitting up on top of his driver's seat in the jeep. "You hear that men? That is funny." His mouth opened wide revealing the flickering proof of his wealth in quick

279

golden flashes. Salizar faced the intruder and yelled to him.

"We have much in common then, Mr. Spaceman. You come in peace, we leave things in pieces." The soldiers around him howled at their commander's little joke.

"But now, you bore me," Salizar said, handing over the two girls from the back of the jeep to the waiting men. "Before I kill you, please tell me why you came. It is quite curious really."

"No, not curious at all," Sturgis said, starting forward. "I came here to kill you and everyone of your murdering slime-crew."

"You kill *us*? We are Cubans man! It is you, *maricone* gringo, who will die!" Salizar said angrily. "Get him!"

The Cuban invaders whipped up their weapons and sent out a deluge of screaming lead at the suited giant. The bullets bounced off, ricocheting wildly in every direction, striking some of the front rows of men. They kept firing, not understanding what was going on as Sturgis continued forward, his right arm suddenly rising and pointing at Salizar and the jeep. The commander of the Cuban force looked in horror as he saw a crackling ball of blue electricity come straight for him like a bee to honey. Somehow he found the reflexes to leap free of the jeep toward the other side. The E-ball tore into the vehicle like the gnashing teeth of death, and spat out little pieces. The white-hot explosion slammed into about 60 of the gathered troops, blasting arms, heads, legs, right off and sending them flying in a red rain of flesh and pulverized bone.

Sturgis waded right into the devastation without waiting for the smoke to clear. With Infra-enhanced visual mode he was able to see what was waiting. "Move — *move*," the C.A.D.S. leader screamed over his helmet mike, just in case they hadn't. The Cubans who hadn't been killed or mortally wounded by the blast tried to

280

clear their heads of the ringing, come to their senses, and fight. They opened up again with another stream of bullet-fire and suddenly Sturgis saw two of them pulling grenades from their belts. He raised his arm, yelling "Mode M," and simultaneous with his words turned his wrist slightly to the right. A scythe of 55mm slugs turned the two grenaders into mush, dissecting both of them at stomach level. Sturgis continued the fire, simply moving his arm across the enemy. Small target-grids, showing human figures, kept lighting up in the lower right-hand corner of the visor, the computer's attempt to assist Sturgis as he sighted each one. But Sturgis didn't have time to aim properly—he was too busy killing. The Cubans went flying left and right, bloody heaps that hit the ground and jerked wildly in spasming death throes. The silicone-coated 55mm bullets with their dum-dum heads didn't leave much to write home to mother about.

Sturgis reached the jeep or the smoking parts that were left of it. The two girls the commander had captured were still alive, cowering on the ground holding onto each other for dear life. Sturgis bent over slightly.

"You're all right now. Just stay here—help will be coming. Don't move." Only one of the two even had the courage to look up and her face turned yet another shade paler as she took in the glistening suited thing with beeps and lights going off all over it. She pulled her head back down under the other girl's arm to hide. "All right," Sturgis half laughed. "I know I'm not pretty. Just as well. Stay put."

He suddenly heard firefights breaking out from every direction. The gunfight was on. Sturgis walked past the smoldering jeep and searched for the leader. "Macro," he said and his vision telescoped down the street. There— two blocks down, the black jacket and cap, disappearing into a building. He heard a whooshing sound above as two of his men rocketed by over the houses, their huge

281

suits looking almost like small planes from this close. A soft but clearly audible warning tone went off in Sturgis' ear. It was the suit's defensive early warning system—PM Mode—the message flashed brightly in large instantly readable letters—"Bazooka attack: 27-19-38. Probability of C.A.D.S. suit destruction within three seconds 58%."

Sturgis knew instantaneously that the numbers the computer had reeled off were code—27 feet ahead, 19 feet to the left, 38 feet up. A code that every man in the C.A.D.S. training had had to learn until it was second nature. There were only seconds of warning time and the numbers told him in a split second where to look.

He stepped quickly to the right with a jump that kicked in the suit's assist so he shot 15 feet to the side. As he left the ground he swung his arm up and around at the coordinates and fired without even checking to see if something was there. Behind him he heard a sudden roar and felt the edge of the blast from the bazooka shell. The suit's gyro went on automatic for two seconds, adjusting for the extra push. Sturgis' electrically-guided globe of mega-death hit the outer wall of a quaint three story colonial home, several feet below the window from which the long tubular weapon emerged. But with an E-ball, giving or taking a few feet doesn't really matter too much. The snapping orange ball's concentrated high explosive tore the whole side of the house out, sending it flying in fragments of white wood. The explosion turned the bazooka man and the whole third floor into a tornado of flesh and bloody sawdust. Sturgis didn't wait to see the results.

"Jump," he commanded the suit, leaping straight up. The rocket assist on the back of C.A.D.S. cut in and he soared over the rooftops of a peaceful little town plunged into hell. From 70 feet up he could quickly see the progress of the fight. Groups of Cubans banding together and trying to set up a counter attack with machine guns and bazookas and hand-held anti-aircraft rockets. But there was no time—the suits moved too fast, in and out of their vision in a second. And the things it fired at them—just one could kill them all. They were terrified. Suddenly, the killers had become the killees and would have tried to flee but couldn't even get out of their various covers. Sturgis, still aloft, quickly scanned each main confrontation with Macro-Mode. His men were working the suits to their optimum.

Sturgis couldn't help feeling proud. He always assumed that they just didn't understand how to use the things to their full advantage—the almost infinite possible combinations of perception modes, attack and defensive systems, and mobility. But they *did*—the team was using the suits like boxers, not waiting to get hit with anything. Moving, always moving. They darted in and out of concentrations of Cubans, dropping from the sky or running at them in a blur—releasing a few choice presents courtesy of Uncle Sam, jumping right out again in the space of a second.

The Cubans were crying, vomiting, even shitting in their pants as these mythic beings came at them from everywhere. They were in a battle with the demons of their ancestors, and they were all heading straight to a fiery hell. Their terror made them fight that much harder, firing whole clips at a burst, madly firing bazooka shells at phantoms that kept disappearing. The odds in manpower were nearly 50 to one on the Cubans' side—but the odds in high-tech destruction were with the C.A.D.S.—a thousandfold.

Whole buildings went up like erupting volcanos of flame as E-balls tore into them on their meteoric paths. And from the flaming windows, burning Cuban deathcommandos, flying through the air like leaves on fire. Whatever barricades the Cubans hid behind the C.A.D.S.-suited warriors were able to blast through with their fists and dispose of the inhabitants in their own personal style.

Sturgis quickly scanned all this in a few seconds, hanging aloft like a black rock just sitting in the air. His warning tone went off again. "Tank 89-5-0. Probability of destruction in six seconds — 76%." The green words danced across the visor. But Sturgis had turned his attention to the coordinates the moment he saw them. There — almost dead ahead below him, and raising its cannon toward him — a Russian K-9 light tank, only 30-feet long but fast. It was bristling with weapons including, as Sturgis knew well, ground-to-air missiles.

"Down!" he commanded the suit and the rockets cut right out, letting him drop straight down until boot sensors knew he was six inches above the street where the jets slammed out a strong burst that gently settled him down. The tank fired a screaming shell from the long muzzle but it soared through the air, missing its intended target and off into the forests to the south. Sturgis saw a forward grid on the tank pop open as the head of a sleek yard-long missile peered out from inside. No time. He raised his arm and twisted to the side sending out two E-balls, one after another like twin comets streaking toward destruction. The small but deadly missile fired and got halfway out of its launch tube when the first of the high-explosive projectiles made contact with it. The tank exploded from without and within at the same instant, sending a shower of white metal slags and nothing recognizable as human hundreds of feet into the air.

Again Sturgis felt the reality of the awesome power of the C.A.D.S. suit sweep through him. It was almost terrifying to possess this much power. One couldn't help but begin thinking like a god. Just point your finger — and whoosh, no more tree or building or hill. Just say it and you're flying. Whether they would ultimately contribute more to good or evil, he wasn't even sure. For in the wrong hands the suits were as terrifying as the nuclear holocaust itself—maybe more so. But he was damned glad he had one.

Within five more minutes the battle was over. Bodies, pieces of bodies, and rivers of red covered the center of the town. Half the buildings in a ten-block radius were burning as smoke from scores of fires poured into the sky joining together in a twisting black funnel that shot straight up. Sturgis prayed that not too many of the townspeople—those who were still left—had been caught up in the action. He instructed his men to meet in the town center where Sturgis had first confronted the Cuban force. The suits came roaring in from different parts of town, most of them coated with grime and soot. Bullet proof they were—dirt proof they were not. Nor blood proof. But the rains and the winds would erase the by-products of their trade.

"How are we doing?" Sturgis asked them when they had all assembled the Tri-wheeler force, leading back a bunch of prisoners, their hands held high in the air. The C.A.D.S. commander looked quickly around at his men for any signs of injury.

"Lynch—your arm. What happened?" The suit's left arm had a large jagged tear in it, with wires and metal hanging out at angles.

"Too close to something that went boom, sir," he answered over his mike. "I'm not hurt though."

"Well get it right over to Rossiter, tell him to work on it pronto." Fenton, Rossiter, and Roberto all served as suit repairmen, having taken special advanced courses on the actual mechanics and electronic components of the suits. And with spare parts, wires, and circuit boards of every kind in the Rhino's storage bins, almost any kind of repair was possible—other than a total wipeout.

"Armell . . . bought it, sir," Roberto said quietly. He was just a few feet away from Sturgis. Armell was—had been — Roberto's friend.

"What the hell do you mean, man," Sturgis half exploded.

"Took one of those fucking ground-to-airs right at the base of his helmet — tore his head right off."

"Shit," Sturgis said, wanting to slam his fist into something but knowing he would destroy it. Another one gone. Another one of the men entrusted in *his* care was just cold pulp now. And one less man to carry out their mission.

"What the hell do we do with these," Tranh asked, pointing to about a dozen Cuban prisoners who had been collected. Sturgis walked over to them.

"Oh *you*," he said reaching forward and slapping a large hat from one of the prisoners. It was Salizar. His mouth instantly snapped open in a golden grin.

"Amigo — some fight, hey? You won, and now you are our respected and worthy captors. And of course, the officers among us," Salizar went on, reaching for a cigarette in his jacket pocket, "will be given special good treat —"

"Shut up slime," Sturgis said with a voice of ice. "I don't have time to stand here and listen to your lies. I can't even stand looking at you. You've killed thousands of people here, in other towns to the south, I'm sure as well. You're not after military bases, and you're not wearing Cuban uniforms. If none of that was true, I might — might, let you live. But it *is* true — you're nothing but *killers*, here to destroy what little remains of our burning country. And we will execute you as killers — now!"

"Please," Salizar said, getting down on his hands and knees. "I have a wife, a child — see?" He reached for her photo from his pocket. "I am just a soldier — doing my . . ."

"By the authority vested in me as a commander of the authorized United States Military Forces in a situation of total war — I hereby sentence all of you to death. Sentence to be carried out immediately."

The dozen Cubans were led screaming and begging for mercy — a mercy they had shown not a single one of their butchered victims. They were lined up against a brick wall.

"Please — a cigarette," Salizar said, fumbling with matches as he hysterically tried to light it.

"No cigarette — no nothing," Sturgis said bitterly as he stood alongside a row of four of his men, their arms raised straight out and aimed at the Cubans.

"Fire," Sturgis said.

CHAPTER TWENTY-SIX

The townspeople slowly crawled out from their myriad hiding places around Carterville. They walked through the streets in a daze, trying to comprehend the enormity of destruction that had occurred. First the war, then the invasion of the Cuban murderers who had killed off half their town in a nightmare of torture and mutilation — and now this, the destruction of their tormentors by yet another bizarre entry into this terrifying new post-war world — giants in black armor. But they hardly cared any more, the human mind can only take so much before it goes numb, putting up a wall of steel around it so that it can't feel any more.

They walked through the streets, stepping over the bloody dismembered pieces that covered everything. It was as if a hurricane spewing human parts had descended on this once lovely town and left it coated red, its quaint and historic houses torn into scrap wood, their roofs, walls, blasted open, lifted from their very foundations and torn into their splintered component parts. The town looked naked with so much gone, so many buildings exposed down to their cracked beams, wiring hanging down like black vines along shattered walls. Even the concrete sidewalks, the asphalt streets, had been taken along to

288

hell in the battle. It was as if they had been pulled apart by an earthquake, with huge cracks reaching feet down to the dirt, bulges and sunken portions that looked more like the cratered surface of the moon than the main street of an American town. Nothing had been spared, everything was scarred.

They walked in small groups of fives and tens, huddling together as they moved slowly through what had been their town, their eyes still as they took in the enormity of the damage. Their own clothes were ripped, bloodstained. They had all lost mates, relatives, children to the Cuban death commandos. Yet something pulls the human being forward. From out of the very jaws of death he will rise and upon unsteady feet start forward once again. Perhaps this is the very essence of the human soul—the good part of it, that is, the life-affirming part. To rise, not look back, and reach out for life with trembling hands. To never give up while there is yet one breath that lingers in the still beating chest.

Sturgis and the others stood stock still in the center of the town square as the townspeople approached them cautiously from every block, moving in slow, stumbling hordes all converging in the center. The C.A.D.S. team didn't move. They knew their appearance was frightening to these gentle people. They had had enough terror. But though they were afraid, the citizens of Carterville knew, that somehow, someway, these strange futuristic giants had saved them.

"We're Americans," Sturgis explained softly, setting his mike amplification system at low pitch and volume, modulated for deep calming tones. He stood in the front of his men, who watched through their outwardly impenetrable visors, their arms hanging loosely at their sides so as not to startle the approaching men, women and children.

"We are not from outer space," Sturgis continued as

the crowds gathered together, stopping about 50 feet in front of him. "We're members of the United States Air Force and we're here only to help you. The only people who need fear us are those who prey on towns like yours. As you can see they paid the price." He swept his hand through the bloody square, corpses hanging from windows, roofs, slammed through smashed store windows.

One of the men, a large muscular man wearing what had once been a three-piece pinstriped suit, now a bloody rag that barely hid the razor marks the Cuban had inflicted on his chest and stomach spoke up.

"I am—was," the man stuttered painfully, barely able to talk "a lawyer here—b—b—before . . ."

"It's okay," Sturgis said, slowly raising his visor so they could all see a human face. They gasped at seeing that indeed there weren't two-headed green things inside the suits. "Don't be afraid of us," he smiled and reached out a large black-gloved hand toward the man who took a few steps forward, managed a weak smile of his own, and took Sturgis' hand in his.

"G-g-god bless you all," the lawyer said, turning slowly toward each of the C.A.D.S. team. "You can't know what it was like here for us—what we went through. All of us, everyone here behind me, have been through their own hell. But I know I speak for all of us when I say, that seeing them all dead—these bastards who did their unspeakable acts of violence—that does give us satisfaction. There was no mercy—but at least there was justice—and vengeance. And for that we are all grateful, eternally."

The other townspeople looked on fascinated as the rest of the C.A.D.S. team slowly lifted their visors and smiled sheepishly at the nearly 2,000 people who had gathered in front of them, now filling the town square to capacity. The people tried to relax their rock-tight mouths to smile back at the first kind outsiders, the first good thing that had happened to them for a week. Some of the young women in the crowd looked desperately into the C.A.D.S. team's eyes, needing them in some deep incomprehensible way. To be protected by their strength—to be held in super-strong arms so they would feel safe enough to release their oceans of tears.

"Although this is hardly an occasion to celebrate," the man went on, suddenly becoming conscious of his official status as the town's de-facto leader—something that in the new world of non-freedom meant more than it ever had before. So lawyer Ed Travers, held his painful body straight and looked with a surge of pride and patriotism at Sturgis.

"You must let us repay you in some way. For, even in the midst of so much death, we must thank you for risking so much to come to our aid. We were sure it was over for all of us. We have some food hidden, medical supplies—you must rest with us now . . ."

"Well, we'd love to stay and partake," Sturgis replied, towering over the man. "But unfortunately, we're on mission of utmost importance and will have to leave immediately."

"Nix that," Fenton said suddenly over his helmet mike. "The Rhino's rear axle is damaged. There's a half-inch space where the wheel shaft enters the body, and damned if a mortar or some damned thing didn't go off within what must have been inches of it."

"How long?" Sturgis asked grimly.

"Well, I've got all the tools and parts. With Rossiter helping me—and if it isn't an actual severing of the shaft—maybe 12 hours."

"Twelve hours!" Sturgis exclaimed, forgetting his mike was also on amplification, so that his voice boomed out over the crowd, startling them.

"Sturgis—I'm not God," Fenton said sarcastically. "I didn't break it—and He ain't gonna fix it. That just leaves me and Rossiter, like I said, with a total of two human brains and four pairs of hands to do what shouldn't even be possible to do outside of a million-dollar repair lab. Okay?"

"Sorry," Sturgis said softly. "Of course—do what you can." He turned back to the lawyer. "Well I guess we'll take you up on that offer. We could use a break." He turned to his men telling them to bivouac their Tri-bikes and suits—post four guards in shifts at *all* times, and partake of what little Carterville had to offer.

In the darkest of times the human heart beats even harder. Though every one of them had lost enough to drive one to madness, they couldn't dwell on it, couldn't mourn it any longer. There was so much death around them it was as if they were floating in a sea of it—every wave, every surge of current bringing more doom, more pain. They had to bring life back among them, if even for just a moment, to walk by their side and give them more than tears.

"I propose we have a celebration," said the lawyer, "God knows we need one. And we have cause to celebrate—the U.S. is still alive, and these brave fighters have freed us from the enemy, saved our town."

"We can have the barn dance that was scheduled for the town's centennial," someone yelled out.

The lawyer said, "That's just fine. We'll get the best celebration we can together, considering, and invite these gentlemen."

Sturgis agreed the C.A.D.S. team would come. Except Fenton and Rossiter, who would be fixing the Rhino. As the C.A.D.S. team walked away for some needed rest, Sturgis heard the lawyer being appointed mayor by voice vote. It was good to hear the cheering.

At eight that evening, showered, shaved, dressed in civvies, the team was headed toward the old barn on the outskirts of town.

They had almost forgotten what it was like to feel the ground give gently beneath their feet, feel the vibrant breeze from the surrounding woods that mercifully swept away the odors of death—at least for tonight . . . feel the cool night air against their faces. The suits were great for fighting, but lousy for living. They laughed and joked with one another as they were taken the half mile to the barn festivities. Only Sturgis, who was growing increasingly worried about their getting to Washington in time, found it hard to relax. It was all on his shoulders, a weight growing heavier all the time. Perhaps they shouldn't have stopped here in this town, he began to wonder. But just as quickly banished the question from his mind. If they hadn't come, every single person in Carterville would be dead. They couldn't come to the aid of everyone, but they also couldn't leave their fellow citizens to the wolves. Otherwise, what were they protecting? What were they fighting for? It was a thin line, a balance that Sturgis prayed he could maintain. One had to care, somehow. One just had to fucking care.

As they rounded a grove of trees, they suddenly saw the big faded red barn ahead of them festooned with paper lanterns on all sides that twinkled invitingly toward the shadowy woods around them. The men were led into the barn, a huge structure, once used for storing grain and stock, for the last 15 years, the town's gathering place. Inside, ribbons were strewn around the rafters, and more japanese lanterns were placed along the walls, lighting the entire 200 by 150 foot barn with bright flickering waves of warm candlelight. The mayor and a small committee waited for them just inside the door, as hundreds of other townspeople, most of them the younger ones, as the elderly had been put through too much of a strain recently for their bodies to even obey their wishes.

Sturgis stopped in front of Mayor Travers and snapped out a quick salute. The C.A.D.S. team gathered behind Sturgis looked eagerly around at the tables of steaming food and the young women dressed in the best dresses they could find, bright ribbons in their hair, sitting together on rows of wooden chairs along the wall. It was all so amazing, so normal.

"On behalf of the people of Carterville, I would like to bestow on you the key to our town," the mayor, now dressed in a crumpled but unbloodied suit, said. He handed a two-foot long key-shaped piece of plywood that had been painted a glossy silver.

"I'm deeply touched," Sturgis said, taking the key. "And on behalf of all my men and the U.S. Government, we thank you and wish you every support possible on the continuation of your town, your democratic government, and your way of life. If there are more like you gutsy people still surviving out there, then I think we've got a chance."

"But enough of all this talk," the mayor said, managing a genuine smile. "We politicians seem to be able to keep our tongues flapping even in the middle of a nuclear war. Now go—enjoy yourselves, there's food, wine, music. Please—it would do all our hearts honor to see your men have fun . . . You risked your lives to save us, and, well, you deserve this truly." He waved his hand and a small band, composed of elderly musicians, began playing foot-stomping country music on fiddle, banjo, and washtub bass. The band sat on a three-foot high stage at the far end of the barn.

The Omega Force rushed around Sturgis and made their way to the food tables where they quickly shoveled gargantuan portions of everything in sight onto their china plates. Sturgis smiled—they looked like kids at Christmas dinner. They'd eat until their stomachs were poking out like pillows. And tomorrow they'd feel it when the powerful vibrations of the Tri-wheelers shook all that roast beef and stuffing and apple pie around their stomachs like a blender. Ah—but let them have their fun. Jesus Christ—for one night. Every one of them might easily be dead tomorrow.

He took portions of each of the big platters of food and headed over to the team, seated on folding chairs at a table, gobbling down their chow. But Sturgis could see by their glances over at nearly 30 of the town's girls seated across the barn floor that they were interested in much more than food tonight. And by the constant gaze of nearly all the females toward his men, Sturgis could see they weren't alone in their thoughts. Before he had even finished a quarter of his dinner, the men were up and across the floor, grabbing partners from their chairs and sweeping across the wide floor to the bouncing beats of the country music.

Yes, let them all live, Sturgis thought, chewing each mouthful slowly. Live, dance, fuck—do it all boys and girls, for tomorrow we die. He felt suddenly old among the exuberant youthful movements of the dancers. And he longed for Robin, to touch her warm female flesh, to bury himself in her scent, in her giving body. He finished eating and sipped a glass of beer, watching with an almost fatherly amusement at the increasingly frantic dancers who seemed to jump higher and higher with each move, the men of the C.A.D.S. team spinning their young, bright-eyed partners high in the air as they doseydoed them around and around, breathless, cheeks flushed with energy and passion.

"Ahem," a voice said just to his side and Sturgis turned with a jerk, startled out of his thoughts. A young devastatingly beautiful woman, no more than 18 or 19 looked at him from the next chair with a coy smile. "Didn't mean to scare you," she laughed. "I just wanted to meet the leader of this team myself." Sturgis relaxed and let out a laugh.

"Although the thought that I could scare *you* after the way you faced those Cuban killers—is rather ridiculous." The brunette's sweet almost purry voice sounded to Sturgis like the song of an angel after hearing nothing but explosions and screams for days.

"Well it just goes to show you," Sturgis said with a sardonic grin, "that even I, the bravest man on earth, have my moments of weakness. I never got to finish my 'How to Be as Tough as Clint Eastwood Course'—a few things got in the way."

She smiled again, showing her even rows of teeth. She was undeniably sexy, very sexy—and she seemed sophisticated in a subtle way, far beyond the norm for a small-town girl.

"You're funny, Mr. Sturgis," she said, leaning a little closer to him, so that her low cut dress revealed the tops of perfectly white ample breasts. "And very handsome." She looked him straight in the face, her almost hypnotic violet eyes staring at him with a desperate intensity.

"And you're very direct," he laughed, taking another sip of beer.

"There's no time to play games any more," she said, the smile vanishing for just a split second before reappearing again, like the sun from behind a wisp of clouds. "All of us girls were talking about it tonight. About what we would do . . . Look!" She waved her hand toward the opposite wall where most of the C.A.D.S. team was engaged in heavy embraces with their town girls, bodies pushing close, lips meeting parted lips. "Death is everywhere," she said. "We are women. Unfulfilled women. We seek life, love, warmth . . . and touch." She reached over and planted the softest of kisses on his lips and then sat back again, looking, waiting.

Sturgis felt his body and mind reeling inside. He felt so tired, lonely, the weight of his command heavy on his broad shoulders. *Robin* . . . but the woman beside him looked like a dream of paradise on this dark night. His blood, his loins reached out for her aching softness.

"What's your name, direct woman?" Sturgis asked.

"Marcy, Mr. Sturgis," she said. "Marcy Aston."

"Well, first of all, if we're going to talk for even one more minute — you can't call me mister or Sturgis. The name's Dean."

"Dean," she said softly, her eyes lowering. She looked back up with a fire burning in those violet eyes and grabbed his hand. "Come on, Dean — let's dance."

He began to say "no," but she dragged him right across the floor and into the crowd of jumping and whooping dancers. He felt self-conscious at first, but quickly got into the swing of things. Within a few minutes he was jumping with the best of them, his body feeling wonderful, as it stretched out and pumped with oxygen rich blood, feeling its strength. His tiredness and dark thoughts vanished behind the flickering lamplights, outside into the real world. In here, he entered the fantasy that all of them were trying to create — a moment, a place where they could be dream lovers floating above the blackness.

They danced for nearly an hour until she breathlessly pulled him over to one wall.

"Can't go on," she said, leaning back and pulling him up against her heaving chest. She put her thin arms around the sides of his chest and heaved a deep sigh. Her lips fluttered up to his neck like a bird settling on a branch and kissed him softly.

He felt his manhood stiffen instantaneously at her moist touch and soft cooing sound. Her mouth rose higher and whispered in his ear.

"I want you, Dean. Now . . . please."

He knew he couldn't resist. He wanted her, had to have her. He felt drawn toward her young flesh like steel to a magnet — unstoppable.

They walked outside into the dark night, dancing with the shadows created by the breeze-blown lanterns.

"There's a nice place that's quiet — behind the barn — the haystack."

There were a few other couples out there, but it was dim and the haypile was huge. They found a place far from the others — behind a hay wagon and thresher — almost in the field.

"You know," she said, "I never — with a man — went all the way before."

"Are you sure you want to go ahead with this?" he asked her, holding her tight, feeling her burning warmth, her softness.

"Yes," she gasped. "Oh yes."

She wrapped her arms around him as if she would never let go and then kissed him more and more passionately. They could hear the caller far off calling out dances as the fiddles played away a mile a minute.

"No, not here," she gasped as he started unbuttoning her dress.

"Is it far?" Sturgis asked.

"Right over there," she pointed several hundred feet away to a darkened unscathed three-story house. We can use the back porch stairs — no one will know. I have a big soft bed with clean sheets." He cradled her in his arms as they walked to the house and up the creaking back stairs.

They went in the unlocked third floor door and she lit a big candle. They went to the bed where she lay down, looking at him with a bottomless desire. He lifted his hand and touched her cheek, and it was a gentle movement that tore at her heart. The touch was a catalyst of her physical being as well. It set loose a storm of desire that swept over her like a tidal wave. She buried her face against his shoulder, moaning. He felt the trembling need of her body as she pressed closer, ever closer. Sturgis threaded both hands through her hair, brought his lips to hers and held her spellbound. In that moment the two civilized people disappeared and something more basic, natural, replaced them. She exhaled a deep shuddering breath as he reached down and began to ease the top button of her dress open. She eagerly assisted him in removing the rest of her clothes, sure that she had found the right man—and desperate to be a virgin no longer. She felt his cold hands run down across her erect nipples like an electric shock, cup her bountiful cream-colored breasts firmly, and then felt his touch trace down to the concave place between her thighs. She shuddered and threw her head back in a gasp. Her tongue swirled around in his eager mouth. Then he lowered himself and kissed and suckled upon her rosy nipples. She couldn't stand the urgent desire. Frantically she tore at the snap to his pants, pulled his zipper down. Her hand slipped into the swelling there, felt the steel hard warmth seething in his enormous erection. She knelt there naked in the darkness and took it fully into her trembling lips. He gasped as Marcy experimented first with one type of tonguing then another. She was hoping she'd do it right, but his responses seemed to indicate she was getting the general hang of it. She wanted to please him, to make sure he would be satisfied with her.

Then he was pulling her naked, lithe form up against him, and she was tearing at his shirt, and pulling it free of his manly chest. Then his pants. He got on top of her, his weight crushing against her. He reached behind and grasped her pale buttocks one cheek in each huge viselike hand and lifted them apart. She felt the moistness dripping between her legs. She felt his pressure—the awful pressure of the enormously swelled male organ between her legs, and tried not to cry out as it slid slowly in, moving inexorably forward into her moistness, entering her tight and narrow vagina and meeting resistance. God the pain, she thought as she felt her insides spreading apart with a sharp pain that made her convulse. But suddenly he was in her—all the way in—and her whole body gave way to a rapture. It was as if the door to another universe, a universe she never knew existed—one of pleasure and fulfillment, were opening for the first time. Her eyes rolled back and she felt her hips convulsing, eagerly and totally uncontrollably jerking forward to meet his now tremendously long and unstoppable thrusts.

She pressed herself up against him, not wanting to lose the pile-driving rhythm for an instant. She felt a volcanic heat burning up inside her, felt the urgent sensation like she had felt the times she masturbated in the hot tub water, but a thousand times more powerful as his body energetically followed her every tremor and movement.

Her moist warmth was making Sturgis delirious. He was without thought now—primitive, a male animal with a female—a force of nature, relentless and unstoppable.

Her cries—were they of pain as well as ecstasy? No—he knew they were ecstasy as her fingernails trailed long deep scratches down his muscular back. Her long thin fingers pulled through his chest hair as he rode her bucking convulsing hips. My God, she has such force in her thrusting hips, he thought, and it excited him in a way he hadn't been excited in a long time.

Running her frantic hands over his hard taut male body now covered with sweat, she felt the imprint of his being impressed upon her soul. It didn't matter what happened tomorrow—the war, the death on a mega-level. It was today, it was now, it was always. That pleasure that was so intense and yet it wouldn't break, wouldn't crest and fall like a titanic wave at the beach. It just rose and rose and then she felt a swaying of rhythm, a contraction of her tight vagina like a tremendous gripping hand upon his member which still managed to slide in and out and in and out. An explosion unlike anything she had ever felt was brewing deep inside her.

"Oh," she shouted, "Oh oh oh . . . Oh God oh God . . ."

Suddenly she arched up, her mouth falling wide open and she seemed to go into spasms of purest ecstasy for nearly 20 seconds, making deep guttural unintelligible sounds.

He came at the same time, buckets of his male energy passed into her writhing pulsing tunnel. He groaned a half growl of animal release and sank down slowly atop her now limp form. She felt utterly exhausted and utterly satisfied and utterly a woman. A Mona Lisa smile danced across her full warm lips.

They gave each other things when they had to part the next morning. He gave her a small pocket watch and she gave him a locket into which she squeezed a picture of herself. He tied it about his neck next to his dog tags.

Then the column formed up in the town square. Resupplied with more than material goods, the Omega Force took off down the street as the townspeople waved and were quickly back on the main highway heading east.

"How'd you do last night Sturg," Billy asked. "Didn't see you much . . ."

"I don't like to talk about those things," Sturgis replied. "But it was beautiful."

Billy grinned. "I felt guilty the whole time but I had a tiger."

Fenton's voice popped in from the repaired Rhino. "Well I certainly don't feel guilty. I would say that I've come to appreciate your American women immensely — especially those twin sisters I met last night . . ."

"*Twins*?" Sturgis and Billy said simultaneously.

Fenton grinned, "Indubitably."

CHAPTER TWENTY-SEVEN

Robin swore she was going mad after just four days inside the armored fortress that Sturgis had built into the rock wall. It wasn't that the living quarters weren't comfortable—nor for lack of water or air, both of which were filtered through charcoal systems that Sturgis had rigged up. It was just the sheer fact of being stuck inside, while the world went on out there—only she didn't know if it was living or dying. She paced frantically around the place, from room to room, moving like a caged tiger, trying to work off her nervous energy. She would stop at each of the wall mirrors as she came to them and stare straight into them from a distance of just inches, searching, peering at every square inch of her skin, trying to find the slightest trace of radiation damage. And when she began finding things—she didn't know if they were real or completely imagined. A few little red dots below one eye, they wouldn't have even caught her notice just a week ago, but now . . . And her gums felt sore, her throat dry and infected. She had looked through some of her *Eastern Studies* and *Holistic Health* magazines and books and found some recommended diets for radiation poisoning including taking iodine pills to give the body a source other than that which might be radioactive—in her food. She switched to a diet of whole grain brown rice and steamed vegetables which, thankfully, Sturgis in his foresight had frozen and stored in zip-lock bags in their freezer that was left constantly on, hooked up to water power/battery operated generators that were capable of running up to six months unattended.

The diet seemed to give her a little bit of strength back. But by the fifth day she noticed clumps of her hair coming out when she brushed it after her morning shower.

"Oh God," she moaned out loud as her beautiful long shiny hair hung from her fingers like dead grass. "Please don't let me go bald. I'd rather die." She just couldn't imagine herself without any hair. She could never let Sturgis see her. It was vain and ridiculous perhaps, but she decided then and there that if she started losing large clumps of hair she would kill herself. With her mind made up to end it all if things just got too bad — Robin suddenly felt strangely better — as if a load had been taken off her shoulders. She whistled and hummed to herself, trying to dispel the bad mood that gripped the house like a shadowy fist. The TV wasn't broadcasting at all other than the one channel the Reds seemed to have firmly in their control, which came on twice each day at three in the afternoon and eight at night, telling people that everything was just fine and that the peace-loving American workers were welcoming their Russian liberators with open arms. Yeah, right — Robin thought, as she watched the charade. But it was the only thing on — and just to see another human face, hear a human voice — was like food and water to her. She would time her meals to the broadcasts and chuckle over them as she ate.

Nighttime was the worst. She had nightmares every night of death, of people melting beneath the onslaught of the star-hot mushroom clouds. Screams pierced her mind; hands, arms, heads melted free of their bodies and floating haphazardly through space, reaching, flexing, trying to re-attach themselves. And she dreamed of Dean—where was he? Why hadn't he come to her? Every night—she saw him dead, killed by a different horrendous fate. And every night she would awaken covered with sweat, crying out in her sleep and sit bolt upright in bed, yelling his name out over and over.

"Come to me—Dean! . . . I need you." She would lie in the soft bed and send out signals to him, signals of her love and her desperate need to see him, to hold him, to know he was still alive.

On the sixth morning she awoke, the bed sheet once again moist with her nightmarish sweat and tears. "I've got to get out of here or I'll crack up," she muttered to herself rising slowly from the bed. She felt like going to sleep forever, just lying there and never moving again. But that was just why she couldn't. Her energy level was low. The radiation had affected her. Only her own life energy could save her now. If she wanted to die—she would, she could feel it in her aching cells. And if she wanted to live, she might. But she would have to fight, fight as hard as she had ever struggled in her life to keep the groping nuclear hands away. Sometimes it takes the worst to happen to human beings before they say enough, before they rise up and raise their fists and say, "as low as I am, as bad as I feel right now, by God I won't give up. I'm a fighter and will be fighting up to the second I die."

The spirit of the warrior suddenly flushed through Robin's blood. Who the hell was she to just moan and lie around like this? As if other people didn't have it bad. Jesus, she was alive, she was in probably one of the best areas, with food and water. Waiting for a man whom she knew in her heart was alive. In this new world of death, she was at the top of the heap, not the bottom.

She got dressed into hiking boots, parka, and weapons. Although she had always been nervous around them, and against them in principle, she knew she couldn't go out

304

there unprotected. Times had changed. She strapped a .45 around her waist—the weapon Sturgis had always made her practice with, saying "it's a monster—but you'll be able to stop anything on two legs with it." She took down the 12-gauge pump shotgun from Sturgis' array of rifles on one wall in the storage room and put nine shells into it. Dean had also taught her to use that formidable weapon. The 12 gauge made her feel safe, slung around her shoulder. Were there any living Americans at all? She had to go out and find out. She headed out through the lightly snow-covered woods, making sure that their farm fortress was sealed up tight as a crypt. The two-inch thick lock that Sturgis had had made specially for the steel door was virtually impenetrable even by bullets. She quickly left the domain of the farm that they owned in both their names and headed over the tree-lined hills to her neighbors' farm a half-mile off. The snowy covering of the ground was mottled here and there with what looked like fine blackish-red powder that seemed to almost melt down into the white stuff. She didn't go near it. She also noticed that some of the trees, particularly those at the very tops of hills where they were exposed to the most fallout—and the most gamma rays from the initial bomb blast—had bark peeling down their sides. They looked almost human, with pieces of their outer surface stripped out in wide gashes and from the inner wood— and oozing sap running down their sides, collecting at the base of their trunks.

As she moved quickly through the field of dead weeds that her neighbors, the Curtises would never trim, she noticed something else as well. There were usually whole armies of birds out in these tangled fields of decomposing thornbushes, and puffs and sunflowers. Usually the chirping and warbling sounds of a dozen species—but today hardly a peep—just the occasional call of a crow soaring jerkily by her. Christ, even the birds had been poisoned. But of course, they would be, as they collected everything from the surface of flowers — the dew, the pollen — it would all be highly radioactive and they would be getting the most concentrated parts. And the birds ate the insects in spring; cows ate the grass — and each one would poison the next, all the way down the food chain. She wondered suddenly if ants, flies, and bees were all heading for extinction, just little fossils to be, cemented in lavic tombs of solidified fallout, preserved for the future, if any, generations to behold. *"Yes, children, once there was a thing called bees, once a liquid they produced named honey."* Everything was turning into myth, Oh God, in this dark new world. Could the human race be far behind? Tears streamed down her cheeks.

She reached the porch of the Curtis' rambling old twelve-room country home and yelled out.

"Anyone here? It's me, Robin from the farm. Hello? Mr. Curtis? Mrs. Curtis?"

There was no answer, just the slapping of a plastic shade inside the house from the breeze of an opened window. She moved forward cautiously remembering what Sturgis had told her about entering dark spaces or dwellings where you weren't sure what to expect. His words echoed in her mind like a racquetball slamming back and forth. "Move slow, ears alert, listen for any sound — any crack of wood. Hold the shotgun with one hand halfway up the barrel and the other on the trigger, ready to snap around. Just move the muzzle hand in the direction of the sound and pull the trigger — all in one motion."

She had practiced it enough times until he approved. It all seemed so unreal to her now, these drills he had put her through a hundred times, shooting at branches, at snowmen — it had all been a game. That was the only way she had been able to deal with it all, or allow herself in spite of her politics to learn it. And now, no more games. None.

She walked slowly inside, moving one foot at a time, placing each down on the creaking wood floors and slowly shifting her weight forward. Everything seemed as it should be, the Curtis' little decoratively shaded floor lamps, their richly textured flower-covering on their armchairs and sofa, their little vases of dried flowers, little round velvet balls of lilac and lavender.

And then a smell — not so pleasant — that of something, meat — rotting, a vile sulfurous smell that made her stomach churn a few times inside. Carefully she peered around the living-room door and into the kitchen.

A growling sound from out of the semi-darkness of the room and two burning yellow eyes made her step backward with a start. She swung the gun around, but just as quickly the growl turned to whimpers and pulled back away from the door. Robin took out a flashlight she had brought along in a pack and turned the beam on and into the kitchen. The lights sliced through the shadows of the room and over the two chairs seated at the kitchen table. There they were, having their — she started forward, a smile on her face which instantly turned chalk white as she saw that they were dead, long dead. Their flesh still hung on the frail old bodies, but it had thickened and rotted away in long hanging strips. Maggots crawled in and out of the eye sockets and nasal openings, and what had been their mouths, long since eaten away of tongue and lips. Cups of coffee, now thick as tar sat in front of them. Together, the way they had always been in life.

She heard a slurping sound and swung the light down below the table where their German Shepherd, Angel, was lying between Mr. Curtis' stiff legs — *eating them*. It had already torn away the thighs of each leg and was now starting on the calves, its face wet with a brownish blood as it tore the hard strips of cold stiff flesh from its dead master. Not wanting to see, but unable to resist the sudden impulse, Robin swung the light toward Mrs. Curtis.

But Angel had already been there, her lower half had been chewed down to the bone. Only what remained above the waist had thus far been untouched, leaving the lifelong couple in their idyllic pose. With a feeling of deepest revulsion and hate Robin raised the shotgun and sighted up the face of the mangy old dog that had served them for so many years. It looked over at her, its eyes caught the beam of the flashlight, and whined a terrifying howl of pain and desertion and confusion all rolled into one. The sound reached into her very soul, sending a wave of the darkest emotion she had ever felt through her backbone. She didn't even know what it was, what to call it — overload maybe. Too much, too many emotions mixed together to even decipher. She lowered the pump. She couldn't kill the pitiful damned dog. It had stayed by its owner's side for days, not knowing what had happened. Then it grew hungry. It knew they were dead, animals know. And, probably feeling its own shame and self-hatred, had begun gnawing on the body which had previously petted and played with it.

Let it live — it wouldn't survive long anyway, that was for sure. And then it too would keel over, next to its master, lying on his bony feet. And they would all be together, the three of them, posed for eternity in their little family tableaux.

Robin backed out of the house, suddenly feeling as if she had intruded on something that shouldn't have been seen, by anyone but God. She breathed in the fresh air greedily as soon as she reached the porch, running out to the earth and away from the house of death. She ran at a medium clip for several hundred yards along the dirt road that led toward the few stores a couple of miles away that was close as the area had to a town. She looked around at everything, the barren trees, the few woods animals scurrying away groggily as she approached, trying to banish the image of the dead couple from her mind. That would be the legacy left for the survivors, to try and forget all they had seen. As if the images of melted faces and rotting children was something that one could ever forget. Just another TV show.

She saw a whole flock of blackbirds in a tree staring down at her like vultures and she waved up to them, happy to see at least one creature thriving in the post-nuke world. The birds just watched, every head turning as she walked beneath them and on down the road. Who would be left, she wondered, when it was all over. It was as if God were throwing dice on every species, and most were crapping out. Who would be the chosen ones, who would get to ride the new Noah's Ark of survival, of extra-immunology to the all-encompassing radiation?

She was about a half mile from the town when she saw the first of the bodies on the road. This one was hardly frightening as it was just a skeleton, a skeleton still wearing a suit. The bones had been stripped ivory white and whatever had been eating it, must have been insect, worms, she thought, as the suit was still in one piece, had also long since vanished. The skeleton man was still holding a briefcase in one hand and had fallen forward, as if trying in his last moment to get home. He must have been coming up from the city and been irradiated but somehow made it back this far, and then . . .

But there were quickly more, most totally consumed already. By the time she reached the three stores that made up Junction, Virginia, there were bodies everywhere, on their faces, kneeling, perched against trees. They all had come out, to meet and console one another in town, and then they died. It was simple, the story was told in bone and dark oozing leathery flesh. The more dead she saw the more she realized how lucky she had been. Somehow she must have missed the first few fallout clouds, and then the filtration system of Sturgis' design had protected her these last days.

She stepped carefully over the skeletons that lined the porch, one still sitting in the old wicker rocking chair that the general store had had perched outside for nearly 30 years. Inside were more dead—and much to her surprise, a fair amount of food left. Shelves of cans and boxes. What was it Sturgis had said—"Anything that can be cleaned off, that is sealed, you can use."

She went around the store filling her backpack with what she thought were the most essential goods: canned fish, batteries, more shotgun shells, a 10-pound bag of rice. She knew this might well be her last shopping trip for a long, long time, and she tried to use her head since she could only carry about 60 or 70 pounds.

At last she was filled with as heavy a load as she could possibly carry. She looked around the old general store, still rich with the scents of coffee and candy and a thousand smells of the country, checking for any last unnoticed item. There, on the wall, the picture of a group of roosters scrambling around a barnyard, their feathers flying in the air. She had always loved the ancient finely drawn print and had promised herself someday she would buy it. She walked over to the foot-square picture and tenderly removed it from the wall, carefully fitting it into the top of her pack. She felt slightly guilty about it, but only the dead would see it here. She would look at it, and love it, and it would be a memory, a good memory of the old world.

She walked out past the rows of calcified gentlemen on the porch, in the positions that they had always been in, talking about the weather, arguing about politics. The wind suddenly howled through their bones, creating an eerie deep note that floated through the air and into her spine. "The song of the dead, sung through bone teeth," Robin mused, remembering some old poem she had read in college. She walked out of the store and across the junction of four dirt roads that formed the little complex.

She couldn't help but check the laundromat to see if Mrs. Chowers was still alive. But of course she wasn't. To the last, working her ten-washer ex-garage, playing with the babies, offering advice to the depressed. The large gray-haired woman lay draped over the top of the folding table atop a half-folded sheet. It was strange, Robin was slowly realizing, but everybody she had seen around here had died doing what they had always done. As if somehow they could cheat death if they just pretended that it didn't exist and that everything was just fine, fold another sheet, make another call, they could sneak into death, doing their daily routines up to the very last seconds. And then as they reached out to do one more thing, they would be dead. Just like that — without even really noticing that it had happened.

Robin was feeling more and more like some sort of thief, coming into town and loading up on everything. But none of *these* people were going to use the stuff anymore, that was for damned sure. And soon it would be gone — from other scavengers, from the elements. Swallowing her pride, she went through the laundry carts of clothes that stood around the floor looking for sweaters, strong pants, stockings. After about ten minutes she had found a few things and somehow crammed them into her pack. That was enough, she thought to herself as she half staggered back toward the road that led to the farm. Another five pounds and she wouldn't even be able to walk. She stood at the turn a few hundred yards away and stared back. It looked so peaceful. And from here, as a cloud passed over the dim sun, it almost appeared that everything was right.

The sky was starting to look overcast again and Robin didn't particularly want to get caught in a downpour that would doubtless be filled with radioactive water and particulates. She hurried down the single lane, deeply tire-grooved dirt road as fast as she could, balancing the mountaineers pack precariously behind her. She was about halfway back, just past the dairy farm, where the cows lay like huge heaps of reddish brown mud, still in their animal shapes but rotted into featureless masses of decayed hide and bone — when she heard a sudden noise from the woods on the opposite side of the road. She dropped quickly to one knee, swinging the pump up in a quick arc. She sighted down the barrel and slowly moved the shotgun back and forth waiting for the least sign of motion. But nothing came at her.

"Who's there?" she tried to yell. But just a hoarse whisper came out. "I said who the hell is there? I have a shotgun trained on you, and you're going to be dead meat in a few seconds if you don't answer."

The tough words made her feel a little tougher. She knew suddenly she would shoot, could shoot, if she had to.

"Uhhh, heellp" an almost inaudible voice croaked out from behind a thick covering of bushes. "I — I," then the words stopped entirely. Whoever was talking was seriously hurt, Robin realized, or else baiting a trap for her. She carefully undid the chest harness of the pack, still keeping the shotgun in front of her and then started forward, circling around about 20 yards to the right, just in case. She pushed the bushes aside, moving as quietly as she could, and came in from behind where she figured the voice was speaking from.

There — a figure on the ground, its clothes shredded away to blackened tatters. She moved closer, looking furtively around in case there were others. But her senses picked up nothing. She walked up to the motionless body and reached out kicking it lightly with her foot.

"Hey you — are you . . ." Somehow the badly wounded figure managed to turn over so its face and chest were facing her. She gasped aloud. It was a boy, couldn't be more than 12 or 13, and he was horribly burned. The entire right side of his face had received third-degree burns that had bubbled and then charred the skin black. It was hardly recognizable as a face, just an oozing mass of twisted pus-dripping crevices and craters. And yet the right side, she could see, as he stared directly up at her through painfogged eyes, was completely normal. In fact he was a handsome boy, with strong features and a square jaw, a face with intelligence and character. He must have caught the gamma rays of a nearby bomb only on that one side, and at that just for a second or two or he would surely be dead. His clothes were burned down to just threads and scraps of charred cloth as he lay nearly naked on the cold ice-patched ground.

"Can you speak?" Robin asked, lowering the shotgun and kneeling down by his head.

"Wa-ter," he groaned, licking his parched lips with a swollen purple tongue.

"Sure, hold on, there," she said, trying to smile, trying to give some kindness to this horribly wounded soul. She pulled the aluminum canteen from her utility belt and held the opened spout to his lips. The poor kid wasn't even able to lift his arms or head, so she slipped her hand behind the back of his skull and gently lifted him. The drops of cool water drippled into his mouth and throat though he was barely able to swallow. She kept pouring it in, trying to get some to go down. After emptying nearly half the canteen, the boy coughed suddenly and she let him lie back down. He managed a thin smile through puffed lips.

"Th-th-h-anks . . . I—I," Even mumbling a few words seemed to cause incredible strain on his entire system.

"Shhhh," she said. "Rest." She looked down at the boy, her mind and emotions in turmoil. What should she do? Sturgis had said never to allow others onto the farm. There would just be too many dead. But—he was just a boy. And burned only on his face, the red patches and blisters on the rest of his body were not that severe. Just that terrible burnt face. But she knew he had a chance. A chance for life. If she took him back to the farm. Out here he would be gone within a day or two. His eyes looked up at her like cold slivers of gray ice. They showed neither fear nor pain nor even desperation. They just looked at her. She felt the boy was saying, "go on, leave me. I understand. See my eyes? They can feel nothing any longer."

With a sudden impulse she made up her mind. She went back out to the road and dragged in the pack of supplies, hiding them deep in the woods. Then she returned to the boy, who, thank God, had not died. His body was on the thin side and small. She grabbed both of his arms and, kneeling down, hefted him over her shoulder as Sturgis had taught her in the fireman's carry. Her knees seemed like they would buckle under the weight but somehow she got herself going forward, and once in movement down the road, was able to hold him up. Over her shoulder she could hear an occasional groan of discomfort, but he was too weak to even complain. A step at a time—that's it, she said to herself over and over, whenever she felt she was about to drop. There—foot forward, now the other. It turned into a rhythm in her head until suddenly without knowing it she was at the farm gate and then up to the cave home. She put him down as carefully as possible and unlocked the door. She hefted him again, feeling she was near passing out herself. She struggled into the living room where she stumbled just as she reached the long couch in front of the fireplace. He tumbled into it in a heap.

Robin retreated to the kitchen to calm her nerves and just sat there looking at the red formica tabletop for minutes. She made a pot of coffee and then got to work. If she was going to bring him in to the damned place, she sure as hell better do everything she could to save his life.

She gave him more water, tried to clean his wounds as best she could, with water and alcohol, then wiped a coat of liquid vitamin E over the entire burned portion of his face, it seemed to soothe him. She got a blanket for him as he seemed to be shivering. Then she went and dragged out every book she could find that even mentioned burns or radiation wounds and sat on the round rug on the floor in front of him so he'd know there was someone with him. She flipped through the pages searching for treatments to prevent infection and scarring. He would be a monster for the rest of his life with a face like that—if he lived. She looked up and he was sleeping, the tiniest of smiles on the white cracked lips. He was in a home again, people, life, warmth. "Yeah, kid, I'm gonna try to help you," Robin whispered softly, "or at least do my damnedest."

Without even realizing it, since she had found the boy, Robin had changed unconsciously from wanting to die—to wanting to live. She had no time now to worry about herself, to muse all the depressing possibilities. The boy needed her. Her spirit reached out to care, to help another live. And thus she came to life again.

CHAPTER TWENTY-EIGHT

The pumpkin-orange dawn lit up a charred hell of burned-out cars abandoned along Interstate 80. A little over one week ago, this road would have been jam-packed with cars and trucks. Today, it was silent; the road was a graveyard of twisted wrecks with decaying corpses as their only passengers.

The Interstate — silent, lifeless. A brooding strip of meaningless lanes divided by a crash barrier. Four lanes *to* nowhere, four lanes *from* nowhere. A highway to hell and from hell . . .

Then the birds heard it; they listened to the rumbling sound that had not assailed them for almost a week-and-a-half. The roar of engines, throaty, voluminous mechanical sounds, the drone of dozens of engines coughing out the lead-tainted blue fumes that had once filled this countryside with a low haze.

They waited until the last moment to take flight, still tearing at the dead flesh.

The roar of distant engines grew louder. Man was coming. Man of fire and death. The tens of thousands of birds that had been feasting on the banquet of corpses grew nervous, craning their bloody beaks, opening their wings. Then, in huge swirling masses of blackness they rose, blotting out the feeble sun. They spiralled upwards, out of the fetid ground-level air, into the low clouds, and became a cloud themselves, a living cloud of fear, still holding red things between their beaks. They hastened to get away from the deafening drone of the approaching humans.

Viking, so called because he wore a helmet with two bullhorns in it, was in the front of the V-formation of 76 bikes shooting down the interstate from the east. All 76 were dented, dirty machines, leaking oil, ill-tuned. Their riders were equally damaged, many with gashes and wounds on their bodies wrapped in filthy bandages soaked with whiskey to keep infection out. The last six riders — in a V-formation of their own, were the most seriously hurt — gunshot wounds. They rode weaving, coughing blood, slumping over from time to time. They would be tolerated for now, but they would eventually be left behind. The post World-War-Three America belonged to the strong, the swift, the *brutal*. To be weak meant to be *dead*. That had always been the creed of these riders, even before the explosions. And was even more so now, after the ruin of death had struck.

Viking rode a Kawasaki 1100, the biggest bike of them all, a bike once all chrome and blindingly shiny. He would make sure it was cleaned and tuned in the next town they hit. He had the best, and *would* have the best all the time. He would pick someone to clean and polish it — and blow their fucking brains out if he found a speck of dirt!

Viking was the leader of The Devil's Horde, a motorcycle gang that was organized in 12 states before the war. The Horde rode with violence in their red eyes, with all-out hell lust in their vibrating flesh down the Interstate. They were 76 strong, down from the 109 of last week.

The people in the last town they hit had been well prepared. Some of *the Horde* had died in the first fusillade of bullets and gasoline bombs. But Viking had exacted revenge on that town, exacted a week of fun-and-games out of the women and children, after killing off the menfolk. And then it was time to ride again.

A tall, lanky man of 29 with stringy shoulder-length blond hair, Viking had been born and raised in violence. His father had been a stickup man, until he was gunned down in a check-cashing place robbery in Albany, New York, back in 1985. The raging alcoholic muscleman had banged Viking around a lot until that day. His mother, a heroin-addicted prostitute, died of cirrhosis of the liver in the filthy Medicaid-ward of a hospital in Middleburg a year later. Viking had been on his own since then, since he was 14-years-old. He had stolen a motorcycle outside a bar at age 15, slitting the man's throat in the process. He never had a license or insurance or any legal papers of any kind for his succession of bigger and bigger cycles. He was a man without a real identity. The pack was his identity. "Too Much Ain't Enuf" was tattooed on his left arm, under the oil-stained leather jacket he wore. On the other forearm was carved into the flesh, by his own Bowie knife, "Born To Kill." And kill he did. But it had been just one here, one there—before the *big blow*. Now the stops were off. *Completely off.*

He smiled inside his black helmet behind the reflective green visor. He *was* death, and his Horde, like the Black Plague of the Middle Ages, was about to visit itself upon Regis, Ohio. Maybe this time he would die. But he and the devil—they were old pals. The devil would welcome one of his own into hell.

Viking signalled the turnoff ahead with a wave of his right hand. The motorcycle gang peeled off onto the ramp, deftly swirling around a pile-up of rusting pick-up trucks and a smashed semi which had burned to twisted

.steel days before. They made a right and resumed their six-row V-formation down the empty County Road 11. Ahead lay the fun-and-games he lived for — women, drugs, liquor. What the hell else was there? You took what you wanted, or you died trying. That's what it was about before the war too. The war proved that *he*, not straight society, was right. *They* had wasted their lives holding back their lusts, their evil desires, their raping, rampaging impulses. And for what? So that some day they could have some wife to support in a little ticky-tacky house? So that they could slave away until they got a pension? Where were those pensions now? Where was that house? That wife? Burned up, man, all *burned*.

He cycled over a hill and saw it ahead — Regis. Excitement tore through his amphetamine-tainted veins. For it wasn't burned. It was still there. The shot that suddenly rang out from a barrier of cars blocking the road ahead meant there was life there. Probably women too . . . Women that someone felt were pretty enough to protect.

The motorcycle gang tore for cover, one of them getting slammed off his bike into a muddy ditch by a high-powered rifle slug. There were many shots now — a dozen perhaps. A dozen against 75. Good odds. Already the cycles were roaring up inclines on both sides of the blocked road. Nothing could stop a good biker who was ready to die.

The roar was deafening as the bikes tore up the farm-fields, sending sprays of dirt behind them. Shots from the barricade were answered by the return fire of rifles and Viking's blazing pistols. Their slugs ate up the paint jobs on the massed cars. A damned good sound to Viking's ears. He flattened out behind his bike and unslung his .30-06 with telescopic sight. He found a face behind a Chevy in the barrier — a farmer's face, all weathered and serious. Viking lined up the crosshairs with the man's nose and pulled the trigger. The head jerked back and out of sight, trailing a funnel of red.

Some of the Horde's riders were upon the defenders of Regis from the flanks now, roaring down from behind them, firing wildly. That must be Farrell, Viking thought, opening up with his SMG. Damned lucky this town's bunch didn't have some Brownings or a fucking bazooka, like that last town. Damned lucky.

Suddenly the firing ceased. War whoops filled the air from the bikers behind the barricade. Farrell came leaping over the cars, holding a scalp, a bloody dripping scalp to tie on his bike's antenna with the others. Viking righted his bike, kick-started it, and rode forward. Members of the Horde pushed the cars off the road and their triumphant leader rode through the opening.

Viking skidded his bike to a stop next to a body. He kicked it over. Dead. He looked around. Farrell had his boot on a man's chest; there was a shiny sheriff's star pinned to the prone man's bloodstained shirt pocket.

"We got us a lawman," Farrell laughed. The man's eyes rolled up out of focus. "He's the only one of the seven still alive."

Farrell looked over at his leader and grinned. "Should we do what we did to that cop in that last town to this redneck sheriff?"

Viking snarled out, "Yes."

They lifted the man, who kept slipping in and out of consciousness, and placed him atop the Chevy's roof. They quickly tied rope to his hands and feet and ran them down to the door handles of the old car, securing them tautly. The sheriff lay bleeding and spread-eagled atop the roof.

"Now the fun begins," said Viking. "Get some gas out of the tank of that-there Ford."

Farrell siphoned off a quart into a coke bottle and ran with it over to Viking, who jumped on the car and looked down at the sheriff. He kicked him in the groin with the

320

heel of his big black boot.

"Time to wake up, old-timer," he snickered. "Time to light a fire." The man's eyes rolled, he grimaced in pain and tried to move.

"Tough luck old-timer. You're still alive. Too bad for you." The sheriff's eyes went to the bottle.

"What . . . what's that for?"

"Oh, just to give you a drink. You're thirsty ain't you? Tell me something, man, why was only you seven protecting the whole town?"

The sheriff smiled a tooth-missing grin. "Cause it's just a few of us left in the whole dang town, that's why. Everyone else — men, women, kids, went off to join the Resistance. We heard the call on the short-wave radio in my jailhouse, and everyone volunteered."

"Then why the fuck is *he* here?" Shark, one of the meanest of the pack asked.

"Yeah . . . Why *you* here then, you dumb shit sheriff?"

"Cause I'm too old, and got a bad ticker, 'Spect I'll be," he gasped suddenly, ". . . guess I'll *die* right soon from this here strain."

Viking smiled. "Maybe I'll help you die."

Viking felt powerful standing there, as the sheriff squirmed for his life. *He remembered* . . . as a kid, having a big magnifying glass and taking it out in the back yard of the ramshackle house they lived in, and finding an anthill in the cracks of the sidewalk. Hundreds of ants, digging, carrying tiny bits of food. He had watched them, fascinated, through the glass. Then he felt the violent stirrings in his gut. He had focused the sun through that lens, until it was an intense white beam on the ant-columns. One by one, he burned those ants alive, watched them squirm and writhe and then shrivel up in agony. Finally, he heard the tiny *pop* as their fluids boiled away and blew them apart. And he had smiled.

Then he had graduated to larger living things. Throw-

321

ing cats off the roof; catching stray dogs and sticking wires in their ears and eyes, hot wires—with the other kids watching in fear.

Then he had seen the bikers. Even when he was ten or twelve, he had watched with envious eyes as they roared by in the street and entered the ramp to the big highway. The motorcycles had symbolized escape for him, freedom. And now he was the leader, the *Führer*, as he liked to call himself. His old name was forgotten. He was Viking. No last name, no age, no address. How many men had he killed before the war? Ten? Twelve? A mere pittance. He had killed a hundred in the last week alone. Someone would get him soon, and he vowed that if he was wounded or came down with the radiation heaves, he would shoot himself. He would not live without his *power*. The power he stared down with *now*.

"What—what are you—going to do?" the sheriff gasped, seeing that *look* in Viking's eyes.

"Old-timer, we want to show our appreciation for your welcoming salute. You got one of my Horde, Daddy, and it's time to pay the price."

"We—we had to shoot at you. We were trying to make you turn away. We had to protect . . ." The sheriff bit his lips.

"So . . . You *do* got women in this town, and you wanted to protect them—and the kids. We heard it before. Well, women belong to the *strong*, Daddy, and you don't look too damned strong. Now, *match*, Jeeves," he said smirking.

"I ain't got no matches. Will a lighter do?" Shark asked.

"Lighter's fine," Viking said, as he slowly poured the bottle.

The sheriff began begging and pleading as Viking saturated his bloody shirt with the gas.

"I'll give you just one chance to tell us where the

322

women folk are hid—and if you ain't right, we light you. Now where they at?"

"Don't—you won't kill them—Will you?"

"Now *what do you think,* Pops? My buddies and me are good guys. We just need dates. Ain't that right guys?"

"That's right, Viking," the gang screamed back as they watched from their bikes.

"Well . . . they're in the church cellar . . ."

"Well ain't that all nice and religious-like," Viking laughed. "Give me the lighter, Shark."

"Stop. You said you wouldn't!" the sheriff screamed out.

The rest of his words were lost in the *whooooooshhhh* of his body igniting. He screamed for over a minute, as the gang started up their bikes and rolled around the Chevy that had become the sheriff's funeral pyre.

When they got to the church on the edge of town, they tore up everything, even the floor boards. But they found nothing.

"Shit," yelled Viking. "We've been sandbagged. There ain't even no fucking cellar at all. Fucking bastard. We're gonna tear up this town, set fire to the buildings. Maybe we can smoke 'em out."

They searched everywhere, but they found only a ghost town. There weren't even any supplies left. "Nothing, nobody," cursed Viking. Finally they found another old man, under the counter of the Regis Diner. He was sleeping off a drunk, a bottle of Chivas Regal near empty snuggled in the crook of his arm.

They kicked him awake. He was more helpful after some painful persuasion. There was *one* family that didn't leave town, he admitted. A sick old man in a wheelchair named Doc Higgins and his five teenage daughters. But the old man wouldn't say where they were holed up.

Shark shoved a blade up to the man's gizzard. "Where

323

them teenage girls? Where?"

The drunk at last gave them directions to the Higgins place. Viking let him live. The cycles pulled up in front of a large old mansion on Maple Street. All seemed silent. Shark, eager to get in there and find the girls, went in first — and stepped right into the firing line of an old man sitting in a wheelchair.

The Doc had been waiting there for days, keeping a vigil. He blasted Shark to putty with his pump-shotgun. Then the Horde heard one more shot. They came in and found the Doc had shot himself, so as not to reveal the location of his daughters, probably. This was one hell of a burg, Viking thought.

"Tear this place apart — maybe the chicks didn't leave. They wouldn't leave their sick old daddy," he grinned.

Viking was sure the girls were there somewhere. But after they went through every room and the cellar, they hadn't seen a trace of them. Finally Viking said, "Maybe this old place is like one of them spook mansions, with sliding doors and all. Rip apart the walls, boys. They've *got* to be here."

Wally was the first to hit paydirt. A false wall. "Shit man. Just like one of them damned horror movies." He stepped in and had his head blown off by both muzzles of a double barreled shotgun. But that was all the frightened girls inside had — two shells.

The gang scrambled in and grabbed them from the small secret room. There were five of them — all young and blonde.

"Let's *do it* now," Dekey said. "They did Wally in . . . ."

"No!" shouted Viking. "First we party, build up a little excitement, see? Like the old days, we dance and party and then the girls take us up on our offer to gang-bang them . . ."

The girls began crying. They ranged in age from 12 to 17. The oldest was very fat. She cried the most, her face

324

red and puffy. Dekey looked her up and down with his one good eye.

"Hell, this one here couldn't dance—she'd take up the whole floor!" Viking roared, grabbing her by the arm and pulling her forward. "What do you think we can do with her?" He smiled.

Dekey licked his lips, "*Pork chops!*"

The girls screamed for mercy as the fat one was led outside. She seemed to sink into a state of shock as if she knew what awaited her. Dekey liked to do this part. Viking liked to do other things.

"Please let us go—you can have the house," said one of the girls, the blondest one. "There's fresh food—even steaks in the freezer—over there . . ." she pointed to a big white chest along the wall.

"Now I know you're lying, Missy. There ain't no frozen nothing. The power's been off for weeks and there's no lights on in here," Viking said. He clicked a wall switch. "See Missy?—So what are you talking about?"

"I tell you it's true," the girl whispered. "There's lots of steaks, everything. We had—had a generator—till we—run out of kerosene yesterday. But the meat must still be good. Please, please bring back Jenny."

Viking smiled. "Zal, you check that freezer, you hear?" Zal limped over on his bum leg and did.

"Hey Viking. This is *fantastic*! It's just starting to thaw—all kinds of goodies."

"Please, please take everything, but leave us alone. Don't harm my sister. She's the oldest—and . . ."

"And the ugliest," Viking winced.

"Aw," said Zal, "she ain't so ugly. For pork chops. Tell you what Viking. I like 'em big. Maybe I'll take a hike out to the barn and have me a little piggy back ride, backdoor style. You know, before Dekey . . ."

"Go ahead," Viking said. "You're the only one what likes 'em fat, you have her, then help Dekey—with his

. . . work."

Viking tried to decide which one he liked best. It had been a while since he'd had a real small one. And virgins were best, for there weren't any doctors to go to if you got the clap from some slut you corncobbed.

The gang tied the remaining four sisters' hands behind their backs and manhandled them onto the seats of their motorcycles for the short ride down to the diner where they had found the old drunk. Maybe they could, Viking thought, still have a pretty good party. And the old guy could be sobered up to cook up some of the steaks—they brought all the food from the freezer along. They rode over in a deafening roar and pulled the sisters off the bikes, herding them inside the diner. Viking was ravenously hungry. He pulled the old man off a stool and said, "Time for some food, man—we got all these steaks outside and we want 'em cooked up."

"Cooked up?" the old man blurted out. "We ain't got no power or gas!"

"Grandpa—we want the grill going and the juke playing in five minutes, or . . ." He left the threat unspoken.

"But, but there's no electricity—there's no lights—no *gas*. How can I do anything?"

Viking squeezed the man's flabby cheeks. "Oh man, did you ever hear of bar-b-que? You've got lots of charcoal in this burg, and I've got lots of lighter fluid, man," he snickered. "So you best get with it."

Funk carried a big bar-b-que grill over from the smashed window of the hardware store, and a 50-pound bag of charcoal. Dexie got some big candles from the church, hundreds of votive candles. Soon the diner was lit up. It was a big place, and when Rapp and Sully got six big radios from the local electronics store and lined them up on the counter with fresh batteries in them, Viking snapped a cassette of *The Doors* into the first one. He led extension-jacks from radio-to-radio so they would all play the same tape.

The sound was deafening when he pressed the ON button, and brought cheers from the Devil's Horde. Soon they were dancing wildly, mostly with each other. The toughest ones had appropriated the four teenage girls they had rounded up.

Notably absent was the fat one. When the old man asked where Jenny was, the Horde just laughed and guzzled their beer. "Man, you just *cooked* her," Bug laughed. "Have a burger." Bug shoved his three-fingered hand holding a bun at the old man who just went pale. Could the meal he prepared actually have been Doc Higgins' oldest daughter? Please God, say it isn't so, he prayed silently. He felt like vomiting. And my God, he realized, what would they do to him?

Rapp, a mohawk-haired ganger, grabbed the 16-year-old by the waist and lifted her up on the lunch counter. "Now dance—little lady. The music is hot and the night is young. Before the night is over, you'll know what a real man feels like—you hear?"

He whacked her ass with a heavy oily hand. "*Dance!*" he yelled. The girl started to move her feet, tears streaming down her cheeks. Rapp ripped the front of her dress down, exposing her small pear-shaped breasts.

"Now that's better, ain't it, Viking?" he said, loudly, so he could be heard over the blasting music.

Viking twisted a cap off a warm Pabst and said "Yup. That's real entertainment, that is. Just like the old club headquarters in Alphabet City." He dug Stan in the ribs with his elbow.

Rapp never understood the amusement Viking saw in everything he did and said, and it made him mad. But Viking was tougher than him . . . tougher and bigger and even meaner. He smiled and said, "Aw, Vike, man, come on. It's fun, isn't it?"

"Sure sure. Why don't you get some of those other

little ladies up there, and have them do some sort of strip or something?"

The other girls were thrust up on the counter and slapped until they began stripping to the blasting music. The sordid strip tease was dragged out by the extreme reluctance of the girls once they were down to their underwear. It took a show of sharp blades by the gang to make them begin the last removals.

Suddenly the door burst open. It was the fat girl, Jenny, the girl that they had all *thought* had been butchered by Dekey. She held the double-barreled shotgun at the bikers sitting on the stools in front of the counter.

Viking licked his suddenly dry lips. The fat girl was dirty and bruised, wearing just a filthy calico dress and had no shoes on. But she held the big shotgun steady and both barrels of the rifle were cocked. "Get down, girls," Jenny said.

"Now easy there, little lady," Rapp said. "No cause to get excited . . ." He moved his hand a bit closer to the .45 in his belt.

The others moved slowly, spreading out. There was dark murder in the girl's eyes. They could see that.

"You," she said between her clenched teeth. "Stay put. Girls, *get down* slowly behind the counter and out the door behind me." Her sisters, who had seemed frozen in place now moved.

"Now listen, little lady," Rapp said. He waited until she blinked to reach for his .45. He wasn't fast enough. His body and those of the two men nearest to him were lifted up into the air and thrown backwards by the twin blasts, which peppered the room with bloody bits of flesh and motorcycle jackets. The fat girl was thrown back out the doorway by the powerful recoil of the weapon.

A hail of bullets flew at the door, but there was no one there. Viking crawled along the blood-splattered linoleum to the doorway and looked outside, holding his silver

9mm automatic at the ready. They were all gone — into the night. The deadly shotgun lay on the floor, still hot and smoking.

"Aw *shit*," he exclaimed, jamming the gun back into his waistband. "Just when the party was getting good. What a fucking *mess*," he said, turning over Rapp's nearly split-in-half body with his boot.

One of the tape-playing radios hadn't been hit, and was still playing:

> "People are strange, when you're a stranger
> Faces look ugly, when you're alone . . ."

It started to rain that night, for the first time since the gang took the road after the nuclear attack. The rain had a foul smell, like piss, and it burned. If the Horde had geiger counters, they would have known that it brought the "puking-death," for the rain was radioactive. When the gang rode out of Regis the next afternoon, leaving the town ablaze, the old man hung on a street light, though they didn't know it, they were mostly dead men . . .

The wind picked up and the church steeple, smoking and ablaze from the torches the Horde had thrown into the House of God, started leaning. Its bell moved and tolled for the last time. They all heard it a mile away as they rode onto the Interstate again. A loud sonorous ringing. At the same instant, Viking felt a nausea erupting inside him, felt the beginning of the puking death he had seen in so many towns they had passed through. Fear clutched at his chest. This was it. For the first time in his life he prayed to God and not to the devil. But there was no answer, only wrenching heaves that spilled last night's booze and burgers out of his nose and mouth.

CHAPTER TWENTY-NINE

General Petrin looked down from the cockpit of a giant Soyuz airlifter onto the Washington, D.C. Airport that loomed ever larger below. He could see the immense destruction that had been leveled on America's capital — the vast burnt sections of houses, the toppled monuments, the once white marble walkways and statues now black. Even though only neutron bombs had been dropped, still, they were powerful enough to do heavy damage and create fires everywhere.

Petrin — one of Moscow's top generals and commander of the notorious Gray Suits. U.S. Intel had heard the dimmest rumors that Russians were working on their own version of the C.A.D.S. suit, but nothing had ever been uncovered. And now it was too late. Petrin smiled smugly behind his closely trimmed silver beard. Whatever resistance was left, whatever defenses the president and his staff had erected in their bunker — it would all be to no avail. The Gray Suits — eight feet of armored/attack combat suits could smash through anything. Developed originally to deal with radiation spills, some obscure scientist had come up with the idea of adding some shielding and weapons to the things — and presto — instant post-nuclear war combat uniforms. Petrin looked forward to seeing the full extent of their powers in real battle over the next few hours. A new era of warfare was about to begin—and he would be its creator. He walked back through the ranks of his men, 125 on this plane. There were another 125 just behind them in another airlifter.

Their immense shiny suited bodies filled the cavernous transport as they waited to release their hell-fire on those below. The general passed every man, making sure all was in full readiness, that there would be no last-minute blunders. The landing lights went on and he returned to the cockpit and strapped in alongside the pilot. They hit the ground roughly as the runway had been cracked with inch- to foot-wide fissures that ran like spider webs across the concrete strips. But the Russian jet's large tires easily rode over them and it abruptly pulled to a stop, its forward thrusters screaming out their power.

His soldiers, like spacemen in their suits, waddled down the ramp at the rear of the eight-turbine jet. The assault on the White House bomb shelter, and the capture of the American president, their primary mission, was to begin as soon as the outer White House grounds were secured. Secured by paratroopers and infantry backed by tanks that had been sent eight days ago. His radio informed him that all was going well despite vainly brave action by a number of American civilians and a few remaining solders. He sighed. It was hard to believe, but General Zelosky, in charge of the advance units seemed to have almost bungled the job. But then Zelosky was an ass.

"Comrades," he addressed them standing out on the tarmac, "your orders are to go in and capture the imperialist clique who began this terrible war—who ordered the killing of your families, the attempted murder of Mother Russia. You are not to—repeat *not* to kill them. Your suits' armor will protect you from their fire so there is no need. We have some maps I am distributing now of the underground bunkers. We do not know if these are completely accurate or not — we only know that they are the best our intelligence could obtain." He handed out contractor's blueprints to the officers in charge of each 25-man team.

"We will move in three waves. We expect opposition — booby traps, surveillance devices. But you all have your specialties, your weapons, so use them. Let's move!"

Petrin got into a suit himself, prepared, if things got problematic, to lead them into battle himself. A general in charge of a tactical unit was unheard of, but Petrin wasn't about to let some jackass bungle the most important part of this damned war. With their leadership in captivity the Americans would be forced to surrender and cut short what was beginning to look like a massive resistance to the Red invasion.

Whoever was in charge of the United States now had done a wise thing. Virtually all U.S. major air bases had been blown to smithereens, making it difficult for the invading forces to land more than paratroopers in most places. Once the bases were captured, engineers were dropped to rebuild the airstrips so transports could land. Even the LST's hitting the coast, and the troop ships, had met with kamakaze-type defenses — being rammed by all sorts of civilian boats, cabin cruisers, yachts. One small PT boat had been attacked by men on *sail-boards*, firing machine guns! These Americans wouldn't give up — Petrin knew that. For years he had been stationed in East Berlin, and seen them tenaciously refusing to give an inch. And Viet Nam — they had bungled it, but they fought like madmen.

He got in the lead APV and roared off. Soon he was on Pennsylvania Avenue — near the White House, his army of suited warriors following behind in troop trucks. Only after they ran into a barrier did he realize that all the street signs had been switched or turned around. Suddenly they were attacked from all sides as men, women, even children opened up on them with pistols, rifles, everything they could get their hands on.

But it was a massacre as the Gray Suits poured from their trucks and fired machine-gun bullets and bazooka-type shells from built-in units on their suits. Within minutes there was just smoke and bodies — bodies of Americans lying everywhere. Petrin took little pleasure in this battle. It was like shooting tin ducks — the fools didn't have a chance. But he was a soldier. And his orders were to destroy all resistance.

They turned and, using his own map rather than following the street signs, General Petrin led his forces toward the White House. As they approached, the sounds of fierce fighting grew louder and louder. Russian paratroopers and regular Red Army advance units were pinned down all around the perimeter of the White House lawn. A rag-tag army composed of local citizenry, what remained of Washington's army units, FBI, CIA, and the Secret Service had all banded together at the White House to make a last symbolic, if futile, battle of it. There were nearly a thousand of them, covering the lawn, dug into foxholes, hanging out the windows of the White House itself. Before the Reds had begun moving in, a quick-thinking Army lieutenant had ordered truckload after truckload of rifles, ammo, grenades, mortars, and hand-held Stinger missiles driven up to the gates of the president's mansion and distributed to all who had come to volunteer their services. When the first Russian commando units had swept down Pennsylvania Avenue, expecting to walk right into President Armstrong's library, they had been wiped out.

Now, many days later, the Regular Red army which controlled large parts of the city was still having a rough time making much headway. They were under strict orders not to blow up the White House itself on the off chance that the president was still inside and thus had to fight foot by bloody foot to take the nation's most treasured building.

General Petrin pulled up the ATV and jumped out, rushing over to the command bunker of sandbags set up out of the Americans' firing range, several blocks down the wide central avenue that was lined with charred tree trunks.

The guards at the command headquarters looked quite startled as the eight-foot tall gray suited figure came bearing down on them. But his Red general's stars and his bearded face which they could see through his opened helmet visor, made them instantly recognize Petrin—one of Russia's most famous warriors. They saluted him with trembling hands. Petrin brushed past them, bending his head as he stamped into the HQ. Inside a half-dozen officers froze as if in a tableau, their mouths hanging open.

"Don't stand there looking like idiots," Petrin screamed, "Where the hell is General Zelosky?"

A short and very stocky man with shoulders the size of a table and a flat red face came bursting out from behind a partition.

"Who the hell dares speak my name like . . ." the general screamed rushing into the main room, until he saw Petrin.

"Ah, General Petrin," he managed to smile, his expression changing in a split second. Although theoretically generals of the same rank, in reality Petrin was far more powerful than Zelosky—and not a man to play games with.

"As I said when I came into this foul-smelling hole," Petrin bellowed again, "just what the hell is going on out there? You've got four divisions of crack troops at your command armed with the most modern weaponry. And yet here it is over a week since your entrance into Washington and you still haven't captured the White House. My men—the Gray Suit Force and I are here. Our schedule calls for us to take the White House and then the bunker below if that indeed is where their cowardly president is in hiding."

"G-g-general," Zelosky stuttered, "these Americans are fighting with a fury I have never seen before—even in the mountains of Afghanistan. They seem to care not a shred for their lives—and are equipped with weapons as powerful as our own. If I am unable to set up an artillery bombardment I don't see how I . . ."

"Bah," Petrin said, waving his huge gloved hand at the Army commander. "I am surrounded by fools. It is the curse of my life. All right then, *my* men will do it. Call your army troops away from the perimeter—we are going in in five minutes. I certainly wouldn't want any of your little boys to hurt themselves," Petrin said caustically, his voice dripping with sarcasm. Every officer's face in the room turned bright red, but no one dared say a word. Petrin turned and strode out of the command HQ and back to his Gray Suits.

The regular army troops were quickly called back to containing positions several hundred yards from the fenced in White House grounds. As they retreated, the dug-in Americans inside let out a cheer of victory, believing somehow, that against impossible odds they had won. Their cheers were short lived. For suddenly a formation of what appeared to be creatures from another world, *huge* figures, came forth. Were they robots or mere men, dressed in shiny gray metal battle suits? They came in a straight line along Pennsylvania Avenue. One of them walked up to the fence and spoke. His amplified voice boomed out over the entrenched fighters, wounded and bleeding, slowly dying of radiation poisoning, but ready to fight on to their last dying breath.

"We are the Gray Suits. If the way we appear frightens

you, I can assure you that what we can do will frighten you much more, and kill you too. My general is an honorable man. We are not here to exterminate America's citizens — just its ruling class. Surrender now and I give you my word as an officer of the Soviet Army that you will be treated well and after re-education, allowed to return to the New Society."

The American fighters answered his words with bullets, thousands of them pouring from every corner of the White House grounds. Although the Russian's suit was armored against small weapons fire, the barrage of slugs almost lifted him off the ground, knocking him backwards off his feet. But as quickly as he fell he rose again and began walking toward them, laughing within his huge helmet.

"You see, Americans — you cannot hurt . . ."

A screaming Stinger missile shot forward from a third-story window of the White House, trailing a straight line of blue smoke. Designed to take out jets and tanks, it flew unerringly toward its target as if eager to cause destruction. The shell tore dead-center into the chest area of the suit blowing a hole clear through to the other side. The violent spray of blood splattered back on the Gray Suits waiting in formation.

From across the street, watching the scene through binoculars built into his helmet, Petrin screamed out, *Kill them!*" over his walkie-talkie. "No mercy — Kill them all!"

The army of giants moved forward on giant plodding legs, making the very ground shake with their numbers as if a fleet of ten-ton trucks was going by. They reached the gate and walked right into it, knocking the steel posts over like toothpicks. From everywhere in their fortified positions the American citizen's army fired a hurricane of lead, spraying across the advancing ranks. But the bullets seemed to not have the slightest effect, pinging off the thick suits and into the air. The Gray Suits raised their menacing arms and from out of them poured automatic machine-gun fire and explosive shells that slammed into the White House defenders, sending them flying in volcanic eruptions of blood and bone.

It was like a nightmare. An occasional American-fired rocket or bazooka would hit one Gray Suit and rip off an arm or leg, but the others kept coming, reaching forward, firing, unstoppable. The Americans fought with immeasurable courage, but in modern warfare courage is a poor man's commodity. Firepower. Technology. These were all that mattered; and beneath the ceaseless barrage of the advancing giants the Americans were slaughtered. The Gray Suits pressed forward, firing everywhere, except at the White House itself. As they advanced they walked right over the dug-in fighters, squashing them as if an elephant had walked on their bodies—as blood pumped out from mouths and cracked skulls.

At last they rushed up the White House steps and splintered the soot-blanketed main door to shreds with a few smashes of their mailed fists. Petrin came right behind them. He glanced one more time at the blueprints for the secret elevator. They would have the shaft booby-trapped, but his experts would defuse it. But perhaps, hearing the Russians coming, they would all take suicide pills. That would be a defeat for Petrin—and Moscow—if they did. For the Reds needed the formality of surrender—a broadcast from the president to his defeated people—to stop their futile resistance. He would move slowly and very cautiously. He had the prey in his trap and he wasn't about to let it escape.

Deep down in the shelter below a technician took off his earphones. "Sir . . . Russian voices above. They're coming."

A surge of adrenaline shot into the president, who was

337

badly wounded from the damage done to the bunker.

"We will hold off until the last damned second. You," he pointed to Arthur Williamson, "will take charge if I pass away or can't function. Whatever we do, we must not fall into their hands for propaganda purposes, paraded around to convince our own people to surrender. We mustn't surrender—ever. Is that all agreed? I can't ask you all to kill yourselves but . . ." His eyes swept the room.

"We're with your decision, Mr. President," the vice president replied. "It's better this way."

Gidley handed around the yellow death pills. The president cupped one in his hand and said, "Again . . . not until the Reds are actually kicking in the door—or sleepgas is pouring in, will we . . ."

They nodded grimly. What would there be to live for anyway? They felt a surge of patriotism as they steeled themselves to die. They had heard the sounds above, seen it all on the closed-circuit TV cameras mounted in hidden slits in the White House walls. The bravery—the sheer bravery of the people up there. They felt proud, very proud, and prayed that they themselves would be as brave when they went into that dark night.

CHAPTER THIRTY

The Omega team came to the Potomac River and crossed by a bridge they found still intact. They scanned the low-lying radioactive clouds overhead for Red helicopters or jets. And suddenly, there, before them, the goal of their long journey. Sturgis whispered, "Telescopic Power 20" to his visor system. Washington D.C. was still there, he could see instantly as its domed buildings come into view. Many buildings were on fire. The Washington Monument had toppled. But the city wasn't just a vast crater filled with atomic water as they had feared. It had been hit with an airburst — a neutron bomb obviously — or a few of them.

Sturgis could see Russian troop trucks and tanks pouring through the streets, and with his augmented hearing, he picked up numerous firefights going on throughout D.C. So the Reds hadn't even been able to take the city nearly two weeks after the nuke attack! Those brave Americans fighting and dying out there may have, unknowingly, bought enough time for them to help the president escape.

They moved through the suburbs of the city at top speed, heading toward their rendezvous with the other C.A.D.S. Teams, at Washington General Hospital. Sturgis prayed they were already there. They pushed on, knowing there wasn't a thing they could do for the moaning survivors behind them, pleading for food and water. Sturgis thought of Robin. Was she a victim in Baltimore, vaporized with the initial blast?

He choked back a wretched feeling in his throat and floored the accelerator. He would take the spearhead position for the advance on Washington. He wanted to be the first to fire at the Red enemy—and perhaps the first to die.

Sturgis led the Omega Team down the car-wreck-strewn streets of western D.C., following directions from Fenton inside the Rhino, who pulled the Washington maps up onto his directional screen. After about 10 minutes they came to it—G.W. Hospital. One of the capital's biggest—and it appeared to still be functioning. As Sturgis pulled up into the driveway he was relieved to see at least some Tri-wheelers there, lined up inside a sheltered parking lot. He pulled to a halt and jumped from his bike, throwing up his visor.

"What's going on here—What unit are you?" he demanded of the C.A.D.S.-suited guards.

"Colonel Sturgis," the closer one said as they both snapped to attention. "Sergeant Jessop, sir. B-Squad. Both B and C Squads arrived. D-Squad has not. Lieutenant Glenner and Colonel Dawkins are inside the hospital seeing to the treatment of our wounded men."

"How many wounded?" Sturgis asked.

"Five from B, 13 from C, sir," Jessop replied, still standing erect in the huge C.A.D.S. suit.

"Don't stand so stiffly," Sturgis cracked, "you'll break something in there. All right now, gather all your men immediately. Tell them to suit up, get their bikes out here in this area. We leave to defend the White House in fifteen minutes."

"Yes, sir," Jessop barked. Sturgis strode through the swinging doors of the hospital and down the well-lit antiseptically white corridors. Bodies littered both sides of the hallway, shaking and groaning as they waited for what little treatment was available. Ahead he suddenly saw two huge black-suited men like himself coming toward him.

"Sturgis here," he said over his throat mike, switching to total suit linkup—so that all the C.A.D.S. men within

340

would hear him.

"Sturgis, thank God," Lieutenant Glenner said. "We were wondering just what the hell to do next, without you to make the command decision."

"Where the hell is D Company?" Sturgis asked, annoyed.

"No idea," Colonel Dawkins strode up and replied. "We haven't heard a word from them since leaving the base. But sir, the situation's very bad. The last transmission we were able to pick up on scramble code from the president's bunker was that the Reds were blasting their way down the elevator shaft. The technician on duty said they couldn't hold out more than a few hours at most."

"We ride now," Sturgis said, turning on his thick booted heels and tearing toward the door. "There's no time to wait. D Company'll have to catch up." Both commanders of the other two teams strode hard after Sturgis, glad that they didn't have to make the decision.

They rode from out of the still swirling smoke of a hundred blazing buildings.

There was no attempt at subterfuge, at coming in under the darkness of night, at complex battle tactics. This would be a war of the fast and the powerful, and the men of the C.A.D.S. team were ready.

"This is it, boys," Sturgis addressed the team as they rode nearly 65 strong onto the outer edge of Pennsylvania Avenue. He took the lead with the two Company B and C Rhinos just behind him, then the rest of the Tri-wheelers with Fenton riding shotgun once again at the tail end.

"From now on all systems are on—pay close attention to your 'early Defense Modes'—they may save a lot of us today. Fire fast and don't spare the ammunition. Use your big stuff. There's plenty more where it came from. We move straight ahead from now on. Straight to the White House where you will go into your pre-arranged positions. Squads B and C, shift a little more toward each other's area as we come in. I'll be going down with my own team to get the president and come back up. Dawkins, you'll get the trucks. If your bike is hit, forget it, leave it. Use your suit. Go to jump mode." He breathed deeply so they could all hear him. "This is it folks — the big time. Let's not fuck up our show, Okay?"

"Okay," they all yelled back over their throat mikes so that for a split second they were almost deafened by the roar. They had scarcely hit Pennsylvania Avenue when Red units along the boulevard opened up with a gauntlet of firepower on the bizarre attack force that swooped down on them. Bullets, streams of machine gun fire, and 120mm tank cannon shells hit them from every side. Two Tri-bikes near the back of the force took direct hits from tank shells and were thrown from the avenue in bloody pieces. The suits could take a lot, but not a foot-and-a-half long shell, dead center.

But within seconds the C.A.D.S.-suited drivers returned their own greetings to the Reds. Sturgis and his men fired back like wild animals, using every mode on their suits, constantly shifting perception and attack systems in split second commands. "Roof 200-300 fire," Sturgis commanded the missile launch of his Tri-bike, whose computer was linked automatically to the suits the moment he sat down in the machine. A shrieking ground-to-air missile tore up out of the front right side of the Tri-bike, and rose toward two large howitzers the Reds had mounted on top a six-story building. The missile tore into the mouth of one, sending the entire rooftop into a funnel-shaped cloud of debris and bone which slowly rained over the entire avenue. Sturgis checked his radar screen. They were surrounded by cannons, mortars, artillery. They could be ripped to shreds.

"Omega Force," Sturgis screamed, cutting in on their radio communications with each other. "Hook into radar. Pick the closest targs, and fire EB mode," he gave them a chance to comprehend his words as the fleet of death vehicles roared forward at 60mph through a living hell of whistling rockets and tracer shells.

"On three," Sturgis said. "One . . . Two . . . Three . . . *now*!"

Every man of the Omega team fired simultaneously, keeping one eye on the road, the other on their radar screens. There was a sudden roar that shook the very air for a half mile as Russian artillery units all over town went up in violent eruptions, stung by the precisely aimed E-balls. The C.A.D.S. team watched glumly as the proud monuments of the nation's capital crumbled under the fury of their own fire.

Sturgis waited a few seconds for the violently swirling smoke and dust of the explosions to blow off. The haze finally cleared and he gunned the Tri-bike back up to 60mph, shooting at every goddamned thing that moved. He felt like a man possessed, not just a soldier, but an avenger, seeking revenge for all those poor bastards they had seen in getting here. Through him and the C.A.D.S. team, the citizens of the U.S.A. were sending their hate for all that had been done to them. Sturgis fired, screaming orders to his computer, turning his head wildly from side to side, to try and get a fix on everything that was happening in the super speeded up time of battle.

Sturgis's Early-Warning System suddenly beeped on as the words "Russian MIGs from northwest 57 degrees."

"Fenton, Fenton—you reading that," Sturgis screamed over the helmet mike.

"I see 'em Sturgis, I'm sending up some Sharks right now." Inside the Rhino, Fenton released two of the four Shark missiles that each Rhino carried. His lit-up control panel beeped out "Enemy craft preparing to fire; weapons away . . ."

The MIGs each got off two rockets which streamed down unerringly into the center of the Omega convoy.

Eight bikes in the middle of the column took direct hits, going end-over-end off the road. Sturgis slowed as the words Casualties: 8 flashed on the visor. The two Red fighters prepared to fire again but suddenly saw the streaks coming up toward them on their radar. Ground-to-air from land vehicles. Their pilots' eyes grew wide with horror as they slammed their jets into missile-escape maneuvers, spinning end-over-end, plummeting to the earth to try and avoid radar homing devices.

But the missiles Fenton had fired were the smartest of the so-called smart missiles. Like dark denizens of the deep the flaming cylinders closed their jaws around the exhaust vents of the MIGs. Fenton saw the two blips disappear from his radar screen.

"Scratch two," he radioed back to Sturgis. "What else we got?"

"We'll find out," Sturgis said instantly. "The road's a bit rough up here. Too many explosion holes. Men, deploy to suit power. Defense unit, stay and guard the Tribikes. The rest of us are heading in on *jump mode. Let's go!*"

Sturgis sailed up into the dark billowing smoke as if into the guts of a bad dream. He could hear the other members of the C.A.D.S. team soaring by all around him. He rose above the gray smoke now, reaching up nearly 100 feet into the air, and looked down on the building they had traveled so far to reach, the White House, still resplendent in its antique beauty, still standing proud in the midst of a soot-covered and flaming Washington.

"Jesus Christ," he blurted out, as the Gray Suited Giants on the White House lawn came into his field of vision. "What the *hell* is that . . . *ID* Mode," he screamed into the computer, his gaze fixed on the warriors.

"Data unavailable," the computer reported. "Some

form of combat suit equipped with offensive weapons. Type unknown, abilities unknown."

His men hovered in the air like a flock of black hawks all around him, unsure of what to do.

"Stay aloft," Sturgis ordered on all channels. "I'm going in."

There was no time to play games. He had to be bold. Were they ours? Members of another top secret team that he didn't know about? Or *theirs*, a parallel development in modern warfare that U.S. Intelligence had missed. He landed on the sidewalk just outside the high steel fences that surrounded the White House. Sturgis looked through the thick bars of the fence at the nearly eight-foot tall Gray Suits who stared back at him with equal amazement and curiosity.

"Who are you?" he asked over his suit P.A. System. At the exact same moment the same words came back at him, only in Russian. The scene was frozen in time for fractions of a second as each side realized with horror that they faced their opposite number—their nemesis in super-tech warfare.

Then all hell broke loose.

Fifty Gray-suited arms rose and aimed toward the strange black-suited American trooper who dared to come down into their midst. They fired a storm of explosives that bore down on their victim in screaming trails of death.

"Jump," Sturgis yelled to the suit which took off a fraction of a second before the combined blasts would have made mincemeat out of him. He rocketed into the air about 60 feet before turning and choosing his attack mode—*EB's*.

"Attack," Sturgis commanded the hovering C.A.D.S. force, now spread out in the air above the White House like a vast flock of black shadows.

It was a battle unlike any the earth had ever seen before. The two opposing forces each armed with the most modern weaponry known to man, each possessed with enough fire power to have taken on whole armies of the past. A battle of giants that made the very heavens streak with lightning and the earth tremble beneath their immense feet.

Sturgis rocketed right over the top of the White House itself to get the full picture of the force they faced. It looked bad. The Gray Suits were everywhere, covering the grounds like a forest of dark trees. He instantly had the visor scan the inside of the building.

"Enemy force inside structure 30 to 74 men," it read back. "Explosive charges being detonated every 80 seconds in tunnel system beneath structure." Great. So they were already blasting their way down to the president. But they hadn't reached him yet. There was still time.

He dropped down low, coming through a haze of smoke that rose out of the smoking bodies of two of the Gray Suits, their guts strewn out across the lawn like blood sausages from the attack of the C.A.D.S. team. He picked up three of the enemy drawing beads on them. "EB," he yelled, waiting just long enough for the laser finder guidance system to home in. He twisted his wrist and shot sideways, tilting his body slightly to the right. Behind him, all three warriors exploded in a torrent of burning flesh that spat out in all directions. He could see that the C.A.D.S. suits were much more maneuverable than their Russian counterparts.

Tranh appeared beside him and the two began working together, making their way up to the White House steps. All around they could see the combatants rising, falling, in the air and on the ground, moving like lightning bolts, in a high-speed digital computer-game-battle where the stakes were not quarters but life or death.

Sturgis saw one of his men take a direct hit from a Red mini-rocket as he flew in low for a strike. The rocket hit dead center and ripped the C.A.D.S. suit to shreds. Sturgis had to look away for a moment as the American fighter dissolved into a chunky red stew that poured down onto the Gray Suits some 40 feet ahead of them. Sturgis could see that the Red unit was capable of taking its toll.

"Sturgis, it's Billy Dixon, sir," a voice rang out through the suit earphones as Tranh signalled that he was going to skip up to the next cover, some 20 feet ahead. Sturgis drew a bead on another Gray as Billy continued.

"Sir, I just took a jump over the place and it looks like they're pulling back on your side."

"Pull in behind me, men," Sturgis ordered, as his team saw the battle develop in their favor, forcing the Reds into a disorganized retreat.

Sturgis could hardly believe it. The Reds were in full retreat after barely 10 minutes of battle. The White House lawn was covered with Gray suited bodies and Sturgis began to realize that his men had taken a far greater toll on the enemy than *they* had managed.

The Reds had fought fiercely and with great power, Sturgis thought, as he looked down on the nearly two dozen men he could see in a glance. Bodies from both sides littered the scene and Sturgis realized that, no matter how complex and sophisticated war became, or *seemed* to become, it always boiled down to the simple fact of spilling your enemies' blood.

"All units," Sturgis commanded over the throat mike, "let them pull back from attack. Repeat—let enemy retreat."

The team began landing around him, dropping from the air like soot-coated eagles from some flaming hell, their suits covered with grease and guts and flesh and chunks of things that were no longer recognizable.

"What now?" Rossiter asked, dropping near his commander. The others gathered closer, keeping a sharp eye out for the attacking forces which for the moment were in too much confusion to do much damage.

"All right, everyone's low on fuel by now, so we're all going to be out of the air-war soon. And that's been our *main* advantage so far. I don't know how good we'd do in a straight ground battle with those big blundering power-houses they got there. Those shells they fire are as powerful as E-balls."

"Build it big and strong and build a lot of them," Tranh muttered into his mike. "That's been the Russian military mind since World War II."

"Well, they are strong—*too* strong. We've got to get inside, but the place is crawling with them. They're in there, laying for us, and there's no choice. We're going to have to . . . have to . . ."

His voice quivered and almost broke for the first time any of the men had ever heard. "Men," he continued, drawing himself together. "We're gonna have to blow up the whole goddamned White House."

"What?" a chorus of incredulous voices shouted back.

"The only way to the president is through that floor. It would take us days to fight our way in, if we could. They'd have time to call in whole squadrons of MIGs with long-range missiles. It's our only chance."

"You're bloody right, you've got to do it," a voice cracked in on the conversation which was being monitored by everyone in the unit. It was Fenton. "Go ahead. Don't let any patriotic bullshit stop you. It's not the building, it's the man, Sturgis, the president—the living symbol of America's strength. If it was my own fucking House of Lords, with the Queen inside, I'd blow it to kingdom come to save her."

"All C.A.D.S. units," Sturgis said firmly into the throat mike. "On count of three, you will aim and fire every weapon on your suit at the White House. Take up attack formation." The men on the ground spread out around the outer fence as those who still had enough fuel in their jet assist packs shot up into their circular mode attack formation. Hundreds of yards off, they could see the Gray Suited Russian troops peering out the windows and doors of the building, raising their arms and sending out volley after volley of big thundering shells that gouged deep craters out of the sidewalk and street as they screamed just over Sturgis' head.

"*Fire*," Sturgis ordered. Every man in the combined C.A.D.S. unit, all 43 of them who still survived from the original one hundred who had left the New-Mexico base, opened up with their heavy guns.

A solid stream of shells of every size and shape tore back and forth across the 50-odd yards of territory separating the C.A.D.S. force from the White House and its occupying forces. Sizzling electro-spheres poured through the white walls of the historic building. First the firestorm ate up the outer walls, blasting huge chunks right off their straight sides. Then the high explosive spheres ripped into the innards of the building, tearing down whole rows of walls, sending the priceless furnishings crashing into piles of burning junk.

The Reds inside continued to send out their missile-like volleys, but the Gray Suits were trapped, and they knew it. Their suits would protect them against the flames for perhaps a minute or two—and then . . .

"Flame units—attack any strays," Sturgis commanded, heading back through the torn gate raising his own LPF cylinder under his left arm. From inside, the C.A.D.S. team could hear the most horrendous screams, as Red troops made the choice to stay inside and die. Others flew out, their backs burning like moths that had strayed too close to a flame, only to be met by a new wall of flame from the LPF's hotter, searing flame that stuck to them, burning deeper, as its plastic fire melted deep into the skin. Trapped between the two fires, the Gray Suits who had remained to hold the White House were destroyed to a man. The merciless flames consumed every part of them, even the bones.

Sturgis rushed forward, requesting the computer to flash the secret blueprint maps he had received before leaving White Sands—that showed the location of the tunnels to the bunker below.

"The Reds thought there was just *one*," said Sturgis to Tranh and Roberto as they marched to the edge of the White House which collapsed before them, the walls gone, the burning wooden supports falling together like charred match sticks. "But there are two."

"Locate entrance," he told the computer, "of point A-B on projected maps."

"30-47-19," flashed across the lower portion of his screen. Sturgis walked to the coordinates and the computer flashed, "Entrance directly below."

"Well, there's supposed to be a whole code and things that should actually make this ground here in front of us rise up," Sturgis said, waving the men to the side. "But I don't happen to know what it is, so . . ."

He pulled back and aimed two EB's dead center and turned his head as showers of dirt sprayed over them from the force of the blast. He walked quickly over to the gaping hole he had created. The top several feet of dirt had blown off, to reveal a concrete walkway below, and a deep shaft that headed down into a vanishing darkness.

CHAPTER THIRTY-ONE

"What the hell do we do now?" Rossiter asked, looking nervously into the seemingly endless pit.

"We go *down*," Sturgis said.

"Suppose it's booby-trapped," Roberto said, his huge helmeted head peering over Sturgis' shoulder.

"It's not supposed to be. The elevator shaft the Reds were trying to climb down *is*. This is an emergency entrance. Let's go. Tranh, Roberto, Billy, come with me. The rest of you watch out for whatever may come out of the other shaft."

"Who the hell goes there?" a voice yelled out over a camouflaged speaker.

"The C.A.D.S. unit, damn it—to take the president to safety. There's no time to fuck around," Sturgis bellowed, lifting his visor in anger.

"The code, *the code*!" insisted the voice.

"I *don't know* the goddamned code," Sturgis growled back. "If I did, don't you think I would have said it?'

"Who won the World Series last year?"

"Chicago—in six games," Roberto, the team sports fanatic, yelled from behind Sturgis.

"The Superbowl?" the voice asked hesitantly.

"How the hell should I know?" Sturgis said, losing his

temper. "If the Reds had one of those record books out here, you dummy, they could recite *all* your answers for you. Now let us the hell in. It's Commander Dean Sturgis, USAF Special Weapons Unit—Omega Force, from White Sands, assigned to this mission by Acting President Christian himself.

"Our computer file says you don't exist."

"Put the president on the damned speaker, you idiot," Sturgis yelled, slamming his gloved hand against the steel door with a resounding gong.

"The president is—indisposed," said the communications technician. "The vice president is available . . ."

"Put him on," said Sturgis, rolling his eyes heavenward. The strong but emotional voice of Vice President Arthur Williamson came over the speaker:

"How do we know for sure who you are? The Reds are blasting their way right now through the main shaft."

"What the hell do you think we're doing out here? Toasting marshmallows? We're up to our knees in red bodies. Up top, I've lost half my force fighting to get to you."

There was silence for a second, then the hiss of compressed air as the vault door in front of Sturgis began slowly opening down the middle, sliding smoothly into the walls. The four C.A.D.S.-suited warriors, Sturgis, Rossiter, Tranh and Roberto, stepped into a wide room which smelled musky and stale. It had been sealed since two hours before the neutron blast killed hundreds of thousands on the surface. The vice president stepped forward and Sturgis saluted, then reached out and shook the Veep's hand. He looked around and counted ten people— two women and eight men, one of whom, the president, lay on a sofa.

Armstrong managed to half sit up as his secretary propped up his pillow. Sturgis walked over to the man and saluted again.

"Mr. President, Colonel Sturgis. I have orders from Acting President Walter Christian aboard Air Force Three, and from my commander, General Knolls, to rescue you and your party, and transport you back to our base."

The president said weakly, "Colonel Sturgis, I appreciate the terribly dangerous efforts you and your men have made to get here. And all your men who died up there to reach us—what can I say?" He coughed up a bit of blood. Gidley limped over, drew Sturgis aside, while the president heaved into a red-stained handkerchief.

"I don't know if we can move him. The neutron blast knocked over those shelves of supplies on him. He had internal injuries, his pulse is weak."

"There's no choice," Sturgis said. "We're not here in large numbers—we're just a commando unit. The Reds will regroup and attack again. Soon. We have to get going immediately. Once out of Washington, our medics, perhaps . . ."

He bit his lip. "I understand."

At the far end of the bunker they could hear the muffled sound of explosions as the Russian Gray Suits blasted their way down through the partially caved-in main shaftway.

Sturgis heard his helmet radio crackle into action.

"Fenton here, Commander, they're coming in again. Choppers, and a whole row of tanks. We're holding—but I don't know for how long."

"Affirmative. We're coming up fast. Are the transport trucks there yet?"

"They just arrived. Two of them."

"We'll be topside within five minutes—prepare the men to move out."

"Roger."

Sturgis sat down for a second. He felt exhausted from the battle—his tense body uncoiling slowly as he breathed deeply.

The vice president spoke up haltingly. "Is it safe on the surface. I mean . . ."

"As safe as it's gonna get," Sturgis said. "The radiation level is 35 around D.C. anyway."

The secretary of defense sighed, "Forty is the maximum per hour for a lifetime dose. We've probably absorbed, we figure, 80 or 100 down here . . ."

"We're way over that, Mr. Secretary," Sturgis said grimly. "We've been out in the worst of it."

They all knew what that meant. The chances of the team developing cancers within five years was over 60% now—and climbing. No one said anything.

"Have our retaliatory strikes done any damage over there?" Williamson asked.

"From what General Knolls could find out we got in a bunch of hits—20, 30 maybe. They got in—*hundreds.*

"Sturgis, are the Americans you've met defeated?" the vice president asked in a whisper, "will they surrender or will they—if the president gives the order, continue to fight?"

Sturgis stared him in the eye. "Give that order," he said firmly, loud enough for all to hear, "and Americans will fight to the death. I'm sure of that. I've seen it out there, and among my men, who are not unique. The Reds will not occupy this country."

"Amen, amen," muttered the white-faced president. His nurse increased the flow of blood-plasma into his arm, shaking her head from side to side.

"Tell them for me," he said suddenly, his voice rising, "Tell America I never thought, never thought the Russians would—do—it . . ." His eyes rolled up and he exhaled a long groaning gasp and lay still. The nurse gently closed the vacant, staring eyes.

Sturgis turned to Williamson. "I guess you're the president now." Williamson a first-term senator from Oklahoma who had been selected to balance the ticket. Sturgis took measure of the man — his jaw firm, eyes clear. He just might grow into the role. He'd have to do it fast.

"We've got to go *now*. Everyone grab clothing and only the most vital documents," Sturgis said, as he directed the rest of the team, carrying charges they'd taken from the Rhino over to the half-blown doors covering the main elevator shaft.

"Leave *him* like this?" the secretary asked, her eyes filling with tears.

"No. We've got to blow the place up — both to stop them from pursuing us and we can't let them get his body." He ordered his men to quickly set the charges, 10 of them, long cylindrical tubes carrying the concentrated equivalent of over a ton of high explosive.

Sturgis and men herded them out to the secondary elevator and put the new president and his top staff aboard.

"Take 'em up," he ordered Roberto. "Call for cover and get them into that transport truck. And get this goddamned thing back down the second they're unloaded."

The platform shot up and quickly out of sight as Sturgis and the others waited anxiously. The booming roars of the still-descending Russians grew louder every second as the granite walls shook all around them. It seemed like an eternity but at last the elevator reappeared, hurtling down from above. They loaded on and rose like a bullet.

The C.A.D.S. team had managed to push one of the parked diesel trucks the Reds had blocked the avenue with out of the way with the Rhino. Sturgis and the rest emerged into the suddenly blinding light of late afternoon and found the entire force of Rhino's and Tri-wheelers waiting for them, their motors roaring.

"*In, in*," Sturgis yelled, pushing the men and women who were all that remained of the U.S. government toward the transport truck and slamming the doors.

"Your bike's here, Sturgis," Dixon said. "We dragged it up for you."

The C.A.D.S. commander leaped aboard the debris splattered vehicle and turned all systems on.

"Let's get the hell out of here," he screamed over the microphone. The fleet raced across the White House's blackened lawn.

How many Reds had his men killed here today? A thousand? Two thousand? Smoking tanks and buildings lay in a wide path all around him. A frown crossed Sturgis' lips. And the realization that he was going to disobey orders — again. Once they got safely out of Washington, he would divert by himself to his farm to see if Robin was there. It would hurt him to leave his men, but the worst part of the mission was over, and it would hurt him a thousand times more to leave her now — when he was so close . . .

They drove for nearly two hours, knocking out some Red vehicles in hot pursuit and two choppers with ground-to-air missiles. When it looked clear Sturgis radioed to Tranh, "Got to check something — back in a minute." Only the Vietnamese knew what was happening and he kept his mouth shut. Sturgis wheeled around to the back of the racing convoy and let his Tri-bike slow down a little until the rest of the team was hundreds of yards ahead. Then he veered sharply to the right and headed off toward the farm — and the woman he had no choice but to try to find — and save — if she was still alive.

CHAPTER THIRTY-TWO

The whine of the Tri-bike couldn't stop him from thinking about what he had done. This was not AWOL, this was desertion.

It had hurt him to leave the C.A.D.S. team like that — just shooting off, mumbling to Tranh, "Take over, I have something I have to do." But this was it — what he had stayed alive for.

Sturgis was just 30 miles from his Virginia farm when the suit suddenly became a suffocating oven. The air exchanger and filter system had broken down. Muttering curses, he watched the systems lights flash off one by one inside the visor. Blue systems off, then red, green. Finally, even visual mode-normal shut down. So aside from baking inside, he had to take the damned helmet off to even see where he was driving the Tri-wheeler. What the hell was wrong with it anyway? A total systems collapse. Did the suit have one of those scratched semi-conductors from U-TroniL Labs? That outfit had sent them so much dangerous and faulty electronics that Sturgis suspected them of working for the Russians. If so, he was out of luck. Of course, it could be the wiring. The suit had been through hell. If it *were* the wiring, he could do the repairs with his little belt kit. But it might take hours. Hours, precious hours.

"Well," he said to no one in particular, screeching to a

halt right in the middle of the macadam. "No time like the present."

He took the entire suit off, breathing in the fresh cold air. He hardly even cared if it was radioactive. The last reading before the systems failure had said it was safe, so he'd best stay right here to fix the contraption.

He felt tense to the point of exploding — probably a result of being so close to finding out if Robin were alive or just some ashes in a nuke-fallout zone. So close, and yet stymied like this. He ripped the repair kit off his belt and opened it up. A maze of miniaturized space-age socket wrenches, screwsets, circuit boards, soldering equipment, and gauges stared back at him, along with a self-illuminating magnifying device to see what the hell he was doing. Plus a 30-page schematic analysis of the internal workings of the suit. He wished Fenton were here. Or Rossiter. Or anybody to help him speed this tedious process. The diagnostic indicator valve stared him in the face: A tiny device similar to the diagnostic machine the garages all had to check engine functions, but tiny as a fingernail. A marvel, like the suit, he thought cynically — and just as likely to break down.

He ran the Optic Scan magnifier down the schematic diagram and found the "red dot" areas — power fuse centers of the suit. The most likely to blow out were fuses R-12 and R-45. They were just under the electroball firing sequence modulator. He took out the mini-phillips screwdriver set and, putting the suit in front of him on the Tri-bike seat, he began the delicate work of removing those fuses. There were *lots* of the 25mm size fuses in the repair kit, if this was all that was wrong, he could be on his way in a half hour.

He was careful not to scar the plastic rims of the mini fuse boxes. If he couldn't fit the new fuses snug, they'd blow out instantly. He moved ever so slowly so as not to make any mistakes, removing the fuses and examining them with the optic scan. One was blown. Could *that* have caused the complete power cut? He doubted it. He replaced the faulty fuse and all the other ones for good measure. The problem was, the suit's fuses might *look* okay but be defective from the contractor. Once, months before, a whole suit had all the wrong amperage fuses in all the right places, and a man had died as a result. Sturgis wished he had some of those fat-faced, double-dealing contractors in front of him right now.

Sturgis heard the crack of a tree branch and froze. His ears tweaked, a cold ball of sweat slid down his neck.

A Kalashnikov rifle's business end was jammed into his back. He winced, but was careful not to move an inch. Russian voices. He knew Russian well enough to pick up the conversation.

"Well, what do we have here? A *sewing* American? Making a spacesuit?"

"Be careful Yuri," his companion said. "There's something strange about this man's gear. I don't like it."

"Nonsense," said the Red holding the gun against Sturgis' back. "He's alone."

You should never put a rifle against a man's back. Before you could pull the trigger a trained fighter like Sturgis could wheel and deflect the rifle merely by the spin of his back. And suddenly you would be face to face with someone with murder in his eyes. Sturgis waited until the second soldier was in a position to the side of him where, when Sturgis spun counter-clockwise, the rifle was deflected right into him. The rifleman pulled the trigger instinctively, blasting his comrade. Sturgis smashed the inept rifleman in the chest with the exploding dum dum bullets of the emergency .45 he slipped from its holster under the Tri-bike's handlebars.

The bullets corkscrewed out of the body at right angles, making nasty exit wounds as the man fell, pulsing blood.

Was that all of them? Time to get the hell out of here. The shots could be heard for miles. Sturgis threw the still non-functioning suit over the back seat with a great heave, jumped on the Tri-wheeler and bucked to a screeching start. He roared down the road barely in control of the lurching vehicle, and swept around a bend, only to be blocked by a big transport truck with its back down and a .55mm machine gun with two helmeted soldiers holding it inside, trained on him. He screeched to a halt and lifted his hands as a half dozen more red-helmeted troops rushed around the truck on both sides, their Kalashnikovs at the ready. A Russian officer stepped forward holding a Turgenov 7.22mm service revolver straight at Sturgis' nose.

"Dismount your motorcycle," the blond man with the single star on each epaulette said, in halting English. Sturgis slowly rose from his seat, his stomach sinking into his feet.

"Put your hands on your head," the officer commanded. Sturgis complied, cursing the damned suit for getting him into this jam. He was sunk. But why didn't they just shoot him? Did they know who he was, what the suit was?

If it was still operational, he could have activated the self-destruct mechanism to prevent it from falling into enemy hands.

He would have died in the process, along with the whole crew. But now, there was nothing he could do. They had him, *and* the suit.

"You're coming with us. Turn around," said the officer. He felt handcuffs snapped on behind his back. "Well, no insignia on this one," he said, looking him over, "you could be shot as a spy."

"The insignia's on my vehicle. I'm Sturgis, Dean, Colonel. U.S.A.F. Serial number 3857293-12. That's all I'm required to say."

"Geneva convention rules?" smirked the officer as a short stocky solider with thick face stubble searched him.

"Yes."

"There is no Geneva, Colonel Sturgis," the officer grinned. "Nor any Switzerland anymore. It's all—how would you say—full of swiss-cheese holes?"

"Sorry to hear that. I hope the same is true of Moscow?"

"I'm glad to say no—"

"Shut the hell up," someone yelled from behind them. He stepped out of the woods—a Russian in an officer's uniform with *two* stars on his epaulette. Unlike these scruffy soldiers in combat fatigues, this man reeked with icy superiority, and the small KGB symbol on his lapel made people jump out of his way in fear. The KGB officer slapped the blond officer holding the pistol on Sturgis. "We are supposed to interrogate prisoners, not have them wheedle information out of *us* you idiot."

Sturgis smiled. The KGB officer, with eyes like an Arctic sea set in a sunken pale face, stepped closer.

"What is your mission?"

"Sturgis, Dean, Colonel. U.S.A.F. Serial number 3835895."

"Yes yes, thank you," the officer said. He gruffly ordered his communications man, carrying a field radio with a whip antenna on his back, to call in Chopper Five. "When it gets here load all this stuff inside, if it fits."

"How about this big suit?" asked the blond officer.

The KGB man stepped over to the suit lying across the back of the Tri-bike. "Curious," he said. "Take it along. Some sort of radiation gear no doubt. Quite sophisticated. This man might be a find. All we get around here are starving peasants with squirrel guns. I want him next to me in the chopper. Maybe we can get to know one another, officer to officer."

The big chopper, black and sleek as a missile for speed,

came shooting out of the northeast in a few minutes and hovered down the road, where the trees didn't come so close to the tarmac. The blades slowed to a stop and Sturgis was pushed roughly forward. Behind him, some soldiers huffed and puffed, pushing his Tri-bike forward, not taking the chance of starting up the bizarre machine.

Sturgis hoped that the cargo door wouldn't take the damned thing, but it did. Lots of room for the suit too. But for now, he was sure this two-bit outfit didn't really know what they had.

The chopper quickly ascended to a height of about 100 feet and wheeled off to the west. Sturgis was blindfolded but he felt the dim sun on his left side and knew they were heading north. They arrived wherever the hell they were taking him in ten minutes. If the chopper was hitting say, 150mph, that meant they had gone one-sixth that far—about 25 miles.

They were careless enough to remove his blindfold when they hit the ground. If there *were* a way to escape, he was picking up valuable information. He saw a few scattered buildings, a broken road full of tank tracks, an abandoned Dairy Freeze with boxes and crates outside it, and a big single-story factory brick building that still said "Auto Parts." He was pushed to its front door. Inside was a bustling wide office filled with clacking manual typewriters, all with Cyrillic script, flown in from Mother Russia for the bureaucrats to make out endless reports in triplicate, probably.

The KGB officer proudly pushed Sturgis along smiling and nodding, showing off his trophy of war to the startled clerks at the typewriters. They reached the far side of the big room and a soldier opened another door for them. Sturgis was led into a cozy office. Damned if there wasn't a full KBG major sitting behind the desk in a black uniform with the collar open. Shit!

The KGB major looked up, apparently in boredom,

362

but his eyes ran covetously over Sturgis' black coverall outfit. The officer saluted and received a casual half-salute back.

"No insignia on his coveralls?" the KGB major asked.

"Just the acronym C.A.D.S. All he'll give is his name, rank, and serial number, sir. Here, I wrote it down for you."

"Thank you, Lieutenant," the major said, taking the scrawled note. "Very good. You may go."

"Yessir." The officer left. The two guards he left behind stood at the ready with their dull metal Kalashnikovs held stiffly in front of them.

The major leaned back and put his hands behind his head as if he were going to say something, but he didn't. He was sizing up this American who stood before him. What the hell was C.A.D.S.? Isn't a cad a *heel* in their slang? A *bastard*? A mystery that could be unlocked by torture no doubt. But, from that determined chin, that unsmiling alertness, this man was a hardened veteran. Maybe a Green Beret or a Seal, or some unknown equivalent U.S.A.F. commando. He claimed to be U.S.A.F. A downed pilot perhaps? A report was brought in to him within minutes with the results of a quick examination of the suit. "Aviator type or radiation type suit — possibly a gravity suit for high-speed flight. Evidently," the report said, "the suit was in some way malfunctioning and the prisoner was repairing it when captured."

"Are you a downed pilot?" the major asked coolly.

Sturgis saw an opportunity here. "Yes. And I demand respectful treatment as a combatant. As our forces would treat your men."

The KGB major looked skeptical. "Downed by *what*, Colonel Sturgis? What were you flying; what hit you?"

"Mechanical failure, I'm sorry to say. I'm the last man alive in my squadron. I found some fuel, was trying to get to Canada."

"Did you have a motorcycle in the airplane?" the KGB man smiled. "How do you account for that strange vehicle?"

"I found it when I parachuted down . . ."

"A strange story. Why have you broken silence, Mr. Sturgis?"

"Because . . . because," he said, feigning cowardice as he whimpered, "I *know* what you are — I know what — what the KGB does if it wants information. Besides — everyone is — is dead. I'm the last of the squadron. There's nothing left, nothing left to fight for. There's no hope. I hope only that you treat me like an officer. I'll tell you everything."

"What *kind* of plane were you flying?"

"RB-1, sir. That's the problem. Two men are needed. I — I tried to do everything, just to keep it in the air. Just to get to Canada."

"What did you think you'd find there? Safety?"

"I — I hoped it wasn't as — as bad."

"Very interesting. It *is* as bad, you know. You're better off here."

The major looked hard at Sturgis — at that face of granite, at those eyes that had seen oceans of death, eyes that deep within, showed no fear — not a trace.

"Somehow, I think you are lying, Colonel Sturgis. Either you are a coward, or a very brave man. But in either case, it is irrelevant. For I shall find out all that I wish to know. We use rather old fashioned methods to get the truth, but amazingly effective. Really, quite amazing. I'm sure you'll be very interested in the procedure."

"N-no, please," Sturgis begged. They led him off to the sound-sealed interrogation room.

CHAPTER THIRTY-THREE

"Know what these are?" smiled the KGB major, pointing to a steel cauldron filled with glowing hot coals into which long metal pincers were embedded, their tips white hot.

"Don't — I'll tell you whatever you want!" Sturgis said. He was tied down naked to a long wooden board coated with dried blood.

"Exactly, you'll talk and talk. You'll betray your mother, your president, your sweetheart — anything — to have me stop. And I have a drug here that will keep you awake, alert, in spite of the pain, so that you can experience it all. There will be no unconsciousness, only an endless burning hell. Your testicles, your lips, your ears. We will start with the smallest little pain implements, and work our way up to the bone-crushing devices, sort of like wire cutters — you see?" He held a big plier-like device up.

"You get your rocks off this way?" Sturgis snarled.

"What? Oh, your slang English. I understand. Very nice. A very nice joke for a man about to become not a man."

Sturgis felt a coldness in his gut. Fear. A sensible man has fear, but a brave man fights that fear. Lets it be but fights it and does not let it dictate his actions. Later will be the time to retch and shake. He had seen that in his own brave men. Men who kept their heads in combat, and then later puked their guts out. He knew that if he survived this man's instruments of torture he wouldn't feel hungry for days.

The KGB torturer moved forward, placing the red-hot metal tip next to Sturgis' face, near his left cheek. "Feel the heat?"

"Yes. Please, I'll tell — everything. I admit I lied, a little . . ."

"Talking already? Such a shame. But I *must* have some fun!"

The major dragged the hot tip across Sturgis' face, searing his flesh. He groaned in real pain. The man moved the implement to his testicles. "And do you wish me to continue? Perhaps shorten your . . ."

"No!" Sturgis yelled. "I'll talk. I'll talk." *Stall, drag it out*, thought Sturgis, let him think he's learning something valuable. He doesn't know what the hell I'm about. He hasn't the technical knowledge to begin to fathom what me or the suit are all about. I've *got to* make him think I'm not as good a prize as I am! Think, think . . .

The major smiled. "Go ahead, you look a bit like that stupid Jesus Christ stretched out naked there on those beams. Only I don't think that God is around any more to save you. But forgive me, you want to tell me *all* about yourself now, don't you?"

Sturgis reeled out a hopefully interesting and revealing story of a secret air force unit of intelligence gatherers, the Central Assistance for Defense Systems Command — C.A.D.S. for short. It parachuted technicians into occupied areas — clad in super-secret radiation suits. The suit broke — true enough, and he was caught.

"Please. I'm not a trained fighter. I'm a technician. I can't stand pain. I had to tell you. I'm sorry—God I'm sorry. I have betrayed my country and myself," he heaved with sobs, giving it his all. It seemed to be working.

The major stood up. "Snivelling dog, you are a disgrace to the Americans I have tortured in the past week. They didn't give in until the last moment. They were heroes. I respect them. You, I spit on. I know what you say is true, for I am not a fool. Anyone could see that cock-and-bull story you told in my office was pure rot. Now that I have the *real* reason for your being dropped here, I want to know how *many* accompanied you, *where* your fellow technician-spies have been dropped, and *where* your base is. In short, tell me everything, and I will not torture you."

He stuck the glowing metal down in the water bucket. It sizzled loudly.

"I'm going to call in one of our *technical* people to be with me when we continue our little question and answer session. We shall meet again tomorrow," the major said, waving his hand at the guards. They dragged Sturgis to one of a makeshift group of cells—a cinderblock room with some empty shelves in it that had once held auto parts. There was a steel door for security to prevent robbers from reaching the auto supplies. Now it held him from escape.

Sturgis looked around. There was only a bed—a thin mattress on a steel frame. The frame was screwed into the concrete floor. There were dried bloodstains on the mattress and on the floor. Probably some of those brave Americans the torturer had mentioned meeting. He had succeeded in buying time. The Tri-bike had been the only thing in his cover story that he was worried about. But obviously the major was not technically sophisticated enough to worry about the strange vehicle. He knew the American intelligence had all kinds of high-tech gadgets.

Sturgis knew he had only bought time. Now he had to use it. But what the hell could he do? His deception would not last after the real technicians got their hands on his equipment. "I'm not dead yet," he muttered through clenched lips. "I will live . . . somehow . . . and reach Robin."

He looked around. The walls were hard and strong. He pried at the steel door, tugged, pushed. Impregnable without tools. But the ceiling—he looked up. Jesus Christ! It was a *dropped* ceiling! The Russians hadn't even noticed, in their haste to create a prison, checking just the walls and the door. The ceiling was plaster-coated foam, about 12 feet from the concrete floor.

Sturgis licked his lips. How the hell do I boost myself up there and find out if there's enough crawl space? He looked wildly around. Maybe if he could work the screws that held the bed free, he could put the metal stand up against the wall and use it like a ladder. He had to have something that could get those screws loose, some kind of screwdriver—but what? He glanced down—the Reds had given him back his clothes—the metal belt buckle on his coveralls looked like it could do the trick. He jammed one of its square edges into the deep set Russian screw heads that held the bedstand down. He hoped he could jam it deep enough into the dirt-clogged groove to turn the bastard.

It didn't work at first, and he bent the first corner of the belt buckle before he stopped. He turned the belt buckle to the next corner, using it to dig out the dirt in the groove of the quarter-inch wide screwhead before he began twisting again. He leaned on the makeshift screwdriver with all his body weight, one-hand on top of the other. It turned. Sweat rolled down his forehead. Sturgis moved to the next screw at the other end of the bed, then to the more difficult ones near the wall, where it was much more difficult to bear down on them. The last edge of the belt buckle broke on the last screw.

"Fuck this," he spat, dropping the broken tool. He grabbed the bed at the end furthest away from the unyielding screw and lifted with all his strength, like one of those Russian weightlifters shot up with cortisone who had won the last Olympic press. It yanked from the floor with a loud groan.

He leaned the heavy metal bedstand against the wall, with the mattress' thin material preventing it from scraping and creaking as he climbed its supports to the ceiling. He shoved at the thin ceiling—asbestos-and-pasteboard squares that moved easily, popping up into a dark space. He pushed his hand straight up and felt only thin air—great—it was at least wide enough to crawl through—if there was enough support in the metal frame work that held the flimsy ceiling tiles in place to support his body. He pushed the rest of the tiles away and felt for the first crossbeam—a good sturdy one luckily, and hoisted himself up into the dusty darkness. He could see in the dim light shafting up from the ceiling below that indeed the wall of his cell didn't even exist up here—it was just a dropped ceiling hanging down from the much higher original factory roof covering the whole one-storied building.

There were sharp metal edges everywhere and snakes of wires and filthy ducts of sheet metal that whirred with the air they were circulating in the big old warehouse. He crawled as fast as he could in what he hoped was the direction of the office he had entered first when he was brought into the building. At last he saw a small leak of light and the flatness of a real brick wall. Judging from the coldness of the tiles, Sturgis located where he thought a window was on the wall just below him. He carefully pried one of the ceiling tiles up. Eureka! The lights were out in the office below. He held tightly to the support beam and swung down like a cat to the floor below. He put his ear to the door. Guards outside passed through the hallway. He worked the lock at the top of the window open and hanging to the ledge dropped to the ground fifteen feet below, onto rain-softened soil.

He could get away now, most likely. Freedom grabbed him like a magnet—the urge to flee—to continue on his way and find Robin. But he put his personal feelings aside with a deep effort of will, for he knew that if the suit and Tri-bike—especially the suit—stayed here, he would have turned over to the Reds the greatest weapon left in the American arsenal. And doomed the C.A.D.S. team members.

He *had* to find the suit. And if he could get it working—an incredibly unlikely possibility—he could just smash his way out of here, take out this whole damned complex. Failing that, he would at least *destroy* the suit at the cost of just one life—his own.

But where the hell was it?

The area outside was lit by a few bare bulbs mounted on poles about 50 yards apart—just enough to see the way to one of the trucks or jeeps without a flashlight. They hadn't gotten around to more than that, thank God. Good old Russian inefficiency. He looked around for any guard towers he might have missed on the way in but there was just the woods beyond and the gravel parking lot that stretched hundreds of yards in each direction. Suddenly he heard footsteps—a lone Russian soldier.

He stepped back deeper into the building's shadow, waiting. The soldier was careless. He was smoking and walking along unconcerned, his pistol holstered, his rifle slung back on his shoulder. A walking dead man, about to finalize his state of death.

Sturgis leaped. The Red didn't get a chance to scream, just gurgle as Sturgis' arm pulled tight around his throat. The guard was nearly unconscious when he let up a bit.

"*Show me,*" he said in his best Russian, "where the

370

equipment I came in is kept, and I let you live."

The Russian looked up with terrified eyes. He was just a pawn in the game, and wasn't about to die in this wretched country. He gave the location. "The third shed to the left," he indicated. "Maybe a hundred meters." He didn't say anything about mines or booby traps.

"How do I get there?" Sturgis asked. The soldier pretended he didn't understand. "Just walk over there of course."

"Asshole," Sturgis snarled at the Red. "*You* walk in front of me."

The soldier's breath came out in deep heaves. "I'm not sure I . . . I don't remember . . ."

"You *know* where the mines are."

The soldier's shoulders sagged. "I will take you. But you will kill me anyway."

"I don't kill for fun. I swear. Take me there. I'll tie you up, you take your chances with your superiors when they find you prisoner."

The soldier nodded. He was young. Perhaps eighteen. He probably didn't know beans about anything. About life, about women, or war. Not survival, obviously. Sturgis didn't want to kill him, but he would if he had to.

They walked in a zig-zag pattern in the near darkness to the shed. The soldier had keys and it was quickly opened. He shut the door tightly and found a battery lamp inside. There was the suit, untouched, leaning on a wall. Sturgis quickly found some rope and trussed up the young soldier as he had promised, stuffing a gag in his mouth. Then he desperately continued where he had left off on his repairs. Fuses, wiring, traced with a desperation that knew no bounds. Then he heard more footsteps. Someone calling out for "Misha."

"Is that your name?" Sturgis frantically asked the tied-up soldier. The kid nodded in wide-eyed fear.

Sturgis thought he might let the kid respond, and tell

them to go away—but they would wonder what the hell Misha was doing in the storage shed.

He had to hope they would go away. He doused the light. No luck. In a moment, the heavy boots were crunching the gravel outside. A voice said in a whisper, "The door's unlocked. Maybe Misha's drunk again."

The door swung wide, and the two soldiers stepped in. Sturgis waited until they were both inside before he slammed the door with his foot and smashed out twice with a steel bar across what he hoped were their heads. A sickening crunch, then another, then the sound of lifeless bodies slumping onto the floor.

He turned the light back on. No doubt about it from their wide open stares and the blood and brain tissue trickling from their cracked skulls, they were as dead as you can get. Misha was struggling violently in his bindings. Sturgis waved the bloodied iron at him and he quieted down like a good boy.

Then Sturgis continued his desperate work, his hands shaking. Suddenly, he noticed that the main lead wire from the suit computer to the power battery was *unsnapped*. That was all—shit—a *loose plug*.

Cursing the contractor once again, and wishing him a speedy trip to hell, Sturgis snapped in the plug and taped it down. It didn't even have the damned little plastic-grip on it that *should* have prevented it from pulling loose.

He got into the suit and pulled on the helmet, watching with relief as all the system's lights blinked on in an array of colors and motion at the top and bottom of the visor.

The kid watched fascinated from across the room. A burst of spray issued from the overflow valve. Water trapped in the gyros being expelled. Now he was ready for anything.

He stepped outside, not bothering to open the door. He just tore it off its hinges, releasing some of the pent-up fury he had contained for hours. A siren began to wail.

"Too late now, comrades," he muttered, taking a visual bearing on the perimeter fence where the truck entrance door stood grimly metallic in the starlight. He hit the jets and flew up off the ground throwing gravel every which way as SMGs opened up on him from several directions.

"Shell Inject System EB2," he instructed the suit, and felt the reassuring tug as the suit complied, loading his right arm sling with a stock of electroballs. His muscular-assist mechanism, not quite warmed up yet, hummed and throbbed. Sturgis pointed at a group of Red soldiers that were blasting away with their Kalashnikovs, and turned his wrist. They were blown to wet Red flecks in a blue-red fireball. Half the building wall behind them crumbled to the ground with a tremendous roar.

He had to find the Tri-bike before he started really tearing up the place. Where the hell would they keep it? He commanded "Strobe On" and the glaring strobe-lights of his suit brilliantly lit up the screen. He saw a flat gray garage-like building far off. He yelled "Power five, Magnify!"

The scene grew instantly in his visor. The Russian words indicating Motor Pool.

He leaned toward the building and shot off the ground, releasing a spray of machine-gun fire at the assembling troops. That silenced the boys down there on the ground as he swept forward toward his objective.

One electroball blew the motor pool's door to shit, together with its two guards. Inside, the strobe illuminated row after row of trucks, then a row of Red motorcycles, crude Russian cycles with sidecars. And smack dab in the middle of them his grease-colored prize, the Tri-bike.

He jumped into the seat—so familiar and reassuring. He started it up, it shot to life. Damned good luck they hadn't disassembled the thing. Probably afraid to do anything before their technical squad arrived. He suddenly realized just how much he had come to depend on the C.A.D.S. suit—and how invulnerable he felt in it.

Sturgis roared out of the garage, shooting out Electro-balls in every direction, one every second with a firepower the Reds could never have imagined existed in a battle-ship, let alone belonging to a single man! The buildings hit with the electroball's fury exploded into orange mushrooming clouds of hellfire. Flying flopping bodies and parts of bodies followed them up into the air. Vehi-cles—trucks, with men inside firing mounted machine guns, roared to cut off his exit at the compound gate. He said calmly to the computer, "Prepare Fire Control mode LPF."

He heard the clicking and whirrings of the servo-mech-anisms setting up the sequence of firings which only his and five other suits had been fitted with.

"Commence firing." The flame thrower shot out a wall of fire from his pointed left arm. The trucks and their screaming passengers passed to the left and right of him as he shot through the center. Drivers clutched at their searing flesh as he bathed them in fire.

He blasted the gate back to powdery ore with a mini-Hawk missile, one of four his Tri-bike held—his ace in the hole.

The screaming Tri-wheeler sped into the dark country-side illuminated in deep silver shadows by his bike head-lights. The firing behind him was scattered, punctuated by enormous eruptions every few seconds that lit up the very clouds above. Some of the fires he had caused were reaching the ammo stored all over the base, and the mines that had been laid down. He relaxed for the first time in hours, smiled and decelerated. Somehow he made it. Jesus. He was on an old country road with a few burned-out farmhouses here and there. At an intersec-tion; he stopped. Damned if there wasn't a roadsign that read "Virginia Bridge, 12 Miles."

He turned the Tri-bike and headed off into the night again at 90mph, hoping to hell the Reds—or the Resistance—hadn't pointed the sign off in the wrong direction.

His heart rate on the readout in the left-hand corner of the helmet read out a figure that would kill a weaker man. He tried to calm down; and slowly, ever so slowly, he did.

The major was jerked out of his thick blankets bolt upright—a concussion ripped the blinds from his window, shattering the glass over the floor. His ears rang as he ran to the blasted window, peering outside. Buildings were burning, Soviet soldiers running every which way. Heavy incoming fire. Artillery? What the hell was happening? Could it be an attack by a large, well-armed force to free the prisoner?

He grabbed his pants off the chair and pulled them on, reaching for his revolver. The hallways was littered with bleeding men. He ran toward the exit on the opposite side of the building and toward—he hoped—safety. There was no way that his men would hold against a massive attack, the kind that apparently was occurring. He must escape—live to fight another day. The helicopters!

He bolted out the door, his bare feet making contact with the cold rough gravel. He ran. He was the highest ranked officer there. He *couldn't* get captured. His heart pounding, he pulled open the pilot's door of the small Volinsky-3 and hit the ignition and the systems switches. His own personal helicopter—it had never let him down—given constant loving care by his own mechanic. But its rotors whined and chugged, failing to catch.

The building he had just exited blew to a billion pieces, shattered brick rained onto his windscreen. *"Come on, come on."*

Thick smoke came out of the chopper's exhaust. The

damned thing was slow to rev up. There—that's it!

He watched the rotation needle come out of the red and instantly pulled the stick toward himself. The black helicopter rose violently off the gravel, leaning away from the burning scene below, rising wildly into the night. My God—he could see out the window the immensity of the conflagration below. Fear gripped his guts like a steel vise. Such a well-equipped force, to do that much damage. They might have ground-to-air *missiles*. He had to get out of range—and fast.

Sturgis heard the thud-thud-thud of the little chopper's rotors, like an annoying bug in the sky, a bug getting smaller every second. But that bug had to go.

"Visor power, 20, track airborne target. Sights on," Sturgis said.

The red readout rolled across the bottom of his visor: "Target acquisition. Laser locked; system?"

Sturgis smiled. It was the major, he could see the blond-haired long face in the pilot's seat. "EB-Five," he said softly. "Fire."

He heard the click of the loading mechanism, the shift of his suit gyros to compensate for the slight shift of weight of the six-inch tube under his left arm. He pointed toward the target as cross hairs swept across the visor before him. A red dot blinked on dead center of the chopper's black wasp body. The small deadly E-ball shot out of the firing tube, then four more!

Sturgis flipped back to normal screen mode and watched as the chopper tried to dive from the sky to below the tree line. But the EB's crackling blue sparks in the night tracked it like a hawk after a rabbit.

What's it like, Sturgis thought, to see your death come screaming at you, to know you'll be dead in one second? The chopper exploded in a single violent flash and then was gone.

The major would never get to make his report, the

records of which would be "sanitized" by fire tonight, along with all personnel and materials at this base. Let the KGB find nothing but charred wood and powdered brick, and wonder.

CHAPTER THIRTY-FOUR

The Devil's Horde shot down the back roads of Virginia searching for victims. For human prey that would feel pain, for women they could release their stores of hatred and lust upon. There were only 37 now, many having died of the puking death since that piss-smelling rain in Regis, that last town they had wasted.

Viking rode the lead cycle, as was his right. He struggled to keep his vision clear—something was happening to his eyes, something horrible. They were full of cracked red veins now, and pus was oozing out of them. His hair under his 'viking' helmet was coming out in big tufts. He was a doomed man. His flesh hung loosely on his big bones, every one of his stringy muscles ached. His teeth felt loose in his gums. Every bounce of the Kawasaki 1100 was pure agony.

Viking's second in command now was Stan—and Stan was eyeing Viking peculiarly—like he was waiting for him to be weak enough to overpower. But Stan didn't look so hot himself. He had gone completely bald, like a Kojak-imitation. Stan drove alongside Viking now and said "Water, man, we've got to have fresh water."

"Yeah—we'll find it, don't worry," Viking snarled from bleeding cracked lips. "Get back in position. I still lead!"

Stan dropped back, but slowly.

Viking peered ahead. It was all a blur now. He had been on this stretch of the Interstate many times before *the Blow*, and he knew that there weren't any exits for miles. He decided to cut cross country—it was flat enough. Out there were farmhouses—isolated farmhouses that might still not have been looted. That still might have living breathing women, and liquor to dull his pain. Damn, he wished he had some heroin, but he didn't.

They were a mile into a plowed field when Viking saw a small sideroad of macadam ahead, and beyond the burned trees a little chain crossing a dirt road—maybe a driveway.

Viking signalled for the Horde to follow him. He drove his big bike around the pole holding the chain on the left, and they all followed single file down the dirt road.

They came to a small clearing, and at first Viking didn't see any house. But then he spotted a shuttered house built right into the rock face of a cliff. Damn, it must be some sort of nuke shelter. And there would be provisions inside.

"Okay, you bastards, lets get out our guns. We have some work to do. Stan, Jake, Bug, bring the crowbars and the sledge hammers—let's take a look see inside that there fucking fortress!

Robin heard the gruff male voice, followed by the slamming of something heavy on the shutters. "Hey, man, come out of there, open it up. It's only us."

Her heart leapt for a second—she was so anxious for it to be Dean. Maybe it was one of his men—that gruff voice.

She peered out a gunslit and saw the Horde. A ragtag bunch of cyclers, their bikes parked every which way in the tall straw outside.

379

Chris, the healing young boy, rushed over to her and grabbed her away. "Shhhh," he said, "Let's be real quiet; maybe they'll go away."

They still had all the steel shutters down, thank God, and she doused the battery driven lights. They might think it abandoned if they were quiet and they might give up trying to get in — *might*.

However, the pounding continued. They watched the shutters dent in, their ears rang from the sound of the sledgehammers — it must be sledgehammers.

Robin realized that they couldn't fight all the men she had seen outside — there were at least two dozen. "Chris, quickly, get matches, extra ammo, and the rucksacks we had packed, the ones with the maps — and blankets — the heavy ones." She picked up the .30-06 and held it ready. She could see the tips of crowbars now in the spaces along the shutters the dents had made. Soon she would have to shoot. Maybe she should warn them — maybe they'll just go away. She almost shouted, "Go away!" then she came to her senses. They probably needed food, water. And this wasn't a neighborly call. They would probably want her — and God knows even Chris — for their pleasure.

Suddenly it was quiet outside. Too quiet. She guessed what that meant in the nick of time, time enough to get Chris and crawl down under a counter in the rear of the shelter house. Then the dynamite exploded against the shutters, tearing one half off its hinges.

She heard the gruff male voice shout, "That'll do it," and warwhoops. A hand started clawing at the twisted steel door, bending it out. She levelled the rifle and sighted.

Then there was a strange *whine* outside, like a taxiing jet. The hand withdrew. She heard someone say, "What the hell —"

There was an enormous report. More explosions. Small

380

arms fire. She heard men screaming out death screams. She had to see what was going on. "Stay here, Chris, keep packing—"

She crawled along the concrete floor to a small hole at the base of a shutter. She peered outside.

There was some sort of black-suited astronaut—or monster. Behind him was a three wheeled motorcycle of some sort—a very strange vehicle. The monster in black was firing something *out of his arm*. My god—it was a *flamethrower*. She watched a cycler get hit and run screaming, his body afire, off into the woods. Other cyclers crouched or were belly down in the grass firing their handguns at the figure, who didn't seem to be affected.

She didn't know what the hell was going on, but there was no time like the present to *escape*!

Chris had the big packs, the blankets all rolled on the metal frame for backpacking, and he had the other rifle, the .45, and extra ammo. She checked to see if the water was in the canteens and led him up the small tunnel to the escape hatch that Dean had built just the summer before. Thank God he had. They came out 30 feet up, on the top of the scrubby cliff, and crawled a distance before they could get up and run. Robin and Chris hadn't tied the backpacks on very well, and they both had to stop to adjust them. The firing continued.

Sturgis had heard the slamming of the big sledgehammers as he drove up to the farm. He saw the cyclers—three dozen or so—laughing and placing the bundle of dynamite against the shelter house. He screeched to a halt, dismounted the Tri-bike and hit his jets, trying to get to the dynamite. But it blew before he made it. When the smoke cleared, the men got up hollering, "Let's go."

He let them have it. God, if Robin was in there—there was no telling if the dynamite had killed her or not.

When he came upon them, he had felt that burst of kill-energy. He didn't just want to kill them—they might have *hurt* Robin—they might have—

"I'll cremate you all!" he yelled over the roar of his electro-ball firing. *"No surrender!"* But the words were garbled as the electroballs shattered the ground in every direction, blasting bikers up into the air in bloody pieces. Two rose still alive, throwing their hands above their heads—he fired the SMG mode, they withered to the ground.

Out of the original three dozen or so, there were suddenly only a half dozen left. He started to train his right arm on one of them when he was blasted off his feet. Dynamite—the group of five to the left flank were throwing dynamite. It hadn't damaged his suit, but it had made his shot toward the running man in the horned helmet go astray, up into the sky.

Sturgis rose to his feet. He pointed his left arm to the group of five horrified bikers. They couldn't believe that he had gotten up—he should have been dead.

Smiling he ordered, "LPF Mode." He felt the slight click, then said "Fire," pointing at the group, who had just turned tail to run. He only let the flames leap out for a second, just enough to set the five men afire. They ran now, every which way, screaming.

Then all was silent.

CHAPTER THIRTY-FIVE

Sturgis looked around at the bleeding dismembered bodies that littered the field in front of the mountain house. They lay everywhere in rising pools of their own blood. The farm had been so beautiful once, and now. So much death. Was this what the post-war-world would be like, he wondered with disgust — just violence at every turn. And yet — if it was — he would fight to live. He would kill all who tried to destroy him. He would struggle to the last second given him on this earth, for Sturgis was a warrior down to the very marrow of his bones.

He walked over the still spasming corpses toward the twisted steel door and pushed it open, stepping through.

"Robin — it's me, Dean," he yelled out, lifting his visor so she could see his face. There was no answer, just the sound of water boiling fiercely in the kitchen. She had been here — he had seen her with his own eyes. His heart began tightening up again in fear. He went through the rooms and then to the bathroom where he saw the lifted ceiling panels. She had escaped. In the bedroom Sturgis found her note.

"Darling, there are two groups of attackers outside fighting for the opportunity of having me. I'm taking the opportunity to slip away. If you find this note I'm going to the place we camped on our honeymoon — remember?

Love, Robin."

She had been here, just a moment ago, so close . . .
His brain reeled with emotion. He wondered if she armed
herself but a quick look reassured him. She had taken the
M-16 and .45. With her skills in the woods and some
luck, she might make it. Might!

He raced outside and flipped on his Scan Mode for
human organisms. A radar grid illuminated his visor
screen and he could see two figures about a mile-and-a-
half off in the woods moving slowly. Could someone be
after her? Who the hell else would be with her? He
started after her on foot, the woods just around the farm
being too thick for the Tri-wheeler. He raced like a madman knocking over small trees, trampling through thick
groves of bushes in his desperate urgency to see her
again, to hold her.

Slowly he gained on them, but as the forest grew
thicker and darker his progress came to a virtual crawl.
But he kept on. If it took hours—days—he would reach
her. He had just come to the bottom of a steep gravel-
strewn hill when the Emergency Beeper in his helmet
went off with a jarring shrill ring. Damn—the signal he
had told Tranh to send if things got hot back in the convoy. Sturgis gritted his teeth in anger. It was as if God
himself were playing games with him—allowing him to
get this close to her and then—. He sat down on a half-
rotted log and put his helmeted face in his huge gloved
hands. Love and duty, his woman versus his country. "It's
not fair. It's not fucking fair," the C.A.D.S. leader
screamed out in pain, as thick tears welled up inside his
eyes and dripped down his cheeks and mouth.

At last he rose, moving as if he were made of stone.
He slowly turned and headed back to the farm—away
from the only person he cared about on this whole
planet. Yet she was one, and the men who counted on
him were many. The whole future of the nation could

well depend on what happened to that convoy to the president and his staff. He couldn't let them down — couldn't. His years of military life, years of devotion to his country, slashed into him like razor blades inside his skull. Sometimes he wished he had never joined the goddamned service — wished he was just a man, a carpenter, a salesman — any damned thing — just a man who could be with the woman who needed him. But such was not the case. He was a warrior and a leader and he was locked into that role as tightly as if he were imprisoned in chains, chains of his own making. Cursing the very country he knew he had to try to save, Sturgis trampled back through the thick woods sick in his heart.

The only thing to do was to try and rendezvous with her in a few weeks. It would take her that long to reach the Smoky Mountain Monument Park and the campsite deep in the woods where they had spent their honeymoon, making love.

He walked back to the bike outside and climbed on. There was nothing for him here now. Flipping down the visor he tried to contact Omega Force, upping the transmission signal to peak. At last a reply came through, broken, hard to decipher. The team was about 100 miles to the west and had suffered more casualties from a Red chopper attack — losing three more Tri-bikes. But the new president was still alive. "I'm coming in," Sturgis replied, hoping they heard him. He had the suit computer calculate a route back to Omega. The blue-green grid came on and a dotted red line designated the path he should follow over the terrain displayed. It was over two hundred miles to intercept point.

The Tri-wheeler's tires spun up a curving spray of dirt as he accelerated out of the field. He shot down the dirt road until he reached the Interstate some 15 miles off where he opened her up to top speed, roaring down the center of the 4-lanes at 125 miles an hour. The world moved by him in a blur of trees blending together into a solid brown line. An occasional burnt out wreck stood in his way but the bike computer warned him and made adjustments as he approached so he barely had to slow down. The groups of corpses he flashed by from time to time were no longer even clinging to life — just skeletons picked clean by what remained of nature's scavengers. Those who had been hurt badly by the bombs were all dead. Now it was the living who would wonder with each day how long they had.

Sturgis rode the Interstate for nearly 150 miles until an immense crater loomed up ahead with sloping walls nearly 200 feet high. Must have gone off target, he mused as he slowed the bike. Out here in the middle of nowhere it looked strangely absurd, a sculpture of death with no victims to kill. Dark dwarfed weeds and plants were already growing up from the powdery soil around the blast site and on the very slopes of the H-bomb crater. Ugly things with spikes and rockhard stems. The new flowers, he thought, gazing down at them with an equal mixture of revulsion and curiosity.

He requested an update on the location of the C.A.D.S. unit and the revised route to follow. The computer fed out a grid map of the country for a two-hundred mile radius. There — he could see them — a band of blue specks tearing ass about 90 miles off. And behind them, an army of amber dots closing in hot pursuit. "Enemy force 20 miles from Omega unit and closing," the computer read out. "Enemy force numbers 200 vehicles including high speed Z-18 assault tanks, armored vehicles . . ."

"Route for closest rendezvous?" Sturgis asked.

"Heading of 87 degrees by 63," flashed on his visor. "Flatlands and small hills on fastest course. Traversible by Tri-wheeler."

Sturgis wheeled off the highway straight up the embankment on the side and headed out over the rolling meadows to the west. A red dot on his bike control panel blinked in the center of a green circle. All he had to do was follow it and he'd reach them. The course the computer plotted was where the team *would* be if he proceeded at present rate of speed, constantly updating itself automatically as it gauged the bike's speed every 5 minutes.

Sturgis flew over the flat bumpy fields blanketed in shrouds of dead undergrowth, through groves of dark burnt bushes, even smashing through wooden fences without slowing. The huge front wheel of the Tri-bike with such a large mass behind it was able to plow right through these small obstacles. He didn't have time to open any fences. And slowly, achingly slowly the blue dots of his team grew closer.

He came over a tree-stumped rise at the very edge of western Virginia and suddenly they were there, tearing along on a vast flat plain below. The C.A.D.S. team shooting up whipping trails of dust in their V-formation, with Rhinos in the lead and Tri-wheelers angling out behind them, protecting the president's transport truck between them. They were only going about 80, Sturgis knew because of the truck which was probably already pushed to the limit. He turned his eyes back to the east and his heart nearly stopped. Coming into view, about 7 miles off, was an armada of vehicles. They stretched as far as the eye could see, taking up half the horizon and coming forward at breakneck speed. It looked like half the damned Russian army was in pursuit of Omega Force. An occasional chopper from the nearly twenty overhead charged forward but the surface-to-air missiles on the lead Rhinos quickly dissuaded such attempts as two of them were blasted from the sky before his eyes. The rest pulled back. They could wait — for slowly they were gaining on the fleeing Americans. And when they were within firing range, Sturgis knew, they would open up with every gun, machine gun and cannon they possessed, like a fleet of warships sending out an unstoppable barrage.

"This is Sturgis," he barked into the suit radio, stopped at the very edge of the 150 foot slope that eased down to the flat land below.

"Sturgis, where the hell are you?" Fenton's voice yelled back. "We're in some hot water—boiling, in fact."

"Yeah, I can see," Sturgis said, watching the motorized Red army. "I'm just off to your right about two miles. I'm going to try and do a little delaying over here. So if you hear some big bangs don't look back."

"Come on in man, we need you," Tranh shouted, cutting in on the transmission. "Don't be a fool, Sturgis, you can't do shit against those boys."

"Maybe I can buy you all a little time," the C.A.D.S. commander said, clicking off and easing back into the seat. Now that he'd said it he didn't know exactly what the hell he *could* do. There was no way he could take on that whole bunch—but if he could jam up the columns— get some secondary explosions—maybe, just maybe . . .

He shot down the slope at an impossible angle, the bike almost tipping forward, and hit the sandy ground below hard. He ripped the bars to the right and tore along the mountainside that sat at the edge of the plain, so he was parallel to both moving forces, set dead between them. Steering with one arm he lifted the other toward the Red fleet, ordering Macro-mode on the visor. The front ranks of the column sprang into view, the commanding officers in their steel-plated armored vehicles, just ahead of nearly 25 of the super mobile Z-18 tanks.

"Fire EB," he commanded, "One per target." He sighted up a tank at the very center of the line until his laser sights slid neatly together, three circles, one atop another. "Fire," Sturgis said. The EB shot out of his arm like a homing pigeon and rocketed in seconds to its nest of steel. The pulsing electric sphere made target acquisition dead center of the tank's turret, blowing the top right off the thing. The ammunition inside followed a split second later and a ball of fire erupted leaping out in all directions. The tanks on each side lurched out of the way crashing into one another. Two of them collided with such force that they knocked each other over on their backs, treads still pumping wildly at the air like the legs of a downed turtle.

"Fire," he commanded again, sighting five tanks away. Again the steel globe whistled in a razor-sharp line toward its goal and hit broadside. The rolling tank disintegrated into a tornado of steaming metal, flying into the vehicles around it. One of the armored cars to its left took the brunt of the blast and rolled on its side igniting in a blinding white blast. The column slowed to about 60, their own more primitive sensing devices trying to track down the source of the fire.

Sturgis edged at an angle toward the Omega force, cutting across the front of the Russian attack about two miles ahead of them. He sighted and fired, and fired again, hitting two more tanks, spaced about 70 yards apart. Suddenly his visor lit up with blinking letters, "Ammunition EB mode — zero." Great, that didn't leave him a hell of a lot of options, just the two mini-rockets in his Tri-wheeler. He'd done all that he could — it was time to rejoin the team — if he could. He charged forward as shells tore through the air blasting up mounds of dirt all around him. Sturgis went into full evasive maneuvers, twisting the cycle this way and that, wheeling around wildly as he slowly closed the ground between him and the team.

Suddenly all he saw was red — a blinding flash that filled his every sense as a tank shell landed just feet ahead, blasting his front tire to shattered dangling shreds. The bike tilted over straight into the ground, throwing him forward through the air at 70 miles an hour. He slammed into the dirt nearly 60 feet ahead as the bike's fuel system went up in a cloud of oily smoke. Sturgis rolled over and over, somehow regaining his senses as the shock of the fall shook his body. He relaxed every muscle inside the suit praying that its internal cushioning could absorb the rough handling. At last he came to a stop and lay there for a few moments tentatively moving his arms and legs to see if anything was broken. But though he ached like the devil, his flesh was still functioning. He rose to his feet, feeling for a moment an absurd pity for his body which he was putting through so much, almost as if it were another person. But there wouldn't be time to make amends, he saw, as he turned toward the Russian attack force which was coming in on him in a tidal wave of dark steel.

It had finally come—his destruction. Somehow he had thought he would make it, once they had reached the president. *That* had seemed like the hardest part. But the plans of man are overruled by the laws of fate. It was over. The whole ball game, 9th inning and one pitch to go. He slowly raised his arm to fire whatever remained of the 55mm supply. Nothing happened. The suit's attack modes were out.

"Status?" he asked the computer.

"Suit musculature-assist functioning—all other systems non-functioning," the wavering words appeared on his visor. Well, the damned thing had served him well. He couldn't even blame the contractors on this one. It had been through a virtual meatgrinder. He was lucky he could still walk. He released a flap near his hip, noticing that the suit's right arm had been almost ripped off at the shoulder, held now by just the internal wiring, and pulled out his .45. He raised the well-worn muzzle toward the rapidly approaching Reds . . . and waited.

CHAPTER THIRTY-SIX

Sturgis heard the sudden high-pitched whine of engines behind him. He turned with a start, tightening his finger on the trigger, wondering how the hell they had surrounded him—and froze. Three Tri-bikes and a Rhino were zipping toward him from out of a cloud of yellow dust. They screeched to a stop just feet away and a C.A.D.S.-suited figure opened his visor and smiled.

"Thought it was time the U.S. Cavalry made its proverbial visit."

"Trahn, you bastard," Sturgis said, not knowing whether to hug them or let them have it for leaving the column. "You shouldn't have come—the whole mission could have jeopardized the president."

"If we hadn't decided to pay our respects," Fenton said, poking his head through a hatch at the top of the Rhino, "the president was about to order us to."

"Anyway," Billy Dixon said, pulling his bike alongside his commander, "we learned from a master how to disobey rules."

"I'll court martial you all later," Sturgis grinned. "Right now—"

"Right now," Fenton yelled down from his Rhino, "we gotta get the bloody hell out of here." Shells dropped from the sky around them like meteors, digging out huge smoking holes in the ground.

"You got any smoke bombs left in there?" Sturgis asked Fenton.

"Maybe 6 or 7," the Englishman replied, glancing around nervously as a 122mm shell landed just yards behind the Rhino sending a sheet of dirt over him.

"Lay down a line of them, 200 feet apart, say a mile." Fenton's head disappeared back inside the immense Rhino and within seconds six shells launched out of the forward tubes. They landed about 200 yards ahead of the column instantly sending up thick clouds of impenetrable smoke. The Reds slowed to a crawl unable to see a foot ahead. Fenton poked his head out again.

"Let's go, let's go man," he screamed down at Sturgis who seemed to be deep in thought. The C.A.D.S. commander looked up.

"No—we've got to stop them—here," Sturgis said firmly. "They'll have us within minutes, hours at most. I know you're not going to like this, but the Rhino is going to have to be sacrificed."

"What the hell are you talking about?" the Englishman asked anxiously, having grown quite attached to the high-tech death machine.

"The nuclear generator for recharging the suit's batteries. It was top secret—General Knolls didn't want word to get back to D.C. in the midst of peace negotiations—but certain modifications were made just within the last month. The Rhino can be turned into a low yield atomic bomb." The three of them looked at their leader, their jaws dropping open. Sturgis jumped up onto the built-in ladder at the side of the Rhino and climbed up to the hatch.

"Out pal, I've got work to do," Fenton climbed quickly out, his suit only half-sealed as he fumbled at the clasps. Sturgis scrambled past him and down into the innards of the super vehicle. Inside, rows of computerized display screens lit up, madly sending out warnings of the approaching enemy. Radar screens, sonar devices, early warning systems all beeped and flashed like a Christmas tree gone mad, signaling imminent destruction. He pressed a code into the keyboarded panel on top of the lead shielded, atomic powered engine and the top of the unit rose up with a low hum. Sturgis reached in and flipped the newly installed "Arm for detonation" button. Instantly a shrill siren blasted into his ears as the words "Self-destruct" flashed in foot-high letters on every screen. A small monitor within the opened engine top lit up.

"Choose arming mode," it read out. He pressed a small button next to one of 8 possible choices—"Proximity detonation," programmed to set off the nuclear core when enemy forces came near. Another set of "Distance of detonation?" choices flashed out and Sturgis pressed "Zero proximity." He stepped back as the covering of the engine lowered back down, and rushed to the front of the Rhino, where he slammed down the secondary safety button, blinking amber. All the warning lights on the monitors switched off and a programmed voice blared out of the speakers. "Atomic pile set for proximity explosion. No recall. Present rate of enemy advance—detonation 4 minutes."

There was no turning back now, Sturgis thought as he shot up the inside ladder and onto the roof of the Rhino. God knew how far the blast would reach and if they had a chance in a million to get away. He jumped down the 12 feet to the ground landing hard and falling to his knees, then rose in a flash. Behind, the billowing smoke was still rising but the plains winds were strong and already the outer edges within which the Red fleet was mired were dissipating.

"Fenton—get on Dixon's bike," Sturgis yelled as he ran over to Tranh. The Vietnamese edged forward as far as he could in the long sloping seat and Sturgis slid in behind him. The two Tri-bikes shot forward with a squeal of rubber, their drivers pressed up against the bars, steering awkwardly with their suited arms pulled far back.

"Go, go, go," Sturgis yelled into Tranh's helmet as the bike spun forward, the accelerator turned to the max. The two three-wheelers rode side by side, some 10 feet apart, their backseat riders hanging on for dear life to the men in front of them.

"How far ahead is Omega Force," Sturgis screamed out. "My suit functions are all out."

"Five-and-a-half miles," the Vietnamese yelled back through his helmet speakers. It was enough—*they* at least would be safe. The effects of the blast, at least as far as Knolls had told him, wouldn't reach more than 3 miles, possibly 4 at the most. Only thing was—it had never been tested. There weren't too many men who wanted to volunteer to see the effects of a low-yield atomic explosion on their nearby bodies. But they were as good as dead if the Reds caught them. Or worse.

The Russian attack squadron emerged from the smoke and immediately built up speed, taking up the chase.

"Now—now we get them," the fleet commander, Major Zarkov, muttered to his second-in-command. "No more tricks." He lifted his binoculars and peered through the bullet proofed glass slit of his armored car. There—perhaps two miles off, he saw the fleeing Americans. Just two of their strange motorcycles. The rest must be ahead—but not far. His claws were closing in. "Begin firing," he ordered the column through the walkie-talkie. A hail of shells shot out from every cannon.

"Can't this fucking thing go any faster?" Sturgis yelled.

"It's up to peak, man," Tranh shouted back. "The gyro, the warning temperature gauges—everything is going crazy up here." Sturgis leaned around in the seat and saw the Rhino sitting like a dark boulder a mile behind them. The Russian fleet was almost upon it—only seconds. He suddenly spotted a sharp drop in the terrain ahead.

"There—to the right," Sturgis said, pointing with his tattered glove about a hundred yards off. "We gotta get the hell out of the direct blast." Tranh radioed Sturgis' command to Dixon and both bikes veered sharply to the side, heading straight for it. They shot over the edge of the eight-foot drop and seemed to almost take off as the bikes flew over 25 yards before slamming into the ground. Both Tri-wheelers flipped over as they struck, sending their occupants soaring off. The men landed hard, knocked unconscious by the crash, spinning end over end before they came to a stop. They lay there like fallen trees, motionless.

Zarkov saw the oddly shaped oval vehicle just ahead, sitting high on its 8-foot tires. A trap? He ordered his gunners to open fire and three shells arched toward the thing, one of them landing just beneath the forward axle. The two front tires of the Rhino blasted away from their bolts as the death machine slammed down into the ground digging in nearly two feet. Zarkov smiled. One down—a handful to go.

"Forward—forward," he shouted to his driver who had slowed slightly, fearing an attack. They shot ahead coming right alongside the downed Rhino lying like some creature of primeval ages, dead in the mud.

Suddenly there was a roar that shook the very earth. A blast of starfire ignited the plains around it for a half mile in a solid sphere of white flame as the nuclear generator shot out its ten kilotons of explosive energy in one millionth of a second. Where there had been an army was now just super-heated atoms flying at nearly the speed of light off in every direction. Not a man had time to scream, or pray to whatever Communist God he worshipped. They were gone into a dimension no living man can know. A small mushroom-shaped cloud lifted proudly into the sky, scraping the bottoms of the brownish clouds that flew rapidly by. The wall of heat and flame rushed across the plain evaporating every rock and cactus, every unfortunate snake and lizard that it touched. Slowly, the flames dissipated, reaching out with dimmer and dimmer hands of fire. It rushed over the embankment where the C.A.D.S. fighters had fallen, in a flameless wind of about 130 degrees—a cloud of heat that passed harmlessly over the suited unconscious men. The sound and shock waves followed seconds behind shaking them like rag dolls.

And then within minutes it was gone. The heat and the gamma rays, the mushroom cloud beginning to pull part beneath the rising north wind. It had left its message of death and departed. Now there was an eerie silence as not a creature stirred. A sound beyond sound. A harmony of nothingness.

CHAPTER THIRTY-SEVEN

Sturgis came to, staring into the open-visored eyes of Rossiter.

"Sir — you're alive," the round faced trooper said with a look of amazement.

"Guess so," Sturgis croaked between dry lips as he rose to a sitting position. "Take my advice Rossiter," he said, "don't get in the way of any A-bomb blasts." He looked around and saw Tranh, Dixon and Fenton lying yards off — but alive, groaning. The rest of the Omega Force, the president and his remaining staff stood around them with looks of sheer horror that slowly changed to relief as they saw that Sturgis and the others were all right.

"We saw the blast," Rossiter said, reaching down with a wide black armored arm to help Sturgis to his feet, "and came in the hopes that — " Sturgis stood up and walked shakily to the edge of the embankment and looked back. Nothing — just the melted sand of the plain fused into a shiny glass-like substance. The Reds had paid the price — just a return on their own nuclear investment in America. But Sturgis knew there would be more, many more. The Reds were out to get them. By now they were probably the most wanted men in America. And there were still two thousand miles to go, back to base. Sturgis felt tired, as weary as he had ever felt in his life. He just wanted to lie down in the nuclear-warmed sand and sleep, sleep an eternity. But not today, never today.

"Let's go," he said softly to the men as Tranh, Dixon and Fenton were helped to their feet. "We got miles to go—and promises to keep," he whispered. Promises of war and promises of love.

THE SURVIVALIST SERIES
by Jerry Ahern

#1: TOTAL WAR   (960, $2.50)
The first in the shocking series that follows the unrelenting search for
ex-CIA covert operations officer John Thomas Rourke to locate his
missing family—after the button is pressed, the missiles launched
and the multimegaton bombs unleashed. . . .

#2: THE NIGHTMARE BEGINS   (810, $2.50)
After WW III, the United States is just a memory. But ex-CIA covert
operations officer Rourke hasn't forgotten his family. While hiding
from the Soviet forces, he adheres to his search!

#3: THE QUEST   (851, $2.50)
Not even a deadly game of intrigue within the Soviet High Com-
mand, and a highly placed traitor in the U.S. government can deter
Rourke from continuing his desperate search for his family.

#4: THE DOOMSAYER   (893, $2.50)
The most massive earthquake in history is only hours away, and
Communist-Cuban troops, Soviet-Cuban rivalry, and a traitor in the
inner circle of U.S. II block Rourke's path.

#5: THE WEB   (1145, $2.50)
Blizzards rage around Rourke as he picks up the trail of his family
and is forced to take shelter in a strangely quiet Tennessee valley
town. But the quiet isn't going to last for long!

#6: THE SAVAGE HORDE   (1243, $2.50)
Rourke's search gets sidetracked when he's forced to help a military
unit locate a cache of eighty megaton warhead missiles hidden on the
New West Coast—and accessible only by submarine!

#7: THE PROPHET   (1339, $2.50)
As six nuclear missiles are poised to start the ultimate conflagration,
Rourke's constant quest becomes a desperate mission to save both his
family and all humanity from being blasted into extinction!

#8: THE END IS COMING   (1374, $2.50)
Rourke must smash through Russian patrols and cut to the heart of
a KGB plot that could spawn a lasting legacy of evil. And when the
sky bursts into flames, consuming every living being on the planet, it
will be the ultimate test for THE SURVIVALIST.